"You're not leaving."

"I have to, the—"

Shy leaned toward Tabby and growled, "You are *not* leaving."

Suddenly, she lost it. Throwing her hands out to the sides, she asked, "Why?"

"This is why." He stalked the three steps that separated them, snaked an arm around her waist, and hauled her into his arms.

Then he slammed his mouth down on hers.

And there it was.

Sweet, God, so sweet.

Also by Kristen Ashley

The Colorado Mountain series

The Gamble
Sweet Dreams
Lady Luck
Breathe

The Dream Man series

Mystery Man
Wild Man
Law Man
Motorcycle Man

KRISTEN ASHLEY

FOREVER

NEW YORK BOSTON

This book is a work of fiction. Names, characters, places, and incidents are the product of the author's imagination or are used fictitiously. Any resemblance to actual events, locales, or persons, living or dead, is coincidental.

Forever
Hachette Book Group
237 Park Avenue
New York, NY 10017

www.HachetteBookGroup.com

Printed in the United States of America

Originally published as an e-book in April 2013

First mass market edition: June 2013
10 9 8 7 6 5 4 3 2 1

OPM

Forever is an imprint of Grand Central Publishing.
The Forever name and logo are trademarks of Hachette Book Group, Inc.

Chasity Jenkins-Patrick
Here we go, baby
Soaring

Acknowledgments

I wish to start my shout outs with Emily Sylvan Kim, my superagent but also a woman who makes the grand feat of diplomacy seem like tying her shoelaces. I'm not sure you knew what you were tackling when you signed me on, honey. What I am sure of is that I'm delighted you're on my team.

Going my own way for so long in the self-publishing world, I was worrying myself silly about forging new relationship with folks who would dig their hands into my stories. I care about my work more than is probably healthy, and I strive to provide stories to my readers that are far from disappointing.

More proof that the star of fortune has finally decided to shine its light on me as it led me to Amy Pierpont and Lauren Plude at Grand Central Publishing. Amy took pains to preserve my voice, listen to and *hear* my meanderings about everything under the sun that meant something to me to share about Tabby and Shy, and put up with my crap along the way. *And* she sent me a bottle of tequila. So you know that's gonna be good stuff. Thank you guys and here's to good things to come.

Own the Wind will be my first book with a bona fide publisher, another in a mess of dreams come true. This beauty would not have befallen me if not for my loyal, dedicated, kick-ass readers who pimp my books, blog like crazy, and shout my name from rooftops. I wish I had the time and space to name you all, but that would take a decade. I hope you know… *down to my bones, mamas.*

Finally, as my life preferences are writing and communing with my readers, not logging sales spreadsheets, updating websites, and dealing with bank managers, so last but oh so not least…

Erika, I love you.

Chas, no way…*no way*…I would be here without you.

OWN THE WIND

PROLOGUE

You Don't Know Me

His cell rang and Parker "Shy" Cage opened his eyes.

He was on his back in his bed in his room at the Chaos Motorcycle Club's compound. The lights were still on and he was buried under a small pile of women. One was tucked up against his side, her leg thrown over his thighs, her arm over his ribs. The other was upside down, tucked to his other side, her knee in his stomach, her arm over his calves.

Both were naked.

"Shit," he muttered, as he lifted and twisted himself out from under his fence of limbs. He reached out to his phone.

He checked the display and touched his thumb to the screen to take the call.

"Yo, brother," he muttered to Hop, one of his brethren in the Chaos MC.

"Where are you?" Hop asked.

"Compound," Shy answered.

"You busy?"

Shy lifted up to an elbow and looked at the two women passed out in his bed.

"Not anymore," he replied.

Knowing Shy and his reputation, there was humor in Hop's tone when he stated, "Tabby Callout."

At this news, fire hit his gut, as it always did when he got that particular callout. He didn't know why, it made no sense, he barely knew the girl, but always when he heard it, it pissed him way the hell off.

"You are shittin' me," Shy bit out.

"No, brother. Got a call from Tug who got a call from Speck. She's out on the prowl, as usual. She's closer to you than me, so if you can disentangle yourself from the pussy you got passed out in your room, it'd be good you go get her."

There it was. Hop knew Shy and his reputation.

"I'm on my bike. Text me the address," Shy mumbled, shifting from under the bodies to put his feet on the floor at the side of the bed.

"Right. Under radar, yeah?" Hop returned, telling him something he knew, and Shy clenched his teeth.

Three years they'd been doing this shit with Tabby. Three fucking years. It was lasting so damned long, he knew, unless she got a serious fucking wakeup call, that girl would never learn.

But no one was willing to do it. The Club didn't normally have any problems with laying it out no matter who it needed to be laid out for, but Tab was different. She was the nineteen-year-old daughter of the President of the Club, Kane "Tack" Allen.

That meant she was handled with care. That also meant when they got word she was out carousing and needed someone to nab her ass and get her home before she bought trouble, they did it under radar. In other words, they didn't tell Tack. And they didn't tell Tack because the first time it happened he lost his shit, but worse, his old lady took off to extricate Tabby from a bad situation and nearly got her head caved in with a baseball bat.

No one wanted a repeat of that kind of mess, so the brothers kept an eye on her and took care of business without getting Tack involved.

"Under radar," Shy muttered then finished, "Later," and touched the screen with his thumb.

He rooted around on the floor to find jeans, tee, underwear, and socks. The women in his bed didn't twitch when he sat down next to them to pull on his boots.

Dressed, he turned off the light in his room and headed down the hall and into the common room of the Club's compound. The brothers' rooms were at the back, doors opening off a long hall that ran the length of the building. A doorway in the middle of the hall led to the common area, which had a long, curved bar and a mess of couches, chairs, tables, and pool tables. Off to the side through another door was their meeting room, a kitchen, and a set of locked, reinforced storage rooms.

As he moved through the common space he saw Brick, one of Chaos's members, flat on his back on one of the couches. He had one foot on the floor and was dead to the world. He also had a woman draped on him, dead to the world too. She had a short jean skirt on, and Shy saw that Brick was sleeping with his hand up the hem, cupped on her ass. Shy also saw the woman wasn't wearing any underwear.

Other than that, the space was empty and currently lit only by a variety of neon beer signs on the walls.

That night, Brick's girl had brought two friends to party.

Brick got his girl. Shy got the friends.

Shy left the Compound, went to his bike, threw a leg over, and drove the six blocks to his apartment. Once there, he didn't bother going upstairs to his place. He never bothered to go upstairs to his place.

He wondered vaguely why he kept it. He was rarely there. He ate fast food that he ordered to go. He slept in his bed at his room in the Compound. He worked in the garage at Ride or the auto supply store attached. He drank and partied wherever there was drink or party provided. He communed with the brotherhood.

All other times, he was on his bike.

This was because Parker Cage only felt right on his bike.

It started with the dirt bike he got when he was fourteen, and it never stopped.

Five years ago, on his thirdhand Harley, he'd cruised by Ride Custom Cars and Bikes, a massive auto supply store that was attached to a garage in the back that built custom cars and bikes. He'd heard of it, hell, everyone had. The Chaos MC owned and ran it, and the garage was famous, built cars for movies and millionaires.

But it was the flag that flew under the American flag on top of the store that caught his attention. Until that day, he'd never looked up to see it. It was white and had the Chaos Motorcycle Club emblem on it with the words "Fire" and "Wind" on one side and "Ride" and "Free" on the other.

The second his eyes hit that flag, he felt his life take shape.

Nothing, not anything in his life until that time, except the first time he took off on a bike, had spoken to him like that flag. He didn't get why and he didn't spend time trying. It just spoke to him. So strong, it pulled him straight into the parking lot and set his boots to walking into the store.

Within months, he was a recruit for Chaos.

Now, he was a brother.

Outside his apartment, he parked his bike and moved from it to his truck. If she was in a state, Tabitha Allen wouldn't be able to hold on to him on a bike. If she was feeling sassy, which was usually the case, she'd put up a fight he couldn't win with her on a bike. So he hauled his ass into his beat-up, old, white Ford truck, started it up and took off in the direction of the address on the text Hop sent.

As he drove, that fire in his gut intensified.

She was in college now, supposedly studying to be a nurse. Cherry, the Office Manager at the garage who also happened to be Tack's old lady and Tabby's stepmother, bragged about her grades and how good she was doing in school. Shy had no clue how Tab could pull off good grades when she was out fucking around all the time. He couldn't say one of the brothers got a Tabby Callout every night but it was far from infrequent.

The girl liked to party.

This wasn't surprising. She was nineteen. When he was nineteen, he'd liked to party too. Fuck, he was twenty-four and he still liked to party in a way he knew he'd never quit.

But he wasn't Tabby Allen.

He was a biker who worked in a garage and auto supply store, oftentimes raised hell and kicked ass when needed.

She was studying to be a freaking nurse with her dad footing that bill, so she needed to calm her ass down.

This didn't even get into the fact that it wasn't a new thing she liked to party *and* take a walk on the wild side. Three years ago, on his first Tabby Callout, she'd been sixteen and her twenty-three-year-old boyfriend had roughed her up because she wouldn't put out. That was the situation where Cherry nearly got her head caved in with a baseball bat, and it happened right in front of Shy. It was a miracle of quick reflexes that didn't end in disaster. Shy liked Cherry, everyone did, the woman was the shit; funny, pretty, sexy, smart, strong, and good for Tack in every way she could be.

If you could pick the perfect old lady, Tyra "Cherry" Allen would be it. She had sass but with class, dressed great, didn't let Tack roll all over her but did it in a way she didn't bust his balls. She was hilarious. She was sweet. She was a member of a biker family while still holding on to the woman she always was. And, honest to Christ, he'd never seen a man laugh and smile as often as Kane Allen. He had a good life, and it wasn't lost on a single member of the Club that Cherry made it that way.

So, during Tabby's first callout, it would have sucked if Cherry was made a vegetable or worse because of Tab's shit. Not to mention, if Shy had to explain why he was at Cherry's back, watching her head get caved in with a bat, instead of taking the lead and protecting her from that eventuality, Tack was so into his old lady it was highly likely Shy would no longer be breathing.

How the fuck Tabby hadn't learned her lesson after that mess, he had no clue, and as he drove it came crystal that she needed to get one.

And he was so pissed, he decided he was going to be the one to give it to her.

Tonight.

Shy pulled up outside the house and he wasn't surprised at what he saw.

He knew that scene, lived it until he found the brotherhood.

In high school and out of it, the other kids had attached him to the "stoner" crowd, the "hoods," even though his affiliation with them was loose. He didn't connect with anyone in high school or after it, not in any real way, but that didn't mean he didn't find an escape. A place to drink beer and find a bitch so he could get laid. So he'd been in many houses just like this with cars and bikes outside just like the ones he saw now.

He still lived that scene but it was better.

It was family.

He saw a couple of bikes parked outside the fully lit and heaving house, and they pissed him off even more than he was already pissed. The bikes were older, the kids inside didn't have enough money for better, but still, they didn't take care of them.

If you had a Harley, you took care of it. You treated it like a woman, lots of attention, lots of TLC. No excuses. If you didn't do that, you didn't deserve to own it.

There were also a couple of new souped-up muscle cars, which meant whoever owned them put every nickel into keeping up the cool.

But there were more junkers and classic cars, the latter in the middle of restoration, all of it loving. Whoever owned them was taking their time, doing it right, saving up and taking care of their baby before they moved on to the next project in line to make their Mustang, Nova, Charger, GTO, or whatever cherry.

Those cars meant that not everyone in that house was a loser.

At least that was something.

Shy angled out of the truck and moved toward the house. Once in, he shifted through the bodies, ignoring looks from the girls and chin lifts from the guys. He was on a mission and wanted it done.

It didn't take long to find her. She was in the living room sitting on a couch, a cup of beer in her hand, her head turned away from him, her pretty profile transformed with laughter.

When he saw her it happened like it always happened. He didn't know why he hadn't learned, why he didn't brace. He always expected he'd get over it, get used to it, but he didn't.

Seeing her hit him in the chest, the burn in his gut moving up to flame in his lungs, compressing them, making it suddenly hard to catch a breath.

He didn't get this.

She was pretty. Jesus, she was pretty. All that thick, dark hair and those sapphire blue eyes, her curvy, petite body, perfect, golden skin still tanned from the summer. Any guy, even if they didn't get into short women with dark hair, could see she was pretty.

It was more and he knew that too, had been around her enough to see it and often. Her face was expressive, she was quick to smile and laugh. She was animated. She was just one of those chicks it was good to be around.

She could get pissed off. She could get feisty.

Most of the time, though, she was in a good mood, but her good moods were the kinds of good moods that filled a room. Even if you were having a shit day, if Tabby Allen wandered into the common room of the Compound wearing a smile, some of that shit would wear off and your day would get better.

But she was his brother's daughter and that was reason number one not to go there. Further, she was too young and too immature. She did stupid shit, like her being with this crowd, drinking beer underage and laughing rather than home studying or hanging with kids from college. So regardless that she was fucking pretty, had a sweet little body, and could light up a room with her mood, he was never going there, but even if he could, he wouldn't, because she was flat-out trouble.

And yet every time he saw her, it somehow rocked him.

He ignored this feeling that he didn't want and didn't understand, and his mouth tightened when he saw how she was dressed. Tight skirt, short. Tight top, cleavage. Lots of leg on show even if she wasn't all that tall. Nice leg. Shapely leg. Fucking great leg.

Shit.

And fuck-me high-heeled sandals that even if she was too young and his brother's daughter, the sight of them Shy still felt in his dick.

Damn.

He ignored this too and moved through the room, eyes on her, determined.

She must have felt his approach because she turned her head, looked up, and that burn didn't lessen at all when her unbelievable blue eyes ringed with long, dark lashes hit his.

He was not surprised when her smile faded, the animation left her face and she snapped, "You have got to be shitting me."

That pissed Shy off too. He fucking hated it when she cursed. Tack didn't give a shit, even when his kids were younger. Shy, though, detested it. There was something just very *wrong* about words like that coming from lips as beautiful as hers.

"Let's go," he clipped.

"Shy—" she began but didn't finish, mostly because Shy grabbed her beer, set it aside, then grabbed her hand and hauled her ass off of the couch.

Surprisingly, she didn't fight.

She followed.

Good, he thought. He wanted this done.

He got her out of the house, down the walk and opened the door of his truck for her. He was pulling her by her hand to get her close to the cab when she finally spoke.

"Shy, I keep telling you guys that this is not what you—"

He leaned in, nose to nose with her, and cut her off. "Shut it."

She blinked even as her head jerked. This wasn't a surprise. Brothers respected brothers, and one of the ways they did that was by showing respect to their kin. Chaos was Chaos, it was all family. Brothers, old ladies, kids. Shy had never spoken to her that way. None of the brothers had. Not to her.

"Get in the fuckin' truck," he went on.

Tabby rallied and started to say, "Can I just explain—?"

Shy interrupted her again. "Get in it or I plant you in it, Tab."

Even in the shadows of night, he saw her eyes flash before he saw her clamp her mouth shut. It was with jerky movements that she yanked her hand from his, turned, and climbed into the truck.

Shy slammed her door, rounded the hood, and folded in.

They were on their way when she tried again, her voice quiet. "Shy, really, those are my friends. It's all cool. Just a couple of beers. A few joints. I'm not smoking and I'm driving so I wouldn't—"

"So all of those kids are nursing students?" he asked.

"No," she answered. "They're friends from high school."

"You're not in high school anymore, Tabby," he pointed out, and felt her eyes come to him but he kept his angry ones on the road.

"You're right," she snapped, the quiet in her voice gone. "I'm not. That doesn't mean they aren't still my friends. We've had a lot of good times together. We're close. What? You think I should just scrape them off?"

He didn't glance at her when he replied, "Uh, yeah, Tab. They're trash. You aren't. Jesus." He shook his head. "I do not get you. I know your mom's a bitch, but for the last three years you've had Cherry in your life. It isn't like you don't have a good role model. Why the fuck you can't be like her is beyond me."

He heard her swift intake of breath before she returned, "Maybe it's because I should be like *me* and, by the way, Shy, Tyra would want me to be like me too."

The members of the Club called Tack's woman Cherry but Tack called her Red. His kids and everyone else called her Tyra or Ty-Ty.

"Anyway," Tabby went on irately, "they're not trash."

"They're trash," he stated firmly.

"They. Are. *Not!*" she stated loudly.

There it was. That gave him his opening.

"You want that life?" he asked.

"That life?" she shot back.

"Booze and bodies, booty calls and bust-ups," he explained.

"Um . . . *hello,* Shy. That *is* my life."

"So you want it," he concluded.

She ignored his question and pointed out, "It's *your* life too, you know. Nothing wrong with it. Never was, never will be."

A nursing student.

Right.

On this path, she'd never make it. On this path, she'd end up like those bitches in his bed. On this path, Tabby was pissing her college education away, and Tack might as well be pissing that money into the wind.

"You want that life," he said softly, "you think that's cool, baby? Then let's roll."

It was perfect timing because he'd flipped on his turn signal to turn into Ride.

"What the hell? Why are we here?" she asked, but he didn't answer.

He drove around the store and through the forecourt of the garage to park in front of the Compound. He didn't delay in folding out of the truck, rounding the hood, and yanking open her door.

"Shy, what are you—?" she started but stopped since he leaned into her, undid her seatbelt, tagged her hand, and hauled her out of the cab. "Dammit! Shy! What are you doing?" she clipped.

Again he didn't answer. He just tugged her into the Compound and straight behind the bar. He nabbed a bottle of tequila off a shelf at the back then pulled her in front of him.

"Ready to let go of that little-girl-beer bullshit?" he asked, holding up the bottle.

Her eyes went to it, then to him. He saw the confusion and he sensed her unease.

He ignored that too.

"Tab, asked you a question. You like to party. You aren't in high school anymore. You wanna grow up and learn how it's really done?"

She ignored him this time and asked, "Why are you being so weird?"

He pulled her closer and tipped his chin down to hold her eyes, now ignoring that it was starkly apparent she wasn't breathing and her body had gone still.

"Didn't answer my question, baby," he said softly and watched her swallow then lick her upper lip.

Jesus. Shit.

He'd never seen her do that. Definitely not this close.

The tip of that pink tongue on the perfection of that rosy lip.

Shit.

"Tab," he prompted, his hand squeezing hers.

"I want to go home," she replied quietly, being smart for a change.

"Too late for that," he muttered then moved away, pulling her with him as he moved from behind the bar, through the room, and into the back hall.

She tugged at his hand and called, "Shy. Seriously. You're more than kinda freaking me out."

Hopefully, in about two seconds, she'd be a lot more than kinda freaked out. She'd be scared straight and out of this bullshit she kept pulling.

Therefore, two seconds later, he yanked her into his room, tugged her to a stop and flipped the light switch.

The two women were still naked, lying head to foot on the bed, having, since he was gone, tangled with each other.

Briefly, he tried to remember their names.

He stopped trying when he felt Tabby's hand spasm in his and she gave a rough pull to try to break away but he just held her tighter and turned to her.

"Usually, we throw some back, get loose, in the mood," he educated her, lifting up the bottle. "I've seen the way you look at me, baby, so if you wanna just get naked and go for it, I'm up for that too. They're out but, we go for a while, no doubt they'll rally and join in. Sounds extreme but, trust me, you try it, you'll like it."

When he started talking, her eyes were on the bed but they moved slowly to him and he saw she was pale beneath her tan. Her eyes were also wide with shock and something else he didn't quite get, and her full lips were parted.

"What's it gonna be?" he asked. "You wanna loosen up or you wanna just go for it?"

"Why are you doin' this?" she whispered, and Shy shrugged.

"This is who you are or who you're headin' to be. Might as well quit fuckin' around, babe, and go for it."

Her eyes slid to the side then to him before she stated quietly, "This isn't who I am."

He looked her down and up and pointed out, "Short tight skirts, too-tight tops. I know it's not lost on you that I can see most of your tits not only through the shirt but spillin' out of it, Tab. Then we got your high heels, lots of hair, lots of makeup. You scream you got a wild side, baby. Quit fuckin' around. You been wantin' to explore it since you were sixteen. The time is right. The stage is set." He pulled her closer to him and lifted the bottle again. "Let's go."

When he said the word *sixteen*, she flinched and her hand jerked at his again.

Also, the look in her eyes he couldn't quite place came clear.

Hurt.

It sucked. He didn't like to do this to her, but he reckoned that emotion stark in her gaze meant he was getting through.

"Take me home," she said softly, and he shifted closer to her

She swung slightly back, but her movements were wooden.

"Come on, baby. Don't bullshit me," he coaxed in a gentle voice. "I've seen the looks you give me. Now's your shot. You're hot, you like to have fun, you shouldn't waste this opportunity."

"Take me home," she repeated.

"If you don't want an audience or this to be a participation sport outside us two, I can rouse those bitches—" he jerked his head to the bed "—send them on their way before we get goin'."

"Take me home," she said again.

"Or we can let 'em sleep. Go to your dad's room," he suggested, and that did it.

With a violent wrench, she tore her hand from his, turned on her foot, and raced from the room.

Much more slowly, Shy put the bottle on the dresser, snapped off the lights, and followed her. He wasn't alarmed.

She didn't have wheels and she was in high heels, there wasn't far shc could go.

Surprisingly, when he exited the Compound, she was sitting in the passenger side of his truck, her head turned to look out the side window.

Yeah, she was ready to go home.

He didn't delay in moving to the driver's side, climbing in and starting her up. Tabby didn't look his way as he reversed out and headed toward Broadway.

They were well on their way through Denver to the foothills where Tack and Cherry lived, where Tab still lived with them and their two new boys before he spoke into the heavy air in the cab.

"You're a good kid, Tabby. Don't let your mother treating you like shit kick your ass. Get off that path."

"You're on that path," she whispered to her window.

"Babe, I'm not. I'm a man and I got brothers. I chose a lifestyle and a brotherhood. It's different for you and you know it. The bullshit you're pullin', the path you're on, no joke, even if you wanted the life, wanted to be an old lady, that wouldn't work for you no matter what respect we got for your dad. The path you're on heads you straight to bein' a BeeBee, and you know that too."

She didn't speak but Shy figured his point was made. Tabby knew BeeBee, everyone did. BeeBee had been banned from spreading her legs and spreading her talent throughout every member of the Club after she stupidly went head to head with Cherry. But even gone, she was not forgotten. Back then, Tabby had been way too young to know BeeBee in any real way other than seeing the way BeeBee hung on and put out. But there was no way to miss her use to the Club, even for a teenage girl.

His point made, he also kept quiet the rest of the way to Tack's house.

He parked outside the front door and she instantly undid her seat belt and threw open the door. He turned to see she'd twisted to jump out and opened his mouth to say something, but he didn't get it out. He had no idea how she explained it to her father when a brother brought her home, but that was her problem, not his.

She turned back and all words died in his throat when he saw by the cab's light the tears shimmering in her eyes and the tracks left by the ones that had slid silently down her cheeks.

His body went rock solid at the evidence of the pain his lesson caused. Deserved, he knew, but it still hurt like a mother to witness. So when she leaned in, he didn't move away.

"You don't know me," she whispered. "But now, I know you, and, Shy . . . you're a dick."

Even with those words, she still lifted her hands, placed them on either side of his head and angled closer. Pressing her lips against his, that sweet, pink tongue of hers slid between his lips to touch the tip of his tongue before she let him go just as quickly as she'd grabbed hold. She jumped out of the cab and ran gracefully on the toes of her high-heeled sandals up the side deck and into the house.

Shy had shifted to watch her move, his chest and gut both ablaze, the brief but undeniably sweet taste of her still on his tongue.

The light on the side of the house went off, and he was plunged into darkness.

"Shit," he muttered before he put the truck in gear and turned around.

As he drove home, he couldn't get her tear-stained cheeks and wet eyes out of his head.

He also couldn't get her taste off his tongue.

* * *

Five months later...

The bell over the door of Fortnum's Used Books rang as Shy pushed it open.

Shy came to Fortnum's for one reason, and it wasn't to buy used books. It was because they had a coffee counter and seating area in the front of the store, and everyone in Denver knew that the man named Tex who worked the espresso machine was a master. Shy liked beer, bourbon, and vodka, occasionally tequila, sometimes Pepsi, but with the way he lived his nights, his mornings always included a whole lot of coffee.

Tex's eyes came to him as he moved through the tables and armchairs scattered in front of the espresso counter and he boomed a "Yo, travelin' man! Usual?"

Shy jerked up his chin in the affirmative, but something caught his attention from the side, and he looked that way to see Tabby sitting at the round table tucked in the corner.

The fire hit his chest.

She had books and notepads stacked around, two empty coffee cups on the table, one half full. She was bent over a book, elbow on the table, hand in her mane of hair at the top of her head, holding it away from her face. Her concentration was on a book and a notepad in front of her, pencil in hand.

He hadn't seen her since that night he gave her the lesson and took her home. She wasn't a regular at Ride or at the Compound, but she was around. She was tight with Cherry; they went shopping together a lot, and Tabby met Cherry there when they went. Sometimes she studied in the office while Cherry worked. She was tight with some of the brothers, particularly Tack's lieutenants, Dog and Brick, and Big Petey, one of the founding members who took a break from the Club for a few years to go be with his daughter while she was fighting cancer. He came back when she lost that fight and Tab, being how Tab could be and growing up with Big Petey, moved in to balm that hurt. So it wasn't unheard of to see her shooting the shit with Pete opposite the counter inside the auto supply store, teasing him by his Harley Trike in the forecourt or sitting close with him and talking at one of the picnic tables outside the Compound.

Then, for five months, she'd disappeared. Not a sign of her. Shy wasn't on Chaos every minute of his day but when he was, she wasn't there.

She hadn't been to one of the three hog roasts they'd had. She didn't even go to the party they threw when they took on their new recruits, Snapper and Bat.

And there hadn't been another Tabby Callout since that night.

Now here she was, studying. Business was bustling and Tex seemed to need to make as much noise as possible when forcing a coffee drink out of the espresso machine, and yet she didn't look around or break concentration at all.

And, Shy thought, there it was. He'd made his point. She'd learned her lesson. Focus on the shit that mattered.

She was taking the opportunity her father was offering to sct herself up with a good life, getting control of that wild side and cleaning the trash out of her life.

He paid the knockout redhead named Indy who owned the place for his drink, got it from Tex at the other end of the counter and moved to Tab's table.

He pulled out the seat opposite her and twisted it around to straddle it, saying softly, "Yo, babe," before her body jerked with surprise and her head came up.

Her eyes hit him and he saw something that made him uneasy flash through them before she shut it down. Her face went blank, and her eyes slid through the room before coming back to him.

"What're you doin' here?" she asked quietly.

He lifted his to-go cup. "Coffee. Best in town. Come here all the time."

She looked at his cup then at the two coffee mugs on the table in front of her before her fingers slid through her hair and she straightened in her chair.

When Shy recovered from watching her thick, shining hair move through her fingers and he realized she wasn't speaking, he asked, "Studying?"

Her gaze went to her books like she'd never seen them before, it came back to him and she answered, "Yeah. I've got two tests this week."

"Harsh," he muttered, though he wouldn't know. He'd never studied for tests. The fact that somewhere in the junk in his apartment was a high school diploma was a miracle.

"Yeah," she agreed. "I need to get back to it."

"What?" he asked.

She looked down at her books, turned her pencil in

her hand and tapped the eraser end to her notepad before repeating, "I need to get back to it."

"You don't want company," he surmised.

"Um...I have two tests. I have a lot of work to do."

Shy nodded then asked, "You come here a lot?"

That sweet, pink tongue came out to touch her upper lip, the burn in his chest magnified before her tongue disappeared and she answered, "No, just trying out places where I can get my studying groove on. It gets a little insane at home."

"The boys," Shy guessed. She had two new brothers: Rider, who just turned three, and Cutter, who was one, meant home was not where she could get that particular groove on.

"Yeah, they're little kids but they're also Allens, so things can get rowdy," she muttered.

He heard Tex banging on the espresso machine, and he knew Fortnum's could get a little insane too.

Thinking that, thinking that it was cool Tabby was finally focused on the right things, and trying not to think about how much or why he'd like her at his place, he offered, "You need space, babe, I got an apartment. I'm never in it. Can't say it's clean but it is quiet."

"Thanks, but I'm good."

He pushed up from the chair, righting it at the table, saying, "Anytime, Tab, you need it, it's yours. Just give me a call."

She nodded, swallowed then mumbled, "Later," to his shoulder before she looked back down to her books, curling in her chair, slouching back to her elbow, hand back in her hair.

It was the swallow, the mumbling, and the talking to his shoulder that drove Shy to round the table, lift a hand, and pull her hair away from her face.

Her head jerked back as her eyes shot to him.

"We good?" he asked.

"Sure," she answered, too quickly.

"You sure about that?" he pressed.

"Why wouldn't I be?" she asked back, too casually.

"Babe, the last time I saw you was extreme." His eyes went to the table then back to her. "I see you got my point but it'd be cool to know we're good."

"We're good," she assured him, again, quickly.

He studied her face. It was carefully vacant.

He didn't know her all that well, but he'd been around her often enough to know Tabitha Allen was never expressionless.

Fuck.

He let it go and reiterated, "You need my place, babe, just yell."

"I'll do that, Shy," she replied quietly.

He jerked up his chin.

She turned so her back was to him and slouched back over her books.

Shy walked out of Fortnum's feeling that familiar burn. Except it wasn't in his gut this time.

It was around his heart.

She never called to use his space.

She never called at all.

And he never again saw her at Fortnum's.

* * *

Six months later…

Shy sat outside the Compound on top of one of the picnic tables, feet on the seat, legs spread, elbows to his thighs, bottle of beer held loosely in his hands, watching.

Tabby was at Chaos for the first time in nearly a year. She was walking out of the office and down the steps, Rider's hand in hers as she steadied him while he struggled to get his little legs to negotiate the stairs. She had Cut on her hip, and Shy could see Cut was slamming his little fist into her cheek as she walked.

She got them safely to the bottom of the stairs but stopped, and Shy watched as she turned her head, jerked it forward, and captured Cut's fist in her mouth.

He squealed. Tabby let his little fist go, and her peel of musical laughter shot across the forecourt and hit him straight in the gut so hard it was a fucking miracle he didn't grunt.

Then it happened.

Rider tripped and Tabby bent to right him and on her way up, her eyes moved through the forecourt, across the Compound, straight through him.

Through him.

Like he was fucking invisible.

Jesus.

Fuck.

Jesus.

There was a time, he caught sight of her, her eyes would shift away quickly and he knew she was watching him. Anytime she'd been around before he did what he did that night, if he saw her, her eyes were on him.

Now he was invisible. It was like he didn't exist.

She moved the kids to her car and strapped them in the car seats in the back, and Shy kept watching, his gut tight, that burn searing his heart.

She had a great ride. Her dad gave it to her when she was sixteen, and she took care of it like it was one of her little brothers. Its electric blue paint gleamed, clean and pristine, in the August sun.

Sweet ride but Tabby, wearing one of those flowy, flowery, loose dresses that went all the way to her feet, so much fucking material, you couldn't begin to guess what lay underneath it, didn't look like she belonged to that car. The dress was saved by being strapless, the top essentially an elasticized tube top covering her tits, but still.

It wasn't cutoff short-shorts and rocker shirts like she used to wear.

And her hair wasn't down and wild. It was braided in thick plaits close to her skull on either side to flare out in a mass of hair at her nape that only hinted at the dense, glossy mane Tack's good genes had bestowed on her.

Yeah, he'd made his point.

Fuck yeah, a year ago, he'd really fucking made his point.

She got the kids strapped in and Big Petey exited the office, lumbered down the stairs, and Shy watched Pete and Tabby engage in a playful argument he couldn't hear. Tab lost, and she faked being pissed as she handed over her keys and stomped around the car.

Pete had one child, his daughter, now under dirt. When he came back after her funeral, he was shattered. The man was not young, but after he lost his daughter and returned to the brotherhood, he looked a thousand years old.

Now, Shy saw, he was grinning as he folded his huge beer belly behind the wheel of Tab's car and adjusted the seat.

Tab did that. Tab brought him back. Tabby put together those pieces and gave Pete something to grin about.

The Tab who looked right through Shy like he didn't exist.

Petey pulled out and he, Tab, Rider, and Cut took off, where, Shy had no clue. Shy'd heard Cherry and Tack talking about it enough to know that Rider and Cut's big sister doted on them and spoiled their asses rotten. So he figured ice cream, park, but whatever it was, it was filled with their sister's love.

He watched the car until he couldn't see it anymore.

Then he jumped off the picnic table and walked inside.

In the cool dark of the Compound, he stopped in the common room and stood, staring at the Chaos flag mounted on the wall at the back of the room.

Cool and dark while his gut still twisted and his heart burned.

He lifted his bottle and with his arm slicing through the air in a sidearm throw, he sent the bottle sailing across the room to smash in a foamy explosion of beer and brown glass on the wall opposite the door by the Club flag.

"Jesus, brother, what the fuck?" he heard rumbled from the side of the room. He turned and looked to see High sitting on a stool at the bar with Snapper behind it.

Shy didn't answer. He prowled behind the bar and nabbed a bottle of tequila.

On his way back around the bar, heading to his room, he ordered Snapper, "Clean that shit up."

Then he disappeared into his room.

* * *

Seven months later…

He rolled his truck to a stop behind the electric blue car on the side of the road.

Shy had gotten his first Tabby Callout in eighteen months.

She wasn't out on the prowl.

She had a flat.

She was standing, jean-clad hips against the side of her car, thermal-covered arms crossed over the poofy vest she was wearing, low-heeled booted feet crossed at the ankles, head turned to him, eyes hidden behind a pair of mirrored, wire-rimmed shades, face vacant.

He'd seen her once since she took off with Petey and her brothers, and that was at the Chaos Christmas blowout at the Compound. He'd shown with a woman on his arm. She'd left fifteen minutes later.

That was it.

Now, as he angled out of his truck and moved toward her, she didn't twitch. Just watched him.

When he got close, even though he hadn't spoken a word to her since they saw each other at Fortnum's over a year ago, she announced sharply, "I know how to change a flat, but I can't get the lug nuts to move."

He stopped a half a foot away from her, looked through his shades down his nose at her and growled, "I'm doin' fuckin' great, babe. Thanks for askin'. How the fuck are you?"

Her head jerked and her shoulders straightened like a steel rod had been jammed down her spine. "Pardon?" she asked.

"Nothin," he muttered. "Do me a favor, step away from the car. Don't need it sliding off the jack while I'm dealin' with your tire because your ass is leaned into it."

She pushed away from the car and Shy headed to the flat. She'd pulled out the spare, had the car jacked up and the lug wrench lying on the tarmac. Shy crouched to it and was grabbing the wrench when she spoke.

"Roscoe phoned. He's ten minutes away. If this is biting into your schedule, he said he'd be able to help out."

"Take me ten minutes. Then you can disappear again," he muttered, putting the wrench to the nut and finding she was not wrong. Those bitches were on there tight.

Tabby fell silent. Shy worked.

He switched the tire with her spare, dumped the flat into her trunk, and was slamming it closed when he stated, "Get to the garage. You got time, now would be good. Don't drive too far on that spare."

"I may be a girl, but my dad's a biker and a mechanic. I think I know enough not to ride around on a spare," she returned. "Though," she went on when his eyes cut to her, "you've given me an idea. All those silly women out there who don't know better, I could give a helping hand, design some leaflets. Pass them out all around Denver. Explain about spare usage. How dangerous it is. I'll be sure to put a bunch of butterflies on it and douse it with glitter so I can keep their attention while they're reading it."

He felt his eyes narrow as his mouth asked, "What the fuck?"

"Nothin'," she muttered, then he felt his gut tighten when she asked, "Is a blowjob acceptable payment for a tire change or does the headboard need to rock?"

Seriously.

He hadn't seen the bitch in months, he hadn't spoken to her in over a year, what was with the fucking attitude?

He was too goddamned incensed to ask her that, all he could force out was a repeated, "What the fuck?"

"Payback, Shy. I certainly wouldn't want to put you

out of your way for nothing," she explained, and he felt his jaw go tight before he forced it loose in order to respond.

"Give me five minutes, baby, hauled ass out here to take care of you, my truck's old, the heat isn't what it used to be. She warms up, a blowjob in the cab would be just fine."

"Is it necessary for me to call a friend or will just me do?" she shot back.

"Hard for two bitches to get their mouths wrapped around my cock, but if you've got a way, sugar, I'm up for the experience."

"Oh, you'll be up," she hissed, leaning in slightly.

"Don't make promises you can't keep," he returned.

She stared at him through her shades, her mouth set, and he knew, he tore off those fucking sunglasses, her eyes would be flaring.

He pulled in a breath, calming the burn in his insides so he was able to request, "You wanna explain the attitude?"

"No," she clipped.

"If you don't, then don't dish that shit out. You got somethin' up your ass, you gotta have the balls to let it hang out. Not dish out shit and expect me to eat it when I don't know your fuckin' problem."

"You're right, Shy. My apologies. You walking up to my car and cursing sarcastically at me threw me off my game. You went out of your way to help me, I should be more appreciative."

Her words were sweet. Her tone was not.

"Babe, you led with snapping out you'd have this covered if you could move those lug nuts. You didn't even fuckin' say hello. How, exactly, would you have liked me to respond to that, seein' as you haven't so much as looked at me in a long fuckin' time."

She threw out her hands in a bullshit gesture of apology. "Sorry, Shy, so, so sorry. I mean, it isn't like I was on my way to do something when I got a stupid flat then I couldn't move the stupid lug nuts and I tried for, like"—she leaned in—"*ever.* So when you rolled up to help out, instead of being understandably frustrated, I should have put the smile on and given you the love. I get that, you hauled yourself out here to help out and me being pissed off that my day is totally screwed, my hands are dirty, my jeans are dirty, and I have to go home and change isn't your problem. I shouldn't make it that way."

Fuck, she had a point.

"Tabby—" he started, but she cut him off.

"And the blowjob crack was out of line. I apologize for that too."

"Tab—"

"As was the friend thing and, well . . . everything. Now, are we good?"

There it was.

His shot.

And he was going to take it.

He took a step toward her and said quietly, "We're good, babe, but since your day is screwed anyway, and we're out in the middle of nowhere, we should take this time to talk."

When he moved toward her, she held her ground. After he made his suggestion, she leaned slightly back.

"About what?" she asked.

"I got the feeling you're avoiding me."

"I'm not," she stated, too quickly.

"I haven't spoken to you in over a year," he pointed out.

"We were never really close, Shy," she replied.

Shy tried a different tactic. "Used to see you all the time, Tab. Now I never see you."

"I'm busy."

"You were busy before and I still saw you."

"Now I'm busy . . . *er.*"

He shook his head and moved closer. She stood her ground but he saw her body go stiff. He ignored that and continued, "You're avoiding me and have been since that shit went down a while back."

"What shit?" she asked, and she was so obviously attempting to pull the wool, he almost smiled because it was fucking cute.

Damn.

"You know what shit," he replied.

"Shy—" she began, moving back, but he caught her by her upper arm and she went still again.

He leaned down so their faces were close.

Jesus, she had a fantastic mouth.

"It was harsh, babe, way harsh, *too* harsh. I see that now, but it's been over a year and you're still freezing me out. This shit can't go on, Tabby. We're family."

He saw that fantastic mouth of hers twist in a way that made his gut do the same before she whispered, "We're not family."

"We're both Chaos," he reminded her.

"We're not family," she repeated.

"Babe—"

She twisted her arm out of his hold but didn't move away when she spoke.

"My *family* talked to me about the shit that went down

with that guy after it happened *years ago*, Shy. Ty-Ty, Dad, Rush were *there* for me. I screwed up, things with Mom were bad, she was always all over me even when I didn't do anything wrong. I was sixteen and stupid so, I thought, what the heck? If I was going to be in trouble anyway, I might as well do something to be in trouble for, and I was with a guy who was way too old for me. He tried it on with me, it flipped me out, and when I said no, he wasn't cool. He hit me, hurt me, and I called Tyra to help me out. She called you to take her back. And, well, you were there. You know the rest."

"Tab—" Shy tried again, now trying to cut in because he could tell going over the past was not somewhere she wanted to be but Tabby kept talking.

"When they confronted me about it, it wasn't comfortable but it was honest and gentle and what I needed. Sheila took me aside and she asked me and *listened* to me when I had to let go of shit about Mom. Arlo took me out for a hot dog and a discussion on how to spot a good guy and when to know when a guy's a jerk. And all of them had my back for years after that went down to make sure nothing like that went down again. It was overboard, overprotective, and annoying but at least it was loving." She shook her head. "But you... *you* made assumptions. You showed you decided exactly the kind of girl I was that night when that guy took his hand to me without knowing one single thing about me. I wasn't what you thought, Shy. I didn't need your shit and I also didn't deserve it. Family doesn't make judgments. They talk. They support. You made a judgment. You acted on that judgment. You doing it hurt me so that means you are *not* my family."

After gutting him, she turned on her boot, stomped to

her car, folded her curvy, little body in and then she was off, leaving Shy standing at the side of the road.

* * *

Four months later…

Shy sat on his bike, pissed. Construction jacking up downtown and some show getting out at the Denver Center for the Performing Arts meant traffic was jammed every-fucking-where.

He watched three cars get through the light and didn't budge on his bike before they were back to red and he was back to thinking he'd ride his bike up on the sidewalk to get past this shit. The cars were so jacked, jockeying for position to make it to the single lane they had to get through, he couldn't even ride between to get the fuck out.

He sat back and turned his head, gliding his eyes through the waves of people crawling over the sidewalks, crossing the street and climbing down the stairs at DCPA, when his eyes passed through her and his head jerked back.

Tabby.

Tabby wearing a tight, strapless red dress covered in lace, the scallops skimming her knees. On her feet were high, spiked black heels that were sexy as all fuck, the same as they were classy. Her mass of hair was pulled softly back from her face, tucked in a complicated arrangement of curls at the back.

She looked like a modern-day princess. Elegant. Sophisticated. High-class.

"Jesus," he muttered.

She was looking around like she was lost, and he was

about to put his tongue to his teeth to whistle when she found what she was looking for and Shy went rock solid.

A tall, good-looking, built blond guy in a suit moved to her, smiling. She tipped her head back, not smiling.

Fucking beaming.

Shy watched as the man slid an arm around her waist, she leaned into his body, and he bent to touch his mouth to hers. He stayed bent, kept his face close to hers, as any man would do, Tabby dressed like that, looking like that, smiling like that, and her mouth moved.

Then his head shot back as he burst out laughing.

Tabby watched for a beat before she dropped her chin and rested her forehead against his chest, her arms moving to curve around him and hold him while he shook with humor.

"Jesus," Shy muttered, that burn back, in his gut, chest, heart, even up his fucking throat.

He wanted to but he couldn't tear his eyes away when the man dipped his chin back down, cupped her jaw with a hand, lifted her face to his, and bent to touch his mouth to Tabby's again.

But it wasn't a touch.

He kept his mouth on hers a long fucking time. Like they weren't on a sidewalk with hundreds of people streaming around them and waiting in cars to get through traffic. Like they were alone, just them.

Shy kept watching as the man broke the kiss. Tabby's hand, now at the guy's neck, moved so her thumb could stroke his jaw and she could gaze up at him like he was the only man on the planet.

It was then Shy tore his eyes away.

And it was then, ignoring the cars that honked and the

shouts out the window, he maneuvered his bike through the cars, nearly jacking up his legs and his bike.

Two seconds later, when the light changed, he roared the fuck away.

* * *

Eight months later…

"Jesus, seriously, set me up," Dog growled as he stalked into the Compound and headed toward where Shy, Arlo, and Brick were sitting, drinking beer, Bat across from them playing bartender.

"What's up, brother?" Arlo asked, as Dog hoisted his ass on a stool.

"Our little Tabby's engaged."

Shy felt like he'd been sucker-punched.

"No shit?" Brick asked, sounding like he'd been sucker-punched too.

"Jesus, God, please don't make it be that blond guy who's built like a linebacker and looks like a cop," Bat muttered.

Dog took a long pull from his beer but did it nodding. Then he dropped the beer to the bar and leveled his eyes on Brick.

"Good dude, I met him. Physical therapist. Played college ball, good at it but not good enough. Though that experience helped. He works for the Broncos."

Shy looked at the beer he was holding on the bar.

Shit.

Fuck.

Shit.

"She's over the fuckin' moon," Dog continued, and

Shy's gut twisted. "Cherry is too. Cherry thinks he's the shit. Can't say I don't like him but he's fuckin' *normal.* Tack's torn. The dude totally thinks our girl walks on water, what father wouldn't like that? He's cool too. Knows us, who we are, where she came from, does not give that first fuck. He'd take her legless and armless if she was still Tab, he don't care where she comes from. That said, he's not anywhere close to the life, he comes from the fuckin' suburbs, and Tack's strugglin' with that."

Shy lifted his beer and took a drag.

He swallowed and found it didn't help the burn.

Dog, unfortunately, kept fucking talking. "They're gonna wait until she graduates to get married. She's bein' funny about it. Dude wants her to move in, she says after the wedding. Don't know why she just don't shack up with the guy. Try before you buy, see if that shit'll work. But she's not down with that so... whatever."

Tabby being theirs, his brothers could talk about this shit all night.

But Shy had had enough.

He pushed his stool back, slid off it, and muttered, "Gotta go."

"Where you goin'?" Bat asked.

He didn't know. He didn't care. Anywhere just as long as he got there on his bike.

"Shit to do," he muttered and moved around the bar, eyes to his feet, mind centered on keeping his jaw relaxed, his hands unclenched.

He walked out the door, swung on his bike, and rolled out.

He didn't hit Chaos again for three weeks.

* * *

Six months later…

Shy was moving across the forecourt toward the Compound in order to grab a shower and head out. His hands were filthy from grease. The car he'd been working on for the last three months was finally done.

Time to celebrate.

He moved into the Compound and felt the heaviness in the air immediately. Boys were moving out, faces alert, even alarmed, the vibe bad.

"What's goin' on?" he asked Roscoe, who was shifting, like all the brothers, toward the door.

"Car accident," Roscoe answered, stopping and catching his eye. "Tab's fiancé."

The force of that information knocked Shy so hard it was a wonder he didn't fall to a knee.

The wedding was three weeks away.

Jesus. Tabby.

"What?" he whispered.

Roscoe shook his head. "Just got the news. She's at Denver Health. He's, brother, this shit is fuckin' crazy, but the guy was DOA. Didn't even make it to the hospital. Gone. Tack says Tab's lost it. We're movin' out, takin her back, Tack's back, seein' if we can do anything." His head tipped to the side. "Comin'?"

DOA.

Didn't even make it to the hospital.

Gone.

Tab's lost it.

Lost it.

"Anyone watchin' the kids?" he forced out.

"Sheila's headin' up there."

"I'll go help her out," Shy offered, turning, digging his greasy hand into his jeans for his keys.

"Help out Sheila with the kids?" Roscoe asked his back.

Shy didn't answer. It was jacked, fucking lame, but it was doing something. Something away from Tabby.

She wouldn't want to see him now.

She never wanted to see him.

But he had to do something.

He wasn't her family.

But she was his.

* * *

Three days later…

Shy sat in his dark living room in his apartment, the first time he'd been there for months.

He was thinking and he was remembering.

Remembering for the first time in a long time that day when the news came.

Remembering that day when his life, at age fucking twelve, shifted and went from good, no *great*, to absolute shit.

Remembering the day years later when he found Chaos and he thought, finally, fucking *finally*, his life would no longer be shit and he was right.

And thinking that, six hours ago, probably wearing black, probably looking lifeless, just like she'd looked yesterday when he saw her walking out of the office with Cherry, Cherry's arm around her holding her close, her head bobbing like she was agreeing to what Cherry was saying when he knew just by looking at her she didn't hear a thing, Tabby stood in a cemetery and laid her man into the ground.

Her man was twenty-seven years old.

Shy's age.

Shy lifted the bottle of vodka to his lips and took a deep pull.

He didn't drop it before he took another one.

CHAPTER ONE

"I Dreamed a Dream"

Three and a half months later…

HIS CELL RANG and Parker "Shy" Cage opened his eyes.

He was on his back in his bed in his room at the Chaos Motorcycle Club's Compound. The lights were still on and he was buried under a small pile of women. One was tucked up against his side, her leg thrown over his thighs, her arm over his middle. The other was upside down, tucked to his other side, her knee in his stomach, her arm over his calves.

Both were naked.

"Shit," he muttered, twisting with difficulty under his fence of limbs. He reached out to his phone.

He checked the display, his brows drew together at the "unknown caller" he saw on the screen as he touched his thumb to it to take the call.

"Yo," he said into the phone.

"Shy?" a woman asked, she sounded weird, far away, quiet.

"You got me," he answered.

"It's Tabby."

He shot to sitting in bed, limbs flying and they weren't his.

"Listen, I'm sorry," her voice caught like she was trying to stop crying or, maybe, hyperventilating, then she whispered, "So, so sorry but I'm in a jam. I think I might even be kinda…um, in trouble."

"Where are you?" he barked into the phone, rolling over the woman at his side and finding his feet.

"I…I…well, I was with this old friend and we were. Damn, um…" she stammered as Shy balanced the phone between ear and shoulder and tugged on his jeans.

"Babe, where are you?" he repeated.

"In a bathroom," she told him, as he tagged a tee off the floor and straightened, waiting for her to say more.

When she didn't, gently, he prompted, "I kinda need to know where that bathroom is, sugar."

"I, uh…this guy is…um, I didn't know it, obviously, but I think he's—" another hitch in her breath before she whispered so low he barely heard "—a bad dude."

Fuck.

Shit.

Fuck.

He nabbed his boots off the floor and sat on the bed to yank them on with his socks, asking, "Do I need backup?"

"I don't want anyone…" she paused. "Please, don't tell anyone. Just…can you please just text me when you're here? I'll stay in the bathroom, put my phone on vibrate so no one will hear, and I'll crawl out the window when you get here."

"Tab, no one is gonna think shit. Just give me the lay of the land. Are you in danger?"

"I'll crawl out the window."

He gentled his voice further and stopped putting on his boots to give her his full attention.

"Tabby, baby, are you in danger?"

"I... well, I don't know really. There's a lot of drugs and I saw some, well, a lot of guns."

Shit.

"Address, honey," he urged, and she gave it to him.

Then she said, "Don't tell anyone, please. Just text."

"I'll give you that if you keep me notified and often. Text me. Just an 'I'm okay' every minute or so. I don't get one, I'll know you're not and I'm bringin' in the boys."

"I can do that," she agreed.

"Right, hang tight, I'll be there."

"Uh... thanks, Shy."

"Anytime, Tab. Yeah?"

He waited, and it felt like years before she whispered, "Yeah."

He disconnected, pulled on his last boot, and stood, tugging on his tee as he turned to his bed. One of the women was up on an elbow and blinking at him. The other was still out.

As he found his knife in the nightstand and shoved the sheath into his belt, he ordered, "Get her ass up. Both of you need to get dressed and get gone." He reached into the nightstand and grabbed his gun, shoving it into the back waistband of his jeans and pulling his tee over it. "You got fifteen minutes to get out. You're not gone by the time I get back, I will not be happy."

"Sure thing, babe," the awake one muttered. She lifted a hand to shove at the hip of her friend.

Jesus.

Slicing a glance through them he knew he was done. Some of the brothers, a lot older than him, enjoyed as much as they could get, however that came, and they didn't limit it to two pieces of ass.

He'd had that ride and often.

It hit him right then it went nowhere.

He'd never, not once, walked up to a woman who looked lost without him and became found the second she saw him. Who leaned into him the minute he touched her. Who made him laugh so hard, his head jerked back with it. Whose mouth he could take and the world melted away for him just as he made that same shit happen for her.

And he would not get that if he kept this shit up.

He jogged through the Compound to his bike and rode with his cell in his hand.

She texted, *I'm okay*, and Shy took in a calming breath and turned his eyes back to the road.

She texted again. This time, *I'm still okay*, and, getting closer to her, Shy felt his jaw begin to relax.

A few minutes later she texted again. This time it was *I'm still okay but this bathroom is seriously gross.*

When Shy got that, after his eyes went back to the road, he was flat-out smiling.

She kept texting her ongoing condition of *okay*, with a running commentary of how much she disliked her current location, until he was outside the house. He turned off his bike and scanned. Lights on in a front room, another one beaming from a small window at the opposite side at the back. The bathroom.

He bent his head to the phone and texted, *Outside, baby.*

Seconds later he saw a bare foot coming out the small window and another one, then legs. He kicked down the stand, swung off his bike, and jogged through the dark up the side of the house.

He caught her legs and tugged her out the rest of the way, putting her on her feet.

She tipped her head back to him, her face pale in the dark.

"Thanks," she said softly.

He, unfortunately, did not have all night to look in her shadowed but beautiful face. He had no idea what he was dealing with. He had to get them out of there.

He took her hand and muttered, "Let's go."

She nodded and jogged beside him, her hand in his, her shoes dangling from her other hand. He swung on his bike, she swung on behind him. A child born to the life, she wrapped her arms around him without hesitation.

He felt her tits pressed to his back and closed his eyes.

Then he opened them and asked, "Where you wanna go?"

"I need a drink," she replied.

"Bar or Compound?" he offered, knowing what she'd pick. She never came to the Compound anymore.

"Compound," she surprised him by answering.

Thank Christ he kicked those bitches out. He just hoped they followed orders.

He rode to the Compound, parked outside, and felt the loss when she pulled away and swung off. He lifted a hand to hold her steady as she bent to slide on her heels, then he took her hand and walked her into the Compound.

Luckily, it was deserted. Hopefully, his room was too. He didn't need one of those bitches wandering out and fucking Tab's night even worse.

"Grab a stool, babe. I'll get you a drink," he muttered, shifting her hand and arm out to lead her to the outside of the bar while he moved inside.

Tabby, he noted, took direction. She rounded the curve of the bar and took a stool.

Shy moved around the back of it and asked, "What're you drinking?"

"What gets you drunk the fastest?" she asked back, and he stopped, turned, put his hands on the bar and locked eyes on her.

"What kind of trouble did I pull you out of?" he asked quietly.

"None, now that I'm out that window," she answered quietly.

"You know those people?" he asked.

She shrugged and looked down at her hands on the bar. "An old friend. High school. Just her. The others..." She trailed off on another shrug.

Shy looked at her hands.

They were visibly shaking.

"Tequila," he stated, and her eyes came to his.

"What?"

"Gets you drunk fast."

She pressed her lips together and nodded.

He grabbed the bottle and put it in front of her.

She looked down at it then up at him, and her head tipped to the side when he didn't move.

"Glasses?" she prompted.

He tagged the bottle, unscrewed the top, lifted it to his

lips and took a pull. When he was done, he dropped his arm and extended it to her.

"You can't get drunk fast, you're fuckin' with glasses," he informed her.

The tip of her tongue came out to wet her upper lip and Jesus, he forgot how cute that was.

Luckily, she took his mind off her tongue when she took the bottle, stared at it a beat then put it to her lips and threw back a slug.

The bottle came down with Tabby spluttering and Shy reached for it.

Through a grin, he advised, "You may be drinking direct, sugar, but you still gotta drink smart."

"Right," she breathed out like her throat was on fire.

He put the bottle to his lips and took another drag before he put it to the bar.

Tabby wrapped her hand around it, lifted it, and sucked some back, but this time she did it smart and her hand with the bottle came down slowly, although she was still breathing kind of heavy.

When she recovered, he leaned into his forearms on the bar and asked softly, "You wanna talk?"

"No," she answered sharply, her eyes narrowing, the sorrow shifting through them slicing through his gut. She lifted the bottle, took another drink before locking her gaze with his. "I don't wanna talk. I don't wanna share my feelings. I don't wanna *get it out.* I wanna *get drunk.*"

She didn't leave any lines to read through, she said it plain, so he gave her that out.

"Right, so we gonna do that, you sittin' there sluggin' it back and me standin' here watchin' you, or are we gonna do something? Like play pool."

"I rock at pool," she informed him.

"Babe, I'll wipe the floor with you."

"No way," she scoffed.

"Totally," he said through a grin.

"You're so sure, darlin', we'll make it interesting," she offered.

"I'm up for that," he agreed. "I win, you make me cookies. You win, you pick."

He barely finished speaking before she gave him a gift the likes he'd never had in his entire fucking life.

The pale moved out of her features as pink hit her cheeks, life shot into her eyes, making them vibrant, their startling color rocking him to his fucking core before she bested all that shit and burst out laughing.

He had no idea what he did, what he said, but whatever it was, he'd do it and say it over and over until he took his last breath just so he could watch her laugh.

He didn't say a word when her laughter turned to chuckles and continued his silence, his eyes on her.

When she caught him looking at her, she explained, "My cooking, hit and miss. Sometimes, it's brilliant. Sometimes, it's..." she grinned "...*not.* Baking is the same. I just can't seem to get the hang of it. I don't even have that"—she lifted up her fingers to do air quotation marks—"*signature dish* that comes out great every time. I don't know what it is about me. Dad and Rush, even Tyra, they rock in the kitchen. Me, no." She leaned in. "*Totally* no. So I was laughing because anyone who knows me would not think cookies from me would be a good deal for a bet. Truth is, they could be awesome but they could also seriously suck."

"How 'bout I take my chances?" he suggested.

She shrugged, still grinning. "Your funeral."

Her words made Shy tense, and the pink slid out of her cheeks, the life started seeping out of her eyes.

"Drink," he ordered quickly.

"What?" she whispered, and he reached out and slid the tequila to her.

"Drink. Now. Suck it back, babe. Do it thinkin' what you get if you win."

She nodded, grabbed the bottle, took a slug, and dropped it to the bar with a crash, letting out a totally fucking cute "Ah" before she declared, "You change my oil."

His brows shot up. "That's it?"

"I need my oil changed and it costs, like, thirty dollars. I can buy a lot of stuff with thirty dollars. A lot of stuff *I want*. I don't want *oil*. My car does but I don't."

"Tabby, sugar, your dad part-owns the most kick-ass garage this side of the Mississippi and most of the other side, and you're paying for oil changes?"

Her eyes slid away and he knew why.

Fuck.

She was doing it to avoid him. Still.

Serious as shit, this had to stop.

So he was going to stop it.

"We play pool and we get drunk and we enjoy it, that's our plan, so let's get this shit out of the way," he stated. Her eyes slid back to him and he said flat out, "I fucked up. It was huge. It was a long time ago but it marked you. You were right. I was a dick. I made assumptions, they were wrong and I acted on 'em and I shouldn't have and that was more wrong. I wish you would have found the time to get in my face about it years ago so we could have had it out, but that's done. When you did get in my face about it, I should have sorted my shit, found you, and apologized. I didn't do that either. I'd like to know why you dialed my number tonight, but if you don't wanna share that shit, that's cool too. I'll just say, babe, I'm glad you did. You need a safe place just to forget shit and escape, I'll give it to you. Tonight. Tomorrow. Next week. Next month. That safe place is me, Tabby. But I don't want that old shit haunting this. Ghosts haunt until you get rid of them. Let's get rid of that fuckin' ghost and move on so I can beat your ass at pool."

As he spoke, he saw the tears pool in her eyes but he kept going, and when he stopped he didn't move even though it nearly killed him. Not to touch her, even her hand. Not to give her something.

It killed.

Before he lost the fight to hold back, she whispered, "You are never gonna beat my ass at pool."

That was when he grinned, leaned forward, and wrapped his hand around hers sitting on the bar.

"Get ready to have your ass kicked," he said softly.

"Oil changes for a year," she returned softly.

"You got it but cookies for a year," he shot back.

"Okay, but don't say I didn't warn you," she replied.

He'd eat her cookies, they were brilliant or they sucked. If Tabitha Allen made it, he'd eat anything.

Shy didn't share that.

He gave her hand a squeeze, nabbed the bottle, and took off down the bar toward the cues on the wall.

Tabby followed.

* * *

They were in the dark, in his bed, in his room in the Compound.

Shy was on his back, eyes to the ceiling.

Tabby was three feet away, on her side, her chin was tipped down.

She was obliterated.

Shy wasn't even slightly drunk.

She'd won four games, he'd won five.

Cookies for a year.

Now, he was winning something else, because tequila didn't make Tabitha Allen a happy drunk.

It made her a talkative one.

It also made her get past ugly history and trust him with absolutely everything that mattered right now in her world.

"DOA," she whispered to the bed.

"I know, sugar," he whispered to the ceiling.

"Where did you hear?" she asked.

"Walkin' into the Compound, boys just heard and they were taking off."

"You didn't come to the hospital."

He was surprised she'd noticed.

"No. I wasn't your favorite person. Didn't think I could help. Went up to Tack and Cherry's, helped Sheila with the boys," he told her.

"I know. Ty-Ty told me," she surprised him again by saying. "That was cool of you to do. They're a handful. Sheila tries but the only ones who can really handle them are Dad, Tyra, Rush, Big Petey, and me."

Shy didn't respond.

"So, uh . . . thanks," she finished.

"No problem, honey."

She fell silent and Shy gave her that.

She broke it.

"Tyra had to cancel all the wedding plans."

"Yeah?" he asked quietly.

"Yeah," she answered. "Second time she had to do that. That Elliott guy wasn't dead when she had to do it for Lanie, but still. Two times. Two weddings. It isn't worth it. All that planning. All that money..." she pulled in a shaky breath "...not worth it. I'm not doing it again. I'm never getting married."

At that, Shy rolled to his side, reached out and found her hand lying on the bed.

He curled his hand around hers, held tight and advised, "Don't say that, baby. You're twenty-two years old. You got your whole life ahead of you."

"So did he."

Fuck, he couldn't argue that.

He pulled their hands up the bed and shifted slightly closer before he said gently, "If he was in this room right now, sugar, right now, he wouldn't want this. He wouldn't want to hear you say that shit. Dig deep, Tabby. What would he want to hear you say?"

She was silent then he heard her breath hitch before she whispered, "I'd give anything..."

She trailed off and went quiet.

"Baby," he whispered back.

Her hand jerked and her body slid across the bed to slam into his, her face in his throat, her arm winding around him tight, her voice so raw, it hurt to hear. His own throat was ragged just listening.

"I'd give anything for him to be in this room. *Anything.* I'd give my hair, and I *like* my hair. I'd give my car, and Dad fixed that car up for me. I *love* that car. I'd swim an ocean. I'd walk through arrows. I'd *bleed* for him to be here."

She burrowed deeper into him and Shy took a deep breath, pressing closer, giving her his warmth. He wrapped an arm around her and pulled her tighter as she cried quietly, one hand holding his tight.

He said nothing but listened, eyes closed, heart burning, to the sounds of her grief.

Time slid by and her tears slowly stopped flowing.

Finally, she said softly, "I dreamed a dream."

"What, sugar?"

"I dreamed a dream," she repeated.

He tipped his head and put his lips to the top of her hair but he had no reply. He knew it sucked when dreams died. He'd been there. There were no words to say. Nothing made it better except time.

Then she shocked the shit out of him and started singing, her clear, alto voice wrapping around a song he'd never heard before, but its words were gutting, perfect for her, what she had to be feeling, sending that fire in his heart to his throat so high, he would swear he could taste it.

"*Les Mis*," she whispered when she was done.

"What?"

"The musical. *Les Misérables.* Jason took me to go see it. It's very sad."

If that was a song from the show, it fucking had to be.

She pressed closer. "I dreamed a dream, Shy."

"You'll dream more dreams, baby."

"I'll never dream," she whispered, her voice lost, tragic.

"We'll get you to a dream, honey," he promised, pulling her closer.

She pressed in, and he listened as her breath evened

out, felt as her body slid into sleep, all the while thinking her hair smellcd phenomenal.

Shy turned into her, trapping her little body under his and muttering, “We’ll get you to a dream.”

Tabby held his hand in her sleep.

Shy held her but didn’t sleep.

The sun kissed the sky and Shy’s eyes closed.

When he opened them, she was gone.

CHAPTER TWO

Waking Up in His Arms

Six weeks later…

THE BELL TO my apartment rang and, standing in front of my mirror in the bathroom, I jumped.

Dad and Tyra were there to take me to the hog roast.

It was time, according to Dad, that I got back into life. I wasn't so sure but Dad was, and when Dad was sure about something, well…you got yourself together and hauled yourself to a hog roast.

I stared at myself in the mirror, seeing my hair out to there, more makeup than I usually wore, a sweet long-sleeved Harley tee I bought just last weekend, the first I'd bought or worn in ages, faded jeans that fit *great*, and a fabulous belt. I couldn't see them in the mirror but I also had on high, spike-heeled boots that I usually wore under smart skirts.

Nice.

Stupid!

I looked awesome, so awesome even I could say I looked awesome.

It was still stupid.

The bell rang again and there was a knock following it but I couldn't move. I just stood there, staring at myself in the mirror, wondering what the hell I was doing.

I heard the door open and I knew Tyra had used her key.

"Tabby, honey, are you here?" I heard her call, and I tried to get my feet to move but I just stood, frozen in front of the mirror. "Tab, you here?" she yelled.

She was closer, moving into my bedroom, I could tell.

My feet finally moved, taking me out of the bathroom and into the bedroom.

There she was, thick, lush, shining auburn hair and lots of it, great figure even after two kids, Tyra Allen, my friend, my saving grace years ago.

My stepmom.

The instant her green eyes hit me, they got wide and a smile spread on her gorgeous face.

"Wow, honey, you look *great*."

See? I looked great.

I was still stupid.

I knew what she saw. For months, I went through the motions of life but I put no effort into it. I got up and went to work, came home, and tried to sleep. I hung with the family and pretended everything was fine but they knew it was all a show.

Especially Dad.

Kane Allen, known as Tack to everyone but Dad to me, was far from dumb, which was cool most of the time but wasn't when I was trying to pull the wool, something which I never, not in my life, succeeded in doing with my Dad.

“I messed up,” I declared and watched Tyra blink.

“Pardon?” she asked.

“I messed up,” I repeated.

“How did you mess up?” she asked.

“I slept with Shy.”

She didn’t blink then. Her eyes got so wide I thought they’d bug out of her head.

She rallied quickly, stuck her hand in her back pocket and pulled out her phone. She jabbed it with her finger and put it to her ear.

“Tack, honey, go on without us,” she said into her phone. “Tabby and I’ll take her car and meet you there later.” She paused, then, “I don’t know yet, but she and I have to talk, and when we get things sorted out, we’ll meet you at Chaos.” Pause, then, “Handsome, I told you, I don’t know yet, but I’ll find out and we’ll sort it out, then we’ll meet you there.” Another pause with an eye roll, then, softer, “I got this, you know I do. We’ll meet you at the roast soon.”

Dad was worried, I could tell. This was not a surprise. He was the kind of dad who loved you so much he hurt when you hurt, and when you lost something precious he lost it right with you.

On that thought, I saw what I saw a lot when Tyra was talking to Dad.

Even though she dipped her chin and turned her head so I got her profile, I still saw Tyra’s face get soft before she said quietly, “Yeah. Will do. Love you.”

Then I saw something else I saw a lot when Tyra was talking to Dad: her face got softer and I knew Dad was telling her he loved her too.

Tyra was the bomb, so I was glad she had that from Dad and I was even more glad that she gave it to him.

She stabbed the screen on her phone, shoved it into her pocket and focused on me.

Then she asked, "You slept with Shy?"

I nodded but clarified, "Six weeks ago, but we slept-slept, not did the business slept." Her brows went up so I further explained, "See, I was in a situation, he got me out of that situation, I asked him to get me drunk, he did, we played pool, we talked, we ended up in his bed, I sang him a song from *Les Mis*, then I passed out and woke up in his arms."

Her head tipped to the side and her eyes grew sharp, and they did this about the time I stated I was in a situation.

As I said, my dad was far from dumb. Being really not dumb, for some reason I didn't get, he married my mom, who was a lot closer to dumb than anyone I knew. However, being not dumb, Dad got shot of her and didn't make the same mistake twice. Therefore, Tyra was also far from dumb, which also worked in my favor most of the time.

Sometimes, it did not.

I knew this was one of those times when she queried, "You were in a situation?"

I licked my lip and she watched.

Then she moved to the bed while motioning to it with her hand. "Right, talk to me."

She sat on the bed, and I sat with her and commenced laying it out.

"Okay, well, what I'm going to say isn't gonna make you happy but here it is. Six weeks ago I was out with Natalie."

She bit her lip, her face went blank, and I got this.

Natalie Harbinger had been my best friend since

forever. I went to college to be a nurse. Natalie went to the same college as me, but she went to party. She put a lot of effort in and therefore excelled at this endeavor to the point she got kicked out of college. She continued to do this and there was nothing wrong with that, except the longer she did it the iffier became the element she did it with.

People at our age started to grow up and get themselves sorted. If they didn't, their lives started spiraling down a path that would mean they never got sorted.

Natalie didn't grow up and get herself sorted.

I got this. Natalie's mom was arguably a bigger bitch than mine. The problem was, Natalie didn't have a dad who gave a crap and a stepmom who was the bomb. I understood doing stuff to get attention, even if it was bad attention, but for me that crap was over years ago. She just didn't seem to be able to pull herself out of it.

Thus Tyra was not a big fan of Natalie's, and even Dad, who was the president of a motorcycle club and essentially had a life motto of 'live and let live,' had issues with her. The short of the long of it was, they didn't like me hanging with her.

Furthermore, Jason had hated her. Unfortunately, Natalie returned the favor. This put me in the middle, which was not a fun place to be. Jason was the kind of guy who pretty much laid it out if the situation warranted it, and he hated Natalie enough to lay it out. Natalie also wasn't the kind of person to keep things buried, so she didn't hesitate to share. This was not comfortable for me, but I was the kind of person who was growing up and getting my life sorted. I was also falling in love so, naturally, rather than making a choice (as such), I started spending less time with her and more time with Jason.

She took the time I could give her without too much bellyaching, and I worked at keeping our friendship close even as it changed with the different paths our lives were taking.

But when Jason died, she'd totally stepped up. She was there for me. She didn't breathe a word against Jason and kept her other crap separate. It was all about taking my back.

Six weeks ago, I needed her to take my back a different way.

I was tired of no sleep. I was tired of the constant reminders that Jason wasn't there and never again would be. I was tired of the empty feeling in my stomach that would hollow out further when some memory hit me or a wedding card from someone who hadn't heard about Jason came through the mail or I got a phone call from someone Tyra didn't know to contact about something to do with the life Jason and I were going to start.

I needed a release. I needed to go back in time when, for Natalie and me, it was all about fun and music and beer and talking and not about how life could go straight down the toilet.

I needed to forget. I needed to remember when life was different, when it was good.

When things went wrong, I called Shy because he wasn't like the other guys. He didn't know Jason and he didn't like me. I figured, like any of my father's brothers would do, he'd come get me, get me safe, and that would be it. He wouldn't look at me with kind eyes, urge me to talk, or give me a gentle lecture about hanging with Natalie, and I didn't need any of that. In fact, I went out with Nat in the first place to get away from that.

I'd programmed his number in when I got my new phone. I didn't know why, didn't think about why, I just did.

What I didn't expect was that he would give me exactly what I needed, be totally cool about it and also unbelievably sweet.

"Six weeks ago you were out with Natalie," Tyra prompted, and I focused on her.

"I just needed...I needed..." I trailed off, and Tyra reached out to squeeze my hand.

"I get what you needed," she said softly then lifted her chin for me to continue, so I did.

"It being Natalie, I'm sure you're not surprised that our company wasn't great company." The look on her face told me she wasn't surprised, but she had no response, so I kept going. "I was a little freaked, I called Shy, he came and got me, and the rest happened as I told you. The problem is, Shy was awesome, really cool, and I slipped out while he was sleeping and haven't seen him or talked to him in six weeks, which is *not* cool."

"Not sure about the not talking for six weeks part, but Shy *is* awesome," she declared, and I blinked.

"You think Shy's awesome?" I asked in disbelief.

"I do, don't you?" she asked.

"Uh...I don't know him very well...or I didn't," I evaded.

"True, noticed that," she murmured. "You're tight with all the brothers but not Shy. Thought it was because of that huge crush you had on him ages ago but, whatever. Bottom line, he's a good guy."

Tyra didn't know about what Shy did to me, no one did. I shared everything with Tyra but not what he'd done.

I didn't even tell Natalie about that, and I shared everything with her too.

That was how much it hurt.

I'd loved him. It was a young, faraway love, but sometimes that was the most intense kind, or it was when you're young and you love someone from afar. He'd crushed me, so bad I couldn't even reexperience it by sharing.

So I didn't.

When I didn't speak, Tyra did.

"I like him. Your dad likes and respects him. He's great with your little brothers, he's actually great with all the brothers' kids. He's smart. He's funny. He works hard and he's loyal. Your dad says that if Dog or Brick wanted to step down as his lieutenant, he'd ask Shy to step up."

I stared at her because this shocked me. That was huge coming from Dad.

She kept talking. "Says he's loyal to the Club in a way that the recruits who didn't live through what the other brothers lived through when your dad was cleaning up the Club aren't because they weren't tested. They don't know how to be. Shy is, though, according to Tack. Shy's all about his brothers, the Club, the family, so I'm not surprised he took care of you, Tab. Any of the boys would do that for you, not just for your dad." She grinned. "Though, not sure any of the boys would put up with you singing a song from *Les Mis*. That shows your dad is right. Shy's more loyal than the rest if he put up with that."

I rolled my eyes.

She ignored my eye roll and asked, "What'd you sing, 'Master of the House'?"

I rolled my eyes back to her.

"'I Dreamed a Dream,'" I answered, and her grin faded.

Dad had never seen *Les Misérables*. Dad would never see *Les Misérables*. Dad got a funny look on his face when I told him Jason was taking me to see *Les Misérables*. To Dad, a man taking his woman to a musical did not say good things. When I told him, he opened his mouth to say something, caught sight of a smiling-so-big-I-knew-she-was-in-danger-of-laughing Tyra, fortunately shut his mouth, and said no more.

But Jason had a mother and three sisters who were into musicals in a *big* way. They dragged him with them and Jason went, but he did this under duress.

But not *Les Mis*.

"Sweetheart," he'd said, "I saw *The Pajama Game* when I was eleven and had nightmares until I was fifteen. We won't get into what *Cats* did to me. But *Les Mis*, Tab, everyone has to see that."

It meant so much to him I went, and I had to admit I didn't get it through the first act. Jason had decided I needed to "experience" it, so he didn't tell me anything, and since they sang all the time, even the dialogue, I couldn't catch it all and I had no idea what was going on. Luckily, there were some kick-butt songs, or the first act would have been wasted on me.

At intermission, Jason saw the error of his ways, filled me in, and the second act rocked my world.

Dad loved me, but he was never going to listen to musicals with me.

Tyra loved me, and she didn't care about musicals, but she listened to it with me in my car all the time when we were off shopping or to lunch or whatever we did.

She'd heard "I Dreamed a Dream" lots.

She knew what I was saying.

"Oh, Tabby," she whispered.

See?

I flopped to my back, stared at the ceiling then moved just my eyeballs to her to see she'd shifted closer and was resting on a hand in the bed beside me.

"It felt good," I told her, and she smiled.

"Of course it felt good, honey. Shy's a nice guy who took your back and listened to you sing a sad song. It was what you needed and he gave it to you."

"No," I whispered and held her eyes. "It felt good waking up in his arms."

Her smile faded again.

"Oh, Tabby," she repeated in a whisper, and I put my hands over my face.

From behind them I said, "It was messed up, crazy, *wrong*." I pulled my hands away, looked into her troubled face, and let it all hang out. "It was wrong, Ty-Ty. It was… it was *messed up*. I *forgot*."

"You forgot what, honey?" she asked gently.

"Everything," I answered, rolling to my side and getting up on a forearm. "*Everything*, Ty-Ty. I was crying when I fell asleep and Shy was holding me, but somehow when we were sleeping he tucked me under him, tucked me close, and I woke up and all I felt was warm. Warm and safe and loved and *right*. That was all I felt. All I thought. All that went through my mind was how good all that felt."

"Is that bad?" Her tone was still gentle but now also cautious.

"*Yes*," I hissed.

"How?" she asked carefully.

"Jason didn't hold me." She closed her eyes and opened them when I carried on, and I did so thanking God I could talk to Tyra about everything, "He was loving and he could cuddle but not, you know, in bed. He was a hug-and-roll guy. After we, uh..." I let that hang then went on, "He hugged me, let me go, then rolled away. He was sweet about it but that just wasn't his thing. He liked to sleep in his space and he left me to mine. I'd never had that, not ever, not from a guy, not until I got it from Shy and *I liked it*. It *felt good*. No, it felt *great*."

"Tab—" she began, but I was on a roll so I blathered on, talking over her.

"It gets worse," I shared. "Even after I woke up feeling safe and right, it didn't all crash over me. It didn't come to me at all. I looked up at Shy and he's, well... you know, everyone knows Shy's really good-looking, but asleep, Ty-Ty, asleep—" I leaned toward her "—he's *amazing*. So amazing, so handsome, so close, holding me, making me feel safe and loved and after he'd been so cool with me the night before, I kept forgetting. Kept forgetting *everything* and I, oh Tyra, God help me"—my voice dropped to a whisper—"I nearly kissed him."

After sharing that, I flopped back to the bed, put my hands over my face and let it wash over me as it did every time I remembered it, which was often, dozens of times *daily* for six weeks.

Guilt.

Shame.

Betrayal.

"Tabby, honey, look at me," she called gently, I pulled in breath behind my hands, then I dropped them away from my face and looked at her.

She was smiling at me just as gently as she was talking to me, and it hit me, not for the first time, not by a long shot, that I loved Tyra Allen a whole lot.

"I'm glad you shared that with me. Your dad has been concerned and even more concerned lately, thinking that something else was not right with you," she told me.

There it was.

Proof my father wasn't stupid and I couldn't pull anything over on him.

"It was a betrayal to Jason," I whispered, and admitting it out loud hurt worse.

She kept talking gently even as she grabbed my hand and squeezed, "It wasn't, Tabby. It's natural. It's proof you're healing."

I shook my head but she squeezed my hand again.

"It is, honey," she pushed. "This sucks, it sucks huge, so huge there are no words for how huge it sucks, and I would say you're too young to process it, losing Jason the way you did when you did. But honestly, you could be a hundred and three and you wouldn't have lived enough life to be able to process that kind of loss. Jason was a good man and he loved you. He deserves your grief. But he loved you and he'd want you to heal, move on, find happiness."

I shook my head again and she dipped her face closer and kept going.

"I understand why you feel the way you do, but what *you* need to understand is that's part of the process. Having those feelings, remembering you're alive, remembering there are good things to look forward to. You're young, Tab, you have a lot of life ahead of you. What happened with Shy is reminding you that life is out there for you when you're ready. Those feelings you had with Shy are natural. They're good. They *are* right. More so for you now because they indicate you've begun the process of healing."

"I totally forgot him, Tyra," I returned. "I *totally forgot* Jason for *whole minutes*, lying in the arms of another man. Worse!" I cried, sitting up and twisting toward her to see she reared back. "It felt... it felt..." I stammered, unable to get out what I hadn't really even admitted to myself. Then I pushed it out, "*Beautiful*. Waking up that way with Shy... it was... it felt..."

Oh God, was I going to say it?

I was going to say it.

"*Better*," I finished. I watched as her eyes blanked, hiding her reaction, and I knew what that meant so I cried, "See! I'm messed up!"

She reached out, snatched up my hand again, and shook it. "You are *not* messed up, Tabby. You're a woman and Shy's a man, a good-looking one who was there for you when you needed him, and he handled you with care. Your feelings are *natural*. They *are* beautiful. They *are* right. There is nothing wrong with forgetting. I want to be gentle with you, honey, I know you don't want to lose Jason now, even only having him in grief, but in all honesty, you'll get to the point when you'll forget for days then weeks—" she squeezed my hand as my heart squeezed and she finished "—and so on. It will happen and that's healing too, and you might not believe it but I do, I totally do. I know he loved you enough not to want you to forget him completely, which you never will, he'll always be a part of you, but enough so you could be happy. I know that, Tab. I also know, God forbid, the roles were reversed, you'd want that for Jason too. Nothing, not one thing you did or felt that night was wrong or shameful. I don't think so, and I don't think Jason would either."

I had to admit, she was right about that. Jason loved me and I loved him, and although it would suck huge for him as it did for me, if he lost me, I loved him enough to hope he'd eventually be happy.

"I get you," she said softly. "I *so* get you, Tab, spending time with Natalie, calling a brother to take care of you, having the feelings you had. You are not doing anything wrong except being way too hard on yourself. In this time especially, my beautiful girl, you need to be gentle with yourself. Please, stop beating yourself up."

Okay, I had to admit she might be right about that too.

"Okay?" she pressed, and I nodded.

"Okay," I replied quietly, and a small smile curved her mouth.

Then she let my hand go but lifted hers to tuck my hair behind my ear before she ran a finger lovingly along my jaw and her hand fell away.

"Now, since I'm laying it out, what I say next does not take back anything I said before, but it has to be said. Shy is a good guy and he did right by you. What you felt was natural and part of healing. Going out with Natalie was what you needed, and when you felt the situation was unsure, you did the right thing and called a brother to take care of you. But I caution you, Tab, to learn from these things, how they went wrong and how they made you feel. I know you love Natalie, but I also know you know she can be trouble. From what you said, I know Shy handled you with care, but I also know you know how he can be trouble for a girl who's lost something precious and may be vulnerable."

One could say I knew *that*.

Tyra wasn't done.

"I can't imagine Shy would ever go there with you, but Shy's Shy and everyone knows all the ways he is, the good and, for a woman, the bad. Don't get mixed up feeling those good feelings you had with him or *any* man. Assess where you are and only move forward in that part of healing when you're genuinely ready. Not going for that hit that is meaningless just because it feels good and makes you forget. Am I making sense?"

She was.

She totally was.

She was also right. Shy took my back and handled me with care.

But Shy was Shy, and that wasn't where it was heading. I wasn't that for him.

He'd made certain to heal the breach but that was as far as it went. I couldn't *really* mess up and mistake it for something else.

"I made him cookies," I told her, and she blinked.

"You made him cookies?"

"We played pool, we bet on the games we played, and he bet me for cookies. I made them for him. They're in the kitchen. I also didn't phone him for six weeks even after he was great with me and now, I...I...well"—I threw out a hand—"I don't know how to face him. What to say. How to excuse the fact I didn't call to say thanks or even hi."

Her eyes moved over my face and hair, I saw

something flash in them before she hid it, caught my gaze, and grinned at me.

"Shy bet you for your cookies."

I grinned back and muttered, "Shut up."

"Maybe Shy isn't as sharp as Tack thinks he is," she remarked.

"I warned him, he said he wanted cookies."

Something else flashed in her eyes again before she hid it—again—and I gave her that play. I did this because when I needed my own head space, she gave it to me. It would be uncool not to return the favor.

"Okay, this is the plan," she declared. "I take your car and the cookies to the roast. I tell everyone you aren't feeling great and ask one of the guys to bring your car back tomorrow. You take tonight to relax and reflect." She grinned. "Or not reflect and just relax. Whatever you need. Then, in your time, when you're ready, you find your way to connect with Shy and share gratitude. He'll know by the cookies you didn't forget."

That sounded like a plan and, as usual, Tyra sorted me out.

"Thanks, Ty-Ty," I said softly.

"Anytime, honey," she replied softly then shifted to move off the bed, ordering, "Right. Cookies."

I rolled off my side, got her my keys and the cookies, got her long hug at the door and locked it after she was gone.

I moved back to my room, changed into a nightie and my robe, washed the makeup off my face and went to the kitchen. I grabbed the leftover chocolate from Christmas that I had a lot of. Tyra went nuts with stockings at Christmas, and not just with Rider and Cut, who expected Santa to go bonkers, but also with me and my older brother, Rush, who were too old for Santa. It was three months old but I was going to eat it.

I took it to the couch, sorted out my Hitchcock marathon, and scared myself silly through *Rebecca* and *Rear Window* before falling asleep among a mountain of green, red, gold, and silver foil during *The Birds.*

CHAPTER THREE

It Was Family

THE BELL AT my door rang. I jumped and foil wrappers went flying.

I saw blue screen on my TV and stared at it fuzzily for a second before I grabbed my remote, hit Off, and the screen went blank. My eyes went to the DVD player and I saw it was just coming on nine in the morning.

The bell sounded again, and I turned my head to look at the door.

"Who could that be?" I muttered, straightening from the couch amid a fall of silver, gold, red, and green.

It wasn't quite nine, and I grew up Chaos. This meant I knew that my people didn't often see that hour and definitely not after a hog roast. Not even if they got a wild hair with being worried about me and popped by, which happened more than occasionally lately.

I moved to the door, rolled up on my toes, and looked out the peephole.

Then I stopped breathing.

Shy was out there, his head tipped down looking at

his boots, but even with head tipped down, face mostly obscured, he still looked hot.

Crap!

Now what did I do?

As I stared out the peephole, his head came up, his brows drawn, and he looked at the door. I was a little surprised he didn't look pissed or impatient. Instead, he looked a little perplexed and a little concerned.

He lifted his hand and no bell this time, he knocked. *Loud.*

Oh God.

What did I do?

Before my mind figured it out, my feet took me running toward my hall, then they shifted me and sent me back to the door while my mouth shouted, "Coming!"

Okay, I didn't know what to do but my feet and mouth did, and apparently that was acting like a dork.

I hit the door, unlocked the locks, threw it open, and standing there was all the hotness that was Parker "Shy" Cage.

My belly flipped.

Crap.

"What are you doin'—?" I started but didn't finish.

I didn't finish because his hand snaked out, hooked me at the back of my head, and yanked me forward into a forced face plant to his chest. The instant I was there, his other arm wrapped around my waist, he shuffled us in and kicked the door closed with his boot.

Then I felt his lips hit my hair and I went completely still.

I did this because my dad put his lips to my hair when he was holding me close and talking to me.

I liked it. I always liked it.

But this, with Shy, I *loved* it.

"Cherry said you felt shit, sugar. You feelin' better?" he asked into my hair.

"Um... yeah," I mumbled into his chest, seeing as this was my only choice since my face was smushed there.

His lips left my hair but he didn't back away when he remarked, "Uh, Tab, just sayin'. You feel shit, eatin' a mountain of three-month-old Christmas candy might not be the way to go."

Obviously he spied my fall of candy wrappers.

He was also being funny but I didn't laugh, though I did smile into his chest.

His hand at the back of my head slipped down to my neck. I pulled my face out of his tee and looked up at him.

Yes, concern, hotness... no, more accurately *extreme* hotness. That was it.

"You aren't pissed at me?"

Yep. That was what came right out of my mouth.

His brows drew together. "Pissed at you?"

He seemed perplexed and I wondered, if he was confused about why he should be pissed, if I should enlighten him.

As was often the case with me, my mouth decided before my brain did and it started blathering.

"For not, um... when you were so cool with me that night, me not calling to say thanks for being so cool, which was *uncool*."

His face relaxed, his startling green eyes grew warm and he replied quietly, "Baby, bein' your safe harbor doesn't come with me gettin' pissed when you gotta do what you gotta do when you gotta do it. It also doesn't come with me expecting you to explain why you did what you had to do. Bein' your safe harbor means lettin' you do what you gotta do when you gotta do it and not gettin' pissed."

That was a good answer.

And cool.

And sweet.

Crap.

He gave me a squeeze, let me go, then moved around me, sauntering with his long, lanky, loose-limbed, biker badass grace toward my couch, saying, "You're feelin' better, I'll make you breakfast."

I wasn't listening, and this was mostly because I was engaged in watching him moving, bending, and scooping up Christmas candy wrappers, balling them into his fist. As I was occupied with this, I also was wondering how he could be all long, lanky, loose-limbed, biker badass while cleaning up Christmas candy wrappers. Further, as I always did around Shy even when I was holding my grudge, I was thinking he was all kinds of handsome. Thick, dark, overlong hair. Strong jaw that was so cut, it jutted out a bit at the hinges. Those green eyes. The Chaos tats on the insides of his forearms. The small silver medallions hanging from thin, black leather cords around his neck. The flat, black leather straps around his wrists that had thick, silver bands punched with insignias. The chunky silver rings on his fingers.

Amazing.

He turned to me, "Tab, honey, you want breakfast?"

I came to with a start and looked up at him. "Breakfast?'

"Yeah, breakfast. You're feelin' better, I'll make you some."

"I don't have any food in the house," I told him, and his brows went up.

"You don't have any food in the house?"

"Well," I did a quick mental inventory, figured he wouldn't want tuna or ranch-style beans for breakfast then suggested, "We could have Pop-Tarts."

His lips twitched and he shook his head. "Not sure Pop-Tarts are good sittin' on a mountain of Christmas candy. I'll take you out."

My belly flipped again.

He'd take me out?

For breakfast?

"Pardon?" I asked.

He tossed the ball of foil on my coffee table, it bounced off the other side, went rolling across the floor, and stopped a few feet in front of the TV.

"I'll take you out for breakfast," he mostly repeated.

My eyes left the ball of foil and shot to him.

"Uh..." I started then found, for once, my mouth couldn't go on.

"Tab, babe." He came at me. "Get a move on. Once you get dressed, we'll go." He made it to me, grabbed my hand, and pulled me to the mouth of the hall.

He stopped us there and I looked up at him, still frozen.

"Get," he ordered softly. "Breakfast."

Then he put a hand in the small of my back and gave me a gentle push.

Seeing as he pushed me, however gently, and my body's momentum was taking me down the hall, I "got" and scurried to my bedroom wondering if I could have breakfast with Shy or even if I should.

But the fact of the matter was, he'd shown at my house

after I hadn't talked to him in six weeks, and he wasn't pissed or in my face. He was concerned and wanted to take me out for breakfast.

So I hit the shower thinking I not only could do this, I *should.*

He'd faced our history straight on, guided us around it, and obviously, with the way he was being now, he intended to keep us firmly on that path.

And Tyra was right. He was Chaos, a brother, family. He'd done what any of the brothers would do that night, looking out for me.

Yeah, I definitely *should* do this.

Forty-five minutes later, I decided not only that I shouldn't but I *couldn't.*

This was because, even though I gave my legs a close shave last night while getting ready for the hog roast, I did it again.

I also couldn't because I pulled out my favorite Harley tee. One that was buried in a drawer. One that I hadn't worn in years. One that fit great and since it was tight at my breasts that made it even better.

And further because I had on faded jeans, a fabulous riveted belt, and high-heeled boots, and I'd fluffed my hair out and spritzed it with that stuff that made it look all beachy and cool. I'd also put on makeup even though I didn't intend to. I had put on a hint of makeup, just blush and mascara, but I decided on liner. Then decided liner looked stupid without eye shadow, so I put on eye shadow. After all this, I decided makeup didn't look good without appropriate accessories, so I layered on the silver and now I was totally made up, done up and (mostly) tricked out.

Which was stupid (again).

And wrong.

And it meant I should not, could not, go to breakfast with Shy.

The problem was, he'd been waiting for forty-five minutes, and I knew from a lifetime of experience that bikers weren't all that patient. To fix the damage, I'd need a new outfit and a face rubdown, and I didn't have time to select a new outfit. That could take twenty minutes alone.

For that reason, I knew I had to do this.

He was being cool and sweet.

It was just breakfast.

So I walked out of my bedroom in order to do it.

I turned the corner at the end of the hall and saw Shy leaning into his arm at the bar, head bowed, hand scratching on a piece of paper.

My first thought was he was left-handed.

My second thought was that I found that extremely interesting.

My third thought was that Shy looked perfectly at ease in my kitchen, like he'd been there dozens of times before. Like he was comfortable there. Like he belonged there.

Crap.

My apartment was in a decent complex that was well taken care of. However, it was old, though not *that* old. It was also worn but not *that* worn. And the appliances weren't great but they weren't *that* bad.

It was as good a place as any to wait it out until my new life started. I wasn't going to be there long (or so I thought), the rent was super-affordable, so why not?

That said, I moved in and made it mine with funky stuff I liked, and I had to admit I was comfortable there.

It was small, cozy, took very little time to clean, and was close to the hospital and Chaos.

Jason lived in a three-bedroom town house that he bought for us to move in together when our lives started. The town house was not worn or old, and the appliances were awesome.

Jason had grown up in a suburb of Denver, and his parents and one of his sisters still lived there. He'd never had worn or old. Anytime something got too old or broke down, his father replaced it.

Jason hated my apartment. Not frequently but often enough to make his point, when we were cuddling on the couch watching TV or he was sitting on a stool at the bar watching me ruin dinner, he'd say something like, "Can't wait until we can get you out of this pit."

It wasn't a pit. It was old and worn, but it wasn't a pit.

Jason thought it was a pit.

Looking at Shy leaning into the counter, he didn't look like he thought my place was a pit. He didn't look like he thought anything except whatever he was scratching on the paper.

"We'll go to Racine's on my bike," he muttered, not looking up. "Tug's bringing your ride back later. When we get back, we'll take it and get you to the store. I did an inventory and seriously, Tab, you need to stock up."

That was when he lifted his head and looked at me. Two beats after his eyes hit my face, they moved over my hair before they went down then they went back up. They did this slowly with a certain look in them that made my belly flip again.

On the way back up, I saw a muscle jump in his jaw.

Okay, maybe I shouldn't do this.

His eyes were on another downward run, caught around the area of my breasts when I forced out: "Racine's?"

His eyes changed direction and came to mine. He pushed away from the counter, pulled the top paper off the pad and, shoving it in his back pocket, he said, "Yeah, Racine's. Ready?"

It hit me then he said he was taking me to Racine's on his bike.

I liked this.

First, Racine's was awesome, especially for breakfast.

Second, he was taking me on his bike.

I had to admit, as much as it killed, that was something I had missed with Jason.

Bikes.

I loved riding on the back of a bike, always did. Loved the growl of Harley pipes. I loved even looking at them.

Jason didn't do bikes, and as our wedding drew nearer, I'd begun to plot how I was going to talk him around to getting one.

I hadn't held high hopes for my plotting.

This was because he'd once declared, though gently, "I know that was your life, sweetheart, how you grew up. It's just not my thing and, no offense to your family, it also isn't real safe."

Well, he was in a car when he died, so apparently they weren't real safe either.

"Tab, babe, you ready?" Shy asked, and I looked at him. He'd come closer during my minitrance, but he took one look at my face, dipped his close and asked quietly, "Hey, you okay?"

I sucked in breath, nodded, and answered, "I will be when I'm on the back of your bike."

His eyes moved over my face, then his lips turned up, and, finally, he caught my hand and moved me to the door.

He held my hand as we moved to his bike. He climbed on. I climbed on. His Dyna Glide roared to life, and I found I was right.

I was okay now that I was on the back of his bike.

I was even better when the wind was rushing through my hair, my front tight to his back, my arms around him, feeling the same things I felt when he came and got me out of trouble six weeks before.

Free.

Right.

I didn't let my mind go to how free and right I felt or why. I just let myself feel it, let the wind whip away my worries, let the pipes drown out anything in my head. I held on and enjoyed the ride.

We got to Racine's all too soon. Shy parked, I swung a leg over, he swung a leg over, and he grabbed my hand. He held it as we walked to the restaurant, and he kept hold of it as we were shown to our table. He only let me go when we were seated.

We got our coffee and ordered before Shy spoke.

"So what was it?" he asked.

I put my coffee cup down on the table and asked back, "What was what?"

"You feelin' shit," he said. "Headache, flu, what?"

I looked him in the eye and decided on honesty.

"It was nothing. Tyra made excuses. I just didn't feel up to a hog roast and I didn't feel up to anyone poking and prodding about why I wasn't up for a hog roast. So I stayed home."

He held my eyes a beat before he said softly, "That's cool."

It was cool he thought that was cool.

He was just plain cool.

And sweet.

Him being so cool and sweet, I decided it was time so I went for it.

"Now that I've got you, I just wanted to say, belatedly, thank you for dropping everything and coming to get me that night. You...I...well, I needed that night to go a certain way, it was going the wrong way, and you were there for me. I...everyone...well, I needed to get drunk and play pool and sing songs from musicals and you made that safe for me. It was what I needed, and ever since you gave it to me, I've wanted to say thank you and now...well, now I can. So thank you."

There.

Good.

I'd finally gotten the chance to say what I needed to say, and although I mostly stammered, I still said it and I was glad I did.

Shy took a sip of his coffee, put his mug down on the table, sat back, looked at me, and commenced with rocking my world.

"Pleased I could give that to you, Tabby. It's what you need, it's what I'm here to give you. Know that. Wish I had someone to give me somethin' like that when my parents were murdered, so I'm glad I can give it to you."

Luckily I wasn't taking a sip of coffee or I would not only have spit it on him but I also would have choked on it.

"Pardon?" I whispered and his head jerked slightly but his eyes grew sharp on me.

"You didn't know?" he asked.

Heck no, I didn't know.

"No, I didn't know," I answered out loud.

He looked to the side and muttered, "The brothers didn't share."

The brothers certainly did not share.

I didn't express this, I stayed silent.

Shy didn't.

He told me his heart-wrenching story.

"New Year's Eve, I was twelve. My brother and me were at the babysitter's spending the night there 'cause my parents were goin' out. Mom was home gettin' ready. Dad was at the liquor store pickin' up a bottle of champagne. Guy came in to rob the store, popped the clerk, popped my dad. Took the cash from the register, the clerk's wallet, Dad's wallet and keys, and he took off in Dad's car. Don't know for sure but I figure no one's luck is that fucked up so I also figure that means some other random motherfucker didn't do my mom. In other words, it stands to reason the same guy used Dad's license to find our house, his key to get in. He got in, popped Mom, took everything he could shove into our car, and took off. Cops got a lock on the shit he pawned a few days later. Found our car three weeks later two states away. Never found him."

My breathing was shallow when he was done but I forced through it, "God, Shy. *God.* I didn't know. That sucks, *huge*, so huge it's impossible to measure how huge that sucks, it's that huge."

He grinned.

Yes, I said *grinned.*

Through his grin, he noted, "That about covers it, sugar."

I ignored the grin that I knew, from experience, hid his pain and blathered, "What...I mean, you don't have to talk about it if you don't want to, uh...you don't have to tell me but what happened after? To you and your brother."

He leaned further back in his chair, shifting his hips so his legs were out to the side. He stretched them, crossed them at the ankles, casual, cool, like this could be any conversation.

"Mom and Dad, Lan, my brother, and me were tight. Dad was cool, there but not in your face, Mom was awesome. You're right, fuckin' sucked huge they were gone and, after, Dad's brother took us in. He was cool, a lot like Dad. My brother and I liked him. We didn't understand until later there were a lot of things about him not like Dad."

This, I thought, wasn't a good beginning.

Shy kept talking and I found I was right.

"My aunt was *not* cool. Dad hated her. Mom detested her. Said straight out in front of Lan and me she was a bitch. My aunt hated us bein' there, and she didn't have a problem lettin' us know. Doted on her two pieces-of-shit brats, acted like Lan and I stole the last slice of bread the family'd ever have and pissed on it." He tipped his head to me. "Your mom, seen her around, Tab, before Tack stopped takin' her shit. She's a total bitch. My aunt makes your mom look like mother of the year. She was relentless. She had enough venom for a thousand snakes and she was not afraid to strike."

"That sucks too," I noted then finished, "Also huge."

He grinned again and that grin, as well as the first one, in the face of our subject matter made me all kinds of uneasy. "You're right about that too, babe."

"I don't know what to say," I told him, and I didn't. I mean, I really wanted to say something, I just didn't know what that was.

He sat up in his chair, put his legs under the table, and leaned into me, all the while his eyes locked on mine.

"Nothin' to say, Tabby. Life was shit. Lost my family, years later, found a new family. Then life wasn't shit anymore."

He was talking about his life but his point was clear.

My life was shit. I lost Jason. But someday, life wouldn't be shit anymore.

He was right, and so was Tyra.

Losing Jason at all, much less at his age and three weeks before our wedding, sucked huge. So huge it was impossible to measure.

But time would pass and, if I was lucky, life wouldn't suck anymore.

To express the epiphany he'd led me to, I whispered, "Right."

"Right," he whispered back.

Our food arrived.

It was time to eat and get out of the heavy, and I knew Shy agreed, because he tucked right in, so I did too.

I was forking into my eggs when it hit me.

I should never have had second thoughts about coming out with Shy because Shy was Chaos. I was Chaos. And Chaos was family.

So being out with Shy was right, because he was family.

"Thanks for draggin' my ass out to breakfast, Shy Cage," I muttered to my eggs then shoved some into my mouth.

"Pleased you hauled your ass out to come with me,

Tabitha Allen," Shy muttered back. I lifted my gaze to his and I saw his unbelievable green eyes warm and smiling at me.

I chewed, swallowed, and informed him, "Just that, I hope you know, you're getting the check."

Shy burst out laughing.

It sounded beautiful.

Good.

Right.

And again, I was right, this was right, this was good.

It was family.

CHAPTER FOUR

Let's Ride

Two months later…

I STOMPED THROUGH THE parking lot of the hospital and stabbed at my phone.

I put it to my ear, it rang once, then he said what he always said when he got me.

"Sugar."

"Where are you?" I snapped.

Silence a beat then, with humor in his tone that I wisely decided to ignore, Shy asked, "Where do you want me to be?"

"My house for dinner. Twenty minutes. And I don't care what it tastes like, Shy, you're gonna eat it and you're not gonna bellyache about it."

"Your place. Twenty," he agreed, still with humor in his tone, which I continued wisely to ignore.

Then he hung up.

I shoved my key into the door of my car and unlocked it.

I only felt better when I turned the key in the ignition and she purred to life.

My dad gave me my car, he restored it for me, and he still kept it purring for me. He did this with love, straight through from before I was sixteen to now, and he'd do it until he couldn't lift a wrench anymore.

Every time she purred to life, I remembered that and it made me feel better.

I coasted on that feeling all the way home, even as my mind filled with the last two months.

In that time, I'd grown tight with Shy.

This was partly because he didn't treat me as fragile like everyone else did. Shy treated me like me, and as the days wore on with Shy in my life, I felt more me than I'd felt in a long time.

This was also partly because there were times when I needed to be treated like I was fragile and with an acute sense that was a little uncanny (and something I was burying in my pit of denial, a place I created after breakfast with Shy that was seeing a lot of action these days), Shy knew when those times were and treated me accordingly.

Twice, I'd fallen sleep in his arms crying about Jason.

Twice, I'd woken up when he'd picked me up, cradling me and carrying me to bed.

I felt it when he laid me down. I felt it when he pulled the sheets over me. Last, I felt it (but was burying it in my pit of denial), when his lips brushed my temple and he moved away.

Incidentally, I was also burying in my pit of denial how it felt to be carried and essentially tucked into bed by a hot guy.

Since we'd gotten tight, it went without saying we spent a lot of time together. He came over and I ruined dinner, we talked, then we watched TV. I went to the Compound and we played pool or sat on a couch, gabbed and sometimes laughed, or we'd sit at the bar with some of the guys and shoot the breeze.

We didn't see each other every day, just four, five times a week, but we talked every day on the phone, sometimes more than once, just checking in, chatting, Shy keeping his finger on my pulse (something I also was burying in my pit of denial).

With Shy's help, I was coming back to myself and I was healing from the loss of Jason. I didn't think of him every other minute, the times when I would feel empty were coming less frequently, and the times when I would smile or even laugh were coming more often.

As the days went by, with Shy in them, I was also realizing, in a way I couldn't bury in my pit of denial, that it had been a long time since I'd been me, truly me, even before Jason died.

I was also remembering things. Like when I'd catch Jason staring a hair too long at my Harley tees in my drawer, his face expressionless, but the length of time he did it speaking volumes that now I was coming to understand but before I refused to acknowledge. I also recalled times like when we were sitting outside a restaurant and a bike would go by, I'd watch, listen to the pipes and when they died away, I'd find his eyes on me. I knew my face was wistful and his gaze was contemplative.

Having these memories, I wondered if Jason wondered if there was some piece of me I was burying that would eventually surface and, without Jason living, breathing, walking, talking, putting his hands and mouth on me, making it all good, I was wondering the same thing too.

He had never judged, never acted like I was anything

or anyone but someone he wanted. He was cool and comfortable around Dad and Tyra, Rider and Cut, Rush, Dog, Big Petey, anyone associated with my family, or Chaos.

Jason didn't make me be not me. It was me who was denying my world, my life, in order to live in Jason's, and I wondered if somewhere inside him he knew it.

Dad knew it and was concerned about it. Before Jason died, he'd talked with me about it, shared that it wasn't an easy choice to step out of the world you knew and live in another one.

But then, I'd had Jason and he was the one for me. I knew it. I had no questions, no doubts, not a single one. So I didn't rethink my decision because I knew it was the right one.

Now I was wondering and it bugged me, these questions, these doubts surfacing when he was gone.

On the drive home, as my mind sifted through the last two months, it didn't settle on happy thoughts about Shy or me coming back to me, but I wasn't thinking gloomy thoughts of doubts about Jason either.

I was thinking pissed-off thoughts about work.

Life was life and kept going even when you were struggling to deal with the crap it hit you with, and sometimes it hit you with more crap before you were ready for it.

And currently, my life was hitting me with more crap.

Namely, Dr. Dickhead.

We had one doctor at the hospital that was more douchebag than your average douchebag. So much so, he'd win Douchebag of the Year if there was a competition, and I'd had a run-in with him that day.

When Shy showed at my house I was still pissed, banging around in my kitchen, rock music blaring loud from my stereo.

He'd used his key. I didn't give him a key—he'd confiscated one in order to lock up the first night he carried me to bed post–crying jag.

I also didn't ask for it back.

His eyes came to me. I glared at him, and then I wisely ignored his lips curving up even as his eyes went to the floor, unsuccessfully hiding his smile from me.

He thought it was amusing when I got in a snit.

I didn't find anything funny about it.

His long legs took his lanky, loose-limbed frame to my stereo and he ratcheted it down from the ten it was at to about a three, a move that was so anti-badass biker, if his brothers knew he did it they would likely have thrown him out of the Club.

Once he did this, he moved to my fridge, where he pulled out two cold ones, popped the caps, and set one beside me. Then he sauntered around the bar, sat his behind on a stool, and leveled his beautiful green eyes with their rims of dark, thick lashes at me.

Before he could say a word, I announced, "We're having hamburgers because no one can ruin hamburgers, even me." I grabbed the beer he got me and took a hefty pull.

When I dropped it and looked at his face, I knew he disagreed. His eyes flashed with humor, and he pressed his lips together. He'd eaten my food. He knew I could ruin anything. It was his turn to act wisely, because even though his eyes disagreed, his mouth stayed closed.

Then he opened it to invite: "Talk to me."

I grabbed the salt, started shaking it on the mound of ground beef in the bowl, took him up on his invitation, and cried, "*Get this!* Dr. Dickhead wrote the wrong order in the chart, which meant I administered a higher dose of medication than was warranted or even healthy. Then, when it all went down, I overheard him telling the hospital administrator that even though the dose was written down wrong in the chart, he'd verbally given me an order with the right dosage and I'd administered the wrong one, which, Shy, he...did...*not*." I slammed the salt down.

The muscle in Shy's jaw jumped, as it had a tendency to do when he was pissed, which happened often during the times I was ranting about Dr. Dickhead.

I grabbed the pepper and started shaking, ranting on, "Luckily, the error wasn't so bad it ended in trauma, tears, lawsuits, and loss of employment, just uncomfortable explanations and me tamping down my desire to commit physicianicide, but *still*!"

I ended my last word on a high-pitched note, slammed the pepper down, grabbed the minced, dried garlic and resumed shaking and blathering.

"The hospital administrator knows he's a douche. She talked to me for all of, like, five seconds before she nodded and took off. Still, it was a pain in my ass."

"Tab—" Shy started, but I chattered on right over him.

"Don't worry. It's all good. Not only does the administrator know he's a douche, everyone knows he's a douche. Even the other doctors think he's a douche, though they wouldn't say it out loud. That's how big a douche he is. And it doesn't matter what he says, if it comes down to it, it matters what the chart says. Still, I don't like the idea of how this could have gone bad. Okay, sure, if the dose was crazy wrong, I'd notice it and question it before I administered it so the bad would never be *that* bad. Still, even not that bad, like today, was no good."

"Sugar—" Shy tried again, his eyes to the bowl but I kept babbling.

"It's just him *lying* about me. That bugs me. Okay, everything about him bugs me but, today, that's the top of the list of all the one hundred and seven thousand things about him that bug me."

His gaze came up to mine and he said, "Baby, I want you to rant, get that shit out, process it so you can move on and have a good night, but you're processing it while ruining our dinner. Gotta say, I prefer it when you ruin our dinner while laughin' and smilin', not rantin' and ravin'."

My eyes shot down to the bowl and I noticed a not-small mound of garlic on the beef.

Crap.

I felt the garlic taken out of my hand and tipped my head way back to find Shy close.

"Get. Sit on a stool, drink beer, and rant it out. I'll deal with this," he ordered gently.

I shook my head and gave him a small smile. "It's cool, Shy, I'll fix it."

He got closer and his voice got gentler when he repeated, "Get."

I buried the gentleness of his voice in my pit of denial along with how it made me feel. Grabbing my beer, I "got" and moved around him and the bar to haul my bottom up on a stool. I sucked back beer while Shy did his best to shake garlic into the sink.

"What are you gonna do about this motherfucker?" he asked.

"Suck it up," I answered, and his head jerked around so he could look over his shoulder at me with narrowed eyes.

I understood this reaction. We were both Chaos. It wasn't lost on me that any member of Chaos would put up with Dr. Dickhead for about three seconds.

I smiled at him before I told him, "I can't exactly plant a bomb in his car."

Shy looked down at the meat, that muscle moving in his jaw, and I knew he was calling up his memory banks to ascertain precisely how to plant a bomb in Dr. Dickhead's car.

I buried that in my pit of denial too.

"Shy," I said quietly, and he turned from the sink. He came back to the counter in front of me as I explained, "I knew this was the gig when I took it. It isn't a secret doctors can be dickheads. They don't warn you in the textbooks in nursing school, but word gets around. I'm lucky, all the other doctors I work with are great, always have been, even in nursing school. It's just him. There's always one."

"You don't eat shit, baby," he told me.

I licked my lip, his eyes dropped to my mouth, that muscle ticked in his jaw again, and I buried that instantly in my pit of denial.

"Life can be shit, Shy, so unfortunately sometimes you have to eat it," I told him.

"Right, correction," he returned. "You eat shit until you're done eatin' shit and then you find a way so you don't eat shit anymore."

I grinned at him. "Okay, how's this?" I began. "I eat shit until I'm done eating shit then I go to the hospital administrator, share my concerns in an official way, and hope."

Shy's hands were forming patties while his eyes remained on me and, again, I knew he didn't agree with my solution.

When he didn't say anything, I continued, "Then, if a miracle occurs and he's prompted to move on, life will be breezy and I'll smile and laugh while ruining dinner rather than ranting and raving. Work for you?"

"Yeah, sugar, works for me," he muttered, and I didn't bury in my pit of denial how much I liked it when he called me "sugar." This was mostly because it was too big to fit in my pit. And that pit was dug deep, not because I was burying stuff deep, but because Shy gave me so much to bury.

He jerked his chin in the direction of the hall and ordered, "Go, change out of your scrubs. I'll deal with this."

"Righty ho, biker boss," I mumbled, grinning at him, grabbing my beer and jumping off my stool.

I was nearly to the mouth of the hall when he called, "What are we havin' with this?"

I stopped and looked at him. "Store-bought potato salad and chips."

"Chips?" he asked.

"Chips," I confirmed.

"You got potatoes?" he asked, and my grin became a smile.

"Only because you bought them for me the other day," I answered.

"You got oil?" he went on, and my smile got bigger.

"Only because you bought it for me the other day."

"Then we'll have fries," he muttered to the patties.

"Fries?" I asked, and his eyes came back to me.

"Fries," he answered.

"Homemade fries?" I sought added information.

"You got potatoes, oil, and a knife. All you gotta do is

cut 'em up, fry 'em up, and, if you're feelin' feisty, season them."

"FYI, biker boss, I'm feelin' feisty," I threw out my thinly veiled order.

Shy grinned as he put the patty on the broiler pan and turned toward the sink, murmuring, "My girl's feelin' feisty, she'll get seasoning."

I buried how that made me feel too. Even so, I still strolled to my bedroom smiling.

I was changed into an old Mötley Crüe tee and cut-off jeans, and still smiling when I moved back toward the kitchen.

Shy was giving me back me. He was guiding me to healing. He was keeping me company in a way I liked. He treated me like me when I needed it, and he treated me as fragile when I needed that. He listened to me moan about work. He stocked my cupboards. And he made me homemade fries.

Seriously, I could love this guy.

I hit the kitchen, and Shy had the oil going and a small mountain of sliced potatoes on a cutting board. I walked to the fridge, got us two fresh cold ones, and put one on the counter beside him, then I moved around the bar and hefted myself up on a stool.

"Thank you for bringing me back to me."

Yes, that was what came out of my mouth, and I knew my words weren't a figment of my imagination (unfortunately) when his eyes came to me.

"Say again, honey?" he asked.

It was out there, I had to go for it. And anyway, this was Shy. He'd proven over the last two months he could take it, take *anything* from me and handle it with care.

"I'm coming back to me," I told him. "And you're helping me. It's been a long time since I've been me, just me. I've been thinking and I've come to realize that even before Jason died, I was burying parts of me."

Shy held my eyes, something working in his I didn't quite get, but he didn't speak, so I hurried on in case he got the wrong idea.

"Jason didn't want me to bury it, just so you know. He wasn't that kind of guy. It was me who buried it. All me. Now, looking back, I'm wondering if it would have surfaced. I'm wondering if he worried about it. I'm wondering if we might have—"

"Stop that, babe," Shy commanded quietly and I blinked.

"Pardon?"

"Way you say it, you were into that guy and he was into you. Don't ask questions that will never have answers. You'll drive yourself crazy with that shit. Just remember you were into him, he was into you, it was all good, and don't fuck up good memories with questions that have no answers and never will."

He was right. Totally.

My head tipped to the side and I felt my eyes go soft when I asked, "How'd you get so wise?"

"Had a good teacher," he answered.

"Your dad before he died?"

"My dad before he died and *your* dad when I found him."

I sucked in a sharp breath.

It was not lost on me that Shy liked my dad, he respected him, and I loved that because that was how I felt about my dad. Obviously more, since he was my dad, but I still loved it that Shy felt the same.

Yes, I totally could love this guy.

"You're done rantin' and got nothin' to do but sit there and stare at me," Shy began, "haul your ass off that stool, come around and help me with the fries."

I was done ranting and it would probably burn out my retinas if I stared at him too long, so I grinned at him, hauled my ass off the stool, rounded the bar, and helped him with the fries.

* * *

"Sugar, you awake?"

I opened my eyes and blinked at the blank TV.

I didn't know what time it was but it felt late. What I did know was that I'd fallen asleep with my head on Shy's chest, my legs curled behind me on the couch, my arm resting over his abs, his arm around me.

The last thing I remembered was being sucked into a marathon of *American Chopper.*

I tipped my head back and looked up at him.

"Hey, is it late?" I asked.

"Yeah, you gotta work tomorrow?" he asked back.

"Yeah," I answered.

He nodded, gave me a squeeze and shifted to move but my arm around him tightened and he stilled.

"Why?" I asked.

"Why what?" he returned.

"Why did you ask if I have to work tomorrow?"

"Goin' for a ride, thought, you didn't have to work, you might want to come with me."

He was going for a ride.

I wanted to go with him.

I wanted to go with him because I liked to ride. I wanted to go with him because he was Shy and I was me and that was what we did. It wasn't rare, it wasn't frequent, but he liked to be on his bike and he didn't hesitate to offer to take me with him. I didn't hesitate to say yes.

This, too, I was denying. How much I liked it that he asked. How much I liked to be behind him on the back of his bike.

I shifted, saying, "I'll get some shoes."

He gave me a squeeze and his fist came under my chin, gently tipping my head up to look at him again. "Tabby, baby, you gotta work. It's cool. Another time."

I held his eyes and replied quietly, "I'm alive. You're alive. I gotta work to live so I do that and I'll have to do that for a long time. But when I'm not workin', I'm livin'. So let's ride."

His eyes moved over my face and then a slow, lazy, sexy as all hell, beautiful smile spread on his face about a millisecond before he pulled himself off the couch, taking me with him and setting me on my feet.

Then, looking down at me still smiling that unbelievable smile, he whispered, "Let's ride."

I smiled back, took off, grabbed my shoes. Shy held my hand all the way to his bike and we rode.

For a long time.

It.

Was.

Paradise.

CHAPTER FIVE

Apocalyptic

Two and a half months later…

"ARE YOU INSANE?"

That came from my best friend Natalie, who not only asked the question but was also staring at me like I was insane.

I was back. Totally back.

I was me.

What I was not was insane.

Life had settled, grown into a pattern I liked with work and family, friends, and Shy.

I was going out again with Tyra, shopping, meeting friends for lunch, hanging with the boys, acting crazy, just like I used to.

I'd even found the time to reach out to Jason's family, see if there were relationships there to salvage.

I couldn't say I was tight with his mom and sisters, but I liked them in a way that I knew if we had the future we were supposed to have, I would have gotten tight with them. Though I didn't like his dad too much. He was too straightlaced for me, and I didn't like the way he sometimes barked at Jason, making Jason's mouth go tight, and then later Jason would take that crap out on me. But his mom and sisters were cool.

We'd clung together after we lost Jason then naturally drifted apart, shrouded in our individual fogs of grief. But when we sat down, it was clear they didn't want the tie to Jason that was me to be cut and I felt the same.

It was all good.

My life with Shy hadn't changed. We saw each other all the time, I ruined dinner, he took me out on his bike, we called each other frequently, and I laughed and smiled even more.

And it had been weeks since I'd had a time where he needed to treat me as fragile and I no longer felt empty inside.

That didn't mean the sucker punches didn't keep coming. I'd drive by a restaurant where Jason and I went, I'd remember, and my breath would leave me. Or I'd be blow-drying my hair, looking in the mirror and remembering how Jason used to come in, dip down, and kiss my shoulder. And going to bed and waking up alone day in and day out, I still wasn't used to that.

But I was no longer going through the motions. I was getting back to life, living it and not pretending.

Thus I was out to lunch with Natalie and sharing with her my scheme.

I looked into her pretty gray eyes framed by flawless peaches-and-cream skin and halo of fabulous ash-blonde hair with kick-ass highlights, and I narrowed my eyes.

"You are," she stated. "You are insane."

I leaned forward. "I'm not insane."

"Wrong," she declared.

"I didn't say *I* was gonna go out and hunt down the man who killed Shy's parents."

This was the reason Natalie thought I was insane.

Although most of the time Shy and I were together I was blathering, there were some times when he talked. He shared. He laid it out. He was as comfortable giving it to me as I was giving it to him.

He talked about his parents and brother a lot, which meant they were on his mind a lot. He did it often grinning, chuckling, natural, comfortable, but as time wore on, I saw this was all an act.

Their loss bothered him.

No, it didn't bother him. It was coming clear it was eating at him.

All his talk was understandable about his brother. He was in the Army and deployed in Afghanistan now, and I knew, even though Shy didn't say it flat out, Shy was worried about him. I didn't even know him but, for Shy, I was worried about him too.

It was more than that, though. It was clear they had a good family, but it was a family interrupted, and the fact that the guy who murdered his parents was never caught and Shy was still talking about it meant he didn't have any closure. He didn't have a way to put it behind him, and I wanted to help him heal and move on like he'd done for me.

So I figured finding the guy, bringing him to justice, if that could happen, would help Shy to heal. Or, at least, it wouldn't hurt.

"No," Natalie cut into my thoughts, "you're not goin' to find the guy yourself, but that doesn't mean you're not insane."

"Why is finding that bastard insane?" I snapped.

"How many reasons do you want?" she snapped back.

"Five," I retorted.

She sat back in her chair, lifted her hand with one finger extended and launched in. "One, you're hiring Lee Nightingale and, girl, you know, that dude has had books written about him. They were fictionalized, but he's also in the paper all the time, so we both know whoever wrote that shit did not tone it down. He's the badass to end all badasses. He's *such* a badass, he's the freakin' definition of badass, and his team of badasses only exist to define alternate nuances of the same thing." Her chin jerked out. "*Badass.*"

"This is good in a private detective," I pointed out.

Natalie ignored me, lifted her hand again, and shook two fingers at me.

"Two, he's the best of the best, and the best of the best is expensive. You got a sweet gig as a nurse, but even so, you also don't have that kind of cake."

I had to admit this was a concern.

When I moved into my apartment, Dad and Tyra sprung for my living room furniture set, the brothers bought me a killer stereo, and the old ladies got together to outfit my kitchen with junk I could use to ruin food. I just had to buy my dining room table and bedroom furniture and I was good to go. My rent was also cheap. And Nat was right, I had a sweet gig. I wasn't a millionaire but my salary was nothing to sneeze at, especially at my age.

Therefore, I was comfortable.

That said, I'd been thinking on this scheme for a while, and I'd called over a month ago to get an appointment with Lee Nightingale of Nightingale Investigations, the premier private investigation service in Denver or, maybe, from their reputation, *the world*. They set me up, but my appointment was next week. That was how in demand this guy was. And usually that kind of thing reflected in fees.

"Three," Natalie went on and I focused on her, "I don't know, it's a guess since I never was stupid enough to hire a badass but, I'd say, when a badass sends an invoice and it doesn't get paid, he gets testy."

Another concern I had.

"Maybe he'll take installments," I suggested.

She again ignored me.

"Four and five, because, girl, when I say it you're gonna know this is worth two numbers, you manage to hire Lee Nightingale, he manages to find this guy, and, Tabby, you know Nightingale is so good, that case could be cold as the arctic and he'll still find this guy, we're talking about Shy Cage and Chaos here. The guy who whacked his parents is unearthed, he's gonna go apocalyptic on his ass. We're talkin' takin' this guy somewhere *no one* knows about, playin' with him for maybe years, then probably tossing him into a pit, dousing him with lighter fluid, and setting him on fire like that stone-cold black dude did to Tig's daughter on *Sons of Anarchy*."

"Chaos is not SAMCRO," I returned, referring to the acronym for the motorcycle club in that TV show.

She lifted her eyebrows.

I decided not to argue that point.

She leaned forward and continued, "Tab, I can see it. My girl is back and I don't want to turn you to that dark place you're leavin' behind, but Shy Cage is not a physical therapist." Her voice dipped quieter. "In other words, girl, he's not Jason."

I licked my upper lip and fidgeted in my chair.

Natalie kept talking, "If Jason's parents were murdered, you found the guy who did it, he'd stand in front of reporters and make relieved statements about justice being done. You know, there is no way that motherfucker was found, Shy, who you're suddenly weirdly tight with and we'll talk about that later," she declared ominously. "*And* your dad, I'll put out there, since Shy is a brother and those brothers are all about the brotherhood, will not lose their fuckin' badass biker minds and let that shit go unavenged the way *they* think it needs to be avenged."

Okay, even though I'd been thinking on this awhile, maybe I didn't think it all the way through.

"Okay," I started. "Maybe I can make a deal with Nightingale that he finds enough evidence that when this guy goes inside, he never comes out."

Natalie sat back, her brows shot up and she cried, "Girl, do you *not* watch TV?"

I glared at her.

She leaned toward me again and stated, "These guys got *networks*. That guy would be in the joint about two seconds before some inmate who owed Chaos a marker got the word and he started carvin' that motherfucker's name in a shiv."

This, too, was probably true.

I leaned toward her and admitted, "Natalie, he's been supercool with me. You're right, we're tight and he talks about his folks all the time. I have to do something."

"Now we're talkin' about what *I* wanna talk about," she informed me. "Tell me, how in the fuck am I in your kitchen for four hours last week helpin' you botch batch after batch of cookies to get one good enough to give to Shy Cage?"

"I told you, we had a bet, we played pool. I lost."

"Bullshit," she returned and shook her head, her eyes moving over me, her face getting soft. "Tabby, I love you. I watched it happen. I watched you tossed into the pit of despair when you lost Jason. I took that fucked-up ride with you, and I'm tickled freakin' pink that you're finding the other side and comin' back to you. And, babe, hear this, it's been months and it's time. Your girl parts are growin' cobwebs. You need to get back in the saddle." She held my eyes and her voice dipped quiet. "But not with Shy Cage."

I felt my back go straight and I told her, "It isn't like that."

"You on the back of his bike?" she asked.

I ignored that question and said again, "Nat, it isn't like that."

She leaned further over the table. "Listen to me, Tab. I gotta give it to you straight and it sucks, but here it is. You know I didn't like Jason. Thought he had a stick up his ass. I knew he didn't like me. I know that was shit for you and I'm sorry. Make no mistake, that apology is straight from the heart. Lookin' back, wish I played that differently. I didn't and I gotta live with that, him bein' gone. I also know, much as I hate to admit it, he loved you. Loved you like I've never seen." I felt my breath hollow out and her hand came across the table to grab mine. "And, girl, burns in me to remind you of this shit but I gotta. You are never gonna get that back. It's gone, he's gone. Still, even havin' that good from him, that doesn't mean you might not find something even better. You just gotta get your ass out there and look."

"I'm not ready for that," I told her.

"You are," she shot back immediately, and I started to get pissed.

"I am?" I asked sarcastically, pulling my hand from hers. "You know? Did you lose your fiancé three weeks before your wedding and I missed a memo?"

"No, I watched my best girl endure that shit and pull herself through, but you can't get frozen in the process and not *see it through*. It's been near on a year, Tab. It's time to see that process though. Sayin' that, girl, you get to the other side and move on, you don't do it with the likes of Shy Cage."

I felt the idea of moving on in life with Shy settle in my belly in a way that I immediately transferred it to my pit of denial.

Then I hissed, "Natalie, *it isn't like that*."

She shook her head, but her eyes never left mine. "Maybe not for you, but that boy is all about pussy. You think with you bein' all sassy and hot and sweet and funny, he's not doin' the time in order to get payback?"

"No," I clipped. "I don't think that."

"Well, you also know I have occasion to rub up close to the circles Chaos runs in and I know Shy Cage. I've seen him around a lot and, babe, he gets around *a lot*. Lee Nightingale defines badass. Shy Cage defines *dawg*."

"He's a brother, he's family," I snapped.

"He's a dawg, Tabby, and you can't forget that. If he's bein' cool with you, awesome. Pleased he's givin' that to you. Take it. You need family. I'm just tellin' you to keep your eyes open and watch your heart. Or, more to the point, watch your ass because if you don't, Shy'll tap it."

I rolled my eyes.

"No joke," she stated.

I rolled my eyes back to her. "I'm thinking I liked it better when you treated me like I was fragile."

"Kiss that good-bye," she retorted.

Great.

I sucked in breath.

"Nat, honestly, we're just friends," I whispered, and she studied me.

Then she whispered back, "I believe you."

I nodded.

"But do you feel me?" she pressed.

"I feel you," I said softly.

She grinned.

I grinned back.

Then I sat back and she did too, turning her head and calling loudly and rudely to no one in particular, "Yo! Check!"

My grin grew into a smile.

That was Natalie. Loud, rude, funny, up for anything, always surprising and mostly always loving.

I just wished she was willing to listen to advice just as easily as she was willing to dish it out, and I determined that during our next lunch, it was my turn to lay it out.

This time, it was my turn to pay the check.

* * *

"Thanks, Lenny," I called to the man under my car.

"No problems, Tab, be done in about half an hour," Lenny called back.

"Cool," I finished and then wandered out of the big garage bay at Ride.

The good part about not holding a grudge against Shy anymore was that I was at Ride more, on Chaos more, with the boys more, my family more, and, obviously, Shy more.

I also got free oil changes.

I was heading toward the Compound to see if Shy was there and he wanted to share a drink when I saw him.

Walking out of the Compound hand in hand with a tall, buxom brunette.

My lungs started burning and my body tossed itself to the side of the cement steps that led to the office, hiding me from the couple.

I crouched and deep-breathed.

What the heck?

What the heck?

Okay, all right, okay.

No. Not okay. Not all right.

What the heck?

I lifted up and peeked over the stairs toward the Compound and my lungs burst into flame at what I saw.

Shy and the woman standing by his bike. Her hand was at his hip. His hand was at her neck. Their mouths were connected.

I jerked down and my lungs turned to ash, I struggled for breath as I heard a Harley roar, and I pressed against the cement at the side of the steps, my eyes glued to the forecourt so I could see them as they drove by, Shy on his bike, the woman pressed to his back.

Fortunately, Shy's head was turned away from me.

Heartbreakingly, her cheek was pressed to his shoulder.

A huge wave crashed over me, pulling me under, whipping me around. I couldn't get myself under control. I couldn't strike out for the surface.

I was drowning.

I'd grown up in the world of bikers and I knew.

I *knew.*

I knew what a piece of tail looked like riding on the back of a bike, and I knew what a biker's woman looked like.

That woman was not tail.

She was Shy's.

I hadn't even recovered and another wave crashed over me, bigger than the first. So huge and powerful, I'd never make it to the top.

I watched until they disappeared and I kept watching, trying to surface, come up for air.

"Honeybunch, what in the frig are you doin'?" I heard Big Petey ask.

I shot up from my crouch and turned to see him moving my way, coming from one of the bays.

"Um..." I mumbled but couldn't go on.

He looked at me and concern washed over his features. "You okay?"

"Uh... yeah," I forced out. "Great."

He stared at me then remarked, "You look like someone ran over your puppy."

Oh God.

His eyes moved over my face, "You look like when—"

I held my breath. Pete stopped speaking then turned to look at the entrance to Ride. Then he scanned the Compound. Then something moved over his features and he looked at me.

"He's been seein' her for three months."

Oh God.

I clenched my teeth together so my mouth wouldn't drop open. It felt like I'd been punched in the stomach.

Three months.

Shy had been seeing her for *three months.*

Three months!

How?

How had he been seeing her when *he'd been seeing me*?

And why didn't he tell me?

I came out of my fevered thoughts but not out of the haze of pain I was trying to deny because I didn't get it. What I was feeling. How huge it was. How deep it hit me. How much pain it caused.

No, I did but I was burying it.

Pete's hand curled around my upper arm. "Let's get you a drink."

My head jerked back to look up at him. "No, that's cool." I said softly. "I'm driving."

His head dipped down to get closer to me. "Tabby, honeybunch, let's get a drink. Promise, we'll get one down you and we'll get you out before they come back."

He held my eyes and I knew, like always, he was looking out for me, even, in this instance (though I was denying it), saving me from myself.

Pete was the grandfather I never had.

Dad's dad was inside, serving life for double homicide. Dad hated him, I'd never met him and, seeing as Dad felt the way he did, I knew I never would.

Mom's dad was a good grandpa, but he didn't understand the biker life. He also didn't have a problem sharing this and frequently. He didn't like his daughter being in it, and he didn't like what he thought was my dad dragging her in. Before the divorce, when we were all together, this made family visits not real fun, and I was close with my dad, so I never really forgave Gramps for being such a pain in the ass.

He was down in Arizona now with my gram, and I never saw them. They sent cards and called on birthdays and Christmases, but they were checked out of the family. So much, for some whacked reason, they didn't have it together enough to call and cancel the gift they bought for Jason and me. It, and the shot to the heart it carried, arrived five weeks after he died, when we would have arrived back from our honeymoon.

So for me it was Pete, it had always been Pete.

And looking in his eyes, I knew, since he only had one daughter, now passed, and no grandkids, it was always me.

So I took the hand he offered and let him lead me to the Compound.

He got me a drink.

He also got me the heck out of there before Shy came back with his woman.

CHAPTER SIX

Tied to Your Strings

Two weeks later…

I WALKED UP the stairs to my apartment, dog tired.

I was exhausted because I'd just had two days of back-to-back double shifts.

I had a shift the next day too, and though it wasn't a double, I needed a break.

Thinking about tomorrow made me even more exhausted.

And as if being dog tired wasn't bad enough, I'd had another run-in with Dr. Dickhead that day and it was bad.

Gossip was running amuck in the hospital that the nurse he was always banging in the supply closet was denying him his piece of tail until he asked his wife for a divorce. This did not make him happy. He was the kind of guy who wasn't happy normally, but he was a lot less happy when he wasn't getting it regular, and some woman trying to yank his chain just made things worse.

Unfortunately, for whatever reason, he was taking this garbage out on me and (mostly) only me. I had somehow earned his focus. Maybe because I was the newest and youngest nurse on the ward and thus fresh meat. Maybe he just had it out for me because he was a douche.

The constant focus of his douche-ness escalated that day when he laid into me in front of a patient. It wasn't cool normally, but in front of a patient meant I couldn't stick up for myself. I had to take it.

So I did and it was bad.

So bad, I wanted to turn my head to the patient, say, "If you'll excuse me," round her bed and knee him in the 'nads. I did not do this. Instead, he finished up, stormed off, and I knew it was as bad as it seemed when the patient asked, "Are you all right?"

I assured her I was, but it stuck in my craw that I was assuring a patient that I was all right when it was my job to make sure *she* was all right.

I was tired of his crap. I was just plain tired, and what made matters worse was that I didn't even have Shy to talk to about it.

Work sucked. Not having Shy sucked more.

Everything sucked.

I had been avoiding him for two weeks, not taking his calls, not returning his messages, not hitting Ride and finding ways to stay away from my apartment just in case he popped by.

I didn't know why I was avoiding him, but I told myself I was doing it because I needed to get my head together.

No, strike that, I *did* know why I was doing it. I just let that fester in that deep place inside me that I was never, ever visiting.

So I had no one to talk with about my work crap, and I had no one to talk to about how I was feeling about Shy, because I wouldn't even admit to myself how I was feeling about Shy.

I was screwed.

I was also beginning to think I was an idiot.

These were my thoughts when I let myself into my dark apartment, locked the door behind me, dropped my purse and keys on the table by the door, and moved through the dark living room to the lamp by the side of the couch.

I turned it on then let out a small scream.

Shy was sitting on the couch, long, lean legs straight out, booted feet on my coffee table, arms stretched out and resting on the back of the couch, eyes on me.

"What are you doin', sitting in the dark?" I asked, my hand at my throat.

"Are you avoiding me?"

I knew what he was asking. I couldn't *not* know, but I didn't know how to explain it to him so I stalled.

"Pardon?"

Slowly, oh so slowly, he lifted his booted feet from the table, set them on the floor, and pulled himself off the couch. Equally slowly, he turned and locked eyes with me.

All of this was pretty scary.

It got scarier when his voice, low and menacing, came at me just as slowly as he had moved.

"Are. You. *Avoiding.* Me?" he enunciated each word with precision, and that was even scarier.

"I've been busy," I told him, and my heart jumped as I saw the muscle jump in his jaw.

"You've sung that song before, Tabby," he reminded me. "Didn't like it the last time. Really don't fuckin' like it now."

"I'm on double shifts. A nurse is sick and another one is on vacation." This was true but it only explained the last two days, not the last two weeks.

Shy was far from dumb. He'd see through that and call me on it.

He didn't delay in seeing through that and calling me on it. "Your phone broke?" he asked.

"What?" I asked back.

He leaned slightly toward me and it took a lot not to lean back. "Is your *phone* broke?" he repeated, his voice back to low and menacing.

"No," I admitted.

"So, explain, if you're not avoiding me, you got a call from me, why you don't take it? And, Tab, I'll throw this out there now so you have plenty of time to come up with another excuse, when I leave a message, I wanna know why it isn't returned."

I stared at him and he stared at me.

I licked my upper lip, his eyes dropped to my mouth, his face got hard, and suddenly the room felt like a silent thunderclap rolled through it.

It was then I knew I couldn't take it anymore.

"I know about her," I whispered, and yes, that came right out, and yes, it sounded like an accusation.

"Say again?" he asked.

"I know about her. Your woman."

His brows went up. "So?"

So?

So?

"So, you didn't tell me about her," I pointed out.

"Sorry, Tab, didn't know I needed to report to you about who I fuck," he fired back.

Ouch.

That hurt but with no choice, I worked through it and rallied.

"We're tight," I said quietly.

"Not that tight," he returned.

Ouch again.

But I got it, I totally got it, and I had no choice but to power through it so, with difficulty, I did. "Okay, Shy, I get it and its cool. All of it's cool. You were there for me and I appreciate that. You helped out a lot. Now you're off the hook."

His eyes narrowed, that thunderclap feeling came back, and he crossed his arms on his chest. "I'm off the hook?"

I nodded again. "Yeah. I... it's... I get it. It's cool. We're cool. I understand and I want you to know I appreciate all you've done but you can... well, you're off-duty now. You can do, uh... whatever it is you do."

"I can do whatever it is I do," he repeated, and I wished he wouldn't do that, repeat stuff I said. It was freaking me out.

"Yeah."

"Let me see if I got this right, babe. You find out I got a woman and you freeze me out, and, I'll point out, you're doin' that shit a-fuckin'-gain. You don't talk to me about it. You don't call me. You don't take my calls. You don't answer my messages. You're not even fuckin' home half the time so I can see you. And now you give me my marching orders?"

"That's not what I'm doing," I replied.

"You didn't have the time to print out the papers but, sugar, you did that shit all the same."

"You didn't tell me about her," I reminded him.

"And?" he returned and at his sharp word, I threw out a hand, beginning to get pissed.

"Shy, you spent time with me while you were spending time with her, for *months*, and you didn't tell me?"

"Seems like it," he retorted and I shook my head.

"That isn't cool."

"What isn't cool is this bullshit, Tab. You got an issue—" he leaned toward me "*—you talk to me.* You got somethin' to say—" he leaned closer "*—you say it to me.* What you do not fuckin' do is freeze my ass out."

Okay, crap, he had a point.

"Right, okay, Shy. You're right," I gave in. "I should have talked to you."

"I fuckin' know I'm right, Tabby," he clipped out, still seriously angry.

"I'm givin' in, Shy," I pointed out.

"No, you're not. You're goin' docile thinkin' I'll back off when you haven't answered my fuckin' question," he shot back, and now I was scared and slightly pissed but also confused.

"What question?" I asked.

"I got a woman, you find out, why the fuck are you freezing me out?"

Uh-oh.

This was not good mainly because I didn't have an answer.

No, that wasn't true, but that answer was lying deep inside. So deep I wasn't even admitting to myself what it was so I certainly couldn't admit it to Shy.

Therefore, I winged it. "I'm just hurt you didn't tell me. You kept it from me and I didn't get that."

"Okay then," he returned instantly. "You want it out, we'll put it out there. Tomorrow night, you meet me and Rosalie for dinner and you'll see for yourself."

It came as a surprise, instantaneous, overwhelming, so huge my middle rocked back with it like I'd been socked in the gut.

I stared at him, unable to breathe, pain saturating my system, and I saw some of the anger slide out of his face as concern washed in.

He didn't miss my reaction.

Then again, Shy never missed anything. Not when it had to do with me.

"You okay?" he asked.

"No," I whispered.

He dropped his arms and took a step toward me.

I took a step back.

He stopped and his head tilted to the side. "You got a cramp?"

I shook my head. "No."

"Tabby, baby, what the fuck?"

"I can't do this," I announced, not knowing where those four words were coming from, just knowing they were coming from somewhere deep, and I meant each and every one like I had never meant anything else in my life.

His brows drew together. "You can't do this?"

I shook my head.

"Do what?" he sought clarification.

I lifted my hand and waved it between him and me. "This."

His eyes went to my hand, then moved to my face, and he asked, "This? You and me?"

You and me.

You and me.

There was never going to be a him and me.

My belly, twisted in knots, screwed up tighter and the pain was excruciating.

He stared at me, his eyes moving over my features, and I watched in horrified fascination through the pain as his face grew terrifyingly dark.

Then he whispered, "You have got to be fuckin' shitting me."

I didn't know if I was shitting him. I didn't know what the heck I was doing.

"Tell me, Tab, that you're shittin' me," he demanded.

"Honestly, Shy, I don't know what I'm doing," I admitted.

"I do," he ground out. "You're standin' there tellin' me, years, fuckin' *years* ago you were into me, I fucked that up, you held a grudge, also for fuckin' years, you lost everything, and only then did you let me back in. Now, you find I got a life without you in it, a woman, and you can't deal. For fuckin' *months* I listened to you talk about him. I held you while you cried about him. Now you're handin' me this shit?"

He had a point about that too.

God! What was I doing?

"Shy—" I tried to instigate damage control.

I failed.

Spectacularly.

The damage was done, no way to control it.

"No," he bit off. "You need to disappear to get your head straight, Tabby? You fuckin' do it. That works for me. I don't take rides I don't like, and I just found out I was on a ride I didn't know I was takin', and I don't like it.

So you go into your head and get it straight, Tab, but you don't come back to me until you got your head straight. No sooner, babe. I do not need that shit in my life. I am not gonna see you through that shit your way, tied to your strings. I'm cuttin' myself loose. You come to me and you don't got your shit sorted, you wanna get your head straight draggin' me along with you, you can go fuck yourself."

With that, he pulled his keys out of his jeans, twisted my key off the ring, and my heart twisted when he dropped it on the coffee table. Then he prowled to the door and slammed it behind him.

Woodenly, I walked to the door and locked it.

Just as woodenly, I walked to my couch and sat on the edge.

I heard his Harley pipes roar, and I stared at my wall unseeing, listening as they growled until I couldn't hear them anymore.

Only then did I collapse, my face in my hands as I burst into tears.

CHAPTER SEVEN

You Are Not Leaving

One month later…

SHY WALKED OUT of his apartment, locked the door, and headed to the stairs.

These days, he stayed there, seeing as Rosalie cleaned it and also seeing as, since he didn't have Tabby's cupboards to fill anymore, he hauled his ass out and bought groceries for his own damned house. He also stayed there because Rosalie was not the kind of woman you banged in a bed in a biker Compound while men were raising hell in the common room or tapping ass in rooms down the hall. She was the kind of woman you banged in an apartment that was two steps up from shithole that she kept clean.

He jogged down the stairs, moved into the sun, and saw Roscoe sitting astride his bike. His brother was there because they had some Chaos business to see to.

Shy tipped his chin up, Roscoe tipped his back, and Shy moved to his bike.

He threw a leg over and was starting the ignition when Roscoe spoke.

"Sucks, man."

Shy turned his head to Roscoe. "What sucks?"

"Tab takin' off to Cape Cod."

That burn hit his chest encroaching dangerously close to his heart. A burn he hadn't felt for four months. A burn that, over the last month, smoldered deep. Now it fanned to life and singed his lungs.

"Say again?" he asked and Roscoe's eyebrows knitted.

"You didn't know?" he asked back.

"No, I didn't fuckin' know," Shy bit out. "Tabby's goin' to Cape Cod?"

"How can you not know? You two are tight. You're not bangin' Rosalie, you're up in Tab's space."

"I didn't know, Roscoe," he clipped. "She's goin' to Cape Cod?"

Roscoe nodded. "Yeah, brother. Some doctor at work was up in her shit, she couldn't take it anymore, so she quit her job. She's packin' up her shit, storin' it up at Tack and Cherry's, and headin' out. Some traveling nurse's program, six-month contract."

Shy's vision went hazy.

He could not believe this shit.

That bitch.

That fucking *bitch*.

She was leaving.

Leaving her family, leaving him, leaving people who had taken her back for a fucking year.

Leaving.

Leaving him.

"Not doin' this," he growled right before his bike roared to life.

"Doin' what?" Roscoe shouted over the pipes and Shy looked to him.

"This. Our gig. You need someone at your back, call Tug or Snapper. I got shit to do."

Before Roscoe could say anything, Shy backed out and roared out of the parking lot.

On his way to Tab's, he did not make one single effort to calm his ass down. He'd need everything he had not to wring her pretty neck when he got there and lit into her.

Leaving.

Leaving him.

Fuck!

Ten minutes later, he pulled up outside her apartment, parked, switched off the bike, and scanned for rides he knew.

Tack's bike wasn't there, neither was his Expedition. Cherry's Mustang wasn't there. Tab's girl Natalie's ride wasn't there either.

But Tabby's electric blue ride that she took care of like it was her baby was gleaming in the sun.

The way clear, Shy swung off his bike, jogged to the steps, took them two at a time, and didn't hesitate to pound his fist on her door the instant he hit it. He also didn't stop pounding until he heard the locks turn and the door was thrown open.

"Jeez, Shy, what's the deal?" Tabby snapped, staring up at him.

He hadn't seen her in a month.

This meant that was the wrong greeting.

The *way* wrong greeting.

Making matters even worse, behind her everything but the furniture was boxed up.

Fighting back his need to explode, he prowled in and Tabby had to jump out of his way. Once in, he turned on her.

"Shut the door, Tabby," he ordered.

"Shy, what—?"

"*Shut the fuckin' door, Tabby!*" he roared and watched her face pale as she shut the door and turned to him.

"Okay, Shy, calm down. We'll talk," she said gently.

"You leavin'?" he asked.

"I..." she hesitated, licked her fucking lip and, Christ, that hit him straight in his dick like that *always* hit him straight in his dick. "Yes, Shy," she admitted. "I was gonna call you next week. Talk to you. Tell you what's—"

He cut her off, "You're not leavin'."

Her head jerked, then she told him, "I am, Shy. I need space to get my head together. The contracts are signed—"

"You," he interrupted her again, "Are. Not. *Leaving*."

She shut her mouth and stared at him.

He kept talking.

"You gotta get your head together, you do it here where I can get to you, not somewhere where I gotta haul my ass on a plane to get to you. Are you comprehending me?"

"But, Shy—" she started.

She was not comprehending him.

"You're not leaving," he repeated.

"I have to, the—"

He leaned toward her and growled, "You are *not* leaving."

Suddenly, she lost it, throwing her hands out to the sides, she asked, "Why?"

"This is why," he clipped, stalked the three steps that separated them, snaked an arm around her waist, drove a hand into the back of her hair, and hauled her into his arms.

He slammed his mouth down on hers.

Then he thrust his tongue between her lips and there it was.

Christ, there it fucking was.

That taste he'd had on his tongue for fucking years.

Sweet, God, so fuckin' sweet.

Beautiful.

He took more and she gave it, her body melting into his, her feet coming up on her toes, her arms circling his shoulders, holding on to him, one hand sliding up into his hair, holding his mouth to hers.

She kept giving it so he took even more and Jesus, the taste of her, the feel of her pressed close, the world melted away. It was more intoxicating than any liquor, a high better than any fucking drug.

Phenomenal.

Better than he would have guessed. Better than years of wondering how good it could be.

The best he ever had.

With just a fucking *kiss*.

He broke his mouth from hers but felt her short, excited pants against his lips when he said yet again, "You are not leaving."

"Okay," she breathed, and he closed his eyes, dropped his forehead to hers and sucked in a breath to gain control over the burn in his chest.

When he had it, he opened his eyes and looked down at her.

Her eyes were unfocused, hazy. She was pressed up against him, still holding him, hand in his hair.

He'd made the world melt away for her too.

That burn came back but it was different, and the change was fucking brilliant.

"You're gettin' your head together here," he demanded.

"Okay," she agreed on another breath.

Fuck, she was cute. Hot and cute.

It was time to talk to Rosalie.

"What are you doin'?" he asked.

"Not leaving," she answered.

Good. It was penetrating.

"Then what're you doin'?" Shy pushed.

"Getting my head together," she answered.

"How long's that gonna take?"

"Two hours."

He felt his lips twitch.

Finally.

Fucking *finally.*

"You got two hours, sugar, then you come to me," Shy demanded. "My apartment. I'll text you the address."

Her beautiful blue eyes held his and she whispered, "Okay."

"Two hours, Tabby."

"Two hours, Shy."

Yes.

There it was.

Fucking finally.

"Good, baby, now kiss me."

Her eyes flashed in a way he also felt in his dick, then she rolled up to her toes, put her pretty, rosy mouth to his, and gave him what he'd been craving for four years.

That sweet, pink tongue of hers slid out, glided between his lips and touched the tip of his.

His tongue pushed it back into her mouth and he took over the kiss. It was a repeat of the first but longer, wetter, deeper, not better but a whole lot fucking hotter.

He broke his mouth from hers and ordered, "Two hours, babe."

She panted against his mouth and nodded.

He let her go. She teetered. He prowled to the door, pulled it open, turned back to her and lifted a hand with his middle and index fingers extended to the ceiling.

Her cheeks were pink, her mouth swollen, her eyes dreamy, and it was a fucking good look.

She powered through the haze and nodded.

Shy grinned, turned, closed the door behind him, and he kept grinning as he jogged to his bike.

CHAPTER EIGHT

Gone for You

I STOOD OUTSIDE Shy's door trying not to hyperventilate and also trying to get my head together.

Two hours wasn't enough time.

I knew one thing. My pit of denial could be denied no longer. Not after a month without Shy. Not after that kiss.

That kiss.

That fabulous, unbelievable, *amazing* kiss.

That wasn't what I had to sort out in my head.

At least I'd been able to deal with the agency that was sending me to Cape Cod. I'd called and told them I had a family emergency that might mean I'd have to back out, which was a total lie, but after that kiss…

That kiss!

After that kiss I knew one thing for certain, I couldn't take off and be that far away from Shy for six months or even for another day. I'd had a month without him in my life and I felt even more lost than I felt when Jason died.

I knew why this was. Unlike with Jason, I didn't have anyone to talk to about it and even I was denying to myself why our separation affected me so deeply. Both of these made it more difficult, so difficult I couldn't deal without escape. Therefore, Cape Cod it was.

So after that kiss, no way I could be most of a continent away from him and stuck on a freaking island for six months.

But we still had things to sort out. Like Rosalie.

One thing I had managed to do in those two short hours was phone Big Petey. I tried to pull the wool, dance around the subject, but I was thinking that he saw through it when I tried to ascertain without coming right out and asking if Shy was still seeing Rosalie.

Pete gave me the bad news sounding like he was giving me bad news, this why I thought I didn't pull the wool. The bad news, Pete told me, was Rosalie got dropped off at the Compound three days ago and they'd gone off together on Shy's bike.

Before we moved on from that kiss, I had to know what was going on with Rosalie.

And last but oh so not least, we needed to have a discussion about him losing his mind when he got annoyed at me.

I'd had a lifetime of watching biker babes and the way they got on with their badass bikers. I knew this was a minefield, and I knew that Shy was not the only badass biker who went gonzo like he did that night we discussed why I'd disappeared for two weeks and like he had again two hours ago when he confronted me about leaving.

As far as I could tell, there were three options for going the distance with a biker and after that kiss that was what was on my mind.

Going the distance with a biker. With Shy.

The options were, one, give up and let them roll right over you.

I didn't think that was me, or I hoped it wasn't.

The next was become a biker bitch, like my mom had become. Mom was just a bitch, so it was bound to happen that she'd let her bitch light shine through. But sometimes when the boys were the boys, bossy biker badasses, instead of setting the boundaries right off, I'd seen women go over the top with attitude, butting up against their man all the time and not talking to him so they did nothing but fight. Loudly. Publicly. Nastily.

I didn't want that either.

Not at all.

The last option was the way Tyra was with Dad. I didn't know how she balanced it, but they were who they were and somehow that clicked. She didn't let him roll all over her even though he had a dominant personality, the kind that pushed out all other personalities unless you were able to hold your own against him. Still, Tyra had to find that middle ground where she gave Dad what he needed to be, well...Dad. A little over, he'd butt heads with you and the results wouldn't be pretty. A little under, he'd take advantage and then lose interest, especially in women, because as much as Dad was about control, he didn't want to control his woman. He liked a challenge. Just not too much of a challenge.

They worked.

Spectacularly.

That said, sometimes things got intense, the balancing act went out the window, it was anything goes, and Tyra didn't take a lot of shit from him.

I'd never forget that night years ago when she came

to my rescue after my ex-too-old-for-me boyfriend hit me and then my ex nearly busted Tyra's head in with a baseball bat. Dad had lost it on her, that she'd put herself in that situation, and I still remember hearing them fighting.

At the time, I was devastated, them fighting over me like that. After it all was good again, I admired her for yelling right back and not taking his crap.

That was what I wanted for me if I was going to hitch my wagon to Shy's biker stud.

So before I blew it and started something with Shy after all our history and it being my first relationship after Jason (who was, it was important to note, my only other real relationship), we had to talk. Get a few things straight.

Depending on Shy's answers I'd know if I had my head together or if I needed time and space to find that.

I took a deep breath, determined to talk it all out with him without losing my head, my patience, my temper, or myself, but I didn't even raise my hand to knock when the door flew open.

All of a sudden I had an arm hooked around my waist, I was in his apartment, and Shy's booted foot was kicking the door closed.

The next thing I knew, I had lips on mine and a tongue in my mouth.

With that, I didn't know anything else. I didn't *want* to know anything else. The only thing I wanted to know was Shy.

He was just that good. So good, when he kissed me, the world melted away.

His mouth broke from mine and my thoughts came back, kind of.

"Shy, we need to talk," I breathed, my pulse racing, my skin warm, my breath coming fast, my arms locked around him, the fingers of one hand in his hair, just like the first time.

Exactly like the first time.

Suddenly, my shirt was gone.

My breath, already fast, left me totally, and my nipples started tingling.

Shy's hands slid up my sides and those tingles went into overdrive.

"Got your head sorted, sugar?" he asked, his green eyes intense, hot and locked to mine, his body herding me backward.

"Yes," I answered. "But we have to talk."

His hands left my sides but he kept herding me at the same time he whipped off his tee.

My thoughts flew out the window.

"We'll talk later," he murmured, his hands settling on my waist.

I got a second to take in his lean, muscled chest and the scrolled, elaborate tattoo that adorned his upper left pectoral that said forebodingly, "Love dies," before I was falling backward.

I landed on the bed.

Shy landed on me.

Before I could get my wits about me, Shy's lips were back on mine, his tongue was in my mouth, and his hands were moving on me.

His hands felt good. His mouth felt good. And he tasted *great*.

I wanted more of him. No, strike that, I *needed* more of him. I put my hands to his body, and the feel of all that smooth skin, soft to the touch, hard underneath rocked through me so thoroughly it felt like it started in my hair and ended at my toenails.

And that was so huge I needed even *more*.

So I took it, arching up, pushing him to his back and climbing on. I put my mouth to him, his neck, his throat, collarbone, chest, nipples, my lips moving, my tongue tasting, as my hands roamed. While I was exploring, Shy's fingers went to the hook of my bra and, with a flick, it came loose.

I only stopped long enough to lift up, pull it off, and toss it aside.

Then I went right back.

I didn't take my time. I was desperate, needing to get in as much as I could as fast as I could like he'd go up in a puff of smoke any second.

I got down to the waistband of his jeans, my tongue licking a line along the edge as my fingers undid the buttons, when Shy suddenly hauled me up his body, took my mouth in another devastating, wet, hard, hot kiss, and rolled me to my back.

Within seconds, my jeans were undone, he broke the kiss, and then they were gone. The sensation of the fabric sliding down my legs caused another bolt of desire and hunger to shoot through me.

Shy moved away but only to lift me up and rearrange me in the bed so my head was on the pillows. He pulled my legs apart and positioned himself on his knees between them.

I stared up at him, my breaths rapid and shallow.

He was staring down at me, his face dark with the same hunger I felt slinking through my body, and his hands were moving down the outsides of my thighs until they stopped behind my bent knees.

"You," he growled, the sound of his rumbling, deep, harsh voice like a touch. "In my bed," he finished and my heart flipped.

Four words.

Four words that said everything.

He wanted me there.

He'd wanted me there for a while.

From the look on his face, the sound of his voice, he even *needed* me there like I needed to be there.

"Shy," I whispered but he jerked up my legs and bent forward, his mouth hitting me at my midriff, it moved down fast until it closed over my panties between my legs.

My back arched, my legs jolted, and my mouth opened in a silent moan.

Paradise.

As soon as I had him, I lost him and my head shot up, but he only moved to pull my panties down my legs. When they were gone, he rolled right back between my legs, tossing them over his shoulders, and then I had him, just his mouth against me with nothing in between.

I was wrong.

This was paradise.

In minutes, Shy nearly took me there, and just as my orgasm was about to tear through me, his mouth was gone.

My head shot up again. "Shy," I breathed and there it was again, need dripping from my voice.

"The first time I make you come for me, you do it with me inside you," he rumbled, and I nearly came just from his words.

One thing I knew in my crazy world, I was down with *that.*

He shifted his torso, reaching toward the nightstand, and I sat up, putting my mouth to his skin as my hands undid the buttons of his jeans. When I got enough undone, I yanked them down his hips and felt an electric shock starting between my legs and emanating outward.

He was beautiful *everywhere.*

He came back with a condom and took over but I kept my mouth on him, his belly, his ribs, my hands on him everywhere I could touch, but I kept looking down to watch his hands work, getting more and more turned on simply by watching him roll a condom on.

A nanosecond after Shy got it in place, he had an arm around my waist, his other one curved under my bottom and I was up. My arms and legs circling him, Shy moved forward two paces on his knees, my back hit headboard, and Shy slid inside.

My eyes closed, my head sagged back then forward, my forehead hitting his shoulder.

Beautiful.

This was what I'd been waiting for.

Not for months.

For years.

To be right here, right like this.

With Shy.

"Gorgeous, baby, you . . . feel . . . fuckin' . . . *gorgeous,*" he groaned into my neck before he started moving.

It must be said, he felt the same way.

My limbs clenched around him and his arm around my bottom moved, drifting up my side, up my arm, pulling it away from him until he had my hand. He shoved his thumb in the palm, curled his fingers around the back and pressed our hands to the wall.

My head fell back, hit wall and Shy's came up. I saw instantly his eyes mirrored how I felt.

Loved.

Right.

Therefore I knew it was safe to share what was in my heart.

"I missed you," I whispered, as he moved, building it further, going deep, sweet, slow.

We'd never had this, not this, but what I said was true. I missed him.

At my words, he closed his eyes, dropped his head to rest his forehead against mine, and kept moving, faster, sweeter, deeper.

He opened his eyes but didn't lift his head even as the power of his hips increased, the burn built, and his hand in mine clenched hard.

"Missed you too, honey."

Oh God.

He missed me.

I loved that.

He went faster, the build sharpened, the burn increased and I gasped, "Shy."

"Wait for me, Tabby," he growled.

Faster, deeper.

Oh God.

God!

"I don't know—" I started.

"Hold on, baby. I'm close," he ordered, his voice thick.

"I don't know if I—"

Faster, so deep. So, so *deep.*

"Let go," he commanded, his voice gruff.

I let go. Twisting my head and shoving my face into Shy's neck, I moaned against his skin at the same time I felt his groan vibrating against my neck as it crashed over both of us, the wave taking us under, drowning us in a way neither of us was going to fight.

I held him close and Shy stayed buried deep, his hand holding mine tight, his breath heavy against my skin, mine the same against his.

Surfacing from under the wave, it struck me that I was wrong both times before.

Shy this close, buried deep, holding my hand, his breath against my skin... *this* was paradise.

Before I could catch a thought, fully process how beautiful the moment was, Shy let my hand go and shifted, falling to his back, one arm wrapped around me, one hand cupped at the back of my head, our bodies still connected.

Okay, before, paradise, but lying on top of Shy's warm hardness was far from shabby.

"Don't ever leave me," he rasped.

I blinked at the corded column of his throat with its kick-ass medallions attached to the thin, black bits of leather resting against his skin.

I tried to lift my head but his hand at the back kept it where it was and he repeated, "Promise me, Tab. Do not ever leave me."

Oh my God.

What did I say?

I didn't lie when he was moving inside me. I missed him when he was gone. Further, it wasn't just sex we had. I didn't have a lot of experience, but I knew enough to know that. It was more. It was a connection. A promise. And when he came to my place just over two hours ago being intense and bossy, not only was that hot, it was *awesome*. It was what I needed to stop denying all I was feeling and finally admit what he meant to me.

But this was too much.

Maybe not too much but definitely too soon.

"We have to talk," I told him quietly, and his hand left my head so he could wrap his arm around my shoulders.

I lifted my head to see his chin ducked down so his startling green eyes could capture mine.

Okay, looking into those eyes, those beautiful eyes that looked sated and warm but intense and serious, all hot, all gorgeous, I thought maybe it wasn't too soon.

"Yeah, Tab, we got a lot to talk about. You're right. This is not gonna go easy."

Uh-oh.

What did he mean by that?

He didn't make me wait for an explanation. "We got a lot to sort through. I gotta tell you how I spent the two hours since I was at your place. We gotta work out how I lose my mind when you need to go into your head and freeze me out. We gotta work out *why* you freeze me out when you go into your head. And, baby"—his hand drifted up my shoulder to curl around the back of my neck—"I know you know and I'm also sure it isn't lost on your dad or Cherry that I got a reputation. They find out we're an us, I don't see good things. Fuck, half the brothers in the Club are not gonna think good things. Pete's already givin' me looks and has been for a while. When we leave this apartment, you and me gotta be on the same page. But sayin' that, sugar"—his voice dropped—"what just happened was somethin' that was bigger than all that. It was bigger than everything. I had a taste of you four years ago that I could never get off my tongue. Now, I've tasted more of you with more than just my mouth and I know I wanna keep it in a way I don't want to think of it bein' done. Not in a few weeks. Not in a few months. Maybe not ever."

Oh wow. It could be said all that was too soon too, but it also had to be said I liked it.

Like, *really* liked it.

So much I melted automatically into his body.

I slid a hand to his neck and whispered, "Shy."

He kept going, "So promise me, right now, my dick still inside you, you naked on top of me in my bed, us sharing what we just shared, us having a taste of what it's like apart and knowin' we're better together, you won't leave me. You won't go in your head and take off no matter what. You stick with me until there's nothing to stick to, if that ever happens."

I could promise that.

"Okay, darlin'. I promise," I said quietly. His eyes closed slowly then they opened, his hand sifted into my hair and pulled my mouth to his.

He gave me a soft kiss then his fingers squeezed my head gently.

I got the message, pulled slightly away and he whispered, "Hate losin' you but you gotta shift off me, honey. Need to get rid of this condom then we can talk about shit I don't wanna talk about with you sittin' on my dick."

My lips twitched, I whispered, "Okay," then I shifted off him, slowly, taking my time, not liking the feel of losing him but really liking the way his eyes got lazy as I slid him out of me.

Once I'd lost him, he rolled me to my back, bent and kissed my chest, then kissed the underside of my jaw and rolled off the bed.

I watched him hike up his jeans as he walked away, appreciating his ass as he did so. Then my eyes shifted to the Chaos tattoo that spanned his back, and I appreciated that too. All of this I appreciated while appreciating the loose-limbed way his lanky body moved before he disappeared though a door.

I moved my eyes to the ceiling and smiled.

He had the same thoughts I had, *exactly*. He knew we needed to talk and he knew what we needed to talk about. He was going to give me that.

I rolled toward the edge of the bed, reached out a hand, and nabbed my panties, and since Shy's tee was close, I nabbed that as well. I shimmied my panties on while lying on my back, sat up, pulled his tee over my head, and my smile came back.

His shirt smelled of him.

Another piece of paradise.

Arranging myself cross-legged on the bed, I looked around and surprise hit me, tamping down (but not forcing out, nothing could do that except, perhaps, the end of the world) my happy mojo.

Shy lived in an apartment that was just that little bit older and more worn than mine. The carpet wasn't great. The walls needed a new coat of paint, and they needed that coat about seven years ago. There were boxes all around and no personal touches at all. It was like he hadn't actually moved in yet.

I'd never been to his place, and I knew he spent a lot of time at the Compound, but I also knew that he'd had his own place for a long time.

Maybe he'd recently moved, though if this was a step up, I wondered where he used to live.

I was in the living room and, weirdly, so was his bed. It was at the wall to the back of the room, but there were two doors on the side of the living room and I figured at least one must be a bedroom. There was a couch shoved up against the side wall, but it was covered in boxes. There was also an old TV on a stand about two feet from the foot of the bed. There was one nightstand with a lamp on it, a bunch of change, packets of condoms, and that was it. No other furniture. No dressers. No bookshelves.

Nothing.

It was somewhat tidy considering any space filled with boxes wasn't exactly tidy. It was also surprisingly clean. What it wasn't was a home. Not even close to it. Not even a bachelor pad.

It looked like it was just a place to crash on occasion and store stuff.

This made me feel uneasy.

What didn't make me feel uneasy was when Shy walked back into the room with his biker grace, his chest on display.

The instant I saw him, I pushed to my knees and moved to the edge of the bed.

Shy, his eyes on me, his face soft, did exactly what I wanted him to. He moved right to me.

I slid my arms around him and pressed my lips to his chest.

He curved a hand around one side of my neck, the

other hand he glided up into my hair to curl around the back of my head.

There it was again, that feeling.

Loved.

Right.

I took my lips from his skin and put my chin there, seeing the "Love dies" tattoo.

I'd seen the two tats he had on the insides of his forearms and I'd suspected, like all the brothers, he had the Chaos emblem on his back. These three tats all the brothers had, the two Shy had inked into his forearms the brothers put wherever they wanted. The emblem on his back, all the guys had on their backs. They got the back tat the minute the Club voted them into full membership.

Having never seen his chest, I'd never seen the only tattoo he seemed to have outside the Chaos ones.

"Love dies?" I asked quietly, my gaze lifting to his.

His hand twisted gently in my hair even as his fingers at my neck dug in slightly, and he broke my heart when he replied quietly back, "Had a mom and dad I loved, they died. Had an uncle I loved who didn't shield us from that bitch and that love died too. One night, I was seventeen, listenin' to them fight, her bitchin' yet a-fuckin'-gain about how they had two more mouths to feed, two more bodies to clothe so they couldn't go to Hawaii or whatever the fuck, and I knew the next day her mood was gonna fuck up my week because she always took that shit out on him first, then on us. He didn't take our backs during the fight, and I knew he wouldn't take our backs the next day. That night, my love died for him. I was holdin' on but it slipped away. I had a fake ID to buy booze so I snuck out the window and went to an all-night tattoo place." He lifted a hand to indicate the tattoo. "Had this inked on me."

My eyes moved to the tattoo but went back to Shy, and I leaned away a bit when he bent slightly.

His face got close and he continued, "I was young, pissed, and stupid, sugar. I don't believe that shit anymore. But ink is ink, it doesn't fade away. Unfortunately, it reminds me of a shitty time in my life every time I see it." He grinned. "It also reminds me not to do anything permanently stupid because I'm pissed."

I grinned back. "Good lesson to learn."

His grin faded and he muttered, "Not sure I learned it."

I knew what he was saying so I whispered, "Shy, don't. We both fucked up and, obviously, it wasn't permanent."

He touched his forehead to mine and sighed before he ordered, "Shift, Tabby. I'm climbin' in."

I shifted. Shy climbed in then he claimed me. Resting with his head on the pillows, he tugged me over his body and turned so he was on his side, his body curled at the waist and knees and my hips were cradled in his lap, thighs over his hip, my back to the bed, head to the pillow. Shy came up on an elbow, head in hand and aimed his eyes at me.

"Rosalie," he muttered.

Oh crap.

I braced and his gaze moved over my face even as his hand hit my belly and slid across, pulling me in and tucking me closer to his body.

He kept talking, "Until about an hour ago, we were seein' each other. Now we are not."

"Shy—" I started and his hand at the side of my waist gave me a squeeze.

"Let me finish, baby." When I shut my mouth, he went on, "It was unpleasant, for her it came outta the blue and she was not pissed. She was hurt. Pissed I can deal with, hurt's a lot harder. It sucked. It's over. She's sweet, nice, pretty, she'll find someone else."

"Um..." I began hesitantly, "being honest, although it's good to know you had that conversation with her before we, uh...officially started things, I have to admit I'm not real sure you being equipped to scrape her off at the drop of a hat fills me with joy."

"I get that, Tab. What you don't get is, she isn't you," he returned, and I blinked, then my belly warmed.

When I said nothing, he gave me another squeeze and went on.

"By the end of our conversation, she admitted she'd wondered about you and me. The time I spent with you. When I'd walk away from her to take calls from you. How you disappeared for a month and I was in a shitty mood that whole month. None of this I hid from her. I knew where my head was at about you but I had no clue your head would ever go there. Seein' as I knew how I felt about you, bottom line, I dicked her over. It was uncool. I gotta live with that. You in my tee in my bed, I think will help."

"That's kinda cold, Shy."

"It's cold but it's real, and it's better that shit is done for her, for me, and for you so we can all move on, rather than me draggin' it out in a pointless effort to cushion the blow for her that, in the end, would only make shit even shittier."

"Yes, but you and I are moving on to something that's good and, obviously, since it lasted a while for you two, when she started it with you, she thought she was moving on to something good too," I pointed out.

"I saw you," he replied, and my head tipped on the pillow as I felt my brows inch together.

"Pardon?"

"With that guy outside DCPA. You were wearin' a red dress."

My heart squeezed, I felt my eyes get big and I stared at him.

I remembered that night. That was the night Jason took me to see *Les Mis*.

"You saw me?" I asked.

"You were alone, looked beautiful but lost. You saw him, he got to you, you leaned into him, kissed him, made him laugh and then he kissed you. I saw it. All of it."

Wow, he really *did* see this, and he remembered it better than I did until he just reminded me.

I didn't know what to make of this or the reminder of Jason when I hadn't thought of him once. Not once. Not once since Shy stormed into my apartment.

Before I could make anything of it, Shy kept talking.

"Didn't like it," he stated.

Not keeping up, I asked, "Didn't like what?"

"Seein' you with another guy. Didn't like it."

My hand slid up his arm at my waist and I whispered, "Shy, honey, I don't—"

"I had the taste of you in my mouth, so sweet, for four years. Your grudge and you hatin' me made that taste as bitter as it was sweet. Didn't get it, what I was feelin', not until I heard you were gettin' hitched. Then I knew I was gone for you. Don't know how it happened, just know it did. Seein' you with another guy cut deep. Then you lost him, and I felt that for you. Even removed, I felt it. And when you called me, I realized if I didn't get my shit together it would be empty pussy and parties for the rest of my life, and I'd never have a woman who was lost without me." His hand moved from my waist to frame the side of my face, and his voice got quiet when he said, "Just to be clear, the point of findin' that is not makin' a woman be lost without me like Rosalie will be for a while until she moves on. The point of findin' that is to have that feeling, be able to give that gift, to work at keepin' it good so my woman never feels lost because she knows she'll never be without me."

I closed my eyes and my fingers curved spasmodically around his forearm.

That was beautiful, amazing, *right*, and the best part about it was, if I wasn't mistaken, he wanted to give that to *me*.

I opened my eyes again when he kept talking.

"I'm sorry I had to bring him up but you gotta know that's where I'm at. That's why I stepped away from the empty pussy and parties and looked for somethin' that meant somethin'. The problem was, I found you a month before Rosalie and I had the somethin' that meant somethin'. I just didn't think you wanted me that way and I liked spendin' time with you enough, I was willin' to take what you could give me." His eyes warmed. "Now you're willin' to give me more and I'm gonna take that too."

Suffice it to say, I was willing to give more to Shy, but he knew that and I had to go over some of the more important things he said.

So I commenced in doing that.

"You were gone for me?" I asked softly and got a grin in return as his face dipped closer.

"You and me may not have been tight since the day we first saw each other, but am I the kind of guy who hangs around listenin' to bitches moan about work while ruining a dinner I gotta eat?" he asked.

No, he was absolutely not that kind of guy.

My belly got warmer and I whispered, "No."

His eyes moved over my face again before they caught mine and he whispered back, "Gone for you."

I closed my eyes and pulled in breath.

Yes, this was right.

"Sugar, look at me," Shy ordered gently, and I opened my eyes. "Let's go over it all. You are not Rosalie. That shit that went down with her will not go down with you. On that, baby, you got my word. When it goes around that we're an us, we're gonna face shit from the Club. How that's gonna come, I don't know, but I suspect it'll come from your dad, even Cherry, and we gotta stand strong and prove to them this is what it is. And last and most important, to stand strong and prove it to them and ourselves, we gotta get our shit together and get outta this pattern where you go into your head and freeze me out and I get pissed and say shit that's outta line. That means you gotta suck it up when I call you on your shit, and you gotta be willin' to call me on mine. Are you with me on all this?"

I nodded.

After I nodded I found my mouth forming the word *Why?*

His head jerked slightly and his brows drew together before he repeated, "Why?"

It came out, I had to go with it.

"Yeah, Shy, why? Why me? Why us? You seem pretty sure, and I—"

I stopped talking when a big, beautiful white smile spread on his handsome face right before he burst out laughing.

He was good-looking always, better when he was laughing, but it kinda peeved me he was laughing when I wasn't being funny.

"Shy," I snapped into his laughter. He sobered, kind of, and focused on me. Then he started speaking.

"Baby, I got a piece of tail, I fuck," he announced, and that didn't make me any less peeved. I figured he noted that because he carried on, "I fuck and I do it hard. I take what I want and if the bitch gets off, golden. If she doesn't let go enough to let me take her there, that's not my problem."

Again, this didn't make me feel much better.

"I'm not sure why you're sharing this with me, Shy," I told him. "I'm equally unsure I feel real good about what you're sharing."

His hand shifted minutely so his thumb could move over my cheek and my lips before his eyes got intense and he explained, "I have never, not once, not in my life, made love to any woman. Not once. Not until what I just did with you."

Oh.

Wow.

That was a good response.

"I had you up against the headboard, baby, but that was not fucking and it came natural. It's what we have. I didn't know that's what I'd get but I'm pleased as fuck you gave it to me. That alone answers your *why* when it comes to the us part. As for why it's you, I don't know, I don't care. It just is. It could be 'cause you're gorgeous. It could be 'cause you're funny. It could be 'cause I like the way you handled Pete when he lost his daughter. It could be 'cause you and me got Chaos in common, it's us, it's in our blood and this was meant to be. It could be 'cause I like the way you are with your family. It could be 'cause you get off on bein' on the back of my bike almost as much as I get off straddling it. I figure it's all that and more. I am not gonna analyze it. I'm gonna feel it 'cause I like it and that's all there is to it."

That response was even better.

"Do you wanna know why it's you?" I asked quietly, my hand gliding up his arm to his chest.

"Don't wanna piss you off, Tab, but I don't give a fuck. I'm happy just rejoicin' that it is."

Another good answer.

"Now," he continued, "you get that I'm pretty fuckin' sure and my guess is, you're here in my bed, my tee, and my arms, you're pretty fuckin' sure. So are we good?"

"Mostly," I answered and his head tipped to the side.

"Mostly?" he prompted when I didn't explain.

"Well, I didn't get the work thing entirely sorted. I have a feeling they'll let me renege on the contract since I told them I had a family emergency, but if I renege that means I don't have a job."

"Can you get your old one back?" he asked.

I shook my head. "They weren't happy to see me go and they told me when I got back from Cape Cod, if I wanted to come back and they had an opening, they'd see what they could do, but I don't wanna go back there, Shy. Since you and me, uh...had our thing, Dr. Dickhead got worse and began to target me. He used to spread his dick-headedness wide, but when I became his focus, I decided I couldn't deal."

"You talk to the administrators?"

"No, Shy and, darlin' "—I kept going quickly, because I knew by the change in his expression and the muscle that ticked in his jaw what he was going to say—"you don't get how it works in that world, but doctors are king. I could get embroiled in a big drama but in the end it would be a lot of headache, time, and stress, and either I'd have to suck it up and carry on or I'd have to get out and move on. It's just the way it is."

"Lucky for you I don't live in that world," Shy replied and my belly lurched.

Uh-oh. I knew what that meant, and what that meant was that it was damage control time.

"Shy, you don't and I don't but I *do* have to exist in it for eight-hour shifts, five days a week."

He leaned a bit away from me and declared casually, "No blowback."

Great.

The guys said that word all the time and then things would happen, like a few years ago when Tyra got kidnapped and stabbed, like, a gazillion times. Granted, that huge drama wasn't Dad's fault. It happened because Tyra's best friend Lanie's messed-up fiancé was, well…totally freaking messed up. So messed up, he got both Tyra and Lanie dragged into it. Still, Dad also got in the mix, and no one had given me the full briefing but however it went down pissed my big brother Rush off so much he refused to approach the Club to become a recruit. This gave me the sense that Dad's involvement upped Tyra's vulnerability.

She survived and she was a fighter, so she didn't let what happened drag her down, not even a little bit.

But still.

"Shy, I don't want you to get involved," I told him.

"And Tabby"—his face dipped close—"you showed up at my door and, unlike other women, you get the life so it's gonna come as no surprise to you when I say, I hear you, baby, but I'm still getting involved."

There it was and it came fast.

I had to do the balancing act.

"Shy, seriously," I said softly, pressing my fingers into his chest for emphasis, "I don't have a good feeling about this."

"I do it right, Tab, you won't feel anything at all, and mark me, honey, I'll do it right."

Fabulous.

I stared at him and it came to me.

Talk to Tyra.

I might have lived in the biker world all my life, but until I was sixteen and she disappeared, my mom was my biker-babe mentor and she was no good at it.

Tyra was the *master.*

I'd talk to her.

That was, I'd talk to Tyra about managing Shy after I talked to Tyra about how it was a good idea I was with Shy and then waited for her to get over the fact I was with Shy and believe in us (or pretend she did until she really believed in us), *then* I'd talk to Tyra about Shy rocking my employment world.

Hopefully, she'd get over the Shy-and-I-being-an-us thing fast, because I had a feeling from the look in his eyes, Shy wasn't going to dawdle.

"You with me?" he asked, and I wasn't.

Still, I said, "Kind of, but can I reserve the right to discuss this with you later, at a time when I haven't just become part of an us with a hot biker guy and brother to my father and a bunch of men who are family to me?"

He grinned and muttered, "Yeah you can reserve that right."

At least there was that.

Then his hand moved from the side of my head down to my chest and kept drifting further down when he continued, "Though, I reserve the right to repeat that I'm still gettin' involved."

Wonderful.

"Shy—"

"Talk over, Tabby, we got things to do."

I blinked and asked, "We do?"

"We totally fuckin' do," he answered.

"What things?"

He didn't answer.

He dropped his torso to mine just as his hand curved around my breast and his lips hit my lips.

Then we did the things we had to do which, to spell it out, was take a few trips to paradise.

CHAPTER NINE

Family Reunion

I HEARD THE knock on the door and I slowly opened my eyes.

It was morning, I could see the sun shining into Shy's apartment and I was in his bed.

More precisely, I was naked on him in his bed. Chest to chest, my body over his, my cheek to his shoulder, my hips off to the side, my leg crooked, knee resting against his thigh, his arm curled around my waist at an angle so his hand could cup my behind.

This position, surprisingly, felt supercomfortable and *very* nice, but I had no idea how he could sleep like that without being crushed or at the very least being able to breathe.

I also had no idea how *I* could sleep like that, seeing as I was naked and I could feel the sheet pulled up to just below my bottom, but mostly I had it all hanging out.

In my groggy, waking-up mind, memories of the day before hit me, and I had the feeling I knew how I could sleep like that and he could too.

I rarely slept naked, but that didn't mean it didn't

happen. Sometimes, when Jason and I went out on the town and I came back tipsy, we'd have wild monkey sex, this would go on for a while, and then I'd pass out naked.

Normally, if having sex was the last thing we did before going to sleep, after we did the deed, he gave me the hug-and-roll, I slid out of bed, cleaned up, and pulled on panties and a nightie before I hit the sack for good.

This was all the experience I had.

Jason was number two in my not-so-long list of lovers. I gave it away to my high school boyfriend when I was seventeen. It wasn't great. It didn't suck. What sucked was, even though he was way into me and told me it was forever and I liked him enough to give him my virginity (which was to say, a lot), he told his friends he did me and that crap got back to me. This did not fill me with joy, and I dumped him. He was devastated, I didn't feel all that great about the situation, but I wasn't going to take that, the looks, the under-the-breath comments, the girls' bitchiness, all of which he caused by doing something as stupid as bragging.

After him, I dated often enough but I was hung up on Shy, waiting for him to notice me, like guys seemed to notice me often so I didn't get too involved and never found a guy I was willing to go there with. Then Shy broke my heart and I decided to concentrate on my studies, not guys.

While doing that, I met Jason.

Although the sex I had with Jason was always good because he went to great lengths, lengths I enjoyed, to make it that way, and it could get wild, we had fun, it was nothing like what Shy and I had last night.

I thought I'd had wild monkey sex.

I didn't know the meaning of it until Shy taught it to me.

He had stamina. He had creativity. And he was so into me, it was unreal. He couldn't get enough of me, wasn't shy about me knowing it, and that worked for me since I felt the same for him.

We took only one break, to order a pizza. When it arrived, Shy walked to the bed and tossed the box on it. He moved to the kitchen, grabbed a couple of cold ones from the kitchen, handed one to me, then fell to his side across the foot of the bed, threw open the box and commenced eating.

I joined in, and when we were done, he threw the box on the floor (where, mind you, it still was), grabbed my ankles and hauled me down the bed to him.

I'd never eaten naked.

I'd never done a lot of the things I did with Shy yesterday.

And the best part was, it was natural, it felt right. I never felt funny or apprehensive or wondered if I was doing it right. It was all about him, his hands, mouth, cock, and body, what they made me feel and how much I could get of them, going for it, building it in him, giving it my all to get a low groan or a growl, feeling like I conquered the world when I earned one.

It was beautiful, amazing, all of it. And there was a lot of it.

So it was no wonder I passed out naked on top of Shy.

Another knock came. I felt Shy's hand tense into the cheek of my bottom, and I was about to lift my head and look at him when his other arm wrapped around me and I stilled. This was because he was holding me gently, rolling me, moving me slowly and carefully, like he didn't know I was awake and he was making a grave effort not to wake me.

Sweet.

Very sweet.

"I'm awake, darlin'," I said softly right before he placed me on my back.

His head came up, my eyes hit his sleepy ones, and my heart tripped.

God, seriously, even sleepy-eyed, he was amazing.

Those sleepy eyes moved over my face as his hand came up, cupping the side of my head. His thumb slid along my hairline, his eyes came to mine and he gave me the best good morning ever.

"You," he whispered, "in my bed."

My lungs compressed but in a good way.

"Yeah," I whispered back. "With you."

His eyes went lazy, dropped to my mouth then his lips dropped there.

We touched tongues when another knock came at the door and this time it didn't stop.

Shy's head came up and he growled, "Fuckin', fuck me."

I grinned up at him. He scowled down at me then kissed the underside of my jaw before he rolled over me and off the bed.

I pulled the sheet up to my neck and rolled to my side, watching the show that was Shy tugging on a pair of jeans.

He looked out the peephole and I watched, captivated

by what I saw at the same time bracing as I watched every inch of his body go still.

Then he moved quickly. Unlocking the door, he threw it open and let out a man howl that shook the windows.

This shocked me so much, I sat up in bed. Holding the sheet to my front, I watched Shy lunge at whoever was outside. He then backed inside, his body now arched way back because he was carrying a grown man wearing fatigues *with* his stuffed-full Army drab duffel at a slant on his back.

Shy bounced the guy a few times as the guy slapped Shy's bare back in a way it appeared he hadn't noticed Shy's back was bare. Then Shy dropped him on his feet, they jumped apart and looked at each other grinning hugely. They jumped back together and there was more man hugging and back pounds.

I took a wild mental stab and decided this was Landon Cage, Shy's brother, home from deployment.

I was thrilled for Shy, and he was clearly thrilled to have his brother back.

What I was not was comfortable being naked in a bed in the same room as a family reunion.

"Fuck, good to see you man, shit, you surprised me," I heard Shy say as I started sliding toward the edge of the bed, yanking the sheet with me.

"A fuckin' peephole," Landon replied, pulling away, they kept hands on shoulders and hands clasped between them as they looked at each other and Landon finished, "Was gonna get the drop on you finally. Kick your ass."

"How many times I gotta prove that shit to you? It's not gonna happen," Shy returned.

I made it to the edge of the bed and saw none of the clothes, Shy or mine, were within reaching distance.

Crap.

I looked back at the brothers, noting vaguely they didn't look a lot alike. Shy's hair was two shades down from black. Landon's hair was about three shades up from light brown and, obviously, cut in a military cut, not long and curling around his neck like Shy's. Shy had amazing, green eyes. Landon's eyes were a warm, dark brown. They were the same height, but whereas Shy's frame was tall with lean, defined muscle, it looked like Landon had maybe thirty pounds on him, all of it muscle, but I couldn't tell for certain under those fatigues.

I took this all in as I considered my dilemma and wondered if I could make an escape to the bathroom with an armful of clothes without being noticed.

Both men's eyes came to me.

Wonderful.

Well, escape was out.

Shy smiled big, sauntered my way and, in typical Shy fashion, didn't hesitate one moment in putting me where he wanted me to be.

In this instance, he hauled me out of bed, tucked my front to his side and shuffled me his brother's way, saying, "Fuckin' thrilled I get to do this. Tab, meet my brother, Landon. And Lan, meet my girl, Tabitha Allen."

Lan was smiling down at me. I was smiling tentatively up at him at the same time frantically tucking the sheet around me.

The problem was, the instant Shy said my name, something passed through Lan's eyes and the clearly genuine smile he had on his mouth turned straight-out fake.

Uh-oh.

Shy had been talking about me, and it didn't appear that whatever he'd said was good.

Putting a courteous face on, he stuck his hand out and muttered, "Cool to meet you, Tabitha."

"Tab, Tabby, uh...whatever you wanna call me. People call me both," I stammered, taking his hand and concentrating on giving it a warm squeeze.

He gave me a squeeze back and quickly let me go.

"This is good. Now I get to take my girl and my brother out for coffee," Shy announced and my body froze solid as his eyes hit Lan. "Tex will wanna see you're back, brother."

"Is he still a whackjob?" Lan asked.

"Tex is Tex, not sure there's another way he can be," Shy answered, still grinning, still badass biker elated and relieved his brother was home in one piece.

"Uh...how about I go home and give you guys some one-on-one reunion time," I suggested, and Lan's eyes cut to me, which was what I saw.

What I *felt* was Shy's eyes come to me. I felt them so much, I turned my head to look up at him.

Uh-oh again.

"You're comin' with us," he declared, his eyes intense, his demeanor stating his declaration brooked no argument.

Unfortunately, I needed to argue. I needed to give Shy time with his brother because Shy should have time with his brother. Selfishly, I also needed to give Shy time with his brother to explain how things were now, not however they were when he last spoke to him about me.

"Shy, darlin', you haven't seen Lan in a year. Maybe

you two can have coffee, I'll go out, get some stuff, and make you guys lunch," I suggested.

Shy's eyes cleared and his lips twitched. "He just survived Afghanistan, sugar, don't think he needs to come home and have you kill him with your cooking."

I forgot Lan's reaction to me and the small fact I was wearing nothing but a sheet and only could think of Shy embarrassing me by announcing to his brother, of all people, the only real family he had outside of the Chaos family we shared, that I couldn't cook.

"My lunch won't kill him," I snapped.

"Baby, I don't know if garlic poisons anyone but vampires but the way you use it, I figure this is a possibility," he returned.

"I'll make sandwichcs," I told him. "You can't screw up sandwiches."

"That's what you said about hamburgers before you screwed them up," he told me.

"Well—" I started to huff but he kept going.

"And tuna casserole before you screwed that up too."

"Shy!" I clipped.

"And those steaks, that roast chicken, and that soupy chocolate pie," he went on.

"Shy"—I rolled up on my toes and got close—"*shut up.*"

He grinned.

I looked to Lan and announced, "You really need to take him for coffee so I have plenty of time to plot his murder. You can't plot a murder distracted by hot guys, and now I have *two* of you on my hands."

Lan was looking at me like the Tabby he met just

minutes ago evaporated, a new Tabby took her place, and he'd never seen me before.

Then his eyes went to his brother, his face softened, they came back to me, he grinned a gentle, sweet grin and he informed me, "Honey, you do know you're wearin' nothin' but a sheet."

"I can't think of that now," I returned. "My biker boss hot guy just told his brother, the brother I *just met*, that I can't cook. I have to focus on plotting murder, or at the very least revenge, and not on how I'm embarrassed I'm in a sheet which, might I add—" I turned angry eyes up to Shy "—is not my choice *either*. Just so you know, darlin', I was headed to the bathroom when you plucked me out of bed, and it would have been nice to get there and put on at least a pair of panties before you hauled me across the room."

"We went two feet," he contradicted me.

"Two feet to you because you're in jeans and you've known your brother since he was born. A football field to me because I'm"—I rolled up to my toes again—"*in a sheet*."

"You're more covered than most women walkin' on the street, Tab," he continued.

"The point right now is, I'd like to be more covered, Shy," I retorted.

"And I'd like coffee, kids, so if you two can quit your bitchin' and put some fuckin' clothes on, we'll go do that," Lan cut in, laughter in his deep voice, and both Shy and I looked at him.

Shy grinned.

I snapped, "Fine, but one of you hotties needs to go out and get me a toothbrush. I have morning breath mixed with pizza breath and it's not a good combination."

I said this while pulling away from Shy, struggling

with my sheet at the same time bending and swiping my stuff from the floor. I bundled it in my arms, pulled the sheet tighter, and stomped toward the bathroom but stopped, turning back to them and flipping the ends of my sheet out behind me like a Hollywood starlet threw back her train on the red carpet. I aimed a glare at Shy.

"Something to know about me, I use electric, always, but if I'm in a situation, say now, where you have to hit Walgreens, I want a pink toothbrush and whitening toothpaste." I cut my gaze to Lan and stated, "I won't take long and we'll get you coffee. Really glad you're home safe. Shy was superworried."

Then I glared through Shy and finished stomping out of the room and into the bathroom.

I was dumping my stuff on the vanity when the door opened, Shy stalked in, pulled me in his arms, and whispered against my lips, "I don't care about morning pizza breath."

He went ahead and proved this by kissing me, deep, wet, and long.

When he broke his mouth from mine, he grinned down at me and, still whispering, said, "You're the shit, Tabitha Allen."

Oh my God, that felt really, freaking good and I wasn't just referring to the kiss.

"And you're a great kisser, Shy Cage," I replied, my words breathy.

He grinned, gave me a squeeze, let me go, and sauntered out of the bathroom, closing the door behind him.

I turned to the mirror and saw I had wild sex hair that even I had to admit looked good, flushed cheeks that helped the overall look, and swollen lips that looked sultry as all get out.

And happy eyes.

Very happy eyes.

Shy's brother was home.

And Shy was mine.

I smiled at myself in the mirror, then I turned on the shower.

CHAPTER TEN

Rebound

"VIP! V . . . I . . . *fuckin'* . . . P!"

This was boomed out by the huge, shaggy blond-haired, russet-bearded guy that stood behind the espresso counter at Fortnum's Used Books.

We had just come through the door, and I noted that he was not only looking our way but pointing a finger in our direction.

I'd only been there once years ago, the time I ran into Shy. But when he told me he was a regular there, I'd never come back for fear of running into him.

So it clearly wasn't me he was declaring a VIP. The man lumbered from behind the espresso counter, pushed through the people standing in front of it and headed straight to Landon who, while I'd showered, had changed out of his fatigues into jeans and a tee.

When the barista made it to Landon, they did the man-hug-slapping-the-backs thing, and I was close enough to hear the crazy guy mutter in Lan's ear in what was still a boom but muted, "Safe. Home. Welcome back, son."

I didn't know this guy but something about that,

probably the deep emotion I heard in his voice, made tears sting my eyes as I watched the crazy guy hold on to Landon like he was something precious for several long beats before he pulled away.

He pulled away but he didn't go too far. He kept hold of Lan's hand between them and curled his other beefy mitt around Landon's shoulder, shaking it slightly, eyes locked to Lan's and muttering in his low boom, "Welcome home."

Shy, who was holding my hand, let it go to slide his arm around my shoulders and tuck me close to his side. This was another demonstration of how he could read my mood without even looking in my eyes.

Watching a soldier's welcome home, that soldier being Shy's brother, I needed him to hold me.

The crazy blond guy took a step toward the counter and declared, a lot louder, "Coffee is free for you. We do that for heroes." His blue eyes swung toward Shy. "Sorry, travelin' man, you and your girl gotta pay. If it was up to me, I'd give free coffee to hero's families too, but when I do that shit, Indy throws a conniption."

And with that, he lumbered away.

"Uh . . . I take it you know that guy," I noted.

Landon burst out laughing while Shy gave me a sweet, sexy smile, and neither man bothered to answer a question the answer to which was obvious. We just moved to the counter.

All went well with the ordering and paying portion of the normally simple and drama-free task of ordering a coffee drink.

That was, until we were waiting at the other end of the counter for our drinks, and the crazy guy suddenly arched the espresso machine filter through the air, which was luckily mostly (but not completely) free of used coffee grounds. He used it to point toward the couch in front of the window and totally ignored the small splash of coffee grounds that plopped and slid across the ordering counter.

Then he boomed, "VIP seating! Move your asses! We got a soldier just got home and his ass is sittin' in that couch!"

The people on the couch stared at the big man for about a half a second then they wisely scurried.

It was then the pretty blonde woman with the unbelievably glamorous smile who was also behind the counter aimed that glamorous smile my way. I suspected she did this since I'd been staring at the crazy guy like he was, well... a crazy guy.

"Tex is harmless," she explained. "It takes a while to believe that, since he's also totally nutso, but, I promise, he's harmless."

What I knew was he was loud and bossy, and he appreciated the sacrifice members of our military made for us, so I could get over the loud, bossy, and crazy bits.

Therefore, I smiled back.

She tipped her head to the couches. "Go, sit before Tex tells you to do it in a way that people at Walgreens a block away will hear. I'll bring these out."

"Thanks," I replied.

"Don't mention it," she mumbled, her eyes sliding back to Tex, who was again banging on the machine that looked like it cost as much as my living room furniture (and more) like it only produced under the most abusive of conditions.

Shy flexed his arm around my shoulders and guided

me toward the couch. We hit the seating section in front of the windows, and Shy again put me where he wanted me, settling me into the corner of the couch. He sat on the arm beside me and pulled me up against him.

The nice woman came out with our drinks, and I had a hopefully undetected mini-orgasm when I tasted my drink. Really, the crazy guy was an artist. Shy and Landon were catching up, which, not surprisingly, didn't give me a lot of opportunities to enter the conversation.

This went on for a while. Long enough for my mind to wander to things I could be doing. Such as, say, ascertaining if I was going to be blacklisted by the traveling nurse's agency for backing out of a job and calling the HR Department of the hospital to see if I could have my old one back and phoning my landlord to see if I could stay in my apartment although I gave up my lease.

Nothing important.

I didn't want to get impatient. I wanted the opportunity to get to know Landon, though that kinda wasn't happening except for me doing that by following their conversation.

Not to mention, I'd never seen Shy like this. Obviously happy his brother was home safe. Obviously happy he and I had moved to another level of our relationship. Obviously happy in a way that made my belly feel warm that he was in the company of two people he cared about.

Not that I didn't want him to have that. Of course I did.

It was just that yesterday I had let a kiss change the course of my whole life. I had crap to do, and sitting and listening to two badasses shoot the breeze was not a high priority.

Nevertheless, I settled in for the long haul while

mentally designing my to-do list when Shy noted our mugs were all empty and he announced he was getting us more drinks.

He kissed the top of my head and headed to the counter.

I watched him go, happy to have something to do that I immensely enjoyed, like watching him move, when I heard Lan call my name and my gaze swung to him.

"So you two are tight," he remarked and I smiled.

"Yeah, we're tight," I confirmed.

He looked over his shoulder toward Shy before he leaned forward in the armchair, settling his elbows to his knees. His expression changed and I braced.

The expression change wasn't mean or ugly. It wasn't even blank, like he was hiding something from me.

But it still wasn't good.

"Park and I are close," he declared, and I nodded since I knew this. He continued, "We talk. The last year, not often, can't do that too often when you're in the thick of shit. But when we do, we lay it out."

Uh-oh.

I couldn't know for certain what was coming, but that didn't mean I didn't have a feeling.

"Okay," I said cautiously, sucking it up, wanting it over and inviting him to share what was on his mind.

Lan took me up on my invitation.

"Last thing I heard about you, Tabby, was that you were about to tie the knot and it was a coupla weeks after that went..." he paused and I knew he was trying to find the right words when he finished "...south."

"Yeah," I verified, still talking softly. "That went south."

"Sorry, honey," he whispered, and the way he said it was almost as sweet as his brother could be. I liked that even though I didn't like our topic of conversation. Still, I nodded.

"That was a while ago, Landon," I informed him. "Almost a year."

"Yeah," he muttered then he asked, "After the..." another hesitation "...other guy, is Park your first?"

I felt a tingle slide down my back, the kind that didn't feel great.

This was none of his business. Okay, he was Shy's brother, they were close so it kinda was.

It also kinda wasn't.

"I'm not sure—" I started, but stopped when he shook his head and lifted a placating hand.

"Please get this, Tabby. He's my brother. He's my best friend. We've been through a lot of shit. In an effort to survive that, we had to learn how to unload and we did that by unloading on each other. After we both left that life, that didn't stop. In other words, I know about you." His eyes held mine. "All about you, Tabby."

This wasn't great news.

I opened my mouth to speak, but he lifted his hand again and kept his eyes locked to mine.

"I know he was a dick to you. When you laid it out for him, he gave that to me and I can see why you thought he was a dick. I also know he talked a lot about his brothers in his Club, and he talked about some of the family attached to that Club, and most of that family he talked about was you and you weren't even talkin' to him. He didn't tell me why that was, but that doesn't mean I couldn't get a read that he was into you. Seein' him with you, the way I've never seen him with another woman, I get now he's not into you. He's *into you*."

Well, that felt nice.

"I'm into him too," I shared.

Lan nodded. "I can tell. I'm missin' somethin' from the last deep conversation I had with Park, seein' as it was a long time ago, I can tell that too. What I gotta know is that this isn't you steppin' out from under grief, usin' him to do it, and then you're gonna leave him behind to go find another clean-cut guy you wanna hitch your star to."

At that, my back went straight.

"I'm Chaos," I reminded him, and he nodded.

"You are. I know that. Reigning princess. It's my understanding, though, you turned your back on that for your last man."

He was correct but he was going in the wrong direction.

"You can't control who you fall in love with, Landon," I pointed out, trying to keep the sharp out of my voice.

"No, you can't. But you can dig down deep and assess if the man you're with now genuinely means somethin' to you, like you do to him, or if you're on the rebound."

I sucked in breath in an effort not to get angry and when I got it under control, I told him firmly, "I'm not on the rebound."

"You didn't dig deep, Tabby," he returned quickly but gently, and I stared at him.

Then I leaned forward and locked my eyes to his.

"You two get a moment alone and, Landon, I'll be talking with Shy shortly to get him to give you that as well as leave me to the stuff I have to do since I made some major decisions just yesterday, possibly screwing up my career, maybe being homeless and jobless, all so I could be with your brother, and I need to sort out my life."

His eyes flashed.

I kept talking.

"But when you two have that moment, he'll tell you what's been going on the last seven months. What he won't tell you is what it meant to me because he can't know. So, if I can manage the herculean feat of sharing all Shy meant to me in the last seven months in the two minutes I have before he returns, I'll do that."

He said nothing, just stared at me intently so I kept going.

"Yes, he helped me get over Jason, and he did it in a just-friends way that was no pressure. Until certain things I'll let him share happened, he had my back every single day since I let him back in after Jason died. My loss was too fresh, I wouldn't allow myself to consider having the same emotions for another man so soon after losing the one I intended to spend the rest of my life with, so I denied what was growing between us."

I hesitated a moment for effect then went on.

"That said, from the very first night I let him back in, I knew what had started growing between us."

This got another flash but I ignored it and continued speaking.

"But I didn't deny the fact that I knew, when I was with Shy or even talking to him, I felt more me than I'd felt in years, after Jason died, before Jason died, before I even met Jason. So I can assure you I am not with Shy now as gratitude for his kindness. I'm also not with him because I'm lonely. Further, I'm not with him to test the waters of putting myself out there again."

I sucked in a breath, held his eyes and laid it out.

For him and for me.

"I'm with him because when I'm with him, I'm free to be me. I'm with him because he's hot. I'm with him because he lets me blather, since I'm prone to blathering, and he lets me rant when I have a bad day. I'm with him because when I rant, he makes me feel better and he does this effortlessly. I'm with him because I live for the times when I'm on the back of his bike and we're riding together, not even talking, just being free."

I shook my hands in front of me and kept giving Landon the honesty.

"Crap went down between us that's my fault because I was messed up, confused, acting stupid and frankly immature, and Shy got understandably angry at me. We were apart for a month and I was lost. Totally. Lost in a way I wasn't even lost when I lost Jason. Now we're back together and I'm found. If I'm misinterpreting things and that all spells 'rebound' to you, my apologies. It doesn't to me. For the first time in a long, *long* time, I'm happy. I'm also happy to take the time to prove to you I'm willing to do my part to see we go the distance. I just hope you won't mess with it in the meantime, because you yourself said you noticed your brother is happy too, he is in a way I've never seen, and it would be nice if you wouldn't fuck that up."

"I hope you know, it goes without sayin' I'll give my brother that," he replied.

"Good," I returned instantly. "I'm glad to hear that, but just a heads-up, it would be good to know you're also going to have his back. His brothers in the Club are protective of me, understandably more protective after what happened with Jason, and I think you might guess, when they find out we're together, that might not go great for us. Shy hasn't exactly lived his life holding it precious waiting for *the one*."

That got me a lip twitch but I ignored that and powered on.

"We could get lucky and they'll accept us with open arms. Unfortunately, I don't see this happening. You know who I am, so you also know my dad is the president of the Club, and if he doesn't feel like welcoming Shy into my life with a smile and a handshake, he can make things difficult for him. So if Shy unloads on you what might happen, I'm asking now that you don't let your misgivings about us shadow the support you'd give to him."

This got me another eye flash and a low, kind of rumbly, "I'd never do that, Tabby."

"Good," I returned. "Then I think we both know where the other stands."

"What the fuck are you two talkin' about?"

Shy's voice was also low and rumbly.

Not good.

"Park—" Landon started but didn't continue when Shy, coffee mugs in each hand, shifted to the side of Lan's chair and turned angry eyes down at his brother.

"Do we gotta go outside and talk?" he asked.

Uh-oh.

I stood as did Landon and, not unusually, my mouth got there first.

"Everything's cool, darlin'."

Shy turned his eyes to me. "Not from what I heard."

"Take two seconds," I began, "put yourself in Landon's shoes, think of meeting the woman who held a grudge against your brother for years and then you hear she lost a fiancé and when you show up and see they're suddenly and inexplicably tight... what would you do?"

Shy set the mugs on the coffee table and turned to his brother.

"What I would do is have a care about the loss she had even if it isn't still fresh and understand my brother isn't a fuckin' moron."

Uh-oh!

"Shy—" I began, but Landon got there before me.

"Park, I don't think you're a moron, but I do think you know where I'm coming from."

Shy's arm snaked out, his fingers curling around the side of my neck and I found myself flying toward him, my front landing hard against the side of his body. His hand moved so his arm could curve tight around my shoulders, his other hand crossed his body so his fingers could curl into my waist and through all this, his gaze didn't leave his brother.

"Look at me, what do you see?" he growled and when Landon didn't answer, he repeated his demand, "What do you see?"

Oh God.

I didn't know whether to feel elated because I knew what Shy thought Landon would see or terrified because I didn't want a bust-up to happen in Fortnum's bookstore, not with that crazy guy behind the counter. He'd side with Landon and Shy would be outnumbered.

My eyes shifted to Landon to see him taking us in then they moved to Shy's face.

"I see it, Park," he said softly.

"Fuckin' brilliant, Lan," Shy bit off. "Now, you get this. Do not"—he leaned us toward his brother—"*ever* blindside my woman like that. I'll let this one go 'cause I'm happy as fuck you're home. It happens again, I won't let it go. Are you with me?"

"I didn't take any offense, Shy, honestly," I told him quickly, hoping to defuse his anger, even as I felt the warm protectiveness of his words settling straight into my soul.

His eyes sliced down to me. "Well I did."

Message clear.

"Righty ho, biker boss," I muttered quickly and Shy's eyes narrowed.

"Don't be fuckin' cute and, honest to God, if you lick your lip, I'll lose my mind. Next time you lick your lip you do it when we are nowhere near a public place and I can let loose the reaction I've had half a million fuckin' times over four fuckin' years every time I've seen you do it, not here, in a bookstore where I can't."

Regardless of the tense situation, that gave me a tingle and an even warmer feeling settling in my soul, but I fought the urge to lick my lip (which was precisely what I was going to do) and I just stared at him.

He stared at my mouth then his gaze went to my eyes then he looked back at his brother.

So did I and I saw him smiling.

"I'm not findin' anything worth smilin' about," Shy warned.

"Sorry, Park, but, gotta admit, I'm smilin' so I don't laugh my ass off, since if I did that, I'm gettin' the sense you'd take a swing at me."

"I'm not findin' anything worth laughin' about either," Shy stated.

"That's because you can't see you two. Seriously, Park, I gotta say it. You're totally fuckin' cute together."

I pressed my lips together in another effort not to lick my lip, pretty sure Shy would never want to be described as cute *ever.*

I was wrong.

"No shit? You just noticed that? Jesus, Lan," Shy replied.

"No. Noticed it at your house but was more focused on your girl bein' cute, hot, and in a sheet. Since she's fully clothed now, it's comin' through more."

This, again, was what I considered not a good response from Landon Cage, seeing as I didn't suspect Shy would like it made clear his brother thought I was cute and hot and got distracted by me being in a sheet, and this time I was right.

"Are you shitting me?" Shy ground out.

"Can we drink coffee?" I jumped in. "I need caffeine. Then I need food. Then I need to make a few calls so I can figure out if I've got a home and a job. Watching you two badasses go head to head, albeit hot, is not helping me sort out my life. So if you'd get a move on from this, I'd appreciate it."

Shy's eyes quickly came down to me and I noted immediately his expression had changed from anger to soothing.

"Sugar, you'll be good," he assured me.

"Yeah, I will, but to be good, I need to make a few phone calls, so can we get on with our morning?" I fired back, and his lips twitched.

"We can get on with our morning," he agreed.

"Awesome," I muttered, rolling my eyes at Shy, but when they hit Landon, I smiled.

He smiled back.

"Travelin'man!" Tex the crazy coffee guy boomed.

"Your drink is gettin' cold. Get your ass over here and get it 'cause I'm not makin' another one unless you pay for it."

Shy gave me a squeeze then gave his brother a look that told him to behave the thirty seconds Shy would be gone, and he sauntered over to get the last coffee.

I gave Lan another smile and sat my booty back down on the couch.

Lan folded his long body into the armchair.

"Uh, Tab, just so you know," he started. "That time it's gonna take for you to prove you intend to go the distance with Park just got a lot fuckin' shorter."

His words hit me in a nice place. I sent another smile at him and even I knew it was huge.

And happy.

* * *

I looked up at Shy as Shy looked down at me.

We were in my bed. We were naked. I was on my back, one leg wrapped around Shy's hip, one leg extended, pressed up against his torso, ankle to his shoulder. Shy's hips were between mine, one hand gliding up my shin at his chest, one hand in the bed, his cock moving inside me.

"Gotta say, baby," he murmured. "You're beautiful always but you're seriously fuckin' beautiful when you're takin' me."

God.

God.

I loved it when he said stuff like that while he was making love to me.

"Gotta say, darlin'," I murmured back huskily. "You're handsome always, but you're seriously handsome when you're giving it to me."

His eyes, already hot, scorched into me even as his mouth curved and his hand moved down, down, down, until it curved around my thigh. His thumb found me as he whispered, "Let's see how much more beautiful you can be."

Then he pressed and circled. I moaned, my neck arched, my leg around him tensed, and his hips drove harder and faster between mine.

"Beauty, unbelievable," he growled.

I tipped my half-mast eyes to him, his face darker, his eyes so hot I thought the bed would combust, and he was right.

Beauty, unbelievable.

Not me.

Him.

His thumb pressed deeper, circled faster as his hips pumped harder, and I whispered urgently, "Shy."

"Come without me, honey. This time I wanna watch."

Free to do as he asked, I did and it was *spectacular.*

It was only when I was coming down that his thumb left me. He rolled us so he was on his back, I was astride him, and both his hands framed my head, moving it so he could look at me.

"Take me there," he ordered roughly. "I wanna watch you move on me."

Without delay, wanting to give him what he wanted, I sat up and gave him what he wanted. Doing it slowly at first, then faster, harder, my hands moving on his chest, my eyes never leaving his face, my excitement building again as I watched what I was giving him build, then his hands at my hips yanked me down, kept me full of him, and he gave it to me.

As he felt his orgasm, I dropped to him, chest to chest,

my fingers drifting over his skin, my mouth in his neck, my tongue darting out to taste.

He closed his arms around me and he kissed me on my forehead. His head righted, I shoved my face in his neck, and we lay there for a while, silently.

I didn't know what Shy was thinking about, but I took that time to savor the last forty-five minutes. Then I took more time savoring my most favorite parts. Since all of the parts were savor-worthy, this took a while.

After that, my mind moved to my day, post coffee with two badass brothers.

The good news was, my apartment was mine again. They hadn't even put in an ad, so they were happy for me to sign another lease.

The bad news was they expected me to sign a twelve-month lease. I was down with that, kind of. I needed someplace to stay at the present moment and, with my job in the air, I was kind of stuck staying where I was rather than apartment hunting and explaining how I'd pay rent if I didn't have income. That said, I felt it might be time to move on to something a tad bit nicer, and if they'd switch to month-to-month and I got my employment sorted, I'd have the opportunity to do that in the not-too-distant future.

Shy wasn't down with it, like, *at all.*

Although I'd asked Shy for time to get my stuff straightened out, which would give the brothers time to reconnect without my listening ear, Shy had refused to give it to me. This kinda freaked me out, because it pissed me off and I was confronted yet again, in less than twenty-four hours, with the balancing act I had to perform to be with a biker.

At least that was what I thought until Shy explained it to me.

"Waited for you for four years, Tabby, baby. *Four.* Spent a lot of that time thinkin' I'd never have you. Now I got you, not even for a day, I'm not big on lettin' you go. Give me that for now, yeah? Make your calls here."

That was sweet as well as loving, so I gave him that.

We quickly hit another danger zone when he heard me talking on the phone about the lease.

I knew he didn't like what he was hearing when he pulled my phone out of my hand, muttered into it, "She'll call you back," then his finger hit the screen and he looked at me.

Feeling pressure building in my head at this maneuver, I opened my mouth to, say, maybe, *scream*, but he beat me to speaking.

"A twelve-month lease is not gonna happen. Your place is okay but only okay," he declared. "It's too small, I'm not thrilled about the 'hood it's in, and this works, babe, we're movin' on together and no way it's big enough for us both. I'm not waitin' out a twelve-month lease. I'm not puttin' up with what I don't want for twelve months. And I don't want you in a place that's not good enough for you for twelve months. So you are not stayin' there for twelve months. Tell them month-to-month. If they flinch, they deal with me."

I didn't like the sound of that, but in order not to have words with him in front of his brother, I did as I was told. They flinched. Shy heard it, took the phone from me again, I glared at him then glared at his smiling brother who was privy to all this, seeing as we were back at Shy's place, and then I listened to Shy try and reason with them.

This didn't work so Shy said in the phone, "Right.

You'll be seein' me in thirty minutes and I suggest you take that time to think real hard on that decision."

Then he tossed my phone to me, muttered, "Be back," and took off before I could say word one.

I stared at the door that closed behind him wondering how he would know how to find my landlord.

Then I stared at the door trying to convince myself that didn't just happen.

Then, when I realized that did just happen, I tamped down the urge to throw something at the door.

Then I stabbed at my phone and called Shy.

I did this repeatedly.

He didn't answer for forty-five minutes and when he did, his greeting was, "Got month-to-month, babe. Tell Lan to load you up in his truck. I'm makin' steaks tonight at your place. Meet me at King Soopers on Colorado Boulevard."

Then he hung up on me.

Yep. Hung. Up. On. Me!

Apparently he used his badass biker ways to find my landlord and strong-arm a month-to-month lease out of him. Although this was what I wanted, contradictorily, the way Shy made it come about (specifically my nonparticipation in that), didn't make me happy.

Lan didn't chime in until I was fuming in his truck. "Let him do what he's gotta do."

I kept my mouth set and my eyes out the side window.

"Tabby, seriously, listen to me," Lan carried on. "He's my big brother and a long time ago, he cast himself in the role of protector and he's good at it. He was scary capable of taking shit and giving it, just as long as he saved me from havin' to do either. He gets off on this crap. Let him do it."

I didn't like the sound of that but I let that part go. I'd talk to Shy about that later.

Instead, I turned to look at Lan. "He can't go around threatening and intimidating everyone in my life to get me what I want or what he wants me to have."

Lan grinned at me and replied jauntily, "Sure he can."

I glared at him.

"Bet your dad does that shit," Lan went on. Dad did, for me, Rush, Ty-Ty, any of his brothers, anyone he gave a crap about.

God.

I was screwed.

On the ride to King Soopers, I decided to let this go and fight another day. Today needed to be a good day for everybody and anyway, month-to-month worked for me and I doubted Shy stuck my landlord with a knife, so I decided that all's well that ends without bloodshed.

We got groceries. We had steaks. We drank beer. Lan took off to crash at Shy's place. I explained to Shy that while he was off terrorizing my landlord, I'd called the hospital and learned they'd already advertised my position so if I wanted it back, I had to apply for it.

His response was, "They'll pick you, baby."

Then he picked me, as in picked me up, and carried me to the bedroom.

Commence making love which led us to now.

I broke the silence with a soft, "You... in my bed."

I closed my eyes when Shy tightened his arms around me and stayed that way, but he said nothing. Then again, the arm thing said it all.

"I'm glad your brother's back," I mumbled into his skin, and he gave me another squeeze.

"Me too."

"It was cool how he surprised you," I noted.

"Yeah," he agreed.

I pulled in breath. Then I stated, "Just for the record, before you go off to play biker badass on something that affects me, I'd prefer it if we talked about that thing that affects me first. There were other ways to solve today's problem. If we decided month-to-month was the way to go and they didn't give it to me, I could have stayed with Dad and Tyra or Natalie until my life got back on track and I found a place I liked or, if we were there when that time came, we found a place we wanted."

"My way was faster and less headache," he replied.

Crap, he had a point.

I sighed.

His body shook, I knew he was silently laughing but I ignored that.

Then he murmured, "Slide off me, Tabby, but do it slow. I like it like that."

That gave me a tingle, but instead of sliding off, I thought about why he needed me to, which was so he could go to the bathroom and deal with the condom.

"I'm on the pill," I told him quietly.

His arms gave me another squeeze but this one felt reflexive, so I lifted up to look down at him.

Then I pulled in another breath and started carefully, "Before, were you—?"

He didn't make me finish.

He quickly cut me off with another squeeze of his arms, the pressure not releasing, before he stated firmly, "Always."

"So we can—?"

He again interrupted me to order gently, "Slide off, honey."

I held his eyes a beat before I nodded then I slid off, slowly, watching his face as I did, which stated eloquently he liked the feel just as much as I did.

Once I'd slid him out of me, he rolled me to my back, leaned in to kiss my chest and then the underside of my jaw, then he gave me a sexy smile, then he rolled off the bed.

By the time he sauntered back into my room naked, I was standing by the side of the bed and had on a pair of undies but had yet to get to the nightie. I didn't get a chance to locate one before Shy had me back in bed with him on top of me, his face serious.

"Right, we'll do this quick and hopefully not painful," he began ominously. "For three months, it's only been Rosalie. The month before that, nobody. I didn't lie, babe, always careful. *Always.* But I'm gonna get tested so you know I'm givin' you nothin' but me when it's only you and me with nothin' in between. We'll wait for the results and then it'll be just you and me. You cool with that?"

I was, totally. It was way beyond what I expected he'd do without me even asking and it made me feel safe in more ways than knowing making love with him would be safe.

"Thanks, Shy," I whispered.

"You're welcome, Tabby," he whispered back.

I grinned.

Shy kissed me.

Ten minutes later, my panties were gone.

Two hours later, I passed out on top of Shy, sated, exhausted, relaxed as all get out.

And happy.

CHAPTER ELEVEN

Thick and Thin

Three and a half weeks later…

"SHY, OH MY *God. Shy!*" I cried, my hands, curved around the edge of the kitchen counter, went to his head between my legs. His hands cupping my behind pulled me deeper into his ravenous mouth. My head flew back, slammed into the elevated bar and I came really, freaking *hard*.

Still coming, I barely processed losing his mouth from between my legs but I didn't miss his cock slamming into me.

I lifted my head and tried to focus on his face, seeing it hard, his eyes burning on me, his cock slamming fast, hard, deep.

Mostly, Shy made love to me, managing the unbelievable task of doing this even when it was wild monkey sex.

Now, he was fucking me.

It was *fantastic*.

"You're comin' for me again, Tabby," he grunted, thrusting deep.

"Okay," I breathed.

His hands were spanning my hips, yanking me to him as he drove inside me, so he ordered, "Watchin' you do it, baby. Touch yourself."

No hesitation, I yanked up the nightie I had on, the only thing I was wearing since it was morning. Shy and I had been shuffling around the kitchen getting coffee and I'd licked my lip for some reason. My tongue barely made the pass before his mouth slammed down on mine then I found my ass on the counter, my panties gone, my man's mouth between my legs and myself coming.

And there I still was. Happily.

I put one finger to my clit. I shoved up my nightie and put my fingers to my nipple.

"Nightie up, Tab. Wanna see what you're doin' to your tit," he growled. My belly dipped, my sex spasmed, he pounded deeper, and I stopped what I was doing at my breast, pulled my nightie further up and showed him what I was doing.

"Fuck, honey," he groaned, slamming in deep then rolling his hips in a way that made a moan slide up my throat, his eyes never leaving me. "Fuckin' hot. Gorgeous."

"Shy," I whispered, close again, the first one huge, this one felt like it might kill me and I didn't care.

"You wait for me," he growled, going faster, driving deep.

"I can't," I whimpered, it was nearly over me.

His voice was rough when he gritted, "Wait for me, baby."

"I—"

Suddenly his hands weren't at my hips. He'd wrapped

his arms around me, lifted me clean off the counter and I flew through the air a moment before my body collided with his and he slammed me down on his cock.

My head flew back and I cried out as the wave crashed over me even as I felt Shy bury his face in my chest and groan into my skin.

Lifetimes passed as I whirled under the surface, Shy right there with me. Then, when we were floating up, he gently laid me back on the countertop, his hand cupping the back of my head so it cushioned me when I hit the bar.

I tipped my chin to look at him and saw him grinning down at me.

"Jesus, sugar, you gotta quit comin' so fast. You're killin' me."

My happy mojo took a hit and I glared at him.

"Uh...just pointing out, Shy, you're the one who *makes* me come so fast."

"I like that, babe, and I get it, my mouth between your legs in the morning after you've had a full eight hours without me takin' you there, but right after I give it to you, you get there again before me? What the fuck?"

He was still grinning, which meant I knew he was teasing.

He was also teasing because he was pleased with himself and didn't mind me knowing it, and this didn't please me.

"You were fucking me hard," I reminded him.

"Yeah, so?" He kept grinning at me.

"On the kitchen counter," I carried on.

"And?"

"It was hot," I snapped and watched his grin spread into a smile.

"Uh, I got that, Tab. You came, your pussy clenched around me so hard, I had no choice but to do the same. That sweet cunt of yours milked it right out of me."

That pissed me off and turned me on, both in equal measure. I gave into the pissed-off part and I kept glaring before I tipped my head to the side and asked fake-sweetly, "Is this a problem?"

Still smiling, he opened his mouth to speak then his smile died completely, his head jerked up, eyes to the door, and before I knew what was going on, he pulled out, yanked me off the counter, set me on my feet, shoved me behind him, and his hands went to his jeans, the only thing he'd luckily pulled on earlier to shuffle around in the kitchen with me.

This was lucky because usually he only wore his boxer briefs and sometimes he wore nothing.

And Shy being in his jeans was lucky because at that very moment a key could be heard in the lock.

This could only be one of five people: Dad. Tyra. Rush. Big Petey. Or Natalie.

And none of those choices were good, because none of them knew about Shy and me.

Shy and I had talked about it, and we'd decided that the best course of action was for us to get used to being an us before we sprung it on anybody.

This was easy considering the guys were used to Shy spending time with me, and he'd begun to hang at his apartment in the final throes of his relationship with Rosalie, so they were also used to him not being at the Compound.

Somehow, they missed the fact that we'd had a month apart but I suspected this was because the brothers didn't really stick their noses into each other's business unless it was invited.

Shy did share around the Club he'd broken it off with Rosalie, but that was as much as either of us shared.

Of course, we had to modify our behavior when we were at the Compound together. Though sometimes, I had to admit, we exchanged looks, he would touch my behind, I'd run the tips of my fingers along the back of his hand, but still, we kept up the charade.

As for my part, when I shared with Dad and Tyra that I wasn't going to Cape Cod, they took it in stride, though they both looked happy that they weren't losing me. I suspected they took it in stride because they suspected I was still trying to sort myself out in some ways after losing Jason, so, naturally, I would make decisions then go back on them willy-nilly. I didn't want them to think this, seeing as it wasn't true, but I had to go with it until it was time to tell them what *was* true.

With all that, it must be said, it didn't take a lot of effort to get used to being part of an us with Shy. We slid into it naturally, likely because we were used to each other, we'd grown tight, the only changes were lots of sex, sleeping in the same bed and more cuddling and all of those were adjustments that came easy.

So, truth be told, at least on my part and Shy gave no indication he didn't agree, I was used to us being an us about two days after that happened.

But we still kept it under wraps and didn't even discuss the next step.

For me, this was because I was holding on to my happy. I woke up happy, I happily passed out on Shy after a variety of orgasms and all I had was happy in between.

I'd even interviewed for my old job two days ago, got the call three hours after the interview that I was back so there was just all around happy.

Therefore, possibly injecting antagonism and aggravation into my life didn't fill me with glee, so I was avoiding it.

I didn't feel guilt about this, because I knew when I explained it to Tyra, she would get me. This was because she always got me. And if Tyra got me, she could explain it to Dad as well as Rush in a way they would get me. Also, Big Petey adored me, so even if he was angry at first, he'd come around.

Therefore, when the door opened and it was Natalie, that meant the worst possible scenario was about to play out.

I knew this instantly when she entered, her head swung to the kitchen, her eyes got huge, her mouth fell open, red suffused her face, and she yelled, "*I saw his bike outside so I fuckin' knew it!*"

Not good.

"Nat—" I started but got no further because she slammed the door and stomped in.

"Same as with Jason, one minute I got my girl, the next minute she's unavailable, but this time it's *worse*. You're hooked up with the dawg to beat all dawgs and *hiding it from me*!" she shrieked the last. "Tabby! What did I tell you about him? How could you be so stupid?"

That thunderclap coming from Shy I'd felt during our conversation nearly two months before slapped the room, but Natalie apparently didn't feel it.

As for me, Shy took his STD test the day after his brother got home. He paid extra for a rush, it came in clean, so at that present moment, regardless of the uncomfortable situation confronting me, Natalie saying words I didn't like all that much that needed to be addressed, the heavy air and the fury emanating from my man, I had on a nightie, no panties, and Shy sliding out of me.

Priorities.

I moved around Shy, got in between them, happy there was also a bar in between them and ordered, "Don't you move, either of you, and neither of you speak. I gotta do something. I'll be back in less than a minute and, I swear to God, you two lay into each other before I get back, it will not make me happy."

Natalie, being Natalie, took one look at me, guessed the situation, and didn't have any problems throwing it out there.

"Shit, seriously? Did I walk in on the aftermath of you gettin' banged by a biker? Let me guess, you did it," she leaned in, "*dawgie style*."

Her meaning was clear and Shy actually growled low in his throat and I felt him begin to move. I put up a hand and planted it in his chest, keeping my glare pinned on Natalie.

"I love you, you know I do. But one more word, Nat, I'll confiscate my key, kick your ass out, and you'll never see me again. Are you feeling me?" I asked softly.

Her eyes bore into me, her jaw clenched, then she jerked up her chin.

I twisted my neck and looked up at Shy. "Darlin', please? For me?"

That muscle ticked in his jaw, his eyes were locked on Natalie, but he also jerked up his chin.

I heaved a sigh of relief and dashed to the bathroom. I

cleaned up in record time, snatched a pair of panties out of my drawer, yanked them up, and tripped on our clothes that were strewn all over the floor on my way out.

They were mostly Shy's clothes, since his entire limited wardrobe was lying there considering his brother had been in Denver for two weeks before going back down to Fort Carson and he'd crashed at Shy's pad, so Shy had crashed at mine and hadn't quit crashing there even after Lan left.

Vaguely, it occurred to me it was time to do laundry and, considering his wardrobe was severely limited, go shopping.

I righted my feet even as I settled my panties on my hips and my nightie was still falling over my behind when I skidded to a halt in the living room to see my best friend and my guy in a scary staredown.

"Right, you're back," Natalie stated, not tearing her eyes from Shy. "Can we speak now?"

"You do, you watch that mouth of yours," Shy shot back instantly. "You say somethin' that pisses Tab off or hurts her, you answer to me."

"Answer to you? Who talks like that?" Natalie returned swiftly with not a small amount of sarcasm.

"I do and you don't, bitch, you'll find your coked-up ass out in the goddamned breezeway."

Uh-oh.

What did he mean?

My eyes narrowed on Natalie.

Oh crap.

Her eyes were bright. Too bright.

Crap!

"Fuck you!" she screeched.

Shy leaned slightly toward her, and he'd done that to me when he was angry, so I knew he was in the danger zone.

"Do not even *think* of comin' into your girl's house who, by the way, is *my woman*, high off your goddamned ass and spoutin' your mouth, so stoked on blow, your brain is a fuckin' whiteout," he growled. "Calm your ass down."

"Natalie," I verbally pushed into the fray and then carefully asked, "Are you doing cocaine?"

Her eyes swung to me. "We're not talkin' about me. We're talkin' about you hookin' up with Shy fuckin' *Cage* when I warned you not to do that shit."

Shy moved, my eyes went to him, and I asked, "Darlin', please, let me handle this."

His gaze cut to me, he took me in, rocked to a halt, gave me an unhappy look that I endured but fortunately cut his eyes back to Natalie and stood firm, crossing his arms on his chest.

I looked back at my friend. "Nat, are you doing blow?"

She ignored me and declared, "You said it wasn't like that with you two when I fuckin' *knew* it was and now he's sayin' you're his woman, Tab, which means you didn't listen to me. You listened to his bullshit lines and now you think you're his woman when you're just like any other woman he's had, and there have been lots, Tabby, and you fuckin' know it. You're just pussy."

"Tab, babe, she didn't hear me," Shy clipped his warning, but I didn't move my eyes from Natalie.

"Natalie, maybe we can talk about what happened with me and Shy when Shy's not around. Let's talk about something important, and that's the fact that I'm a nurse and I can see quite clearly you're high."

"How about we talk about the fact that not weeks ago I know he was bangin' a bitch named Rosalie?" she returned.

More unhappy growling from Shy but I again ignored him. "I know. Now he's with me."

She threw up her hands as her eyebrows went up. "So he dumps that bitch and now you're his woman?" She looked at Shy. "Congratulations, sport. Record time. One down, the other one set up, good to go. How long's Tab gonna last?"

Considering more unhappy thunder was rolling off Shy, I knew he was about to lose it but I'd already lost it. I, however, did it a whole lot quieter which meant they both felt me. I knew it because the air in the room stilled and I felt both their eyes on me.

But I only had eyes for Natalie.

When I had her attention, I said only one word:

"Don't."

"Tab—"

I shook my head, she processed the look I knew I had on my face, and she shut her mouth.

I carried on talking.

"You put me in the middle of you and Jason. He did too but he's dead now, so he can't right that wrong. You're alive and you're doing it again. Don't."

I saw her jaw flex.

I kept going. "Jason and you rubbed each other the wrong way. This time, starting right out of the gate, you are makin' it impossible for Shy to like you, much less eventually be able to forgive you for the stuff coming out of your mouth. You know him, who he is, what he is. You go head-to-head with a brother of Chaos MC, you won't come away unscathed one way or another. Don't do that either."

I watched her swallow then kept right on talking.

"He means something to me, you already know that, but what he means to me has changed. The reason you don't know how it's changed is demonstrated precisely with how you charged in today and behaved."

"Right," she hissed.

I ignored that and kept going. "If you'll calm down, we'll plan a time when we can talk like adults about what went down with Shy and me. Once we do that, it's up to you to decide if you feel me or if you feel I'm making a mistake."

I gave that a moment to sink in and when Nat made no response I kept right on going.

"You also gotta be you, so be you and tell me then, rationally and without being a pain in the ass, why you feel that way. But I expect you to respect my decision, since I'll warn you now you won't change my mind. I'll also expect you to suck it up and get along with my man instead of putting me in the middle. You pull that crap on me again, Nat, like last time, you know you're gonna lose. And this is not because I don't adore you. You've never had a man"—I powered through her flinch—"when you do, you'll get it. If you have a partner who grows to mean the world to you, I'm sorry, girl, but he'll win every time. The thing you gotta get is, a sister's any sister at all, she stands by her sister's side or takes her back no matter how she feels about her sister's man or the shit that goes down between her sister and that man. You have got to learn that but learn it now. I'm not going through that bullshit again."

I watched her pull in breath and her eyes slid away.

"Nat," I called quietly, "look at me."

Her eyes slid back to me.

"You have got to pull yourself together," I whispered, her shoulders went straight and I lifted a hand. "Hear me out."

She stared at me, her eyes slid to Shy then they came back to me, and she jerked up her chin.

I took her invitation but kept at it gently.

"You're in free fall, Natalie, and you know it. You have been since high school. Right now, I'm telling you and I want you to listen to me, you need to reach out and catch hold of the hand I'm extending and let me help you pull yourself out."

"I'm cool," she returned, and I shook my head.

"You're coked to the gills. That doesn't indicate cool to me."

"It's recreational," she spat.

"Recreational?" I asked. "Coked to the gills at ten in the morning?"

"I've got it under control," she retorted.

"Jeez, Nat!" I threw up my hands, suddenly exasperated. "Listen to yourself! They all say that!"

"I live my life the way I wanna live my life and *you* live your life jumpin' from man to man 'cause you can't seem to live your life without clutchin' on to some dick that makes you feel complete. Your dad ruined you, controlling your every move, so now you can't exist without findin' some guy who will do the same."

"Tabby, I'm losin' patience," Shy warned in a low voice, as I suspected he would when she pulled Dad into it. Something, incidentally, I didn't much like either.

"Nat, that isn't true and you know it, but I'll point out you're turning the focus on me so we won't focus on you."

"It's my life, under my control," she fired back.

"I'm Chaos," I reminded her. "We were at that party and *you* know that *I* know that those dudes were not good dudes. I had to climb out a freaking *window*, they flipped me so bad."

"They're fun to party with," she returned.

"Booze, drugs, and stockpiles of firearms right out on display for all to see is not a good combination, and you don't have to have a college degree to know that's just the God's-honest truth," I shot back.

"Oh"—she leaned back, waving a hand out in front of her in a wide sweep—"now you're better than me because you got your degree?"

I shook my head and looked to Shy, wanting to find a hint of calm so I could keep dealing with her. From all appearances, I was looking in the wrong direction. Shy looked happy to rip her head off.

No help there.

Crap.

I looked back at Natalie and pulled in a calming breath.

Then I said softly, "I'm with you, thick and thin. I've proved it. I'll keep doing it. You're a beautiful person, Natalie, you deserve better. But the person who has to believe that is you. No one can give it to you, especially if you won't let them. Stop doing this to yourself, realize your beauty, quit treating your body like shit, hanging with people that could get you in trouble or worse, and find your better."

"Maybe I should rub up with Chaos. Get myself invited to a threesome, like Shy here likes so much." She flicked a hand out to him as my breath caught at the unwelcome, long-ago memory her words brought crashing back. "Maybe I'll get lucky, perform like a prize pony, get noticed and get myself an old man for a spell. That work for you, Tabby?"

I powered through the painful memory and shot back, "Any of the brothers of Chaos wanted to take your shit on, Natalie, and you didn't put it out that you're no more than ass to tap when they got a hankering for empty pussy, then yes. That would work for me great, Natalie."

She leaned in to hiss, "You're unbelievable."

I didn't hiss, I whispered, "And you're in denial."

She glared at me and I took it.

Finally, she spoke. "You can take your thick and thin and fuck yourself with it, Tab. We're done."

My heart lurched but my mouth pleaded, "Don't do that either, Natalie."

"Too late, bitch, it's done," she declared, sent an acid look to Shy, turned on her foot, and stormed to the door. She stopped there, twisted my key off her ring but was smart enough to throw it at the couch and not me when Shy was standing two feet from me.

Then she slammed out.

I stared at the door for about a third of a second before Shy curled his arm around and pulled me close.

I deep-breathed into his chest.

"Babe, your best girl is a fuckin' bitch."

I closed my eyes.

Then I mumbled into his chest. "That didn't go well."

"Nope," he agreed.

"That also doesn't fire me up to tell Dad, Tyra, and the rest."

"Nope," he again agreed and my shoulders slumped.

"Though, sayin' that, sugar, none of them are cokeheads with a life complex, so at least we got that going for us."

I chuckled but it didn't hold a lot of humor.

Shy's other arm closed around me tight so I wound mine around him.

"Fuck," I whispered in his chest.

"She loves you, Tabby. She just doesn't love herself. She'll come back."

God, I hoped he was right.

Then he muttered forebodingly and not helpfully, "Let's just hope when she makes that call to mend fences, she isn't in a situation where she's fucked one way or the other and we gotta save her ass."

"Maybe you should stop talking," I suggested, still speaking into his skin.

Shy was silent a moment, his arms tight around me, then he murmured, "I'll give you that, sugar."

I sucked in a deep breath and let it go.

Then I tipped my head back, saw him tilt his chin down and caught his eyes.

"I need coffee."

Shy's hand slid up my back, my neck, into my hair. He tipped my head down, I felt his lips at the top of my hair, where he whispered, "Then I better get my girl some coffee."

I liked it like that.

He kissed my hair, his arm gave me a squeeze, I returned the favor, and he let me go.

Then he got me coffee.

And, it must be said, I liked it like that too.

CHAPTER TWELVE

Goin' Through the Motions

One and a half weeks later...

WE WERE AT FlatIron Mall when it happened.

And we were at FlatIron because it was far enough away, it was unlikely we'd run into anyone we knew. Not that bikers went shopping, but their babes did.

We were leaving because Shy had had enough of shopping. I knew this because after I tried on my third pair of high-heeled, kick-ass, sexy-as-all-heck boots, as much as he appreciated the show, he didn't have a lot of patience with my indecision.

He demonstrated this by turning to the clerk and saying, "The first pair and this one, ring 'em up." Then to me he said, "We're done."

I could really only afford one pair, but since Shy bought them (after a brief verbal tussle at the counter), I got two. Part of letting this go was that I bought Shy all three pairs of his new jeans and two of his four thermals, so I thought that trade-off worked. Anyway, I knew I was pushing my luck just with him agreeing to go shopping, therefore I didn't push it further.

So just then, we were walking through the mall, Shy with his arm around my shoulders, me with my hand shoved in the back pocket of his jeans.

Things were still great, even after the Natalie debacle. She hadn't called and she didn't pick up any of my calls or return any of my messages, but when I expressed my concern to Shy, he just said, "Keep tellin' you, sugar, she'll come back to you. Just give her time to burn it out."

I took his advice, as difficult as this was, and decided to focus on riding the happy wave that was us.

That said, Shy was getting impatient with us keeping our relationship under wraps. He'd informed me of this two days before.

"At the Compound, gotta fake it with you. Bite my tongue when I wanna say something that would expose us. Life's too short to fake it this long, babe. We both know that shit. We're solid. We gotta come out."

He was right. As time wore on, it was beginning to seem less an effort to test the waters of us, which were totally solid, and more a lie. However, considering Natalie's reaction, I wasn't all fired up to move on to the next portion of sharing the news and what that might bring. So I'd begged for another week, just one, then I told him I'd start the process by telling Tyra.

He'd relented but he didn't pretend to like it.

In that time, I'd been rehearsing what I was going to say to Tyra and this was what I was doing, my mind going over my speech, when she came out of a store and we ran right into her.

Literally ran *right into her.*

Rosalie.

Shy went solid even more than bumping into someone would make you go solid.

She had her eyes aimed the other way, she turned to us, starting, "Oh, sorry—" then she saw who we were and went solid too.

Crap.

The instant her eyes hit Shy, her face paled and my heart clenched, seeing her expression.

She was into him, big-time.

Still.

Shy breaking up with her had marked her. Even over a month later, the pain was close to the surface, right there for anyone to see. She didn't even have it in her to hide it.

Oh God.

Her eyes moved over his face, hair, shoulders, the kick-ass necklaces he was wearing, and she also didn't try to hide the longing that infused her gaze during this journey.

I was selective about my country music listening and one of the artists who made the cut was Jana Kramer. I'd never been dumped, but she looked *exactly* like what Jana's lyrics to "Why You Wanna?" put out there.

Hideous.

Shy recovered first and muttered, "Rosalie."

She started, and her eyes darted to me then back to Shy.

"Shy, uh . . . hi. Wow. You're, um . . . shopping."

She looked at me and, without knowing how to handle this, I decided to try to smile a gentle smile. I was uncertain if I managed to pull this off before she spoke.

"And you must be Tabby," she stated, lifting a hand my way. "Shy and I are, uh . . . old friends."

This was killing her but, I had to admit, she had it going on.

"Yeah," I pulled my hand out of Shy's pocket and took hers. "Hi."

Totally lame, but what else did you say?

"Hi," she whispered, then looked at Shy. "You, uh… look good."

"You're lookin' good too, Rosie," Shy replied gently.

Fail!

I knew, and I was sure if the kick-ass country singer Jana Kramer was there she'd confirm, that was the wrong thing to say. That kind of thing would make a girl wonder, if her ex thought she looked good, why he broke up with her in the first place.

I figured I was right when she dipped her chin to hide her wince, tucked her hair behind her ear and mumbled, "Uh… gotta be somewhere." She slid her gaze between Shy and me, still mumbling and also, I was guessing, still lying, "Good to see you Shy, and to meet you, Tabby."

Then she took off.

Shy didn't move. He also didn't watch her go. He just stood there for a few beats, staring into space, and I gave him that time.

Then he set us to moving again, muttering under his breath, "Didn't wanna come this time, not fuckin' shoppin' again. *Ever.*"

I decided the wisest response to that comment was not to respond at all. I just shoved my hand in his pocket again and walked as close to him as I could get.

We were in my car on the road when, from behind the wheel, Shy broke the long silence, "Need a fuckin' drink."

"Okay, darlin'," I replied. I could see the run-in with

Rosalie cut him deep. I had to admit, seeing that wasn't real comfortable.

We drove a good long while and ended up in a honky-tonk between Boulder and Denver that still managed in that populated area to be out in the boonies. I'd never been there before. And since it was just going on four in the afternoon, when we pushed through the door, I noted the honk and tonk had not yet been injected. The jukebox was playing low, and there were three other people in the bar, two of them bartenders.

Shy guided me by my hand to the bar then, as was his way, he firmly guided my behind to a stool.

The bartender came over and Shy spoke immediately, "Two Coors drafts, one shot of tequila." The bartender jerked up his chin, moved to fill the order, and Shy looked down at me. "I get slaughtered, you drive."

Uh-oh.

I didn't have a good feeling about that.

He blew off Rosalie for me and, fresh from that, he didn't seem to have a problem with it. Not at all. But I just saw close-up that she was gorgeous and she looked pained. Obviously what they had ran deep for her, and Shy's need to drink now said that, perhaps, he'd been denying that what he felt for her ran deep too.

And, if that was the case, I didn't know how I felt about that except not good.

The beers arrived, the shot arrived, Shy downed it in a gulp then said to the barkeep, "Another'a those."

He got another, he downed it and chased it with beer. Then he stared at his mug.

I sat beside him and worried. This went on awhile, and I was about to wade in when he spoke.

"Mom left Dad."

Okay, one could say that was not what I expected to hear.

"Pardon, darlin'?" I asked quietly, and he turned just his head, his body stayed hunched over the bar and he pinned me with those green eyes.

"I was ten. Lan was eight. We got home from school, she had suitcases packed for us, said her and Lan and me were stayin' with Grams for a while. Lan asked if Dad was comin', and I'll never fuckin' forget her face when she said, 'No, hon, you'll see your dad on the weekend but Momma needs a little time with just Grams and her boys. Okay?'" Shy shook his head and finished on a muttered "Fuck."

He turned back to his beer and threw back a slug. I lifted mine and sipped.

When I put it back to the bar, I asked carefully, "I'm glad you're sharing but, sorry, darlin', I don't understand *why* you're sharin' particularly this, Shy."

"Lan and me had no clue," he continued, looking at his beer, and I knew he had to get his story out without interruption. "Came outta the blue. They were the kind of parents that hid any bad shit. They didn't yell at each other in front of us. They didn't even shout at each other in their room when we were in bed, or at least if they did, we didn't hear it. He was, Dad was, fuck, I was a little kid and I knew he was into her. Always kissin' her, her mouth, cheek, neck, shoulder. Touchin' her ass, her waist. They walked, he had his hand on her back or his arm around her or he held her hand. She walked through the livin' room, he'd grab her and pull her into his lap. They laughed a lot. Gave each other looks a lot. We'd go to bed, they weren't camped in front of the TV, but sittin' at the bar in the kitchen, sittin' close, talkin'. Not about heavy shit, air wasn't like that around them. Not ever, that I can remember. They just got off on talkin' to each other. It was fuckin' cool. I loved that shit. Made the house feel safe. So I had no clue why she'd need time from Dad."

"Obviously she went back," I prompted when he stopped to take another tug off his.

He stopped hunching over the bar, straightened and turned to me.

"Yeah. She went back," he confirmed.

"So that's good," I noted stupidly.

"Heard her talkin' to Grams."

Uh-oh again.

"Yeah?" I asked.

"To this day, I thought it was stupid shit. He wasn't steppin' out on her, gamblin', drinkin', takin' his hand to her, hidin' money from her. And since they died, I always had this pit, this poison pit in my gut 'cause we were at Grams's for three weeks. She lost three weeks of Dad just two years before they both bit it and, fuck, the reason why was so goddamned stupid."

"Okay," I said when he stopped again.

"What it was, I get now, was woman shit. As stupid as it was to me, it was not to her. It drove her from him. It meant somethin' to her. Enough to put all that good they had in jeopardy. So it actually wasn't stupid. It was serious as shit."

I wrapped my hand around his thigh and gave it a squeeze, guessing, "And you were reminded of that when you saw Rosalie and it was so obvious that she, uh... wasn't good about what went down with you two, and you're thinking you misjudged the situation?"

"Yeah," he bit off. "She looked exactly like she looked a month ago when I broke it off. No healing. Nothin'. Same pain. Same hurt. She hadn't moved on at all so, yeah, Tab, I misjudged the situation."

"That sucks, darlin', but there's nothing you can do about it now. She'll move on. It just may take more time than you would imagine."

"Yep," he murmured, turned to his beer, sucked back the dregs then caught the bartender's attention and jerked up his chin to order another. He looked back at me. "So, when you figure it out, and you'll figure it out 'cause I know you haven't yet and I'm about to lay it on you so you will, after that shit went down with Mom, after seein' Rosalie, I got a bad feelin' the pain is gonna stick with you and drive you away from me."

How did we get here?

No, strike that, what on earth was he talking about?

"Shy, I don't—"

"You blamed his ass and I shoulda come clean about it then. I didn't. I'm comin' clean about it now."

I tipped my head to the side, confused.

"Blamed who about what?"

"That guy," he stated.

"That guy? What guy?"

"Your dead guy."

Something struck me then and it hit me like a sledgehammer.

He never called Jason by his name. He was never mean about him, never cast aspersions, was totally cool when I talked about him and when he guided me through my grief or wayward thoughts.

But he never, not once, said Jason's name.

I felt my stomach knot.

"Shy, I'm not understanding where you're leading me," I said quietly.

"You said that you were back to you, I led you there, you weren't you with him or before. You weren't you for a long time. And you gave me credit for helpin' bring you back to you without cottoning onto the fact I was the one who took you from you in the first place."

I blinked and asked, "What?"

"That shit, Tab, that went down with us four years ago when I acted like a dick and did and said serious-as-fuck stupid shit that drove you away from me? You changed after that. *I* did that to you and I don't want that shit to come back up, you to figure it out and—"

I got it then.

"I'm not leaving you, Shy," I cut him off to say firmly, giving his thigh a firm squeeze.

"Shit festers, Tab, and—"

"Shut up," I ordered and his head gave a slight jerk.

I ignored that and kept going.

"Shy, I was nineteen. I had no idea who I was. I *still* haven't discovered all of me. You didn't see it but between that time and when you came back into my life, I went through a whole load of phases. Music. Friends. Places I'd hang. Clothes I'd wear. I don't know why I did it." I grinned at him. "I do know it was fun."

"Don't bullshit me," he returned. "That shit started when I came down on you unjustified."

I felt my grin leave me and I leaned in in an effort to cushion the blow when I admitted, "Yeah."

I watched a shadow drift over his face so I went on quickly.

"But Shy, darlin', it would have happened anyway. Maybe differently but anyone at that age goes on a journey to discover who they are. You did and it took you to Chaos. I did and, in a roundabout way, it brought me back home and to you."

The shadow lifted but only slightly before he said softly, "First, what I gotta live with is it took you away from me and led you to that guy. Yeah, babe, it led you back to me but I almost lost you and, in the meantime, you had to suffer losing everything. Second, and what's on my mind right now, I do not want you goin' back there for any reason and lettin' what I did get under your skin."

I shook my head and leaned so close, my breasts brushed his arm and I lifted a hand to rest on his chest. "Shy, that's done. All of it. Jason's gone and that's not anyone's fault. It's just what life had in store for me. And we're past that bad history we had. It is not gonna come back."

"The shit Mom left Dad for he did to her in college. Over a fuckin' *decade* before she left him for it."

There it was.

"I'm not your mom, darlin'," I told him carefully.

"Shit festers," he repeated.

"They died," I announced and that pain he thought he hid behind grins or casual conversations, shot through his eyes. Still, I pushed on, "They didn't leave you, Shy. They died. I promised I wouldn't leave you and, honestly, you strong-arm my landlord against my wishes and haul me around where you want me to be, and if there were reasons for me to be pissed, for us to butt heads, somewhere along the line in the last month, with our personalities, they would have come up. But I get that's you. You get whatever it is is me and we both know what we have. We also know how it feels not to have it, so we don't let that shit get in between."

His brows went up. "You don't like it when I haul your ass around?"

"At first, it freaked me." I grinned again. "Now, I think it's kinda hot."

He studied me a moment before his eyes cleared and his lips twitched.

I let my smile fade and pressed my hand into his chest.

"I'm not leaving you, Shy. You're not gonna lose me, because to do that I'd lose you, and that isn't going to happen."

He held my eyes two beats, I saw his turn warm and intent then he whispered, "You're the fuckin' shit, Tabby."

"I know," I told him airily on another smile. "My man tells me that all the time."

His eyes dropped to my mouth and his lips ordered, "Kiss me, baby."

There it was. All was good.

I leaned forward and did what he told me.

He tasted of beer with a hint of tequila.

All Shy.

All mine.

All amazing.

* * *

We stayed at the honky-tonk for more beers, dinner, and ten games of pool. I won four, Shy won six. However, the bet we'd waged this time was a lot more interesting and included me sucking him off regularly.

Since I did it regularly already and I liked it, this was not a hardship, and I wouldn't admit it to him, but I threw that last game purposefully.

I was thinking about giving him his winnings when he let us into my apartment, my thoughts so pleasantly occupied I didn't notice the kitchen light was on. I also didn't notice Shy stop dead until I ran into him.

"Shy, darlin', what on—?" I started, stepping to his side and following his gaze toward the kitchen.

What I saw made me go statue-still.

Kane Allen, my dad, was sitting on a bar stool.

I was his daughter, but Dad was hot in a way that even I knew he was serious hot. Dark hair salted with a bit of silver. A kick-ass biker goatee that was long at the chin that also had some light in it. He gave me my eyes, sapphire blue, his, I knew, could be warm or piercing. He had a big body that his good genes kept fit, since he sure as heck didn't work out and drank and ate what he wanted. He also had lines going out from his eyes that I loved because they deepened when he laughed.

He was not laughing now.

He had his heels up to the highest rung on the bar stool, his legs splayed wide, elbows to his thighs, a bottle of beer held loosely in both hands and his eyes to us.

He knew. I knew he knew by the feel of the room and the look on his face.

He knew.

Oh God.

"Dad—" I started, taking two steps toward him.

"Pete told me," he cut me off, and his tone made me stop dead. "My daughter didn't tell me. Pete came by here yesterday mornin' for a visit, saw Shy leave. Saw you two suckin' face by Shy's bike. Pete sat on that for a night, wonderin' if he should tell me. Then he told me."

I pulled in breath and opened my mouth to say something, but Dad got there before me.

"Lied to me. Lied to Tyra. Your brother. My brothers." His eyes moved to pierce Shy. "*Your* brothers."

My blood ran cold and I began, "We just—"

"Lied," Dad clipped, putting his beer bottle next to the three that were already on the counter indicating he'd been there for a while and then he straightened from the stool, his eyes going back to Shy.

"She's my fuckin' daughter, man."

"I'm aware of that, brother," Shy said in a low rumble.

"I get that so what I don't get is what... the... *fuck?*" Dad returned, his voice lower and very scary.

This was not good.

"Dad, please, let me explain why—"

His brows shot up and his eyes sliced to me. "You lied. Told you, Tab, long time ago, you did that shit again, you would not like the consequences." He pointed to the floor. "Now you get the consequences." He started walking and his gaze moved to Shy. "You do too."

He stopped close to Shy, nearly nose to nose, and kept talking.

"My daughter, my brother. Not cool. You know it. That's why you hid it. Do not think for one second this shit washes. Brace, brother. I'm all over your ass. You fuck up, even minor, I'll jump all over that shit to get... you... *out.*"

I sucked in a harsh breath that burned, Shy's body jerked and I watched as Dad stalked by us, straight to the door.

Shy turned to him.

Then he opened his mouth and blew my mind.

"Tack, brother, I'm in love with her."

Dad already had the door open, most of his body out of it, but he turned and leveled his eyes on Shy.

He didn't hide his disgust.

"Brother, you do not know what love is."

And with that, he was gone.

I stared at the door, too much happening to process it all.

Then it all slid into place, the thing that happened that was priority hit me like a bullet, and I turned woodenly to Shy who was also staring at the door, that muscle ticking in his jaw.

"You love me?" I whispered.

He turned slowly to me and the muscle in his jaw kept ticking until his eyes locked on mine.

"You lost that guy, respect, you found the strength to carry on. Know this, Tabby, I lost you, it would be sixty years of goin' through the motions. I know that in my dick. I know it in my gut. I know it in my heart. I know it deep down in my goddamned soul."

Oh my God.

Oh my God!

Tears filled my eyes and I stood frozen, staring at his lanky, tall, biker badass gorgeousness.

"Your dad just threw down and I just laid it out," Shy stated when I didn't speak. "Now's the time to share, Tabby."

"I love you," I whispered.

"Good, but don't say that shit to me three feet away. Get the fuck over here."

I launched off on a foot, took one step and flew through the air.

Shy, as he'd been doing awhile, caught me.

I wrapped my limbs around him and looked down in his beautiful green eyes.

"I love you," I whispered again.

"Good," he whispered back, his hand sliding up my neck, into my hair. He pulled my face to his and he kissed me.

And he kept doing it until he laid me in bed.

He only stopped to make love to me.

CHAPTER THIRTEEN

Home No Longer

Three days later…

I DROVE INTO the forecourt of Ride, scanning the space. I saw Shy's bike, Dad's bike, Big Petey's Trike, and Tyra's Mustang.

"Excellent," I muttered under my breath, irately. "The gang's all here."

Suffice it to say, I was in a mood.

This mood had part to do with the fact that I just got off work and, in my absence, Dr. Dickhead had not taken time to reflect on the error of his ways (not a surprise). I wasn't his sole target anymore but he was worse than before, so it still felt the same. The problem was, now that I'd jacked them around, I felt I had to prove that I was stable, they could count on me, and part of doing that wasn't moaning about a douchebag doctor right after I put them through the hassle and expense of an unnecessary hiring process.

This mood also had to do with the fact that Natalie *still* hadn't called, even though I'd phoned her every day since she took off.

And last, this mood had to do with the fact that neither Dad nor Tyra had returned my calls, calls I'd made repeatedly, and that ticked me off.

Although Tyra and Dad were not taking my calls, Rush called me, reamed my ass for ten full minutes without letting me get a word in, saying some crap about Shy I was trying to block out so I would maybe be able to forgive him sometime in the distant future, then he hung up.

Hung up!

On me!

I'd called Big Petey and asked him why in *the* hell he talked to Dad before he talked to me.

"Honeybunch, this kinda shit, I know your dad, he'd wanna know," he explained to me.

"Pete, this kinda shit, you think maybe there's a reason he *doesn't* know and the only people who can explain that reason would be *Shy* or *me*?"

"I weighed my actions, Tabby, and in the end did the right thing," Pete replied and I knew he had his back up at my tone because, although he was a great guy, I adored him and he adored me, his ass was stubborn. Not to mention, he was a biker and not a young one. He wasn't used to women giving him crap, thus the reason he'd been divorced (three times).

"Well, you would be *wrong*," I told him before I hung up on him.

That was yesterday, two days of messages that went unreturned from Dad and Tyra, Rush's tirade, and Natalie's continuing grudge. And this didn't even include the fact that Shy was trying to gloss over things were not so great at Chaos for him. Not that he'd come right out and said that, but I could tell by the look on his face and *his* mood.

The brothers were about as pleased as Dad upon the

news spreading that there was a Shy and me, and when those men got ticked off about something, they didn't go gab with their psychologists about it. All hell broke loose.

So by the time I got Pete on the phone, I was over it.

Now I was *totally* over it.

Ycs, okay, Shy was a brother, I was the president's daughter, this had ripple effects on the family.

But, to coin Shy's phrase, I was twenty-three years old, and I really did not have to report to my Dad, stepmom, and extended motorcycle family who I was fucking.

Seriously!

So I was raring to go when, still wearing my scrubs, I stomped up the steps to the office and stormed right in.

Fortunately, I saw my little brothers Rider and Cutter weren't there, like they often were, hanging with their mom while she worked.

This was the only good thing.

The bad thing was Tyra turning to the door with a smile then seeing it was me. Her face went blank, her mouth set, and she lifted a hand and announced, "Tabby, I was hoping you were getting the message when I didn't pick up your calls. I need a few more days to process what you've done before I talk to you."

She could not be serious.

She was talking to me like I was sixteen.

Uh-uh.

No way.

I stared at her in her cute little top and I knew she had a slim, smart but tight skirt and high heels on behind the desk that hid her. Even after years as the office manager of Ride, a garage run by bikers, she didn't give up her professional sex-kitten look. I knew Dad (and all the other guys) totally dug it. I also knew, staring at her right then, that was a look I had once adopted. Another phase, the phase I was in when I was with Jason. A phase that was Tyra, not me.

I walked fully in, closing the door behind me, stopped a couple feet from her desk, and repeated, "You need a few more days to process what I've done?"

Her eyes narrowed on me and I knew she was pissed but I also knew I was *more* pissed.

"You heard me," she replied.

"Oh yeah, I did. I just don't understand you. What, exactly, have I done?"

Her head jerked with anger before her eyes got big and she stated, "You lied to your dad and me."

"When did I do that?" I asked. I saw her nose scrunch, it was cute but it was also an indication of anger.

"Don't be smart. You know lying by omission is the same thing as lying."

"Okay, now that you're talking to me, tell me, when did we go back in time, because as far as I know, I'm twenty-three, I have a college degree, a job, an apartment, a dead fiancé, and a man in my bed. So I kinda wanna know why you're talking to me like I'm sixteen."

Her voice got quiet when she warned, "Be careful, Tabby."

"Fuck careful, Tyra."

She blinked. I'd never talked to her like that. Heck, I didn't know if I'd ever talked to *anyone* like that. Actually, I never thought I would, not to Tyra, we were that tight.

But in this instance, having had days to think on it (okay, stew on it), I knew she was in the wrong and I was in the right.

I didn't respond to her surprise.

I kept going.

"How dare you?" I asked.

"Pardon?" she asked back, but quietly.

"How dare you think you deserve to know who I'm sleeping with when I want to keep that private, between him and me, be happy for a little while, just get used to him, the relationship we're building, the life we're going to share? How dare you think that is not my choice to make but it's yours or Dad's or anybody's? How dare you not take my calls like you're putting me in the naughty corner when Dad's pissed, on a rampage, and something this important is on the line? And how dare you sit there and act like I owe you pieces of me that are not yours to own unless I deem them something I wish to share, like who's in my bed?"

She stared up at me, lips parted.

I was so angry, I refused to register her hurt. I kept talking.

"You wanna know why we didn't share?" I leaned toward her and threw out an arm in the direction of the Compound. "*That's* why. We both knew that would happen, Tyra, and we were so fucking happy, we wanted a piece of that before we had to face your judgment."

"Tabby," she started, standing from her chair and I was right—tight, smart, sex-kitten skirt. "Shy is—"

My hand shot up. "Stop right there," I snapped. "I'll warn you now not to say anything you'll regret. Rush already spouted that shit to me, and the grudge he has to bear from me is currently scheduled to last years. You have no clue what Shy is. You know who knows?" I jerked my thumb toward my chest. "Me!"

"You've suffered a grave loss," she reminded me quietly.

"Yeah, Tyra, *a year ago.* I had a grave loss a year ago. Now I'm found."

She shook her head. "I don't think—"

I cut her off again. "You don't get to think. Dad doesn't get to think. Big Petey. Dog. Brick. Boz. Natalie. All you all..." I lifted a hand and circled it in the air before I dropped it "...don't get to think. I live my life, no matter how much you or Dad or anyone loves me, or how much I love all of you, you don't get to live my life for me, tell me how to live it or judge me for the decisions I make. I know what I have with Shy. Shy knows what he has with me. If I thought I wouldn't be facing this, right here, with you, explaining why I fell in love with the man I love, I would have shared with you *while* I was falling in love with the man I love. And, frankly, Tyra, you're my stepmom but you're also my friend, I thought a true friend who got me, and not only did I miss sharing that with you, it hurt when the time was forced on us to share and you wouldn't let me."

She flinched.

"But I'll give you a tidbit. He's good to me. When I say he's good to me, Tyra, I mean *he's good to me.* He's good *for me.* He doesn't care if I ruin dinner. He doesn't care that I talk too much. He thinks I'm the shit, and you know why I know that?" I leaned into her and didn't wait for an answer. "Because he *tells me.* All the fucking *time.* I'm precious to him and I know it because he *shows* me and he *tells* me. It's beautiful. It's real. It's *right.* And, if you'll think back, I knew all of that and shared it with you when it started happening. It was too soon then, that's true, I wasn't ready. But that doesn't mean it didn't happen."

She started to round the desk, eyes on me, speaking carefully, "Honey, you can get confused and I think—"

Oh God.

Seriously?

"No," I whispered. "Don't say another word."

She stopped moving and talking.

I didn't.

I moved to the door and turned to her.

"You know, I'm not pissed because you worry about me and you'd act on that even if you do it judgmentally. I know you're in the middle. You love me but you're Dad's old lady and your loyalty is with him, you have to take his back in what he's feeling and stand at his side when he does what he feels he has to do. That said, you should know the reason I'm pissed is because you and Dad and even the guys, you didn't even give him a chance." Her face paled, I knew my aim was true but I still drove that home. "You didn't give him a chance."

I saw her face soften when that sunk in then I went in for the kill.

"You know you're Dad's one-and-only, Tyra, and if you don't know this, seeing as he had kids before he met you, I'm sorry to tell you but even though you're his one-and-only now, you weren't his one -and-only."

Her head jerked, she flinched, and I finally saw it.

Understanding.

"You feel me," I said softy. "I get I'm not Shy's one-and-only but I still . . . fucking . . . *am*."

I pulled open the door, moved through it, and turned back.

"I'll leave you with this, since you all are so up in Shy's business. How many women has he fucked since he came into my life? You can think hard and you can ask around, but I know the answer. Two. A woman named Rosalie and *me*. People change, Tyra, he changed, and part of that change was for me. If you don't see that as beautiful, then you're fucking blind."

On that, I slammed the door and stormed down the steps toward the Compound.

I gave Tyra an earful, now Dad was going to get one, and if I had any fire left, I was going to lay into Big Petey.

I heard the door to the office open behind me and my name called but I was in Crocs. She was in heels. No way she was going to catch me.

I raced across the forecourt and felt the vibe the minute I opened the door to the Compound. Bikers had auras, and even at rest they forced out other auras, they were so badass dominant.

Now, they were not at rest and the vibe inside the Compound was so far from happy, it was unreal.

I didn't care because I had an idea of why and that was *not* happening.

I stormed in and saw the bad vibe was centering around a faceoff with Shy and Dad in the common area with all the men at Dad's back.

All of them.

"What the hell is going on?" I snapped loudly, and all eyes came to me, including Dad's and Shy's, and those two, scarily, had been nose to nose.

"Compound's closed to anyone but brothers," Dog growled, moving toward me.

"You put one hand on me, I swear to God, Dog, I will never even look at you again, and ask Shy, he knows I hold a mean grudge," I told him, my voice lethal.

Dog rocked to a halt, his expression ferocious then

he turned to Dad, as I heard Tyra's heels clicking up behind me.

I didn't turn to her or look at Dad.

I looked at Shy.

"Are you okay?"

"Babe, go home. I'll be there in a while," Shy said quietly.

"You didn't answer my question," I told him.

"Then no, I'm not okay," he gave me the answer I already knew. "So do me a favor, honey. Go home. I'll be there in a while."

He was not okay. I was not going anywhere.

I looked at Dad.

"Why is Shy not okay?" I asked Dad.

"Club business, Tabby," Dad said to me.

"And how does Club business make Shy not okay?" I asked.

"You wanna know, Tab?" Boz, one of the members cut in. "Not cool, daughters aren't safe. Daughters are always safe and Shy should know that."

"And how am I not safe?" I shot back. Boz's chin jerked but he didn't speak. "Apparently you have no answer to that, seeing as I'm standing right here"—I swung my arm out to the floor under me—"obviously totally safe, healthy, and, by the way, even though you didn't ask, also deliriously happy but, I'll point out again, you, not any of you, *asked*."

"Tab. Out. Now," Dad growled.

"Meeting. Vote," Arlo put in, and my stomach twisted.

That was not good.

"Oh no," Tyra whispered behind me.

Yep, not good.

"Vote about what?" I asked.

"Club business, Tabitha, move your ass out," Dad clipped.

Oh no, that "Tabitha" business was not going to work on me. Four years ago, yes.

Now, absolutely *not.*

"Vote about what, Dad?" I clipped back.

"Shy, she's yours, that's what you say. Control your woman," High demanded. "Get her ass out."

My eyes went to Shy to see him looking at High, and he wasn't looking pissed.

He was looking reflective.

Then he said, "Tab and I don't play it that way. You wanna order your old lady around, do what you do, not for me to say. I asked her to go, she didn't go. Not gonna make her. But you try, you'll deal with me."

God, I loved my guy.

"She don't mind you?" Boz asked, brows to his hairline but Shy ignored him and looked to Dad.

"Vote," he agreed, and my throat got so tight, I suddenly was having trouble breathing. What he said next didn't make it any better. "You want my cut, vote doesn't swing my way, I'll leave it with you and you'll see the back of my bike. I'll black out the Chaos ink. What I won't do is give up your daughter. So fuckin' vote. You don't want me there, text me the results and send a man to pick up my cut. You know where I'll be. I'll be with Tabby."

Oh God. Shy's cut, any of the boys' cuts, were held sacred to them. They were given the leather jacket with the Chaos patch on the back upon induction to the Club. Their "cut."

Once they earned it, they never gave it up.

Never.

Not for anything. Not unless forced, say, should they do something heinous to get kicked out of the Club.

"No. No, no, no," Tyra breathed behind me, but I couldn't move or speak.

"You'd give up your brothers for a woman?" Brick asked incredulously and Shy's eyes moved to him.

"Abso-fucking-lutely."

"Seriously?" Boz asked.

"Not any woman," Shy nodded my way then invited, "Now, ask again."

God.

God!

God, I *loved* my guy.

"Holy fuck," Tug whispered.

Shy looked at Dad. "You vote. Let me know. But you move to take my family from me, Tack, know this, you're dead to me. Tab loves me, it'll suck for her to have a man separate from her family but she'll deal. But you call this vote, no matter which way it goes, *you* will be dead to me."

Oh my God.

"No. No, no, no," Tyra breathed again.

"Shy," I forced out.

He ignored me and his eyes moved through the men standing behind my Dad. "I do not get in your business. I might make a call about what you do and who you fuck but I keep that shit to myself. And some of your shit is almost as close to home"—his eyes pinpointed Hop—"and you know it."

What did *that* mean?

Shy didn't explain but he did continue to look through the men and speak.

"Not once has this Club had a sit-down about how they feel about who a brother has in his bed. Tack calls that sit-down, you boys sit down, I'll say now, it doesn't matter how the vote goes. You sit down, your message will be clear. You'll get my cut. Part of bein' in this family is me bein' free to be me. Not me answering to my brothers about the woman I fall in love with or, actually, any-fucking-thing. You take my freedom away from me, there is no longer any reason for me to be here. So I won't be."

Shy looked back at Dad.

"Just so I'm clear, if you make it Tab or my cut, I pick Tab. You'll get my cut and you, personally, will not ever, brother, not ever again see me."

"Well, fuckin' hell," a familiar voice I hadn't heard in years and wished it had been decades said from behind me. "I'm gone for-freakin'-ever and it looks like Tabby's still causin' mayhem and heartbreak."

Woodenly, I turned to see my mother, defying all reason because I knew that not only Dad but all of Chaos threw down with her and told her she was banned from their property.

I felt the unhappy vibe ratchet up to apocalyptic levels then I felt movement, looked over my shoulder, saw Dad shifting toward Mom but Shy was already on the move.

I'd never seen anyone move that fast.

One second he was six feet behind me, the next he was passing me.

I knew why. Even though it happened well before Shy and I hooked up, all the brothers knew my mom and I didn't get along. They knew how she tore me down. They knew how relentless she was with that. They knew the hateful things she'd said to me, done to me, how it made me feel and how it made me act out when I was younger.

It was my doing, my fault, but it was my mom who made me feel like nothing, and then I found myself at sixteen with a boyfriend way too old for me who hit me when I didn't put out.

It wasn't just me. Mom threw down with Tyra, they even had a catfight in the forecourt of Ride, and she was always a screaming bitch to Dad.

In the end, she tried to sell custody of me *and* Rush to Dad in order to get her now-dead husband out of debt with drug dealers. I wasn't supposed to know that, but family talked and Chaos was family, so I found out. Dad had made the deal in order to get her out of our lives, mine especially, because her abuse cut me that deep.

Dad succeeded. She'd disappeared. But her memory lingered.

As for me, everyone in the Club knew if it wasn't for their love, Dad's love, Tyra's, things might have gone differently for me. Acting out against the unrelenting cruelty from Mom, I was on the wrong path and if I didn't have their care, right now, I could be like Natalie, coked up or doing ice, hanging with people that were no good for me.

Or worse.

I knew this. Everyone knew this.

And my man loved me.

With him advancing on Mom the way he did, I would get an indication of just how much.

"She does not..." Shy's hand hit Mom in the chest and Mom scuttled back, face filled with shock, arms wheeling "...see you..." he shoved Mom straight into the door so her back banged against it loudly before it swung open.

Shy pushed her off. She went reeling and Shy finished, "Unless she fuckin' wants to see you. Heed me, bitch, you are not the mother of my children, so I do not have to go gentle with you. I do not know why the fuck you're here. I also don't care. All I know is, Tab does not see you or hear your voice unless *she* wants to. Now, I can teach you that lesson now or you can get in your fuckin' car and go. Decision. But remember, not a man in this building will step up for you, so take that into account when you decide how you're gonna spend the next five seconds."

I hurried through the still-open door, my mouth open to say something but I didn't get the chance. Mom stared at Shy for one of those five seconds then she actually raced to her car the other four.

As she slammed her car door, started up, screeched out, and sped away, I looked at Shy's profile and I pressed my lips together, getting why Mom did not dillydally.

Shy turned to me. I braced. He lifted a hand, hooked me at the back of the head, and pulled me to him.

Lips to my hair, he said quietly, "See you at home."

I tipped my head back, caught his eyes, and nodded.

He let me go, didn't look back, sauntered to his bike, and I watched him start it and I kept watching him, my heart racing, my throat burning, my brain not functioning, as he roared off.

"Tabby," Dad's rumbly voice came from behind me, and I whirled on him.

I looked up at a handsome face I adored, into eyes I saw in the mirror every day, and before he could say another word, I gave it to him.

"I love you. I couldn't live without you. But if you take away the only family Shy has outside his brother—"

I pulled in breath and finished "—I will never, ever forgive you."

On that, I turned and raced to my car, running flat out in my Crocs (which, frankly, wasn't easy). Then I got in it, wasted no time, and drove away from a place that had always been home to me.

But it would be home no longer if they took it from my man.

Therefore, I cried all the way to my apartment, but I sat parked outside, sucked it up, yanked napkins out of my glove compartment, and cleaned up my face before I went upstairs to my place.

Shy's bike was there, and I had to be strong for my man.

* * *

I ran my tongue up the underside of Shy's cock and was just about to wrap my mouth around the tip when he knifed up. I suddenly was hauled up his body. He rolled us and when he got me on my back, his head came up, his eyes holding mine, he slid slowly inside me.

My eyes drifted half closed and my lips parted.

Shy moved, slowly, his strokes loving caresses. One of his forearms on the bed, his other hand came up to frame the side of my head. He moved his thumb along my hairline, and his eyes held mine as he made love to me.

I pulled my legs back, knees bent, and he slid in deep. As my hands moved over his skin, I lifted my head to get his mouth, and he didn't make me work for it. He gave me his mouth as he kept slowly, sweetly, beautifully taking me.

After my kiss, his lips slid down my cheek to my ear where he whispered, "Love you, Tabby."

Oh yes.

I pressed the insides of my thighs to his hips, wrapped my arms tight around him, and whispered in his ear, "Love you too, Shy."

His mouth moved below my ear and he murmured against my skin, "Everything to me."

God, *God,* I loved my guy.

"And you're everything to me," I breathed then suddenly, out of the blue, it came over me. Fierce and huge, I cried out and sunk my teeth into the skin of his neck.

He kept taking me through my climax and when I was done, he lifted his torso from mine, giving himself more leverage to slam his hips into me. He moved his hand over my cheek, his fingers drifting over my mouth, then down to my jaw, my neck, my chest, where it curled around my breast.

All the while, his eyes never left my face.

He was, quite simply, beautiful.

His strokes deepened, got faster, his face darkened, and I knew it was building for him, so I lifted my hands and ran my fingertips low over his flat abs. His thumb slid over my nipple, sending shivers through me, and my tongue came out to wet my upper lip.

"Gorgeous," he growled, pumping faster, harder.

"Yeah," I agreed breathlessly.

Not me.

Him.

Amazing.

"Fuck," he grunted, and I knew he was close.

I was right. His head jerked back but his hips kept slamming in, even harder. He kept thrusting as I watched his head drop forward and his teeth sink into his lower lip and, seriously, watching him come nearly took me there again.

Finally, he drove deep, stayed there, and collapsed on top of me.

I took his weight happily, my arms surrounding him, holding him close.

He didn't make me take it long. He shifted to a forearm and breathed heavily in my ear.

Finally, as his breathing evened, his hand, still curled around my breast and crushed between us, slid up to my neck. He lifted his head and looked at me.

"Like you comin' with me, Tabby," he said gently.

I knew he did. He tried to make me hold out every time unless he was in the mood to watch. Usually, I could manage this, though I had to admit, sometimes I failed.

"Well, I had no control over that, boss," I replied quietly. "It came out of the blue but, that said, sometimes I like watching too."

He grinned, bent his head, touched his mouth to mine and lifted up, still grinning.

Then he asked, " 'Boss'?"

" 'Biker boss' is too wordy."

His grin hit smile level, then he remarked, "You know, no condoms means I don't have to haul my ass outta bed after just comin' hard and deal with it. I get to be lazy."

He was teasing.

This was good and bad. Good because he was obviously in a mellow mood regardless of what went down that day. Bad because I had a feeling he was searching for that mellow mood, keeping hold of us and only us so he wouldn't have to think about what went down.

"You could be a gentleman and haul your ass out of bed anyway in order to get a washcloth and take care of me," I suggested, and something hot and phenomenal moved through his eyes even as his hips gave a slight jerk and his face got closer to mine.

"You want me to do that?" he asked.

I was being flippant, going with his mood but suddenly, I wanted him to do that. Like, *a lot*.

"Yeah," I whispered.

His face got closer so he could kiss me, wet and deep. Then he lifted his head to watch my face as he slowly slid out. I gave him a show I suspected was a lot like what he gave me when I was sliding him out of me. Then he bent, kissed my chest, the underside of my jaw, and he rolled out of bed.

I shifted to my side, curled up, and watched him move to the bathroom. I stayed where I was so I could watch him coming back.

He climbed in, settling on his side in front of me and ordered softly, "Hitch your leg over my hip, baby."

I did as he told me. His body shifted slightly but his eyes never left my face, and I felt the warm washcloth between my legs.

It felt nice.

I knew this registered on my face when he leaned in closer. "You like that."

It was a statement.

My hips pressed into his hand. "Yeah."

His head slid even closer, his lips hit mine, and his tongue slid in my mouth. The washcloth moved between my legs, then Shy shifted it somehow and there was no washcloth, just his fingers between my legs. He slid one finger inside and I moaned into his mouth, my hips twitching. I moaned again when his finger slid out and lightly glided over my clit before it and the washcloth were gone.

He lifted his lips from mine. "Be back, sugar."

I held his eyes and nodded.

His lips curved and he rolled off the bed.

Repeat of lying there, happily, watching him leave and come back but this time, when he slid in beside me, he settled on his back. He pulled me over him so my chest was to his chest, my cheek was to his shoulder, my face in his neck, and his arm was around me, hand cupping the cheek of my behind.

"We're doin' that every time," he declared, and I smiled.

"Works for me."

His fingers at my bottom squeezed.

I pulled in breath and trailed my fingers along his opposite shoulder.

"You okay?" I asked.

"Healthy or unhealthy, I'm not gonna think about it now," he answered instantly. "Just came. Just shared something special with my girl. You're naked on me. Gonna think about that. What happens will happen. I'll deal with it then."

"Okay," I said softly.

His other arm curled around my back.

I looked for something else to talk about, and something came to mind I'd wanted to ask him since he mentioned his grandmother days ago. It might not be the best conversational gambit, but at least it wasn't talk of what was happening at Chaos.

Still, I requested first, "Can I ask you something?"

"Anything," he replied immediately, and I smiled into his neck.

"May not be fun," I warned quietly and his arms gave me a squeeze.

"Not always gonna be fun, baby. Ask anyway."

I nodded, my cheek sliding against his skin then I asked, "Why didn't you go to your grandparents after your folks died?"

His arm around my back moved up, his fingers tangling in my hair then drifting through before he answered.

"Don't know. Mom and Dad made provisions. They picked my uncle. I figure they didn't get my uncle was weak or they never woulda left us to that. Mom didn't have any brothers or sisters. Her mom and dad were divorced. Gramps lived up in Wyoming. Mom grew up there until her folks divorced, and Grams moved them down to Denver 'cause she found a job here. Grams was cool, she was also around, took Lan and me to dinner, out to do shit. We never shared how bad it was 'cause we were kids. We didn't know how, and by the time we could the damage was done. That said, I think she knew shit was not good 'cause she was around as often as she could be. Gramps was cool too. He wasn't around as much 'cause he was in Wyoming. But he came down, got me my first bike for my fourteenth birthday, a dirt bike. He also gave me my first Harley, bought it thirdhand from a friend, fixed it up, got a buddy to help him bring it down to me. I'm still tight with both of 'em, even though he's still up in Wyoming and she moved to Arizona a few years ago. Dad's parents moved to California when he was in college. We didn't see 'em as much and still don't."

"Until you mentioned your grams the other day, I'd never heard you mention them," I noted.

"There's no reason for that, sugar. They just never came up." He wrapped an arm around my shoulders and offered, "You get to a place where you can take some time off, I'll drive you up to meet my gramps. He'll like you."

"That'll be cool," I replied softly.

"Maybe, if Lan can get the time, we can all go down to Arizona this winter. Get away from the cold. See Grams."

I smiled again. "That'll be cool too."

"It's a plan," he muttered.

Yeah, it was.

I pressed closer, took in a deep breath, then said what I had to say to get it out of the way, "You don't wanna talk about it, we won't. I'm just going to say, I'm gonna have a chat with Dad—"

He closed his arms tight around me and cut me off by saying, "Tabby, baby, look at me."

I lifted my head to look at him and I saw his eyes serious on me.

"He's gotta decide, as my brother, if he trusts me. Not you gettin' in his face and puttin' pressure on, not you takin' time to explain it rationally. I made the decision I wanted to join. I approached them. When I did, I put myself out there so, before they took me on, they knew everything about me. I did my time as a recruit. I do my part at the shop and in the garage. I take my orders when they come and I have never questioned them. When I get the call, I take a brother's back and I never question that either. I have not given them one reason to question me. I get where your father is at. I also know he's gotta get his shit together, think this through as a brother as well as a father and make the right decision. What I said at the Compound today is the God's-honest truth. I didn't become a member of the Club to have anyone tellin' me how to live my life. So that's a brother thing, Tab, and, it sucks if you don't like it but that's how it's gotta be."

I lived the life all my life, I knew enough to know this was true, so I nodded.

Shy kept going. "More, he's gotta come to terms with the fact that his only girl is all grown up and he's gotta give her the freedom to live her own life. What he's doin' to me is uncool. I get him bein' angry. He thought we were hidin' for the wrong reasons. But what he's doin' to you is more uncool. What he needs to get is that there are now parts of your life that are none of his business. I am not a father. I don't know how it feels to let go of a child in that way, especially your only girl. What I do know is, I acted on assumptions about shit about you years after it happened, it was wrong and . . . justified . . . I lost you. Now, he's doin' the same thing seven fuckin' years after it happened, and he's gotta clue in you're not that girl pullin' shit because things with your mom are extreme. You're an adult making decisions about your future, and you get to decide when you'll share."

That was the damned truth.

"You're right," I agreed.

"Yeah," he replied quietly.

"Okay, I'll let it be," I gave in, and his lips curved as his eyes got soft and his arms gave me a squeeze.

"Thanks, baby."

I smiled at him. Then I tipped my head to the side and asked, "What was that with Hop at the Compound?"

His eyes held mine, he waited a beat, then he shared, "Hop is nailin' Lanie."

I blinked.

Lanie was Tyra's best friend. Lanie was the one who lost her fiancé when all that crazy stuff went down that eventually got Tyra kidnapped and stabbed. Lanie had moved to Connecticut to lick her wounds after Elliott, her fiancé, got whacked and Lanie got shot. She did that until Tyra flew out there, gave her some honesty, and then Lanie moved back.

Lanie was tall, slender, and model gorgeous. She also made a lot of money, she ran her own advertising agency, was pure class, and could be (frequently) pure drama.

What she was not, in any way, was Hop's type.

"You're kidding me," I breathed.

"Nope. They're hidin' it too. Don't know why, but I do know neither Tack nor Cherry know shit." He grinned. "Not the same as bangin' one of the brother's daughters, but figure they're hidin' it for a reason. Also, whatever they got is not runnin' smooth. I heard them goin' at it in his room at the Compound. Was in the hall when I saw her strut out, pissed as all fuck, Hop tearin' out after her, not looking any happier. He saw me so he knows I know. We had a chat, he told me to keep it under wraps, I have not said shit."

"I...I don't know what to do with that," I told him. "Has Lanie been with anyone since that Elliott guy?"

Shy smiled and replied, "I'm not one of her bitches, so I have no clue. I just know he's had her in his bed awhile."

"Oh God," I whispered, "Ty-Ty might freak."

"Don't know why, he's a good guy," Shy remarked.

Hop *was* a good guy. I loved him. Everyone did. But he also had an ex, Mitzi, and when she became his ex, it got ugly. I was not one of his brothers, so I didn't know why but it got so ugly it was hard to miss.

"He's a good *brother*," I clarified. "What went down with Mitzi was messy. So messy, no one missed it and definitely not Tyra, seeing as she works there."

"What went down with Mitzi was deserved by Mitzi. She was a pain in his ass," Shy returned.

"Shy—" I started, my body tensing.

"Tabby," he interrupted me. "You know, some shit with the boys, I'm not gonna share. Just know this, a woman doesn't treat men like us like Mitzi treated Hop. They do, they'll find themselves where Mitzi is now."

I studied him, then asked, "Was it bad?"

"Bad enough for him to roam," he confirmed, and I sucked in breath, shocked at this news.

Hop was a good brother. As I already mentioned, Hop was also a good guy. I liked him. He had his imperfections, everyone did. And it wasn't unheard of that some of the men would do whatever they wanted with whoever they wanted even if they had an old lady at home.

But I did not think Hop was like that.

"Hop roamed?"

"BeeBee," Shy grunted, and I sucked in another breath.

BeeBee had not been around for a good long while but the ghost of BeeBee remained, such was the power of BeeBee. I had been a whole lot younger when she used to hang at Chaos, but I'd seen her around and I knew she was a biker groupie.

Her mission, as jacked as it seemed, was to collect every member of the Club, become a notch on their bedposts, the more notches the better.

The old ladies detested her. It wasn't like Chaos didn't have biker groupies, but they knew their place and they knew the place an old lady held and never the twain shall meet. That said, I'd been to enough hog roasts to see BeeBee communicating with her eyes, and sometimes with her mouth, she'd had a woman's man. My guess was, since

BeeBee's tenure was long, the old ladies sucked it up and this never got back to their men. Unfortunately, this could be the way with motorcycle clubs, and old ladies learned when to keep their mouths shut.

That was until BeeBee went head-to-head with Ty-Ty. It kinda grossed me out to know my dad went there (though, admittedly, she was gorgeous with a fabulous body, just skanky) and from the argument I overheard Tyra having with Dad, he and BeeBee had been together before Tyra's time, but still.

Dad found out BeeBee even looked at Tyra, much less spoke words to her (which she did), sent Dad over the edge.

Exit BeeBee.

Forever.

She was also the example Shy threw in my face way back, that night he was a dick to me. None of that night was pleasant, though it was over and I wasn't going back there. However, I remembered quite clearly that him even suggesting I was going the way of BeeBee was a hurt that dug deep.

On the exhale, I breathed out, "Oh my God."

"Yeah. Even I think that play was fucked, but when it happened Hop and Mitzi were on a break, a bad one, the break they had just before all hell broke loose and Hop ended it with Mitzi for good. Enter BeeBee, who could sniff that shit out like nobody. Why Hop took Mitzi back, don't know. Just know he didn't take her back for long before it was really over."

"I'm not sure any of this is good," I told him.

"I'm not either," he agreed, then his eyes grew intense on me. "What I am sure of, it's nobody's fuckin' business."

That, I knew, was very, very true.

His arms gave me a squeeze and his voice went soft when he reminded me, "You got work tomorrow, and we both don't know what the day will bring. We should get some shut-eye."

"Yeah," I whispered then dropped my head to touch my mouth to his.

When I lifted it, he rolled me to his side and reached an arm across me to turn out the light. He settled in and tucked me close.

I snuggled closer.

I was about to enter dreamland when it hit me.

And although near sleep, what hit me, Shy had to know.

"You did it," I said, my voice quiet and drowsy.

"Did what, sugar?"

"Today, at the Compound, what you said, you did it."

"What, baby?"

"I dreamed a dream."

His arms spasmed.

I drifted to sleep, muttering, "You promised to get me to a dream, you got me to a dream. Thank you, honey."

Then I fell asleep.

* * *

Shy

Shy Cage did not sleep.

He held his slumbering girl in his arms and he struggled with the urge to howl at the moon.

It took a while to control that urge.

Then, no matter the shit that went down that day, Shy fell asleep smiling.

CHAPTER FOURTEEN

Make Her Happy

SHY'S MOUTH WORKED between my legs, my back left the bed, my heels dug into his lats, I ground my hips into his face, and I came hard.

Still coming, I found myself on my stomach, my hips were jerked up, and Shy's cock drove inside me.

"Again, Tabby, hand between your legs," he growled, his hands at my hips, yanking me back as he thrust forward and took me.

I was still coming but I managed to get my hand between my legs. I moaned into the pillows at my touch and his strokes.

Oh God, this was brilliant.

"Push up, baby, want your tits," he ordered.

I pushed up, he kept driving deep even as his mouth hit my neck and his hands covered my breasts. Then his fingers did things to my nipples that made me gasp and my entire body jerk.

"Wait for me," he grunted.

"Shy, no way," I panted.

He drove up and ground in, rumbling against my neck as his fingers twisted my nipples, "Wait. For. Me."

"Oh God," I moaned, grinding down. "Hurry."

He started thrusting.

Oh God.

"Are you close?" I breathed.

"Gettin' there," he muttered.

He kept thrusting, his fingers working my breasts.

"Honey, are you close?" I begged.

"Fuck," he groaned into my neck. "Give it to me, Tabby."

Thank God.

I let go and gave it to him, my head flying back, slamming into his shoulder as his mouth closed over the skin of my neck and I felt him sucking deep.

That would leave a mark.

I came down and I felt his breath against my skin as he did too.

Then I lifted my hands to his that were now just holding me, curled around my breasts.

"That was awesome," I breathed.

"It's always awesome," he murmured.

He was right, and I was glad to know he felt the same way.

My hands moved with his hands as one of them slid up to wrap around my chest and the other one slid down to cup me between my legs where he was still buried deep.

"Love you, Shy Cage," I whispered.

"Love you too, baby," he whispered back.

After the day before, I didn't know what that day was going to bring.

I just knew however it carried on, it started *great.*

* * *

Shy and I were shuffling around in the kitchen, me in my scrubs, Shy in his jeans. We were sipping coffee, sucking back bowls of cereal, chatting, touching, kissing, our usual routine, when my phone rang.

I'd turned my cell off and the ringer to my house phone the night before. Shy needed my concentration so I gave it to hm.

I'd turned my phone on that morning and found I had seventeen missed calls and nearly as many voice-mail messages. Five were from Tyra, three from Dad, two from Rush, one from Big Petey, and the rest were from various brothers or their old ladies. All of them were asking me to call them.

I knew the day was going to go downhill from there.

Luckily, it started at a way-high point. The problem with that, the higher you are, the farther there is to fall.

I looked at my phone on the counter, saw the screen said, "Tyra Calling" and heard Shy say, "Pick it up, babe."

I looked to Shy to see he had his eyes to the phone.

"I don't know if I'm ready."

His eyes came to me. "She wasn't ready for you to lay into her yesterday either. You took your time to talk, give her hers."

He was right.

Crap.

I grabbed the phone quickly before it went to voicemail and put it to my ear.

"Tyra," I greeted.

"Tabby," she whispered, and my heart squeezed.

She sounded relieved and something else that didn't sound great.

Learning from what I lost with Shy, I didn't delay and extended the olive branch.

"Listen, I know we have a lot to talk about but I'm getting ready for work. Can we set time to talk after work? I'll meet you someplace and I promise, I'll come prepared not to be a bitch."

"Honey, I'm so sorry to have to tell you this, but your grandmother died."

My middle shifted back as my breath left me in an audible *whoosh.*

My phone slid out of my hand, and I heard Shy growl, "You got Shy. Whatever else you gotta say, you're gonna say it to me."

My eyes lifted to his, I saw he mistook my reaction when his angry eyes that were riveted to my face changed. They went soft, his hand came up and curled around the side of my neck, and he pulled me close.

"Right," he said into the phone, his voice no longer a growl but a soothing rumble. "Okay," he went on. "I'll tell her. She's bein' careful at work 'cause of what went down. I'll talk with her, see how she wants to play this. One of us will call you back." Pause then, quietly, his eye still on me, "Later, Cherry."

He didn't take his gaze from mine when he took the phone from his ear, touched the screen with his thumb, and whispered, "Your mom's mom. Massive stroke. Your mom told Rush, he told your dad. They've been callin' but didn't approach 'cause things were not good."

I nodded.

"You tight with her?" he asked.

"She hated my mom, acted mean to her, but although

she could do stupid crap, she was usually great with Rush and me."

His hand slid to the back of my neck, he pulled me into his chest and his other arm slid around me.

It was then I started crying.

Shy held me, gave me time, and only spoke again when I was pulling myself together.

"Your dad wants to see you," he said gently, and I sucked in breath and nodded. "How you wanna play this, sugar?"

I pulled my face out of his chest and tipped my head back to look at him. "Unfortunately, I really do need to go to work. I'll explain what's going down, read the pulse, and then I'll know. I'll, uh . . . call Dad on a break or something."

He nodded.

"I knew this day would turn shit," I whispered. "I knew with how great it started, there'd be farther to fall."

His eyes flashed, his hands moved to cup my jaws, he tilted my head way back, and brought his face to mine.

"May feel like you're fallin', Tabby, but remember, I'm at the bottom ready to catch you."

At these beautiful words, I burst into tears again.

Without hesitation, Shy yanked me back into his arms and held me.

There it was.

I'd reached bottom and I was crying, because I didn't realize it at the time, but he'd already caught me.

And it felt beautiful.

* * *

Shy

Shy stood on the sidewalk and watched Tab pull out to drive to work. The minute she started rolling, turning to give him a wave, he jerked his chin up to her, waited for her attention to go back to the road, then his eyes moved to the man on the bike across the parking lot who he'd seen the minute he'd walked her down.

Luckily, she didn't notice.

Shy stood where he was and crossed his arms on his chest as he watched Tack throw a leg over his bike and move his way.

It wasn't until he stopped three feet away that Shy spoke. "This gonna get ugly, or can you contain your shit so we can do this in Tab's apartment?"

Tack held his eyes then said quietly, "Not ugly, brother."

Shy jerked up his chin, turned, and led the way up the stairs and into Tabby's place.

He moved in five steps, turned to Tack, and watched him close the door.

"It would be cool," he started the minute Tack turned to him, "if we can keep things good while Tab deals. You know more than me she isn't tight with her grandma, but she's still feelin' this. I haven't had the chance to talk to her about it, but she's also feelin' the fact that her mother showed to share this yesterday but instead she led into that by layin' into Tabby. You also know she's got other shit on her mind. You, me, the Club. One last favor I'll ask of you is you don't make her feel that until she's done feelin' this."

He watched Tack's mouth get tight before the man spoke.

"You don't have to ask me that shit."

"Wouldn't think so until the shit you've been pullin'. Now I feel I gotta ask," Shy replied.

Tack's mouth got tight again.

"We good on that?" Shy prompted when Tack said nothing, and Tack jerked up his chin. "Good," he finished on a mutter.

"That other shit, brother, we gotta have words," Tack declared.

"You've said your words, Tack. You got other words, I'll listen. But, mark me, I've heard every word you've said the last four days."

"I think you get me," Tack returned.

"Oh yeah, I get you," Shy agreed.

Tack studied him. Then quietly, he stated, "She's my only daughter, man."

"And she's the only woman I've ever loved, Tack," Shy shot back instantly.

"I'm seein' that," Tack murmured, his lips twitching.

Shy didn't find one fucking thing amusing so he clipped, "Well, brother, finally."

"I was pissed as all fuck when I said that shit to you about not knowin' what love is," Tack explained.

"Know that," Shy returned. "Also know four days have passed since you took it back."

"Three days passed before you showed me you walked the walk, not just talked the talk," Tack retorted.

Fuck, he had to give him that.

Shy said nothing.

"You know me. She knows me. You knew the way I'd react and that's why you both hid that shit from me," Tack continued.

"Yep," Shy confirmed. "And you know me, brother, and, outta respect for you, you know I would never, not fuckin' *ever* go there with Tabby unless it was real. I get your reaction. I just don't get that days have gone by and you haven't seemed to get why we would move to manage it."

"Yesterday, Tyra explained some things to me," Tack shared.

"Thrilled, brother," Shy replied, and Tack's eyes narrowed.

"You're missin' this," he warned low, "but I'm wavin' a white flag here, Shy."

"I'm not missin' shit," Shy bit out. "It has not been lost on me, since I've been fuckin' *there* watchin' her girl Natalie lay into her about us and, seriously, man, that woman has got a mouth on her. It was not easy not tossin' her ass out the way she talked to my woman, but Tabby felt it was time for a fuckin' intervention so she wouldn't fuckin' let me. I've been there too, dealin' with her worry that her girl has not returned one single call she's made and, brother, she calls that bitch every day to smooth the waters and she's got nothing. I was also there to overhear my brother givin' her shit, testin' her to see if she's on the rebound from that guy and usin' me."

Tack's eyes flashed but Shy was far from done.

"I was there, watchin' her take her brother's shit when *he* fuckin' called and laid into her. I was there, watchin' her worry 'cause you and your woman would not speak to her. And I saw her pissed off and in pain yesterday when she saw what you were doin' to me and she was stuck, torn between her man and her family. Honestly? I do not give one fuck what you or any member decides to do to me. What I give a fuck about is that you're puttin' my woman through the fuckin' ringer a year after she went through the fuckin' ringer and, brother, I am not down with that. So wave your goddamned white flag, but if Tab isn't feelin' you, I won't feel you."

Tack's eyes were intense but his lips were twitching again when he muttered, "She'll feel me."

"I suspect she will," Shy agreed. "You're a hard act to follow. Luckily, when I got my shot at beauty, I had a blood father who showed me the way with the way he treated my mom and a brother of the cut who showed me the way with the way he treated his family and his old lady. Until recently," Shy stated, and saw Tack's jaw get hard so he knew the man didn't miss his meaning. "Then I had to wing it," he finished.

Tack unclenched his jaw to share, "Your point is made, brother."

"Good."

"You don't have a family, a daughter. When you do, you'll get it," Tack went on.

"I hope to fuck I will," Shy told him and watched Tack's head jerk with surprise, and he didn't quite hide his look of fatherly pain. The thought of his girl as a woman was clearly something he had not quite processed, even if she had once been engaged.

So Shy lowered his voice and reminded him, "She's not your little girl anymore, not like that. She may always be your little girl in some ways, brother, but not like that. You gave me the chance, I would have told you, this is solid. We started out and it was friends. That wasn't what I wanted, it was what she needed, so I gave it to her. We built on that. The foundation is laid and it's the kind that holds fast. This is it, brother. We're livin' together. Soon's we can do it, we're movin' to a better fuckin' place so I can provide her a decent home. I'm puttin' my ring on her finger, I'm givin' her babies, and when she's laid to rest, that ring I give her will still be on her finger. I see you're accepting this now, so you need it all and there it is. I was a part of an us and I was happy. Some motherfucker killed my parents and took that from me, so life forced me to become nothin' but a me. Now I'm an us again, and that's what I'll be with my woman and the family we make until the day I fucking die."

"Christ, Shy," Tack whispered.

"I think now *you* totally fuckin' feel *me*."

Tack's head tipped to the side. "The Club doesn't factor into that?"

"You know you're my family, Tack, but don't bullshit me. You know exactly what I'm talkin' about and you also know, you find her, you'll give up anything to keep her. You walked through bullets to do just that and when you walked through that hail of gunfire, brother, you were not thinkin' of Tab or Rush or the Chaos MC. The only thing on your mind was Cherry. So I also know you understand what the Club means and, when it comes to Tabby, you get me."

Tack held Shy's eyes.

Then he said quietly, "I wanted that for her. That other guy was a good man but I couldn't know, way he was raised, if he would give that to her, and I wanted just that for her."

"Then lucky you, that's what she eventually found," Shy replied instantly.

Tack again held Shy's eyes. Then he jerked up his chin and stated, "Guess we'll see if Tabby feels me, then you and me can mend fences, brother."

"Yep," Shy replied, and Tack's lips twitched again.

He turned to the door, opened it, then turned back to Shy and shared, "Givin' you honesty, thought that business with Tab over the Club was bluff. The way you bore down on her mom, I knew."

"Rush or you speak to that bitch again, I'd advise reiterating my message, because I was not fuckin' joking."

Another lip twitch, then, "I think she got that, brother. Not sure anyone missed that."

"That's good, 'cause Tab isn't real hip on her mom, but I don't think she'd like what I have planned."

"Probably not," Tack muttered then his eyes locked on Shy's. "Gotta say it, my duty, gettin' you know it without me speakin' the words but, you have a girl, you'll understand."

"Say it," Shy invited.

Tack's eyes stayed locked on Shy's two beats then he said quietly, "Make her happy."

Shy held his gaze as, for the first time in fucking *months*, he began to breathe easy.

There it was. Tack just gave it.

His blessing.

Shy took it by jerking up his chin.

It was then, Tack straight out smiled a half a second before he disappeared behind the door.

Shy sucked in a breath.

He let it out, muttering, "Jesus."

Then he pulled out his phone to call his brother.

* * *

"I'm good, Lan, thanks. It's cool you're willing to come up, but I'll be okay," Shy listened to Tab, who was curled in the couch beside him, her head in his gut and talking on the phone to his brother. "Though, you wanna come up, Shy would love to see you and I promise, I won't cook. Restaurants and takeout the whole time."

Shy grinned.

There it was.

She was good.

"Right," she whispered. "Thanks, Lan. You wanna talk to Shy again?" Pause then, "Okay, I'll tell him. Later." She touched the screen, lifted her head, and looked at him. "Lan says he'll call you later."

"Cool," Shy muttered.

She tossed the phone to the coffee table, settled with her head on his gut again, and aimed her eyes to the TV.

His girl took her fall this morning but, as was their way, Chaos as a whole cushioned the landing.

Not surprisingly, there would be no vote. Shy took call after call from brothers who wanted to mend fences. He didn't make them work too hard. If it was just him, he'd be thinking on things. Even respect and loyalty to Tack and thus, in a twisted way, Tabby didn't take away the fact not one single one of them took his back. Right now, he needed smooth for his girl. Time would pass and they'd again earn his trust.

Or not.

Tab had sorted things out with her dad, and when she called Shy to tell him she'd talked with Tack, it sounded like it lasted about five seconds before it was all good. He was not surprised about this. She loved her old man, and he'd led the conversation with sharing he'd wasted no time and flown the white flag with Shy. Shy had told Tack he was good if Tab was good. She was good because Shy was going to be.

She'd talked to her grandfather and explained that she couldn't get off work. He, too, had been cool, asked her schedule, and told her he'd plan the funeral when she had two days off. Shy and Tab were going to fly down for the funeral and fly back up the next day.

She'd met Cherry for a drink after work and that was also good. Again, not a surprise. He knew Cherry didn't have it in her to be a bitch, hold a grudge, or fuck with a good thing. And she and Tabby had a good thing.

The only person she had not patched things up with was with her brother Rush. He'd called repeatedly and she hadn't taken his calls. This *was* a surprise.

"I'll see him at the funeral and deal then," she'd muttered.

It was time, Shy decided, to push her to deal with the situation with Rush.

"Babe, you gotta call your brother."

She lifted her head from his gut, twisted her neck and looked up at him. "Shy—"

He cupped her cheek with his hand. "You lost family, both of you. Do not let this fester."

She held his eyes a beat, two, then she whispered her admission, "He said things about you."

"I don't give a fuck. He repeats 'em and doesn't get over shit like everyone else is doin', you got a case to be pissed and hold a grudge. Now, you both lost your grandma. He doesn't have a woman. He only has a sister. Honest to God, is *my* girl gonna take that away from him now?"

She licked her lip.

He hauled her up his chest to touch his mouth to hers.

When she lifted her head away, she was grinning a sexy little cat-got-her-cream grin.

"You pull that shit now deliberately, don't you?" he muttered.

"Actually, no, but it's a good idea," she replied, still grinning.

He ignored her sexy grin and looked in her eyes. "Rush," was all he said.

She held his gaze. Then she murmured, "Oh, all right."

"Call him now," he ordered.

She rolled her eyes and muttered, "Righty ho, boss."

He grinned, then he rolled her to her back in his lap and took her mouth, leaving her clutching his shoulders and panting when he lifted his head.

His eyes went to the mark he put on her neck that morning then to her eyes.

"You get off the phone, you thought the day started good, I'll give you an ending you won't fuckin' believe."

"I foresee my forgiveness phone call to Rush lasting all of thirty seconds."

Shy burst out laughing. When he quit, he saw she was smiling up at him.

And it hit him.

All of it.

Waking up to her. Going to bed with her. Making love to her. Eating with her. Laughing with her. Kissing her. Going shopping with her, and when she was in a store and wandered away, he saw her looking over the racks, looking for him, and when he came to her at her back, she'd turned to him, looking lost, and leaned into him the second he got there, suddenly found.

Jesus, he had it.

All of it.

"I never dreamed any fuckin' dream," he whispered, and the smile faded from her face as tears filled her eyes.

She understood him.

"Shy—"

"Didn't dream it, saw it, waited my time, and then you gavc it to me."

"Shy," her voice broke on his name.

He looked into her blue eyes swimming with tears, feeling her fingers digging into his shoulders, her weight in his lap, the smell of her hair, the taste of her still on his tongue.

Yes, he fucking had it.

When he was twelve he lost it.

Now he had it again.

All of it.

Everything.

"Call your brother," he muttered. She pulled in a breath through her nose then nodded.

She then lifted up and touched her mouth to his, one of her hands sliding into his hair so when she pulled back, she held him at the side of his head.

"Love you, darlin'," she whispered.

"Love you too, honey."

She grinned a wobbly grin and broke from his arms as she rolled off his lap.

He listened to her patch things up with her brother.

When she was done, he turned off the TV, took her hand, guided her to the bedroom, and gave her what he promised. An end to the day that was exactly what he intended it to be.

Unbelievable.

CHAPTER FIFTEEN

Lucky

One month later...

I STOOD OUT in the cold, a beer in my hand, next to a steel drum filled with fire giving off a wave of heat. I felt an arm slide along my shoulders and I tipped my head just in time to hear Landon, who'd claimed me, say, "Jesus, Tab, what's goin' on with that? It's like a hippie hookin' up at a Tea Party rally."

My eyes went to where his were aimed and I saw Lanie and Hop, not quite hidden by the steps that led up to the office that they were behind but mostly hidden by the dark of the November night. She looked glamorous, as usual, her glossy, thick dark hair gleamed even in the distant fire and floodlights. I'd gabbed with her earlier and saw she was casual for Lanie, wearing jeans, but her killer, expensive boots, elegant sweater, and the pashmina she had wrapped around her neck screamed class.

Hop, on the other hand, was in beat-up, faded jeans (that still looked good on him), a black thermal, and his battered cut, a black leather jacket with the Chaos insignia on the back. His dark hair was overlong and falling in his face, and his kick-ass, biker mustache that ran thick across his lip and down the sides of his mouth needed a trim. Something, knowing Hop for ages, I knew he'd get around to when he felt like it, he had a classy dame in his bed or not. This could be the next day. This could be next month.

I watched as they talked, then Hop suddenly grabbed Lanie and I held my breath when he kissed her, hot and heavy.

I had to give it to her, she struggled.

For about five seconds.

Then her arms wrapped around his shoulders, he arched her further into the shadows, twisting his torso so I could see nothing but the indistinct Chaos emblem on his cut, and I knew they were going at it.

My eyes darted around the forecourt of Ride, where we were currently engaged in the eating and drinking portion of a Chaos hog roast. The raising-hell portion would come in about half an hour after the pig was decimated and there were more bottles passed around than plastic cups being filled from kegs.

I spied Dad, his eyes pinned to the stairs and thus Lanie and Hop, and his eyes were narrowed.

Uh-oh.

My gaze moved, and I located Tyra talking with Dog's woman, Sheila, and she had her back to the couple.

Shoo.

"Don't know, sweetheart, but thinkin' that right there flies in the face of all that's holy," Lan muttered, and I burst out laughing.

Through my laughter, I saw him grinning down at me.

I kept laughing even as I felt something warm hit my belly, my eyes wandered from his, and I saw Shy fifteen feet away, standing with Boz, Roscoe, and Bat, looking at me, his lips curved up, his face, clear in the floodlights, happy.

His brother and his girl were getting on and just with something as simple as that, all was right in Shy Cage's world.

Knowing that, one could say all was right in mine too.

Suffice it to say, Landon had been true to his word. The time it took for me to prove to him that he trusted me with his brother didn't last long. It happened close after all hell broke loose with Chaos.

As for me, I knew I'd fall in love with my man's brother when Shy, Rush, and I hit Denver International Airport to fly down for my grandmother's funeral, and Lan was at the gate. Shy hadn't said a word, probably because he knew I'd try to talk him out of Landon taking time out of his life and money to buy a plane ticket in order to be with me during what the Cage brothers thought was my hour of need.

Seeing Lan there, I was shocked.

Lan simply gave me a hug and muttered in my ear, "Family looks after family."

That was sweet and all, but flying to Arizona to attend the funeral of a woman he didn't know and, obviously, seeing as she was deceased, he'd never meet?

I would understand during the funeral why he was there when I discovered what the Brothers Cage had arranged.

This was, while Rush and I hung tight and Shy gave me his support, Lan wasted no time in his approach to Mom. I didn't know what he said. I just knew by the look on her face when he was saying it, she heard him. He lurked close to her the entire time I was in her space, at the funeral home, the gravesite, and at Gramps's after.

His message was clear: Don't get any ideas about being a bitch to Tabby (and she would, it was Mom's way, even at her mother's funeral). You do, I'll pounce. Seeing as he wasn't exactly small but he was obviously a badass, Mom, who could miss the most blatant of hints, didn't miss Lan's message.

Therefore, I endured Gram's funeral without having to endure my mom being a bitch. She didn't even chance throwing a bitchy look at me. She stayed well away.

That did it for me with Lan, but I didn't know what did it for Lan with me. I just knew I'd been let in. When he called Shy, or Shy was talking to him and I was around, he asked him to pass the phone over and we gabbed. Not forever and not deep but friendly, warm, and sweet. And now that he was up for the weekend, he joked and teased, all genuine, all real, nothing watchful, nothing fake.

I knew Shy loved it.

So did I.

The good part of that awful visit to Arizona was that Shy and Lan got a chance to see their grams. We met her for dinner. I loved her on the spot. This was because she was beside herself with joy at the surprise chance to spend time with her boys and she didn't hide it. This was also because she flirted audaciously with Rush. It was funny. *She* was funny, and something else she didn't hide was that she clocked Shy loved me and folded me into the family immediately.

My grandmother dying sucked but, it had to be said, gaining Shy's grandmother was awesome.

"Good to hear you laughin', Tab. You been quiet," Landon observed. I gave Shy a smile and then looked up at his brother.

"I'm good."

His head tipped to the side and his eyes held mine. "Sure?"

I shrugged but his arm didn't leave me. "Just shit at work," I admitted.

"Dr. Dickhead," he stated knowingly.

As an FYI, bikers were not taciturn. I'd known this my whole life. They were in the life to be who they were and do what they wanted and that included, for those of that bent, saying whatever the heck they wanted to say whenever the heck they wanted to say it to whoever they wanted to say it to. Although some could be quiet, introspective, or mysterious, most of them let it all hang out.

And I knew from him telling me and listening to them talk that Shy let it all hang out with Lan.

Therefore, it wasn't a surprise Lan knew about Dr. Dickhead, because Dr. Dickhead had not calmed down. Gossip, proved accurate by his mood, stated his supply-room piece had called Dr. Dickhead's wife and broke the news that her husband was a cheater. This did not go over very well and included him sleeping on the couch in his office for a week while he found a new apartment.

For me, it meant I was again, for some unfathomable reason, his target, and he'd ratcheted up the nastiness pretty significantly.

At first, I shared the misadventures of Tabby and Dr. Dickhead with Shy. Now, I did not. He was pissed, and the more I talked, the more pissed he got. Considering that my landlord simply pressed to have a twelve-month lease and Shy got up in his face, I wasn't fired up to drive him to intervene with Dr. Dickhead, something he already promised he'd do.

So I quit talking about it.

Suffice it to say, the all good parts of Shy and I building a friendship on which we fell in love and began to build a relationship had ended. This was not to say things still weren't amazing. It was just to say that life was life and not everything was perfect all the time.

For instance, Shy threw his clothes all over the floor, and this drove me nuts. I decided to put up with it but then, after I gathered them and put them in the hamper, Shy disappeared anytime I was going to the Laundromat.

This, I decided *not* to put up with.

"Did I get a biker badass who's great at serving up orgasms and has a natural talent with sweet, or did I get that *and* an unpaid laundress's job?" I'd asked irately the last time I came back from the Laundromat to see Shy in front of the TV with a beer.

"Don't do laundry, babe," he told the TV.

Not me, the TV. He didn't look at me, and he certainly didn't look at the hamper I was lugging in.

"Did you have a magic spell before me that you could cast over your clothes to get them clean?" I sniped, dumping the clean, folded hamper of clothes in my armchair.

His eyes finally shifted to me. "No."

"So *someone* did your laundry, because your clothes are worn but they weren't filthy before me."

His eyes went carefully blank before he advised quietly, "Don't go there."

Oh God.

I went there and did so by planting my hands on my hips and stating, "Your bitches did them for you."

"Told you not to go there," he muttered, eyes going back to the TV screen.

"Shy," I called. He sighed and looked at me. "Seeing as you're here, your clothes are here, you sleep in my bed every night, come home to my place every evening, we're essentially living together. So we have to figure out how to do that without me getting pissed."

"All right, sugar, but like I said, I don't do laundry."

"Okay, boss, what *do* you do?" I shot back.

"Nothin'," he stated and I blinked before my eyes narrowed, something Shy didn't miss. I knew this when he warned, "Do not go off on one. I've pretty much crashed at the Compound for the last nine years, so I didn't even take care of my own place. That bitch who raised me after my mom died didn't do shit for us. We didn't only keep our room clean and did our own laundry, we did *their* laundry and cleaned *their* house while her kids sat on their asses and watched TV. So I've had my fill of laundry and cleaning, and I don't intend to do any fuckin' more of it. I'll take out the trash. I'll get the groceries, since you seem allergic to the grocery store. I'm in the mood, I'll clean up the kitchen. You got somethin' you want me to do that doesn't include washin' clothes or pushin' a vacuum, we'll talk. But, babe, you can get pissed, you can rant, you can try sweet, I am not washin' clothes and I'm not pushin' a vacuum. Do you understand me?"

Pulling the bitch aunt to Shy's future biker Cinderella card unfortunately worked, so I retorted, "Fine. I don't like pumpin' gas, therefore it'd be cool, when you use my car, if you would top her up."

"I can do that," he replied, lips twitching.

"And," I went on, not liking the lip twitch, "put your clothes in the hamper, not on the floor."

"Can do that too."

"And—"

"Tab, quit while you're ahead," he warned me.

"Not feelin' ahead of anything yet, darlin'," I shared.

"I'll pump gas, change your oil, get groceries, take care of the garbage, and dump my clothes in the hamper. Mind, I also do most of the cookin'," he reminded me. "That's what you got. You nag or bust my balls, I can dump my clothes wherever the fuck I want at my place or the Compound, and I won't have a woman gettin' up in my face about it."

Was he serious?

"Are you threatening me with leaving?" I asked.

"I'm sayin', quit while you're ahead," he returned.

"So you're threatening me with leaving," I surmised.

"I'm sayin', you want me here, you are in the know about the kind of man you picked. I laid it out. It's the way it is. If you don't like the way it is, I can make alternate arrangements."

"Therefore threatening to leave," I finished for him.

"You either want me like I am, babe, or yeah, I can find a place where I don't have hassle."

"Which, just for your information, Shy, would mean me having a home without the additional hassle of cleaning up after two people and doing two people's laundry."

"Yeah, sugar, you'd also go to bed alone with no one to eat your pussy," he retorted.

Since that nearly made my head explode, I decided, because he wouldn't clean it up if brain and skull fragments were splattered all over the living room, I should extricate myself from the conversation pronto.

This I did, grabbing the handles of the hamper, storming off, slamming the bedroom door behind me, making a lot of noise when I put away the clothes, then locking myself in the bathroom with my phone.

Of course, I hefted my behind up on the vanity, called Ty-Ty and shared with her, at length, about Shy and my fight.

This conversation didn't go much better.

"Tabby, honey," she started, using a cautious tone that made me brace, "your father has not vacuumed a floor in the years we've been together. To be honest, I haven't even asked. Kane Allen is not a man who vacuums floors."

"Well, I'm not you and Shy's not Dad and I didn't ask him to vacuum floors. We were negotiating and he cut me off before things were balanced and that's uncool," I fired back.

"No, you are not me, but Shy *is* Tack but younger, and I know this isn't what you want to hear but he's also not wrong. You've lived your whole life with your dad and his brothers, honey, so you also know it."

This sucked but it was true.

"Love you, Tabby," she went on quietly. "And I'll listen to anything you want to share with me. I'll also have a mind to not oversharing with you. What I will say is, there are a variety of ways your father makes putting up with all his extreme, uh... *man-ness* worth it. You need to hang in there and see if Shy makes it worth it."

I got her though I kinda blocked out some of the parts I got.

She was right, of course. Shy already made it worth it,

of course. But I was too stubborn to admit defeat (yet), of course.

I rang off with Ty-Ty, called Natalie (again), got no answer (again), and avoided Shy by hanging out in the bedroom until bedtime.

Or, I should say, I avoided Shy until Shy was done with me avoiding him.

I knew he was done, because he made this clear by walking into the bathroom while I was brushing my teeth. His hands at my hips, he turned me, lifted me, planted my behind on the vanity, pulled the toothbrush out of my hand, and tossed it into the sink.

Then he leaned into me, hands on the counter on either side of me, and ordered, "Stop bein' pissed. You know you don't give a fuck if I vacuum the fuckin' floors."

Truthfully, I didn't. Rush used to vacuum until I made him stop because he sucked at it. It wasn't like I didn't know this was his ploy. It was just that it wasn't worth the headache of calling him on it when I could just vacuum and be done with it. And I discovered it wasn't worth the headache because I'd spent years getting a headache calling him on it before I got smart, gave up, and just did it myself.

At that moment, however, I had a mouth full of toothpaste foam and face to save.

Priorities, I twisted, spit the foam in the sink, reached and grabbed the hand towel, wiped my mouth and tossed the towel on the counter.

Then I glared at him and shared, "Just so you know, there's really only one kind of biker. He might share his feelings, he might not. He might fuck around on his woman, he might not. He might carouse a *wee bit* more than is healthy, he might not. But down deep, a biker is a biker and I know you're a biker."

"All right, and...?" he prompted when I shut up and didn't keep going, so I kept going.

"There's only one kind of biker, Shy, but there are three kinds of old ladies. One lets her man walk all over her. One turns into a bitch like Mom or Mitzi. And one is like Tyra, who gives but also expects to get her take. I'm like Tyra. I'm not *Tyra*, but you should know, I've considered the options and chosen that biker-babe life plan. You don't wanna vacuum, I'm not gonna make you. But don't cut me off by making asshole remarks because you've decided the conversation is over. Respect me or, truthfully, I love you, you know it, you mean the world to me, but that will dig deep, fester, and there will come a time when I don't mind your clothes are on the floor at the Compound."

His face changed, I held my breath at the change as he growled, "There will never come a time when you don't mind my clothes are on the floor at the Compound."

A vow.

Absolutely.

Not an apology but I got him and I'd take it.

I was smart enough not to gloat.

"Right, so, I've brushed my teeth, you haven't, so you're free to eat something before you go to sleep," I declared. That intense look left his face, his eyes flashed with heat, then I was off the vanity, in the bedroom, tossed on the bed, my panties were gone, and Shy ate something before he went to sleep.

Truth was, I used my mouth before finally falling asleep too, but fortunately what I used it for wouldn't give me any cavities.

Also, before falling asleep, Shy proved he intended to make it worth it, and it wasn't by giving me two orgasms (or it wasn't only that).

It was by muttering right before I fell asleep, "Just so you know, babe, the kind of biker I am does not fuck around on his woman."

Other women might not think it was worth knowing she was the one who would be cleaning the toilets without a break for the rest of her life, but it worked for me.

That was the worst run-in we'd had. Although we'd butted heads a couple of times, it was nothing that sent me to fuming alone in my bedroom.

And in an effort to continue that run, I was not sharing with Shy about Dr. Dickhead.

Shy, like all the members of the Club, got a monthly cut of the profits from Ride Custom Car and Bikes as well as the three auto supply stores they ran, one in Denver, one in Colorado Springs, and one in Fort Collins. The boys moseyed their badasses into the store to work the counter, stock the shelves, keep the inventory, and those, like Shy, who had the skills worked in the garage on the cars and bikes. No one scheduled it but such was the loyalty to the brotherhood, not to mention their livelihood, no one sluffed off either.

The cut of profits was only graduated as to whether you were a full member or a recruit.

Every member had to pledge the Club and put up with however much crap the brothers made him do for however long they decided it lasted. Chaos wasn't into rules, so it wasn't like if they pledged, they'd be facing six months or a year and the boys knew when the torture would end, they'd get their cut, ink their tat on their back, and they could sally forth as full-fledged badasses. It was never six months or less, but it could be over a year before the boys sat down and voted a new man in.

And by crap they had to take from the members, I meant anything.

Anything.

And anything was really anything when you lived in a biker world.

So recruits got paid because they also worked in the store or the garage but they got paid less.

The Club made no distinction on pay according to terms of membership for full brothers. Although the cut went up and down with the profits, according to Shy, the checks tripled between recruit and member. The amounts, even in leaner months, were also not shabby.

This meant, with Shy keeping a low-profile apartment and not buying clothes for about six years, he was sitting on a mountain of money.

So Shy, like all the brothers, did his bit at the store and he also worked in the garage. As far as I could see, he pretty much did both in equal measure. Therefore, he didn't keep a schedule, he went when he went, came home when he was done working, but he was at Ride often.

He also did things with his brothers and for the Club in daylight hours and sometimes at night that he didn't share with me, and I knew enough about the life not to ask. No, strike that, *never* to ask. If he wanted me to know, he'd tell me. I'd heard my mom and dad fighting enough to learn that lesson.

I knew the Club was clean, Dad fought to make it that way.

But the golden rule for any Chaos old lady was to

take her man's back when needed, stand at his side when needed, ask no questions in order to get no lies, and know the goodness of her man outweighed the things he might need to do to keep the Club thriving. If she didn't follow this golden rule, she would find herself no longer an old lady.

In other words, Shy was around, we spent time together, we talked, we made love, we ate together, we watched TV together, but Shy also had his own life, his own things to do, and his own things on his mind, so not sharing about Dr. Dickhead had been successful.

"He still fuckin' with you?" Lan asked, and I focused from my thoughts onto him.

"It's his way," I tried to blow it off, but his eyes narrowed on me.

"Better or worse?"

"Depends on the day, Lan." I shook my head. "It's just him. He does it to everybody."

Though not as much as he does it to me, I thought, but didn't share.

"Not cool, you're quiet, off work, at a party with your man and family, and it's on your mind," Landon pushed.

He wasn't wrong.

Still, I shrugged again and muttered, "That's life."

He dropped his arm from around my shoulders and turned to me. "Tab, I know you wanna make sure you don't have a reputation as flighty or trouble at work, but if a bunch of folks are eatin' this guy's shit, maybe someone should do something. Maybe you can talk to a few of 'em, strength in numbers, so it isn't just you swingin' your ass out there."

That, actually, wasn't a bad idea.

So I nodded and replied, "I'll think about that. I know some of the other nurses are over it, so I'll talk with a few of them. Test the waters."

"You do that, honey, but you quit 'cause of things with Shy but also because you couldn't put up with that asshole anymore. I don't know if you told them then but even if it rubs you wrong, life's too short for that bullshit. So if you gotta look for another job, you do it no regrets. If they were loyal to you, they wouldn't let this guy fuck with your head. So you just be loyal to you, yeah? Find somethin' that won't make you quiet when you should be havin' fun. You with me?" he finished on a gentle question.

"I'm with you, Lan, thanks," I replied.

He grinned down and me and, seriously, Shy told me he didn't have a girl and I thought that was miraculous.

Then his eyes wandered over my shoulder and stopped. I looked over my shoulder, saw a big-boobed, full-hipped, big-haired, blonde biker groupie giving Lan the eye, and I knew it wasn't miraculous.

He was like his brother, chasing tail, enjoying gathering lipstick, but I suspected when he settled, he'd find ways to make his badass *man-ness* worth it.

"Right, Tab, gonna take you to my brother. I got things to do," he stated.

Oh yeah, he had things to do.

"Luckily, Shy's at my place all the time or I foresee I'd need to change his sheets," I mumbled through a grin as Lan hooked his arm around my shoulders and started us toward my man.

"Absolutely," he muttered, I looked up at him and gave him my grin.

He looked down at me and smiled.

Then he looked at his brother. "Your girl needs company."

His arm fell away.

Shy's replaced it instantly.

Then he pressed his lips to the top of my hair and kissed me.

Seriously. Loved my man.

Lan jerked up his chin, and I encouraged, "Go get her, tiger."

He shot me another smile, took off, and Shy asked, "What?"

"Landon is about to see if he's lucky," I shared.

Shy's eyes went to his brother and mine followed. The girl was looking under her lashes at him as he approached. Lan was grinning at her.

Something caught the corner of my eye, I turned my head and saw, in the shadows at the edge of the revelry, Hop dragging Lanie toward the Compound. He had her hand in his and was definitely dragging her, but her high-heeled boots were moving double time and she didn't appear to be struggling.

Quickly, I scanned the crowd and saw Tyra laughing with Big Petey, her back to the Compound. She still had no clue.

But I also saw Dad, and I knew he had a clue seeing as he was following Hop and Lanie with his eyes, his mouth tight. I knew my dad's looks and that one didn't say angry, it said impatient.

My gaze went back to the doors of the Compound to see that Hop and Lanie had disappeared inside.

Them keeping things under wraps confused me. They were both consenting adults, and Lanie wasn't anyone's daughter.

But in that moment, I found that I hoped like hell that worked out for them, no matter how, on the face of it, it never could, what with Hop being a rough and ready badass biker and Lanie being chic and sophisticated.

I hoped this because, after all that happened to Lanie, she was still Lanie. Crazy. Fun. But there was something off about her that I found troubling, and I knew Ty-Ty worried about it and even Dad did too.

Also, I didn't think she'd had one single man since she lost Elliott. Not one. And it had been *years*. For a woman as beautiful, crazy, fun, not to mention sweet as Lanie, that was sad. She deserved a good man in her life that could make her happy.

And Hop was a good man, no matter the ugliness of his break with Mitzi and that business with BeeBee. I'd known him a long time. I knew he would never go there with Lanie, knowing who she was to Ty-Ty, if he didn't intend to do right by her.

Further, like good women, good men deserved happiness. So Hop deserved all the crazy, fun, sweet, beauty Lanie could give him.

Staring at the Compound door, I sent invisible good vibes to two people I cared about that they'd find happiness together.

And, of course, that what they were doing wouldn't tick off Dad and Ty-Ty too much.

"He's lucky," Shy muttered, taking my mind off Lanie and Hop, and bringing my attention back to Landon and the biker groupie close in each other's space, and I mentally agreed. Then Shy's lips came to my ear. "I'm gonna be lucky in about five minutes too."

All thoughts of Lanie, Hop, Landon, and his groupie

fled, a shiver went over my skin but I turned my head and caught his eye. "You are?"

"Time it takes me to walk you to my room, yeah, I am," he whispered.

Another shiver, then, "But we haven't even started raisin' hell."

"Somethin's gonna rise but it won't be hell."

I knew that.

It would be paradise.

I grinned.

He bent his head and brushed his lips against mine.

Five minutes later, in his room in the Compound, Shy got lucky.

* * *

"At the risk of pissin' you off, gotta share. More than once in the last five years, laid on my back in this bed, my hand on my dick, thinkin' of you doin' what you just did to me."

That did not, in any way, piss me off.

It turned me on.

I lifted my head from his shoulder and looked down into his green eyes.

"What else did you think of me doin'?" I asked quietly, my legs shifting restlessly.

His eyes went to the ceiling. "Got her off, seconds later, she's rarin' to go again."

"It's been minutes, Shy," I pointed out, he aimed his eyes at mine and grinned at me.

Then his grin faded and he declared, "Right, before we tear each other up again, gotta talk to you about something."

I registered the grin fade, sensed his mood, and therefore melted into him.

"Okay," I said softly.

"Boys voted. We're takin' on the mountains."

I felt my brows draw together. "Pardon?"

"Expanding Ride, sugar. Boz and Brick went out, scouted locations. Durango or Grand Junction. It's lookin' like it'll probably be Grand Junction. We're movin' out of just havin' places along the Front Range and opening a new shop out west."

I smiled and cried, "Wow! That's cool!"

His lips twitched and he replied, "Yeah."

I studied him. His lips twitched but I got the sense he wasn't committed to his "yeah."

So I asked, "What's on your mind, darlin'?"

Shy didn't hesitate to share. "Brick, Dog, and Boz are goin' out next week, makin' the final decisions on the locations we might buy. They'll bring the info on the options to the Club, big meeting. All the boys from Fort Fun and C. Springs will come to town, we vote on one, it's a go. Dog and Brick have already volunteered to up stakes, head out, and oversee start-up. We'll be findin' new recruits, gettin' 'em started, since more boys will be needed when the store is up and running. Bat, Arlo, and Tug have already made it clear they're good to go out and be part of that team. Leaves us down in numbers, so it's time to build the Club."

I nodded.

Shy kept talking.

"Brick and Dog both say already they wanna stay in the mountains for a while, change of scenery."

"Right," I prompted.

"That means Tack's losin' his lieutenants."

My heart flipped.

"Right," I said again but this time slowly.

"Deal's done. Those two brothers are goin' and gonna be gone at least a year, probably more. So Tack is makin' decisions. He asked Hop to step up when they go."

My shoulders drooped.

"He also asked me," Shy finished.

My face split into a grin, Shy's eyes dropped to my mouth then he rolled me so I was on my back and he was up on a forearm, looming over me but bent so our faces were close.

His other hand framed the side of my head and his thumb slid along my hairline when he muttered, "Don't get excited, babe."

"But that's cool. That's respect. That's an honor, Shy."

"Yeah. It is," he agreed. "But you gotta get that, for you, that also means I might not be around as much. It isn't like Dog and Brick are called to duty daily, but they got extra shit to do the other brothers do not."

"Okay." Again I said this slowly and when he didn't speak, I asked, "What aren't you saying, honey?"

"Not sure I wanna do it."

I blinked.

Then I asked, "What?" I paused, but before he could speak I asked, "Why?"

He sighed, looked at my throat, then looked back at me as his hand drifted down to curl around the side of my neck. "My commitment to the Club is there. My commitment to the brothers..."

He let that hang and didn't go on but my stomach tied in a knot.

"Really?" I asked quietly.

"Really," he answered firmly.

The knot in my stomach twisted.

"Are you thinking of leaving the Club?" I forced out.

"Absolutely not."

Well thank God for that.

"Okay, then, why?" I queried. "Why are you questioning your commitment to the men?"

He shook his head and looked at the pillow beside mine. "Thought I could, couldn't."

"Couldn't what?"

He looked back at me. "Do not wanna drag you over old ground when shit is good, babe, but not one of them took my back when it went down and they found out about you and me. They made their calls, they patched things over, but I didn't forget it, and I find they want more of me, I'm thinkin' they gotta prove respect before I give it back."

I beat back the urge to lick my lip before I asked, "Do you have issues with Dad?"

He shook his head. "Fuck no."

At least that was firm.

Shy kept talking. "He had his reason and it was a good one. Them, parts of it I see, parts of it I don't. Not one of them spoke up for me. That went down, I wasn't a recruit. It wasn't like I'd been in the Club two years, three, but near on a decade. They knew me and no one spoke for me?"

He shook his head but went on.

"Gotta say, your dad feelin' that for me, thinkin' I got what it takes to handle shit for the Club in his stead when he calls on me, speakin' for him, the Club when they need me, that's tight. I like it. That's a tribute I didn't expect, not at my age. I know the history with him and High.

High seriously butted up against him when Tack was tryin' to clean up the Club. Luckily, that shit got sorted but I know Tack didn't forget, so I know why he doesn't go there when High's got more time in with the Club than me. I know Hound can go off on one, doesn't have the disposition for diplomacy. Still, he could stick with Hop, have only one man he calls on and he called me up. I like that. But I'm thinkin' I need more time with the brothers, I need it to feel solid again before I give more back."

"Okay, then take your time," I agreed and his head gave a slight jerk.

"Say again?"

"I feel you," I told him. "It's not like you're being a dick. You're being real. You're right, that was uncool. Hop spoke for you when you came forward to recruit. He's also totally nailing Lanie, still, and, by the way, Dad saw them going at it by the garage, so that cat's gonna be out of the bag soon. So he knows the shoes you were standing in. Roscoe and Tug did their time at your side, not one of those three put words forward for you when they all should, Hop especially. If you need to feel more solid, do it. Take your time. If Dad chooses another lieutenant, High isn't trustworthy, Hound is possibly clinically insane, Dad may soon be looking to fill those motorcycle boots and Chaos will feel it if those men don't represent their brothers well. When it's your time again, they'll be ready for you, but you need to be ready to give it to them."

He studied me a beat before asking softly, "You're not ticked I'm turnin' down your dad?"

"It's your time, your life, your standing with your brothers, honey. Your decision. My job is to stand by it, not get ticked about it."

He studied me for five beats before he whispered, "Fuck, but I love you, Tabby."

I grinned. "Good, darlin'. That works for me since I love you too."

Shy did not grin. His thumb moved out to stroke my jaw as his eyes burned into mine.

I lifted a hand, curled it around his wrist, let him have his moment, and enjoyed the warmth he was giving me.

Then he was done with his moment, his brows went up, and he asked, "Tack saw Hopper and Lanie?"

I smiled and answered, "Yep."

"Brace, baby," he muttered.

"I guessed that," I told him.

"No, *brace*. Cherry knows about Hop and BeeBee. Apparently, Cherry actually saw them doin' the deed, which is somethin' I do not wanna picture."

I curled my lip in disgust because it was something I didn't want to picture either.

Shy continued, "Cherry doesn't know Hop and Mitzi were on a break, but I don't think she'd care. Hop had a chat with her and she and him have moved past that, but that doesn't mean she's gonna be big on him bangin' her best friend, who happens to be the woman who took bullets for her dead old man."

Well, that might explain why they were keeping things under wraps.

Shy kept going, "Until tonight, Hop has managed to keep this from Tack and Cherry, but most of the boys know, they're talkin', and they're bettin'. The odds are with Cherry losin' her mind not only with Hop, but with Lanie for makin' what she thinks is another poor choice."

My head tipped on the pillow. "Did you place a bet?"

"Fuck no. Lanie is beautiful but she's a fuckin' nut. There's no guarantees with her in the mix, and Hop's not sayin' it, but he's gone for her. I caught sight of them late one night standin' by his bike and I can't say I'm an expert at readin' bitches but, body language, she's gone for him too. Cherry or Tack get in his face, Cherry butts up against Lanie, there's gonna be fireworks."

"Well, we're old hands at that," I muttered, and Shy grinned.

"Bet it's more fun observing," he muttered back.

I was not going to take that bet because I knew he was right.

"He's gone for her?" I asked quietly.

"Had a dad who loved his wife. See what Tack has with Cherry. Dog and Sheila. Feel what I have with you. When they're together and not yellin' at each other, that's what I see."

I felt my chest get warm.

There it was, maybe they didn't need my invisible vibes. If Hop was "gone" for Lanie, he'd do right by her.

Or at least I hoped so.

"I like that for Lanie," I told Shy.

"And I like it for Hop, baby. Mitzi was a bitch. Lanie'll keep him on his toes, but if they have those tender times, it's worth it."

It *so* was.

"Yeah," I whispered.

"Yeah," he quietly repeated after me.

I slid my hand down his back. "So, if we're done talking, are you gonna tell me what you thought of me doing while you were lyin' in this bed?"

His face got dark as it got closer.

"Definitely."

I tightened my arm around him, using it to press my body up into his, and I whispered, "How about you show me what you did while you tell me?"

His eyes flared, his mouth moved to mine, and he replied, "My girl wants it like that, that's what she'll get."

Awesome. I not only wanted it like that, I . . . couldn't . . . *wait.*

"Though, sugar, I'm ready for you to climb on, you swing astride me. I'm finishing in you," he ordered.

I grinned against his mouth.

I could do that.

CHAPTER SIXTEEN

It's Me

Four days later…

I WAS AT the nurse's station reaching for a chart when I heard, "Ms. Allen, may I have a moment to speak with you?"

I knew that voice. My back went straight, I turned to look up and my mouth dropped open.

Dr. Dickhead was standing there, eyes to my shoulder, his face messed way the heck up. We were talking *massive.* Both eyes black, blue, and very swollen, a bandage on the bridge of his engorged, reddened nose, fat lip with three angry cuts and yellowish bruising around both of his cheekbones.

Oh God.

"I, um… of course," I said quietly, my gaze skimming through my colleague, Peggy, who was sitting behind the desk at the nurse's station and who also was staring at Dr. Dickhead with an expression on her face that I was certain mirrored mine.

I turned back to Dr. Dickhead to see him extending an

arm for me to precede him. I moved, he shifted to let me by, and I noticed that he was holding his body very carefully.

Shy had fucked him up.

Shy had totally fucked him up!

Oh God.

My mind blanked of everything but walking as he guided me to an empty patient's room. I walked into the room and he followed, closing the door behind him.

Eyes to my shoulder, he launched in, "I want you to know I apologize for my behavior. I've had some problems at home, I took them out on you, and that's inappropriate. From now on, I'll be more mindful of how I treat you and, erm... all the nurses, and be certain to show you more respect."

Yep, Shy so totally fucked him up.

"I, uh... okay," I whispered.

His eyes slid to mine then quickly moved away and he asked, "Is that acceptable to you?"

"Um... yes, uh... that would be great."

"Excellent," he muttered. "I appreciate your time."

"Well, uh..." God! What did I say? "Thanks for that."

Lame!

He extended his chin, winced, hid the wince, turned while holding his body stiffly and opened the door.

It swung closed behind him and I stood there staring at it.

I didn't know what to do about this, and I didn't know what to feel about it. I just knew, at that very moment, it felt weird and not in a good way. I also knew I had three hours to the end of my shift and I couldn't do anything about it until then.

When I hit the nurse's station, Peggy was still there, her eyes still wide, she leaned in and asked, "What was *that* about?"

"Uh, something about a patient. No biggie," I lied.

She looked down the hall, obviously where she'd last seen Dr. Dickhead and asked, "Do you have any clue how he got that messed up?"

Oh yeah, I did. I totally did.

"He didn't share that," I told her. Fortunately it was the truth (in a way) and she looked back at me and grinned.

She was loving this. Yes, that was how big a douchebag he was.

"I bet he didn't," she muttered.

I pulled up enough professionalism to move on with my day and it was only when I was walking to my car that I took my phone out, my thumb moving on the screen, automatically calling Shy.

I put it to my ear and within a ring, I heard Shy's, "Sugar."

"Where are you?"

He didn't answer immediately and when he did, his tone was quiet.

He'd read me.

"Where do you want me to be?"

I stopped at the door of my car, pointed my eyes to my shoes, and said, "That didn't answer my question, Shy."

"I'm at the Compound, havin' a drink with the brothers."

Okay, not home. That was good.

Maybe I could get my thoughts sorted before he got home.

"Tab?" he called when I said nothing.

"I'm here."

"You okay?"

No, I wasn't. I just didn't know what I was.

"Sure," I lied.

"Tabby—" he started.

"Listen, uh... it's been a hectic day. I'm standing outside my car. I just wanna get home. I'll see you when I see you, yeah?"

"Tabby—" he began again, but I cut him off.

"Later, Shy."

I ended the call, got in my car, started her up, and ignored the two times my phone rang on the way home.

I was in jeans, a long-sleeved Harley tee, bare feet, had my hair up in a sloppy ponytail and my head in the fridge to get a much-needed beer (though, I was thinking more along the tequila lines) when Shy got home.

I twisted from the fridge to look at him and saw his face was serious, his eyes intense and they were on me.

I closed the door to the fridge coming out with my beer, taking two steps away from the fridge and deeper into the kitchen, I asked, "You want one?"

He walked into the kitchen, stopped and his eyes moved over my face.

Then he said quietly, "No. I want you to talk to me."

"Shy—"

It was his turn to cut me off.

"Tab, heard it in your voice, see it all over your face. Somethin's up and I figure I know what that somethin' is. Now, talk to me. Why are you lookin' at me like you're lookin' at me right now?"

Okay, suffice it to say I hadn't got my head sorted before he got home.

It would have been nice to have the chance to do that, but with the way Shy was looking at me, I knew I wasn't going to get that chance.

So I whispered, "You beat up Dr. Dickhead."

"Yeah," he copped to it immediately.

I blinked.

Shy shook his head then spoke. "Babe, we may not be an old married couple but we got a lot of time in and, just pointin' out, at first, I was into you so I paid attention. Then I was fallin' in love with you so I paid more attention. Then I was in love with you, so I figure you get where it went from there. What I'm sayin is, I know you. I know you were keepin' shit from me. I also know why. And last, I know that motherfucker was fuckin' with your life and it was bad, because I sensed your mood and it was deteriorating. After the hog roast, Lan had a word with me and what he said sealed it, so I did what I'd been thinkin' of doin' for a while. Somethin', I'll add, that needed to be done."

That was debatable, but I decided it best at that juncture not to debate it.

"You didn't talk to me about it," I told him.

"No, I didn't," he told me. "But I told you flat out what I'd do to that asshole if he didn't leave you alone."

"You didn't even tell me after you'd done it," I kept fighting my corner.

"No, I didn't," he repeated, and again said no more.

Crap.

"I'm not sure how I feel about that, Shy. This affects me, my work—"

Shy interrupted me, "He apologize?"

I was losing it, therefore my voice rose when I answered, "Yes, but that's not the point."

Shy crossed his arms on his chest and his voice went low when he replied, "Oh yeah, it is."

"Shy—"

"This is not a surprise to you, Tabby," he stated low. "It's not a surprise but it's a shock, and I know on the face of it that doesn't make sense, but I also know you get me."

I stared at him and kept my distance.

Shy didn't miss much and he didn't miss this. We were the kind of couple that got close. Even shuffling around the kitchen, we touched, brushed mouths, stood near when we were both doing something at the counter.

So he didn't miss the unusual distance I was putting between us. He also didn't approach.

What he did was order, "You take time to come to terms with this. You need me to help you, I'm there. Now, I'm gonna give you time alone to sort your head out. Not much, we're sleepin' together, we're wakin' up together, so now you got a sense of how much time you got. Use it wisely, honey. This is me, you knew that was what you were gonna get, you can't expect me not to be me and I'm not gonna lose you over somethin' as meaningless as that douchebag."

On that, he gave me a long look and sauntered with his tall, loose-limbed biker grace to and through the door.

I sucked in breath.

Then I moved to the phone with only one person on my mind.

My dad's rough voice came at me after one ring. "How's my girl?"

"Dad, I need to talk to you."

He didn't answer immediately and when he did, his tone was quiet.

"You had dinner?"

"No."

"Buyin' my girl dinner. See you at Lincoln's in twenty."

"Okay," I agreed.

Twenty minutes later, I walked into Lincoln's Road House, a biker bar off a slip road on I-25 that doubled as a neighborhood watering hole. I didn't know how they managed to mix bikers, booze, and often live music with the staunchly middle-class 'hood that surrounded the joint, but they did it. Likely because the food was good, the waitresses were friendly, and the music, when they had it, was great. Not to mention, Denver was eclectic and folks were used to rubbing shoulders with just about anyone. It was one of the reasons I loved my town.

I saw Dad sitting at the bar with a beer, and his eyes were on me the moment I came through the door. I moved through the bar, slid my bottom up on the stool beside him, and plopped my purse in front of me.

His eyes moved over my face then they moved to the bartender. He jerked up his chin and waved a hand toward the beer in front of him.

Nonverbal badass speak for, *Get my daughter a beer.*

The bartender clearly spoke badass because he got me a beer. I took a pull, put the bottle on the bar, and looked at Dad.

"Talk to me," he demanded.

"Shy beat up a doctor at work who was giving me a hard time."

Yep, that was what came straight out.

"No, he didn't," Dad stated, and I stared.

After staring awhile, I asked, "He didn't?"

Dad shook his head. "Nope." He lifted his beer, took a

pull, put it back on the bar, and looked at me. "Shy, Roscoe, and Hop fucked him up. Not just Shy."

Oh my God!

Three of them?

I leaned in and hissed, "Are you serious?"

"Yep."

I sat back and threw up my hands. "Already, it was bad. That's totally overkill. No wonder he was totally messed up."

"Not overkill, Tabby," Dad told me and I glared at him.

"Dad, he's a doctor. They do that shit. It wasn't that big of a deal, and by the way, I was *dealing*."

"No, they don't do that shit. Not to my girl and, obviously, not to Shy's old lady. An old lady doesn't *deal*, darlin', she breathes easy."

I hated it when these bikers had good, albeit lunatic, answers for statements that had no good answers.

I didn't give up. "Okay then, Dad, he's a doctor, not a heavyweight fighter. Three guys? That's insane!"

"Not insane either, Tabby."

"Dad!" I snapped and he leaned in, his voice going low.

"Lesson," he started and I drew in a sharp, annoyed breath but at his tone, a tone I'd heard often in my life, I knew to shut my mouth. "You do somethin', you do it right and you do it so there's no blowback."

There it was again. *Blowback*. A word which I was beginning to think they didn't really know the meaning of, but since it was a brand-new word coined by, my guess, Hollywood, perhaps it hadn't made it to the dictionary.

My eyes narrowed.

Dad kept talking.

"To make his point Shy needed firepower and he needed presence to make certain that weasel didn't hightail his ass to the cops. Shy needed to make certain all his messages were clear. Those messages being, one, he does not fuck with you. Two, he does not fuck with the other nurses. Three, he does, Shy's got the backing to fuck him up worse than he did during his first lesson. Four, he does not go to the cops and report the assault or he buys Chaos displeasure. Shy's lean but he's tall, fast, smart, and he's got one fuckuva power punch. He could have taken care of that asshole on his own but if he did, he wouldn't get his point across." Dad dipped his head to me. "He did it smart, doin' what he had to do to get his point across, and he got his point across."

I ignored Dad knowing Shy had "one fuckuva power punch" and, more to the point, how he might come about that knowledge and instead, snapped, "I'll repeat, that's insane!"

Dad's brows went up. "He apologize?"

Oh. My. *God!*

Ty-Ty was totally right. Shy *was* Dad, just younger.

"Yeah, he did, but that isn't the point," I answered. "Shy didn't talk to me about it and, I'll add, he didn't tell me about it after the fact either."

Dad's face registered surprise and he asked, "Jesus, why would he do somethin' stupid like that?"

I stared at my father.

Then I replied sarcastically, "I don't know, maybe because it's *me*"—I jerked my thumb at my chest—"who has to work with this guy."

"Bet that'll go better," he muttered.

I rolled my eyes.

"Thinkin'," Dad continued, "we're gettin' in the zone where you should be talkin' to Red."

"Well, Tyra isn't here, so you're going to have to guide me through this one, Dad," I pointed out, and Dad's gaze locked to mine.

"He loves you."

I sucked in breath as that hit me in the gut.

Dad was far from done.

"He loves you, Tabby. Boy's totally gone for you. He don't like you eatin' shit, he can do somethin' about it, so he did. He let you have your time to sort it, let you have your time to stew about it, but you didn't make a move, so he did."

"But—" I started, but Dad shook his head.

"This is the life. It's the only thing you know. It's different, when you're a kid, you're shielded from a lot of shit but that don't mean, darlin', that you don't feel the umbrella of protection that Club provides to family. I know my girl's not dumb, she's not gonna sit there and tell me she doesn't know every brother in that Club was willin' to have her back every breath she took on this earth. Now, you got a different position in the Club, one you chose, one you fought for. You're still shielded but you are no longer a kid. You're an adult and you're puttin' things together and you now are seein' how they can directly affect you. Do not fall down at this first hurdle with your man. As his woman, you got a job, that's to let him be who he is and do what he feels he's gotta do. You find common ground in your home with the life you live together day to day. But what it takes to make him the man he is, you give him."

I pulled in another breath.

Dad still wasn't done.

"That other guy, your Jason, I liked him."

Another hit to the gut, and I pressed my lips together.

Dad kept talking, his tone gentle, his eyes on me the same.

"He loved you. I liked the way he treated you, liked the way he looked at you, liked the way he handled you. I hated you losin' him. But I'll say this, what Shy did to that asshole who was makin' work an unhealthy place for you to be, I like more. You asked me five years ago what I'd want in my daughter's life, I'd pick a man like Shy. I told him that after we had our fallin' out. And, as far's I'm concerned, him steppin' in and sortin' your problem, Tabby, darlin', proves I was right."

One could not say I didn't like his words (as lunatic as they were).

Still, I turned my head away and took a drag of my beer.

I was contemplating it in my hand when I heard Dad order, "Cajun popcorn and two meatloaf cheeseburgers. We're eatin' at the bar."

Well, at least dinner was going to be awesome.

I sucked back more beer.

"Tab," Dad said, and I looked to him just as his hand came up, curled around the back of my neck, and his face got close. "You made the conscious choice to step back into our world. You live here again with all of us. And you made that commitment when you took on the Club and Red and me to have Shy. You knew what you were gettin'. You can't pick the parts you want and force out the parts that make you uncomfortable. He is the man he is. With men like us, you accept him as that or you don't take him at all. You gotta decide, what's it gonna be?"

"I love him," I whispered, and his eyes lit immediately as he smiled.

"Then that's what it's gonna be."

I sighed.

Dad pulled my head to his, tipping it down and he kissed the top of my hair. Then he let me go, turned to the bartender and ordered us another round of beers.

I guessed that was that, that was how it was going to be, and I knew my guess was right.

Dad was not dumb.

I made my choice and that was how it was going to be, and sitting next to Dad I realized, really, after the shock wore off, I wouldn't have wanted it any other way.

* * *

Two hours later, I walked into my apartment to see Shy on his back on the couch, one leg bent, bare foot in the seat, the other leg to the side of the couch so his foot was resting on the floor.

His head was turned, eyes on me.

I walked to the back of the armchair and threw my purse on the seat.

"Come here, Tabby," he ordered gently.

I went there.

When I got close, he grabbed my hand, pulled me closer, so I put a knee on the couch between his legs, moved in and settled on him, hips between his legs, chest to chest, cheek to shoulder.

His arms curled around me.

"Where you been?" he asked, still quiet.

"Dinner with Dad," I answered, and got an arm squeeze.

Then I got a murmured "Good choice."

I sighed.

It was. Then again, Dad was always a good choice.

"Get your head straight?" Shy asked.

"Yeah," I answered.

He was silent a beat, then he wrapped his arms tighter around me and stated, "You got that, let's get it all."

Uh-oh.

Shy continued, "You fuck up food more than you don't. You talk a lot. Coupla days before your period, sugar, you can get bitchy. It is not lost on me the way you slam the toilet seat down when I leave it up. That statement you intend to make without usin' the words is clear. And no one should get as ticked as you do that I don't rinse out my beer bottles before puttin' them in the recycle bin."

I didn't really like where this was going.

And, seriously, you didn't rinse stuff out before throwing it in the bin, that made the bin stink. Who'd want that?

When he stopped talking, I prompted with a slow "Okay."

Shy went on, "I get all that's you. I love you, so I've decided, instead of findin' it annoying, to find it cute. 'Cause it's you. So that's what it is. Cute. Except the part when you're bitchy 'cause you're goin' on the rag, but that has more to do with the fact I'm gonna lose your pussy for a few days and that is not my favorite time of the month."

Okay, well, I liked all that and I was with him.

Still, I said to his throat, "Beating someone up isn't cute, Shy."

"No, but it's me."

He was not wrong about that.

I pulled in breath in order to help that thought settle. When it settled, I shifted and kissed his throat.

His arms got tighter around me, and I figured that statement was clear too.

"He was fuckin' with you, Tabby. Anyone fucks with you, I'm steppin' in and I'm gonna do it how I feel it needs to be done. This time, I gave you time. I'll warn you now, I might not give you time if it happens again. All I need is for you to understand where I'm at and roll with me."

"I'll roll with you," I agreed and got another squeeze.

"I'll also say that I gave you the option of goin' quiet about it this time 'cause we're still gettin' used to each other. But, sugar, in future, I'll have a lot less patience with you goin' into your head and keepin' shit from me. And the only way I can think to get that across is to ask you to think about how you'd feel if I did the same to you. Somethin' important was goin' down, I didn't let you in, give you a chance to help me deal even if I eventually decide not to deal the way you advise me to deal, how would you feel?"

I wouldn't feel good, that was for sure. I'd want the chance to help him deal, but more, I'd want him to trust me to do that.

When I said nothing, he asked, "Did I get that across to you?"

"Yeah," I answered.

Shy went quiet.

I did too.

Then I told him, "You were there but, just sayin', I saw the aftermath and he was totally fucked up."

"Had a point to make, didn't fuck around. I made it," Shy muttered.

He certainly did that.

"Peggy thought it was a hoot," I shared. "I didn't know she was so bloodthirsty. She told everyone about it. She's dying to know what happened."

Shy was speaking with humor now when he said, "Least somebody got off on it."

"Yeah," I mumbled.

Shy again went quiet and I did too, tipping my chin to stare at the TV.

My body was settling deeper into his, relaxing when Shy asked softly, "We good?"

I slid my arm around him, tucking it tight and I replied just as softly, "Yeah, we're good."

"Good," he murmured.

Again, I sighed.

There it was. No going back. I just went through the unofficial ceremony.

I was an old lady.

Just like with anything in life, there was good and bad. To get the former, you put up with the latter. So I decided, bottom line, Dr. Dickhead was clearly not going to mess with me anymore, and although the path to that eventuality was not paved with stuff that made me want to do cartwheels, that journey, at least, was over.

Minutes slid by as this settled deep before Shy called, "Sugar?"

"Yeah," I answered, now sounding drowsy, and this wasn't a surprise. Two beers, Lincoln's for dinner, Dad's wisdom, and a life epiphany were a great recipe for a good night's sleep.

"Got a lock on a house."

I blinked, suddenly not even close to drowsy. I lifted my head and looked at him. "Pardon?"

His chin was dipped down so his eyes were on me. "Got a lock on a house. In Englewood. Little bungalow. Big yard. Three bedrooms. Great deck. Two-car garage, big enough to fit both our vehicles and my bike. I wanna take you to have a look at it."

"Like... *to buy*?" I asked.

"Yeah," he answered.

"Um... I don't have—"

"I do."

"A down payment?"

"Yeah, and enough left over to get some shit, make one bedroom an office, another a guest room for when Lan comes up, deck furniture, a grill. The fridge isn't all that great, so we'll get a new one."

"Shy, I—"

"This place is too small," he told me.

He wasn't wrong about that. I liked our togetherness though, in my apartment, it was kind of a forced togetherness. It must be said, it was also time for both of us to move up accommodation-wise. I was a nurse. He was essentially a partner in a highly successful business venture. There was no reason we weren't looking to be on the property ladder and no excuse for us not to be in something that was nicer. Furthermore, he was never at his apartment and essentially kept it so Lan could sleep there when he came to visit, which was a total waste of money.

"Okay," I said softly, and he grinned.

"Okay."

Then he lifted his head and touched his mouth to mine.

When he settled his head back against the toss pillow, I settled my cheek back to his shoulder and aimed my eyes at the TV.

More minutes slid by and he stated offhandedly, "Haven't had a home in sixteen years."

I closed my eyes tight.

I saw the boxes in his apartment. The bed in the living room. The old TV at the end of his bed. I heard his voice saying he mostly crashed at the Compound and I knew that to be true.

I opened my eyes and replied, going for offhanded but my voice was husky, “Then let’s get you a home.”

“Sounds good to me, baby,” he muttered back on another arm squeeze.

Yeah, he was right.

A home with Shy.

The opportunity to make it a good one for him.

That sounded good to me.

CHAPTER SEVENTEEN

Blowback

Two and a half weeks later . . .

It was after work and I was walking to my car.

I had my mind on a bunch of things. Christmas shopping. Furniture shopping. Dinner. The fact I needed to get to the Laundromat. What Shy and I were going to do with Rider and Cut that weekend, since we were watching them because Tyra and Dad were heading off to someplace in the mountains for a weekend away. The conversation I'd had with my brother three days before, when he told me Dad had called a meeting and Rush was now the newest recruit for Chaos. I was elated about this, but Rush still seemed conflicted, though he didn't share. What he did do (surprisingly) was go off for a beer with Shy.

When Shy came back, he didn't share either but he did say, "He's close. Lives the life, not the edge of it, he'll get closer."

I decided to leave it at that, since the way Shy said that meant I needed to leave it at that.

I'd also viewed the bungalow that Shy had scouted for

us and, unfortunately, I didn't like it. Mostly because the bedrooms were too small, it didn't have a master bath, and I just didn't like the feel of it because it didn't have stairs. It didn't even have a basement.

I shared this with Shy and he didn't get pissed.

He just pulled me to him and said against the top of my hair, "Needs to be right for the both of us, honey."

So totally loved my man.

Even though the first place didn't work out, I was now on a mission to make Shy a home, so I spent every available minute looking at places online.

Shy clearly was on the same mission since he came home last week saying he'd scouted two more places. I looked up their pictures on the Internet. They looked awesome, so we didn't delay in going to see them.

The bad news was, I loved the first one but Shy hated it, and even at that early juncture, I had begun to despair we wouldn't find a happy medium.

The fantastic news was, we both totally dug the second one. It was perfect. So we put an offer in. Shy negotiated like he bought houses for a living, we got a good price, and we put the deposit down.

All was a go.

I was totally excited.

Shy was too, I could tell. It was badass-biker excited but it was still excited.

I was also excited about Christmas. I loved Christmas, loved it more when I had two little brothers to buy for, and now I had a feeling I was *totally* going to love giving Christmas to Shy.

It went without saying that since life wasn't good at his bitchy aunt's house, Christmases weren't much better. So

I got to give something for Christmas, not only to Shy but also to Lan, that they hadn't had in a long time.

Real, honest-to-goodness family.

These were my happy thoughts as I settled in my car, and I was about to start her up when my phone rang. I pulled it out of my purse and took the call.

"Hey, darlin'," I greeted Shy.

"Where are you?"

My stomach dropped.

He sounded pissed.

No, strike that, he sounded *furious*.

"In my car, ready to drive home," I told him cautiously. "Is everything okay?"

"Drive to the Compound, babe," he ordered, paused a scary pause then finished, "*Now,*" and hung up.

I looked at my phone wondering what on earth was happening. He didn't sound furious as in, furious in general or furious at someone else.

He sounded furious *at me*.

I didn't get this. Things were good. I hadn't done anything that I could think of that would make him angry or not *that* angry. Since the big to-do with Shy and the boys over beating up Dr. Dickhead, all was cool.

I mean, we did have that conversation about how I really wished he'd put the seat down (and the lid) on the toilet but he'd grinned through that, and since then, only once (yeah, I counted) he left the seat up.

He listened. He got me. He made an effort. So it couldn't be that. And anyway, if Shy was that pissed about the toilet seat, then I'd put the danged thing down myself.

As I started my baby up with shaking hands, my mind moving feverishly, I couldn't think of anything it could be.

I drove carefully to the Compound, considering I was freaking and although I wasn't all fired up to find out how I'd ticked Shy off so royally, I wanted to figure it out and move on.

I turned into Ride, drove through the forecourt and parked outside the Compound seeing there were a goodly number of bikes there, which was surprising. The boys tended to be busy, out and about, not all of them at the Compound at once unless they had to be. It was like they were having a meeting and instinctively I did not see this as a good sign.

I also saw a big, black, shiny Ford Explorer.

Tyra's car, however, was not to be seen.

I didn't take this as a good sign either. Tyra should be at work, unless she was told, for some reason, to clear out.

I got out of my car and moved toward the Compound, hoping, if Shy had words for me, he'd take me to his room rather than lighting into me in front of the guys. That would only serve to piss me off, and I had a feeling one of us needed to be calm.

I walked in and saw I was right. The boys were all there.

All of them.

I stopped dead when I realized, possibly, though it had to be said I didn't get it, why Shy was ticked.

Lee Nightingale was standing in the middle of the room.

Although I'd had my conversation with Natalie about hiring Lee Nightingale and his team of badasses to find Shy's parents' killer and was rethinking things, I still took the meeting mostly because it took so long to get it in the first place, and if I changed my mind back, I didn't want to wait another six weeks.

The meeting with Nightingale verified all my worries. Lee Nightingale and his team cost a lot, and not just hourly. They also charged expenses.

That said, I was there so I sallied forth, gave him my story and his face got kinda scary. He then told me he knew my dad, knew Shy, and he'd "look into shit" (his words). I told him I wasn't comfortable with him "looking into shit" unless I paid him. So we made a deal. I gave him a retainer which was the totality of my savings, and that wasn't dinky. I'd been putting money in and not taking it out since Dad took me to the bank to set up my savings account when I was eleven. I'd meant to use it to help set up the house I would share with Jason, which didn't come about. I then lamented losing it because it would have helped with the down payment on the house I bought with Shy and I would have felt better, doing my part. Alas, by then, it was gone.

So we made our deal, Lee told me they'd look into shit, keep track of time and expenses, and call me when the money ran out.

Not surprisingly, since the case was very cold, ages ago he'd called me and told me the money had run out.

Therefore, I thought it was over. It was disappointing and perhaps a stupid waste of money, but I held on to the fact that I tried to do something important for Shy, something huge, even though it didn't work out and he'd never know I did it.

Now, taking in the room, the vibe, all of the angry eyes on me, including Shy's, I had a feeling he knew.

I just didn't understand why Shy, and everyone, was so freaking angry.

"You forget to tell me somethin', babe?" Shy asked when I came to an uncertain halt.

"Uh..." My eyes slid to Lee Nightingale, who looked scary but he kinda was that way normally. He was just one of those men who gave off the vibe you didn't mess with him. This didn't take away from the fact that he was tall, dark, built, and seriously hot. He was still scary. My eyes went back to Shy. "Not really."

His eyes narrowed on me. "Not really?"

That was the wrong answer, I could tell.

"Well, um...no. I mean, obviously you know I hired Lee to, uh...look into things, which, by the way"—I chanced a disapproving look at Nightingale hoping he wouldn't take offense—"I thought was confidential."

"Shit went down, wasn't on your dime. If you're not paying, it's not your case, you're not my client, so it's no longer confidential," Lee explained to me, and that made sense. It sucked with Shy's present mood but it made sense.

"You hired him to find that motherfucker," Shy pushed into our conversation and I looked back at him.

"Yeah," I said quietly. "But—"

"Wound like that never closes, you tear it wider? What the fuck, Tabby?" Shy bit out.

His words slashed through me.

That wasn't what I was trying to do. He had to know that.

"I thought I was—" I started but didn't finish.

"You thought you were what?" Shy clipped, his words harsh, coming from someplace ugly.

A place he'd clearly been keeping locked down and I'd inadvertently opened.

God, why hadn't I listened to Natalie when she told me not to hire Lee Nightingale?

I had to go into damage control. I just had no clue how.

Still, I had to try.

"I...you..." I looked around then back at Shy, knowing what I had to say, needing to tell him what he exposed when he talked about his family and thinking he wouldn't want an audience. So I asked, "Can we talk about this somewhere else?"

"No, darlin', you talk about this shit here," Dad growled, and I turned surprised eyes to him to see he looked just as angry as he sounded. "After Shy gets what he needs outta you, I'll be askin' some questions about why you took shit like this outside the family."

What?

"I—" I started.

"Tabby, eyes to me," Shy ordered tersely and when I looked back at him, he repeated, "What the fuck?"

"You talked about them," I explained.

"Yeah. So?" he clipped.

I studied him wondering how this had turned so bad.

Then I tried, "You...you were doing a lot for me. I wanted to do something for you."

"So you fuck me up?" he asked and I flinched.

It took a lot but I recovered and pointed out carefully, "Obviously, I didn't think I was doing that, Shy. I thought I was giving you closure."

"Well, you didn't think right, sugar. You didn't give me closure, you reopened a nightmare," Shy fired back.

"How?" I whispered and looked around. "How?" I repeated then I looked at Lee. "What's going on?"

"We found him," Lee told me.

Oh my God!

"Seriously?" I whispered.

"Seriously," he didn't whisper.

"You're sure?" I pushed.

"Absolutely," he stated firmly.

"I see you're not gettin' this, darlin'," Dad put in at this point and his voice was now gruff but gentle. He was also angry at me, but he saw I didn't understand why so at least he was giving me a break. "Nightingale's got this guy in his holding room and now he has a difficult decision to make 'cause he knows we got a job to do. We also got a relationship with Nightingale and his team. If we don't agree on what goes down now, there'll be friction. We try to avoid friction. But there's only one thing that can go down now, so if we can't negotiate with Nightingale, we got a problem."

I didn't get it.

Then I got it.

Just like Natalie said, the Club wanted this guy so Shy's loss could be avenged, and Lee Nightingale knew it and he might not be hip to being involved, even on the periphery, of what they had planned.

"This is not a we," Shy declared, his furious gaze now on Dad. "This is a me."

"Brother, this is a we," Dad told him.

"Was," Shy spat the word out. "If this shit happened a coupla months ago. Now this is mine." Dad's brows snapped together, but it was Hop who spoke.

"This is not somethin' a brother does alone."

Shy looked to him. "Yeah it is. This is about me. My family. I deal."

"You got another family now," Dog put in.

"I do?" Shy asked and my heart sank. "Didn't feel that way when you all made your call about Tabby."

Oh God! There it was.

Something bad was getting worse. I knew that by Shy's words, the tightening of the mouths of some of the men and others looking away and shuffling their motorcycle-booted feet.

Shy looked to Lee. "You turn him over to me."

Okay, there it was again. Now it was even worse!

"Authorities would make him pay longer, Cage," Lee said quietly.

"Authorities didn't get their mom and dad popped. You turn him over to me," Shy shot back.

"Shy—" I started and his eyes sliced to me.

"Quiet, Tabby, we'll have our words later."

Okay, and now it was even *worse.*

I decided the best thing to do at that juncture was shut up, so I did.

Shy looked to Lee. "You turn him over to me. Whatever happens, whatever blowback, it's on me. Not you, and this does not have fuck all to do with Chaos."

I turned pleading eyes to Dad, but Dad had his eyes locked on Dog. Then he moved his gaze to Lee.

It was then Lee said to Shy, "Don't make a mess."

Oh God, God, *God!*

Worse!

Shy jerked up his chin.

"Usual Chaos drop-off, bring him there. I'll be waiting," Shy ordered.

Usual Chaos drop-off?

Yikes!

I didn't have a chance to process the scariness of that. Shy shifted, his eyes moved through me, through the brothers, all of this like we weren't even there and he prowled out of the Compound.

I will repeat: his eyes moved *through* me.

Never, not once, not even back in the day when I had a crush on him and he was too old for me, did Shy make me feel invisible.

Never.

My feet moved to launch me toward Shy, but I didn't even get a step in before Dad's hand locked on my arm.

I tipped my eyes up to look at him.

"Go home, darlin', wait it out. It'll be okay," he said softly.

"I think he's going to—"

Dad's face dipped close, his eyes were dark, intense, he was feeling a lot of things but still his gaze was somehow gentle on me, and he reiterated, "Go home, Tabby. I got this. The brothers have this. It'll all be okay." He held my eyes and when I licked my lip he whispered, "Tab, trust me."

"I don't want to be visiting him in the penitentiary," I whispered back.

"You won't," Dad told me.

"You either," I went on.

"You won't be doin' that either," Dad assured me.

"Or anyone," I carried on.

Dad's look, still gentle, flashed with impatience. "Tabby, honey, your message is clear. I get you but we got this. Do you think we don't got this?"

I held his eyes.

Then I nodded.

He had this.

I hoped.

"Okay, Dad."

"Got shit to do, darlin'. Go home." His fingers tightened on my arm, they didn't hurt but they sent a message. "Your man will be home tonight."

I stared up at Dad and read it in his eyes.

My man would be home that night. What would happen when he got there was up to me, but my dad and his brothers were going to get him back to me.

I nodded.

He held my eyes before he said, "I see your play and it was filled with beauty. But, darlin', I'll say this once, we won't go over this ground again. Shit like this is kept in the family."

I got him. Boy, did I get him.

Luckily, there was only one man who murdered Shy's parents and thus messed up his life, so this wouldn't happen again.

"You won't have to say it again, Dad," I assured him.

"That's my girl," he muttered then used my arm to start propelling me to the door. "Now, get home."

I looked through the guys. They were moving, shifting, huddling.

Planning.

They had this.

I looked up at Dad. "Love you," I whispered.

"Same," he rumbled.

I smiled and it was shaky.

Dad didn't smile, he jerked up his chin.

I took in a deep breath and got the heck out of there.

* * *

Tack

The Harleys roared around them as Lee Nightingale and Kane "Tack" Allen stood close next to Lee's Explorer.

"Not stupid, man," Tack said, his eyes locked to Nightingale's.

"Know that, Tack," Lee replied.

"You still got my girl's money?" Tack asked, and Nightingale jerked up his chin.

"Every penny."

"You gonna pay that back or hold it?" Tack queried.

"Your call," Nightingale answered.

Tack studied him then remarked, "You told my girl you stopped lookin' but you never stopped lookin'."

Nightingale's face went hard. "Man loses his family, he should know who took them from him."

It was Tack's turn to jerk up his chin. "Do as he said. Take him to the drop-off. You won't see any brothers but we'll be close."

Nightingale nodded.

Then he asked, "My team delivers him, we're clear of this. Our part in this didn't happen. Can you assure me of that?"

"Absolutely," Tack confirmed.

Nightingale nodded again.

"Chaos marker," Tack offered.

"That'll do," Nightingale accepted. "I'll return the money to you."

This time, Tack nodded.

Negotiations over.

Deal struck.

Lee Nightingale swung up into his truck.

Tack prowled to his bike, threw a leg over, made it roar, then he headed out to take his brother's back.

CHAPTER EIGHTEEN

Breaking the Circle

"DID SHE BEG for her life?"

"Man, I got clean."

"Did he?"

Shy Cage was sitting on his ass on the dirt floor of a shed in the foothills. He had his knees up, his elbows on his knees, his blade hanging from his fingers. His knuckles were split, torn and bloody.

The man in front of him, wrists behind him held together with plastic restraints, had fallen to his side. His position was awkward seeing as his feet were also bound together at the ankles. His face was mangled and bloody. Eyes nearly swollen shut. Blood was oozing from an ear.

At Shy's question, the man didn't answer. He simply moaned.

Shy kept questioning.

"She have time to tell you she had two boys at a babysitter's, playin' games and eatin' junk food and watchin' late movies, havin' no clue...no...*fucking*...*clue* that they'd wake up in the morning with no family?"

The man took in a wet, sloppy, pained breath but didn't answer.

Shy kept at him.

"Or did you pop them quick? Did they even have the opportunity to say, 'please'?"

The man shut his swollen eyes and whispered, "I was messed up back then."

"Yeah, talk to me about that," Shy said, his words an invitation but his tone was cutting.

The man opened his eyes, kept his head to the dirt but his eyeballs slid up to Shy. "Smack, man. I would do anything."

"I know," Shy agreed. "I know, 'cause to get your fix, you fuckin' killed my family. That, man, that's any-fuckin'-thing."

"I'm clean now," the man told him again, hurriedly. "I made my way out of that and, bro, I'll tell you, not a day has gone by where I haven't remembered how far I stooped and it haunted me."

"You lose sleep?" Shy asked.

"Every night, man, every single night. I see them every night."

"So, you remember. You see them, tell me. Did they beg?"

The man closed his eyes.

"He got her earrings, every Christmas," Shy told him. "Not shit, they were diamonds, emeralds, rubies. After you plugged her, when you rifled through my home, you didn't get that shit, did you..." he hesitated before he finished with a disgusted "...*bro?*"

The man opened his eyes and whispered, "No."

"No," Shy whispered back. "I know. My bitch aunt got

them. The aunt my brother and I went to after you murdered my family. The aunt who made us her slaves. Who treated us like shit. Who hated us and let us know every fuckin' day for six fuckin' years. *She* got my mom's earrings."

"I'm sorry," the man replied brokenly.

"So am I," Shy agreed. "I've been sorry for sixteen fuckin' years."

"If I could take it back, I would," the man told him.

"You can't," Shy replied shortly.

The man shifted, his eyes locked to Shy's. "I'll do anything you want. Anything. I get you. I deserve this. I knew this was coming. My penance. It was gonna come, I always knew it. You can't do what I did and breathe easy. You need to know I'll do anything you want but please, please man, don't kill me."

"If you'll do anything I want then fuckin' answer me, did they beg?"

He sucked in another wet, gurgling breath and answered, "No."

"Tell me," Shy ordered.

The man again shifted uncomfortably. "I... they, both of 'em... he surprised me. Didn't see him. I was dealin' with the clerk, he showed and I just, I just freaked and I..." He trailed off, but Shy knew what he did. He knew exactly what he did. He killed Shy's father. Then the man told him, "She was in the kitchen. I surprised her."

"Quick, right? It went quick?" Shy pushed.

"Yeah," he said swiftly. "It went quick."

"They didn't suffer?"

"No," the man shook his head against the dirt with difficulty. "No, man, they didn't suffer. She didn't..." his voice dropped near to nothing "...she didn't even know I was there."

Shy closed his eyes.

In his low voice, the man said, "I shot her in the back of the head."

Shy's head dropped forward.

"She didn't know anything," the man finished.

Shy lifted his head and looked at him. "One minute alive, two boys she loves, a husband who pulls her into his lap for a kiss, she's just walkin' through the room, a husband who gives her earrings, the next she's nothing."

The man nodded, his voiced hitching when he said, "I did that. I did it."

Shy tipped his head to the side. "You got family?"

The man's body jolted and his eyes, even swollen, went wide, filling with fear. "No, man, no. No family."

"You have family," Shy said.

The man shook his head. "No. Not before I got clean. After I got clean. Not before, man, they don't know that me. They don't even know I was that me."

"They should know," Shy told him.

The man shook his head in the dirt, his body shifting with agitation. "They don't know. They only know the me after I got clean."

"You took three lives, destroyed two more I know of, don't know what you laid to waste for that clerk. You think they shouldn't know?" Shy asked.

"I did that. I admitted it. I admitted it to that Native American dude who found me. I admitted it to those guys he set to guard me. I did it and it haunted me, man, it haunted me," he said quickly. "It haunted me so much, what I was capable of, what that shit drove me to, I got clean."

"So my parents died so you could learn your lesson and have a good life. You think I'm happy with that trade-off? My brother? You think that will mean shit to him? You think that means shit to me?"

"No, I don't. I just... I don't know, man, I just, since then, I got my act together. I got family. I got a reason to stay clean. They need me and I'm just sayin', I get you, do what you have to do but I don't wanna die."

"Right now, you want that gift from me. You wanna keep breathin'."

"Yes," the man whispered.

"And you think," Shy leaned forward, "you think, you shot my mother in the back of her fuckin' head, you took that gift from her, you think you should get that gift from me?"

"No," the man was still whispering. "I don't deserve that. I know it. I just hope you have it in you to show mercy."

Shy changed the subject. "Too young, cops didn't tell that shit to kids and my aunt and uncle didn't share fuckin' anything. So you tell me. Where'd you shoot my dad?"

"Man, don't do this to yourself."

"Tell me," Shy pushed, leaning further in, moving the hilt of the knife into his palm, his fingers curling around the shaft, movements the man didn't miss. "Where... did... you... *shoot my Dad?*" he ended his question on a roar.

"Tell him," Tack rumbled and Shy's head jerked around.

Jesus, he didn't hear him.

The brothers moved in behind Tack.

Fuck, he didn't hear any of them.

"Oh God, oh fuck, oh God," the man chanted, scooting fearfully away but he stopped when Boz, Hound, and High rounded him at the back and the rest of the brothers circled around him.

Shy pushed up to his feet to stand by Tack.

"I said," Shy stated, his eyes on Tack, "private party."

"See you don't get this, brother, but we're crashing," Tack replied.

"Answer his question, motherfucker," Hop growled, nudging the man on the ground hard with his boot. "He wants to know where you shot his dad."

"In the aisle," the man said hurriedly.

"That the info you were lookin' for, Shy?" Tack asked, his eyes pointed down at the man.

"No," Shy answered.

The man shook his head.

"Uh...you're not gettin' this, dude, but you were in a world of hurt," Boz spoke up then leaned down toward the man and clipped, "Now you're in a world of *pain*. Tell my brother where you shot his fuckin' *dad*."

"Face," he whispered.

"Jesus, fuck, once we kill him, can I keep stabbing him?" Hound asked.

The man let out a terrified squeak.

Shy stared at Hound then he looked at Tack.

"You been out there awhile," he guessed.

"Brothers don't go it alone," Tack replied, and Shy held his eyes.

Then Shy drew in a deep breath.

Finally, he told Tack, "He's got family."

"I heard. Do you care?" Tack returned.

"I been the survivin' part of a family," Shy reminded him.

"Vengeance," Tack shook his head. "Brother, that shit is messy. This fuck we got here doesn't mean shit but his family, you're lookin' at two things. They learn who he was, what he did and know he paid, or they live to have you where he is right now. Difference is, you got your brothers. That kind of shit"—he swung a hand toward the man in the dirt—"unlikely to happen to you. Way it's goin', my guess, you'll have a new family soon. You carry through, suddenly, they're vulnerable. Vengeance is a circle. There's no corners to turn, there's no end of the line. You feel lucky, we'll deal accordingly. You want this to end here, we get creative in taking his penance and the circle is broken. Your choice. Whatever you choose, your brothers stand with you."

Shy looked down at the man but felt a presence get close.

"This is not a case for mercy," Big Petey rumbled.

Shy turned his head and looked into the man's eyes.

Big Petey kept talking. "But, boy, you make this decision, you get on your bike, you go home, you lie down by your woman. So, right now, ask yourself, next time you touch her, how you gonna feel doin' it with blood on your hands?"

Shy's mind filled with all things Tabby. This meant it filled really fucking full.

He drew in another deep breath and looked down at the man in the dirt.

Then he declared, "I'm feelin' creative."

The vibe in the room shifted, Shy's head lifted, he looked to Tack and he found him smiling.

* * *

Shy rode hard, his mind blank except for one thing.

Or pairs of them but they were all the same.

All the same.

He hadn't thought of them for years. They'd been lost a long time. So long, he almost forgot about them.

Tonight, he was getting them back.

He drove his bike up into a driveway he hadn't seen in years. He didn't even drive down this street. He got nowhere near this fucking place.

He walked to the door, pressed the doorbell and didn't let go.

It was late, dark, it had to be well past midnight so he knocked. Loud. Hard. And he didn't stop.

He saw a light go on in the window high in the door, the locks turned and the door was thrown open.

"Park, son, jeez. What on earth? Are you okay?" his uncle asked and Shy stared at him as saliva filled his mouth.

Then he pushed through him and prowled into the house.

"Park! What the heck?" his uncle yelled after him. "Where are you going?"

Shy took the steps two at a time.

He rounded the flight at the top and stalked down the hall, his uncle still yelling after him.

There she was, in her shapeless nightie, hair ratty from sleep, standing in the door to her bedroom staring at him, pale-faced, eyes wide with surprise.

"Parker, what on earth?" she asked.

"Where are they?" Shy asked back.

"Who?" she queried.

"Not who, what," Shy clipped and didn't stop. He

pushed right through her, ignoring her startled, strangled screech. “Where are they?”

“What?” she asked, her voice now pitched high.

“Park,” his uncle called, his voice sharp. “Son, what in the hell are you doin’?”

Shy saw the jewelry box on her dresser and went right to it.

“Oh my God!” his aunt cried. “Timmy, he’s going for my jewelry.”

Shy stopped and turned.

“I knew it,” she hissed, her eyes on him as his uncle moved toward him. “You’re on drugs, aren’t you?”

“Where are they?” Shy asked.

“Where are what?” she snapped, her tone ugly.

The same shit as always.

Exactly.

“My mother’s earrings.”

Her hand flew to her throat and her face again got pale. His uncle stopped dead two feet away.

“Son?” his uncle called Shy’s attention to him so Shy gave him his attention.

“I am not your son.”

He watched his uncle wince.

His eyes went to his aunt. “Where are they?”

“I... they—” she began to babble but Shy’s uncle cut her off.

“Park, please. Come back at a decent hour. Obviously you have something on your mind. We’ll talk.”

Shy looked back to the man who failed to raise him after his father died. “We are not talking. I’m never fuckin’ seein’ you or that bitch again after I leave. But I’m leavin’ with my mother’s earrings.”

"Although I can see you're in a *mood,*" his aunt bit out, and Shy looked to her, "and I hate to fly in the face of that mood considering who you are and who you spend your time with, but I have to say that not only is this highly inappropriate, you barging in on your uncle and me in the middle of the night, but also you asking for those earrings."

"My mother's earrings," Shy corrected, and she leaned in.

"*My* earrings," she sneered, and Shy's chest started burning.

The bitch wasn't done.

"Didn't get much for taking you in, at least I got that."

Shy stared at her. He then turned to his uncle. "I am not leaving without those earrings."

"Parker—" his uncle started.

"I'm calling the cops!" his aunt announced loudly.

Shy ignored her and repeated, "I am not... *leaving*... without those earrings."

He watched his uncle swallow.

Shy kept his eyes pinned to the man. "You give me those earrings, or I swear to fuckin' *Christ* you will not see the end of this. I will make every fuckin' day of your life a misery either by makin' it a misery or makin' you wonder how I am next gonna make it a misery. You will know every one of my brothers, and you'll know them well because they will make it a mission to make you, that bitch, and your good-for-nothin' children miserable. Now you control that fuckin' woman, get that goddamned phone out of her hand, and give me my mother's earrings."

"Ellen, put the phone down," his uncle said instantly.

"I will not," she snapped.

"Woman, put the goddamned phone down," he clipped, shocking the shit out of Shy, who never, not once, heard his uncle speak that way to anybody. Especially not his aunt.

Shy didn't look at the bitch but he felt the air in the room, already wired, go heavy.

He heard the phone hit the charger then his uncle ordered, "Get Parker his mother's earrings."

"Tim, that's—"

"Don't," his uncle whispered. He drew in a deep breath, his eyes glued to his woman, then he went on, "For years, you rode me about this. Give me some goddamned peace. Give Parker some peace. Just give him his mother's earrings."

There was silence then movement and a hissed "This is just unbelievable."

Shy shifted out of her way, not wanting to be anywhere near her.

Moments went by then he felt her standing close.

"Well? Take them," she snapped.

His eyes moved to her, she looked into them and quailed.

He looked back at his uncle. "I'll need a bag."

"Do you want us to wrap up the silver so you can take that too?" she asked snidely.

Shy looked at her again. "I want you, for once, to put away those goddamned fangs, and by that I mean, shut the fuck up."

"I knew you were a bad seed," she shot back.

"Like usual, not payin' a lick of attention," Shy returned.

"Really?" she asked sarcastically. "Oh. Right. In the

circles you run, threatening middle-of-the-night visits are probably mandatory."

"No, but when they happen, they're fun," Shy replied casually.

She snorted.

"Ellen just, please, go get him a bag," his uncle cut in.

She threw his uncle a look and stomped out.

Shy dropped his eyes to his boots.

"Is there something that prompted this evening's visit, Parker?" his uncle asked, and Shy looked to him.

"Yes," he answered.

His uncle waited. Shy was quiet.

The man tried something else, "Landon home safe?"

"Yes," Shy stated but said no more.

"Well, thank God for that."

Shy didn't reply.

His uncle lifted a hand his way. "Son, I—"

"Save it," Shy bit out and he shut his mouth.

Seconds slid by.

Then his uncle tried again. "Maybe, with your aunt not there, we should find a time to sit down and talk."

"And maybe that's never gonna happen," Shy returned. "Maybe I like it better knowin' that my brother's a soldier, a brave man, puttin' his ass on the line for this country. Maybe I like knowin' that I got a woman, gettin' a house, and soon we're gonna make a family. Maybe I like knowin' that you know that you had not one thing to do with the good that's in us, the good that came to us, the good we deserve, the good we're gonna make. Maybe I like knowin' that you know that we had to escape this prison in order to carve out that goodness. Maybe I like knowin' that your kids don't give one shit about you because they think you're as weak as I do, and they only have time for their mother because they know she'll give them shit they ask for."

His uncle's eyes flashed and Shy knew his aim was true.

"Bet those assholes don't even send birthday cards," Shy continued.

"Don't think I haven't thought on things, you boys gone, and—"

"Don't care what you thought when we were gone," Shy interrupted him. "The time for you to think and fuckin' *act* was when we were fuckin' *here*."

He watched his uncle close his eyes in defeat as he heard his aunt coming back down the hall. Shy moved to the door, stopping and turning to his uncle.

"Last, and best and it isn't a maybe, it's a definite. I like knowin' you'll finish your life at her side. You deserve that shit. And that's what it is that anyone gets from her. That's all she's got to give. Shit."

He heard his aunt gasp in affront, turned back to the door as she slid in, careful with her body like being too close to him would rub off criminal vibes and she'd be arrested on the spot.

He reached out a hand, yanked the bag out of hers, opened it, looked inside, and counted boxes.

When he needed to move some to keep count, he reached in, and she snapped, "They're all there."

Shy looked at her then to his uncle. "They aren't, another visit."

Then, without looking at either of them again, he walked right the fuck out.

* * *

He rode home feeling something he didn't get, something he hadn't felt, not once, not in sixteen years.

He realized what it was when he got to Tab's apartment and saw her electric blue car shining in the streetlamps illuminating the parking lot.

He felt *free.*

The feeling was overpowering, suffusing him, forcing everything else out and allowing him nothing but that.

Feeling free.

Fucking *free.*

He swung off his bike, jogged to the stairs, took them two at a time and turned the handle on the door. He knew by the light coming out the bottom it wouldn't be locked.

It wasn't.

He walked in and saw her curled into herself on the couch.

She shot to her feet the instant she saw him. Her eyes on him, her expression concerned, cautious, even scared, she whispered, "Shy."

He closed the door, turned, locked it, and then turned back to her.

Free.

He was free.

He thought his brothers gave him that, and they did.

At the same time, they didn't.

True freedom came from Tabby.

He stalked toward her.

"Bedroom," he growled. "Take your clothes off on your way."

Her body jerked but other than that she didn't move.

He rounded the armchair, positioning to herd her to get

her on her way to where he wanted her to go, and when he was a foot away, she stumbled then started backing up.

"Bedroom and clothes off, Tabby."

"Shy, I... what...?" Her head tipped to the side as he rounded her wide and changed her direction, aiming her down the hall. "Are you okay?" she asked.

"You aren't taking your clothes off."

She licked her lip and Jesus, he was hanging on by a thread.

"Clothes, Tabby," he growled, rounding her wide again to move her to the bedroom.

He moved her through the bedroom doorway and she stopped when the backs of her legs hit bed.

Shy stopped too.

She held his gaze.

Then she said, "I love you."

Only then did she whip her shirt off.

Shy drew in a breath, he closed his eyes, opened them, tossed the bag with his mother's earrings to the foot of the bed, yanked his own tee off, and then he lunged, taking her to her back in the bed.

He didn't hesitate to take her mouth.

Then he didn't hesitate to take her.

He did not waste time getting rid of their clothes and then he used his hands, mouth, tongue, teeth, knees, thighs, everything he had, to take everything he could get.

He didn't have to take it, she gave it.

He took it anyway.

It didn't take long before he was ready, she was fucking ready, he knew because she was panting so he yanked her up, moved her, shifted on his knees, slammed her back to the headboard and surged inside.

His dick sheathed in her tight, slick, hot silk. Connected to Tabby.

Fuck, always, *always*, gorgeous.

Her arms and legs rounded him, his hand moved up her side, up her arm, pulling it away from him, finding her hand, and he shoved his thumb in the palm, wrapped his fingers around the back and pressed their hands to the wall.

His eyes were locked to hers and he was moving inside her.

"Just like the first time," he murmured against her mouth.

"Yes," she breathed.

"Do you love me, Tabby?"

"Yes," she again breathed.

"I know you do, baby, fuck, I know you do," he muttered, then took her mouth, took her cunt, took her there. She cried out her orgasm, driving it down his throat as her pussy convulsed around his dick, then he shoved his face in her neck and groaned his climax against her skin.

He stayed that way, planted deep, his body pressing hers to the headboard, his hand holding hers, her other limbs tight around him, holding her close. He kept his face in her neck, smelling her skin, her hair, and he didn't say anything.

Slowly, he pulled out, liking the little mew she gave that sounded sweet in his ear as she lost him. He moved back, set her on the bed. Reaching out an arm, he grabbed the bag.

"Shy?" she called but he didn't answer. He dug into the bag.

He pulled out a box, flipped it open, flipped it closed, and dropped it in the bag. He did this again and again until he found a pair of diamonds.

He gently flung the bag to the nightstand, carefully freed the earrings from the box and flung that aside too.

"Shy?"

"Got earrings in, honey?"

Her head jerked on the pillow, her eyes were curious, confused and cautious, maybe still a little scared but she shook her head.

"Pull your hair back," he ordered.

She did as he asked as Shy settled on her body, careful to brace on an elbow even as his hands moved to her earlobe. He slid the post through her ear then slid the back on. He moved to the other side and did the same. Then he got up on a forearm on either side of her and looked down, his eyes moving side to side, the diamonds twinkling against her glossy, dark hair.

"Shy, darlin', talk to me," she pleaded.

He looked at her. "Those are my mother's earrings."

Her body tensed under him as her thighs pressed into his hips.

"Went to my aunt and uncle's house tonight, got 'em," he went on. "All of them. Dad gave a pair to Mom every Christmas since they were married. Fourteen pairs. Seven for you, seven for Landon. I picked those for you. Lan picks the next pair. We'll go back and forth until we each got our piece of our parents."

Her eyes were brimming with tears, her nostrils flaring with the effort to contain them as she asked, "You went to your aunt and uncle's?"

"First time in years, last time for forever." He watched

as she lifted a hand to touch the gem at her ear. "Diamonds," he finished.

A tear she couldn't hold back slid out the side of her eye.

"Are you mad at me?" she asked so quietly he barely heard.

But he heard.

"Was," he told her, saw her lips tremble then moved close, his hand going to cup the side of her head, his thumb sliding down her hairline and ending, pad to her earring. "Was also wrong," he told her gently. "Feelin' too much, knowin' he was found. Lost it, took that shit out on you. Shouldn't have done it but I had so much shit coursin' through me, baby, I had to get it out. So I piled it on you."

"Okay," she said quietly.

"It wasn't cool, Tabby," he replied just as quietly.

"It's okay," she told him, her hands hitting his chest, pressing in.

"No, it isn't. What it is is done. I hope to God I learn from makin' that mistake, freakin' you out, scaring you"—his thumb moved through the wetness at her temple and his voice dropped—"makin' you cry. Can't promise I won't do it again but I can promise to try."

"I'm glad you promised, honey, but you also need to know that I understand. That was a lot to handle. I didn't expect you to be surprised by it. I expected I'd get to tell you about what I'd done going to Lee. But I do understand why you reacted the way you did, and I've gotta be there to help you deal when life lands a sucker punch, even if it's me who unintentionally landed it."

"That's cool, baby, that's sweet and you're right. But when you do that, you do *not* have to take my shit. And you did what you did to give me something beautiful. I didn't get it at the time. I didn't get it until it was all done and I was sittin' outside this apartment. You didn't land a sucker punch, and I don't want you thinkin' that shit."

She held his eyes a couple of beats before she nodded and took in a breath that broke in the middle.

"I get it, sugar. You wanted me to have it," he said gently. "I have it. You gave it to me, but you gave me something else too."

Her wet eyes stayed on him and she murmured, "Pardon?"

"Closure. Freedom."

Her eyes closed, he felt her chest heave and tears slid out both sides. Shy shifted his other forearm up so he could put both thumbs to work.

She drew in another breath and opened her eyes.

"Do you want to tell me what happened?" she asked.

"Broke the circle," he answered.

"What does that mean?" she went on cautiously.

"Means I beat the shit out of him, found out he had family, found out how he killed my parents, found I wanted his life in return and found I didn't want to be in a circle of vengeance. Didn't want to drag you in. Didn't want to be in your bed, touchin' you, blood on my hands." He paused, his eyes looking into hers and he shared, "My brothers took my back and helped me find the way."

She got him, he knew when her entire face wobbled as she tried to hold back tears, then she lifted her head and pressed it into the skin of his neck when she failed.

Shy dropped his weight on her, rolled, curving his arms around her and taking her with him so they were on their sides.

She yanked her face out of his neck, took two hitched breaths and asked brokenly, "Are you…are you all right?"

"Best I've been in a long time, baby."

She took another uneven breath as her eyes moved over his face. Then she nodded.

"You gave me that, Tabby," he reminded her, and she gave him another wobbly smile she couldn't quite pull off.

"That's what I was goin' for," she told him.

He grinned at her and pulled her closer.

His grin faded and he admitted, "I was a dick again."

"I'll forgive you sooner this time, like, say—" her hand slid up so her fingers could stroke his jaw "—now."

His lips twitched. "It'd help for me to know I got your forgiveness, you quit cryin'."

She nodded, breathed deep, and got it together.

"Are you…" she hesitated "…good with the Club?"

It was Shy's turn to nod.

"Good," she said softly, ducked her face, and shoved it in his throat.

He dipped his chin and against her hair, murmured, "Gotta clean you up then I gotta call Lan."

"Okay."

He kissed her hair, rolled her to her back, moved in to kiss her chest then the underside of her jaw, then he met her eyes, gave her a smile, and rolled out of bed.

He got a washcloth and took care of his girl. He took the washcloth back, grabbed his jeans, tagged his phone, and joined her in bed.

She snuggled closer.

He called his brother.

Shy told Lan the story, not leaving anything out, which

meant Tabby heard the story. She pressed closer and closer as he talked but she didn't make a sound.

When he was done, Lan asked, "Tab's wearin' Mom's earrings?"

"Yeah," Shy answered.

"Fuck, man," a pause then low, rough and fragmented, "fuck."

Shy gave him a few beats then asked low, "You okay?"

Landon cleared his throat. "Forgot about those. Totally blocked 'em out. Cannot believe you got them. Cannot believe I forgot them." He was silent a moment then he said, "Glad you got them back, Park. Fuck me, so fuckin' glad you got Mom and Dad back from that bitch."

"Next time you come up, we'll divvy them out."

"Right, works for me."

Neither brother spoke for a long time. They also didn't break their connection.

Tabby burrowed closer.

Finally, Shy announced. "It's done."

"Done," Lan agreed.

"Over," Shy went on.

"Now we can move on," Lan replied.

Shy tightened his arm around Tabby and repeated, "Now we can move on."

"You know I love you, Parker, and that shit runs deep," Lan told him.

"Feel the same, Landon."

"Never forgot what we had, still miss it," Lan shared.

"Then do what I'm doin', Lan, and rebuild it."

There was silence, a short chuckle, and then finally, "Not sure I'm done havin' fun."

Shy tipped his chin down to see the top of Tabby's

head, her profile, her eyes open staring at his throat, her hand at his chest, fingers drifting aimlessly but soothingly, giving him time with his brother but not giving him space, something at that moment he did not need.

"That's your problem, brother, you don't get that this side is a fuckuva lot more fun," he returned.

"Take a little somethin' special to convince me of that," Lan retorted.

"God, I hope you find it," Shy replied.

Lan was silent, then Shy got a quiet "Me too, Park."

They let that hang, then Shy said, "Lettin' you go."

"Right. I'll find some time to come up for a weekend."

"Cool, see you then."

"Yeah... and Park?"

"Yeah?"

"You did right, you did good, now they can rest easy."

They can rest easy.

Shy felt his throat close so he had to force through it, "Yeah."

"See you in a coupla weeks."

"Later, Lan."

"Later, brother."

He touched his thumb to the screen, twisted just enough to throw his phone on the nightstand, then reached out to turn off the light and rolled into Tabby.

She snuggled closer, hitching her leg back over his hip, her arm winding tight around him.

"You good?" he asked into the dark.

He felt her nod then she asked, "How you feelin', honey?"

He thought about her question and the answer was fucked. It made no sense. He had a woman wrapped around him, trapping him to a bed. He was facing a mortgage payment. He had plans to plant babies inside her, build a family.

Still, there was only one answer and he dipped his chin, put his lips to her hair, and whispered that answer into her hair.

"Free."

At his answer, his girl, his gorgeous girl, pressed even closer.

Shy Cage never dreamed a dream.

Still, he knew, without a doubt since he was holding one in his arms, dreams were real.

CHAPTER NINETEEN

Tightrope

Four months later...

"How were they?" Tyra asked in a whisper, running her finger lightly along a sleeping Cutter's cheek as he lay in bed.

"Exhausting," I replied. She turned her head and smiled at me, unrepentant that her two offspring were hellions.

Then she looked back down to Cutter and pulled the covers up to his shoulder. "Like you and Rush, they both got their dad's hair, so I know where they got their temperament."

I was glad they got Dad's temperament along with his hair, though both of them had Tyra's green eyes. If either of them added Tyra's hair and the temperament that came with it with some of Dad thrown in, we'd be screwed.

"Happened again tonight," I said. Tyra straightened from Cut and looked at me with brows raised, so I went on, "Took them out for dinner and a couple of people commented. They think they belong to Shy and me." I looked down at my little brother. "Those green eyes, that hair."

"I see that," she murmured. I looked to her and grinned before I started moving to the door, Tyra coming with me, saying, "Fun to pretend, though, also time to plan."

I watched as she carefully closed the door behind hcr but, at her words, my brows drew together and when she turned from the door and looked at me, she smiled.

"Playing house, honey," she explained. "You and Shy have been together awhile. You've done the living-together thing. You've done the holidays-together thing. You've done the buying-the-house together thing. You've fought out the buying-a-fridge-together thing. When's the next step?"

She was not wrong.

With Ty-Ty's help, I gave Shy and Lan an awesome Christmas. We had a blast. I could tell both men enjoyed it, and the things they enjoyed most were waking up to two overexcited little boys who were in fits that Santa came and, later, sitting down to a huge dinner that tasted great, family all around, food and beer plentiful, conversation free and easy, and laughter coming often.

It was a blessing, they felt it, and neither man hid it.

It was awesome.

As for Shy, I learned he also gave good Christmases. His version of this was handing me my present right in front of everybody, his eyes locked to mine, his lips murmuring, "Every year."

In the box was a pair of sapphire earrings.

Of course, I burst into tears but luckily, doing that on Christmas with family close meant I got Shy's arms around me to comfort me, my little brother Cutter crawling into my lap to do the same thing and, not long after, my father bending deep to brush his lips against my hair to do the same thing.

There were tears but that didn't negate the fact that it... was... *fabulous*.

Then, just weeks after, Shy and I moved into our new house.

Not long after that, Shy and I had a rip-roarin' over our purchase of a new fridge. Although the house was great, there were things that needed updating, and one of them was the fridge.

At the store, Shy declared the kitchen was not my domain and therefore he got to say what fridge we bought and he chose a good model, dependable, but it was not deluxe.

In other words, it didn't crush ice.

I said that bringing him beverages *was* my domain (which it was—once his behind was on the couch, it didn't move), so I would be utilizing the fridge as much as him and I wanted the deluxe model that crushed ice.

Shy informed me that we were not going to spend extra money on having the ability to crush ice when we could spend it on something important, like saving up to build on to the garage so he could tinker with his bike there.

In other words, he wanted a man cave, not crushed ice.

I told him that after getting my money back from Lee Nightingale and putting it into outfitting our home, we were balanced partners and we should do something with the money that was balanced, say, a crushed ice mechanism on a deluxe fridge that we both could enjoy.

Shy said he didn't give a fuck about crushed ice but he did give a fuck about his bike. He also took this opportunity to point out that I *also* gave a fuck about his bike, like, in a big way.

This ticked me off mostly because he was right.

Therefore, I had no ready response, and as I was trying to come up with one, Shy threw out that he also didn't give a shit about balance. He told me, even if I didn't get that money back, we were square. What was his was mine, what was mine was his, he didn't keep track or keep score, and we weren't starting out a life where I did either.

Although I liked it that he thought this, he communicated it in a bossy way that ticked me way the hell off, so I told him to stop being so bossy.

He told me I sucked bossy dick and never complained unless I wasn't getting my way, so I needed to get over it.

Of course, at this, my head nearly exploded, so I promptly ended the conversation by retreating into it and freezing him out for three days, which was difficult seeing as we were living together. That said, I put a lot of effort into it so I succeeded. This, not surprisingly, caused him to lose his mind. My deep freeze ended in a blowout that ended in really great sex and, right after that, Shy telling me a story that sorted me out.

"My mom and dad both worked, sugar," he told me, lying on top of me on the living room floor, still inside me, his thumb tracing my hairline. "She didn't make a lot. He didn't make a fuss. It wasn't about that. It wasn't about balance or partnership or sharing. It was about unity. They didn't keep score, they just gave, and I figure that was why they didn't fight. Because if you give, the other person is gonna give because they get that back. So the balance comes natural. I put the money down on the house. You vacuum and clean the toilets 'cause I hate that shit. So, baby, we already had balance before you kicked in with your cash. You just didn't see it. And as far as I'm concerned, that's always gonna be the way. I'm gonna give to you, Tabby, 'cause I love you. You're gonna do the same. You just gotta feel the natural balance, not work for it."

There were sometimes I hated it when he was right, like, say, when we were shouting at each other.

There were other times I loved it. Like, say, when he was inside me after giving me an orgasm or when he told me sweet stories about his parents. The best was, like just then, when I had both.

So, obviously, after that, the fight was over.

And, by the way, we got the fridge that crushed ice.

I came out of my thoughts and back to Tyra.

"What are you saying? Marriage? Babies?" I asked.

She nodded and replied, "It's time. You've been together for a while, and Shy's awesome with the boys. It's clear he loves kids, and I know this because he loves my boys like they're his own little brothers, and he acted like that even before you two got together. I'm not saying you have to get married if that's not your thing. But you two need to be on the same page about both, since they're important." She tipped her head to the side and asked, "Have you talked about it?"

We hadn't and she knew that. She now knew (nearly) everything about Shy and me.

So I had a feeling this topic of conversation came up because of something else. I also had a feeling I knew what that something else was, since Shy and I were babysitting because Dad and Tyra went out with Hop and Lanie that night.

Therefore, I asked, "Um... Ty-Ty, where's this coming from?"

She hesitated before she replied, "Big stuff, honey. Too big for now after I've had a few margaritas and it being so late. Tomorrow, I'll give you a call and fill you in."

As ever with anything Lanie, even just stories, I was looking forward to being filled in. Especially when it had to do with Hop now that they were "out" just like Shy and I.

Suffice it to say, Lanie still took drama to extremes, and apparently Hop got off on that much like Dad enjoyed Ty-Ty's attitude. I had to admit, Hop and Lanie were kind of cute, because Hop seemed happier than I'd ever seen him, and Lanie had that light back in her eyes that had died when her fiancé Elliott bought it. No way, looking at them separately, would you think they worked, but they totally did.

"I'll wait for your call but tell me now, is everything okay?" I asked.

"Yeah. Everything is good." She smiled a small, knowing smile. "Hop is willing to do anything to make his woman happy. He'd walk a tightrope with no net if she was on the other side, cheering him on. And he just proved what we already knew, and he did that in a big way."

This, I'd noticed watching those two, was the God's-honest truth.

This, I noticed right then, made Tyra Allen happy.

"Though, Lanie feels the same about him," Tyra added.

I'd noticed this too.

"Back to you, though, just to repeat, it's crucial that you and Shy agree about important life stuff."

She was right about that.

Tyra hooked her arm in mine, got close, and moved us slowly down the hall toward the kitchen.

"You don't have anything to worry about," she said. "I know another man who'd walk a tightrope. It's just, you seriously butted heads over crushed ice. You may need to share your thoughts about holy matrimony and what you foresee with building your family."

She was right about that too. There had been heartbreak and drama, and now Shy and I were coasting on a wave of goodness broken only when we fought about fridges, or his bossiness hit the danger zone and we had to have words. We hadn't talked about any of this, and it was important.

"He wants to build a family," I told her.

She stopped us before we hit the kitchen and looked at me. "I know that, honey, but he could be thinking six kids while you're thinking two."

Yes, Shy and I needed to have this conversation, because no way I was having six kids and he missed his family so much, this was a possibility.

I nodded. "You're right, Ty-Ty."

She grinned and we both moved down the hall.

Once there, I saw Dad and Shy in the kitchen, both taking pulls off their beers. Both wearing black tees, faded jeans, and motorcycle boots. Both exuding badassness. Both beloved by me.

It was a happy sight.

It had been said, repeatedly, that women found their fathers in their men.

Luckily, when I did just that, I had a good man to find.

It had also been said that men found their mothers.

I hoped, with the way he talked about her, Shy felt the same.

I hoped this for about a second when he dropped his beer, his eyes came to me and his chin dipped, saying nonverbally I was to go to him.

I went there, he curved an arm around me, pulled me in close, and bent to put his lips to my hair. "You ready to go home?" he asked and I melted into him.

I loved it when he held me and spoke into my hair.

I loved it when he called the house we shared our home.

And I loved it that he finally had a home.

"Yeah," I mumbled into his throat, and he kissed my hair.

I looked to Dad and Tyra and saw Tyra had a small smile playing around her mouth, her expression warm.

Dad wasn't smiling. I saw his eyes were intense but they were not conflicted.

He was happy. He was happy I had someone and he was happy that person was Shy, a man he understood, a man he could trust, a man who would go all out to protect his daughter.

A man who would walk a tightrope for me.

A brother.

"You have a good night, Dad?" I asked, and his eyes moved from Shy's arm around my shoulders to me.

"Yeah, darlin'," he answered then, "Come here and give your old man some love before you go, yeah?"

I moved out of Shy's arm into my father's. He tucked me close and kissed the top of my head.

"Thanks for lookin' after the boys," he murmured into my hair, I closed my eyes and nodded.

"Anytime," I whispered.

"Love you, Tabby," he said, giving me a squeeze. He curled me out and back to Shy before he looked to Shy and said, "Safe home."

"Right," Shy said, leaned in, kissed Tyra's cheek then, amidst waves and good-byes, we went out to my car.

We'd pulled out of the drive and were winding through the curving roads that led down the wooded mountain from Dad and Ty-Ty's house when Shy announced, "Three and, babe, firm on that."

I looked from the wooded darkness outside the car to my man.

"Three what?" I asked.

"Kids," he answered then continued. "And marriage. Firm on that too."

My stomach flipped.

Shy went on but when he did, it wasn't an announcement. It was soft.

"I know you lost it all right before the big event, sugar, and you said you weren't gonna do it again. I'm just sayin', it means somethin' to me so you are."

"Shy—" I tried but he kept going.

"You lost that guy, that's always gonna sting, I get that. But that is not gonna happen again and I want a ring on your finger, my ring. I wear yours. I want every time you look at your hand to remember you belong to me. I want every time I look at mine to remember I belong to you. Same when we see each other's hands. You want a small shindig, I'm down with that but I'll say now, I'd rather have a blowout."

I was stuck on something he said earlier.

That guy.

That guy.

He always, but always, called Jason "that guy".

"His name was Jason," I said gently and carefully.

Shy glanced my way before glancing back to the road and asking, "What?"

"His name was Jason," I repeated. "He wanted two kids. He'd never own a Harley even though I had schemes of finding ways to get him to buy one. He loved me. We were getting married and now he's dead."

Shy reached out a hand, found mine, and squeezed. "Tabby—"

"He loved me and would want you for me."

The air in the car went still.

Then Shy started again, "Sugar—"

I squeezed his hand and interrupted, "That's how much he loved me. He'd want you for me. He'd want me to be this happy."

Shy was silent.

I let the car be that way for long moments before I looked to the road and told him, "Three kids is perfect and I want a big shindig, so it's all good."

"I wouldn't want that," Shy declared, and I looked back at him.

"Pardon?"

He glanced my way, his hand tightened around mine then he looked back to the road and stated, "No other man. Not anyone but me."

"Shy—" I began but it was my turn to get cut off.

"I get you believe that. I get why you need to believe that. It might be wrong that I tell you this but I also saw him with you that night at DCPA, and I know you wanna believe it but it's not even a little true. He would not want me for you. He wanted only you for him and he wanted to be the only one for you. Now, baby, you're right. Jason's dead. He doesn't get to want anything. But I'll tell you, I love you so much, I'm selfish and I only want me for you, not you with anyone else, if I'm breathin' or I'm dead. And Jason felt the same fuckin' way. I know that might suck hearin' it but the truth is, there's beauty in that. He didn't love you enough to sacrifice you to another man. He loved you enough to want there to be only him for a lifetime 'cause that's the way he felt about you. He didn't get a lifetime. But, I'm tellin' you now, I want a lifetime."

I felt a stinging in my eyes as I admitted, "Shy, I don't know what to do with that."

He kept holding my hand tight when he replied gently, "Nothin' to do with it. We don't always get what we want, Tabby, and life goes on. I know you'll always love him. I know you'll always feel his loss. I gotta live with that. But luckily, love doesn't have limits and you're you, you got a lot of love to give. So I'll take what I got since it's everything. But, Tabby, baby, the point I'm making is, this is the only conversation we have where to me, that guy is Jason. He's that guy. I am not bein' a dick. I'm giving this to you real. I need that and I need you to give it to me 'cause he has a piece of you I'll never have, so let me take what I need from him." His voice dropped to low and sweet. "Do you get me, baby?"

"I get you, honey."

He squeezed my hand, released the pressure and murmured, "Good."

I looked to the windshield.

Shy drove in silence.

Then he broke it by declaring, “Settled. Three kids and a big shindig.”

“Settled,” I whispered.

“We’re not doin’ any of that ring-shoppin’-together bullshit. I’ll take care of you and you get the question and the time it’s asked as a surprise.”

I liked that. Something to look forward to.

All of it.

“Okay,” I agreed.

“Though I know the answer,” he went on, his voice soft but there was a smile in it.

“Yeah.”

He knew the answer. He so totally did.

“Yeah,” he repeated.

We went quiet.

Time passed, we hit Denver and I called, “Shy?”

“Right here, sugar.”

“Love you.”

He lifted my hand, touched his lips to my fingers, and then dropped my hand to his thigh.

Then he drove us home in silence.

There it was.

He loved me too.

CHAPTER TWENTY

Stuck with Me

Early the next morning...

I HEARD MY cell ringing, my eyes blinked open as I felt Shy's hand on my behind give a reflexive squeeze.

I sleepily noticed it was still dark.

My cell kept ringing and Shy growled, "What the fuck? Who's callin' at three in the fuckin' morning?"

I didn't know but to find out, I had to get my cell, and I also had to get my cell because any call at three in the morning was a call you had to take. Unfortunately, this meant I had to roll off him and away, which I did, reaching toward the nightstand. He rolled with me so his front was pressed to my side, his thigh between my legs. I grabbed my phone, looked groggily at the display, and, at what I saw, sleep left me completely.

I slid my finger on the screen and put it to my ear.

"Natalie," I greeted.

It was the first time I'd heard from her since we had our big fight.

"Tabby," she replied, her voice small, scared, a way

she never sounded and it sent shivers crawling over my skin. "I'm in trouble."

Oh no.

I knew Shy felt my panic because I was no longer holding my phone to my ear. Shy had taken my phone and he was pressed into me in order to reach out and switch on the light.

I winced in the sudden brightness as Shy spoke.

"You got Shy. What's goin' on?" he said into the phone.

I blinked to adjust my eyes then stared at his face which was scary hard.

"Right, where are you?" he asked and his tone sent my hand shooting up to curl around his jaw. His eyes came to me, they were scary hard too, and I held my breath. He kept talking. "How many are there with you?"

Oh no.

No!

"Firepower?" he asked.

Firepower? God!

"Okay, hang tight," Shy ordered as he rolled over me and got to his feet. I rolled to my side as he kept ordering. "Do not say anything stupid. Do not do anything stupid. But stall 'em. I'm makin' the calls, the brothers are rollin' out. It could be thirty, it'll probably be forty-five."

I swung my legs over the side of the bed and searched the floor frantically for my nightie even as Shy wound things up with Natalie.

"Woman, hear me. This phone is comin' with me so you can't call and freak Tab any more than she's already freaked. Be smart, for fuckin' once in your life. I'm takin' care of your shit once. This is the only chance you get.

Don't blow it now and know you won't get the chance to blow it later. You fuck up again, even somethin' not this big, you're done for Tabby. Hear me?"

This big?

She must have heard him for he touched his thumb to my screen and commenced dressing.

I had my nightie on, and since he didn't say anything to me, just started tugging on clothes, I called, "Uh... hello? Freaking out here, Shy."

He looked at me and did the worst thing he could do at that moment.

He took two long strides to me, lifted his hands and cupped my jaws, one hand still holding my phone. Then he dipped his face so he was all I could see.

Okay, I knew this was serious.

Now I knew it was *serious*.

"She's hit bottom, and I'm seein' from your girl that when she does somethin', she goes big," he explained.

"Wh... what? What's she done?" I stammered.

"Not a lot of time. You need to get dressed and to the Compound, which is where I'll be takin' her after I get her ass. It's also the safest place for you if there's blowback."

Blowback! I freaking *hated* that word.

"Shy—"

He cut me off to lay it out for me. "She got in deep with a dealer. She owes him big. He's takin' his money back from her in pussy and when I say that I mean, her eating it, hers getting fucked, and all of this happening on camera. She's right now dolled up and ready to give her first performance on a porno set."

"They film pornos in Denver at three in the morning?" I breathed stupidly, focusing on that rather than the fact my best friend was preparing to make her film debut and not in a good way, and Shy stared at me.

Then he said, "Babe, pisses me off fuckin' more than I am already that you didn't know that and now you do. This bitch of yours, she's not teachin' you any more of these lessons. She shared with me she doesn't feel like girl on girl or takin' cock from a guy she doesn't know and havin' all that on film. She wants an extraction which means, she's your girl, she gets one." His hands pressed gently into my jaws as he emphasized, "*One*, Tab. I know these assholes, and Chaos is gonna buy a shitload of trouble for intervening."

Suddenly, I had scores of worries and one was my mind suddenly dredging up the word *firepower.*

"What do you mean, Chaos is gonna buy trouble?" I asked but I knew.

Crap, I knew.

I was going to *kill* Natalie.

"That, I'm not gonna take the time to explain," he replied, yanked me to him, kissed the top of my hair, let me go, turned, nabbed his boots, his tee, and prowled out the bedroom door.

I stared at the opened door. In order not to focus on the matter at hand which had my heart racing, I took in something that never failed to calm me.

I looked around our bedroom, taking in our new kick-ass bedroom furniture (my old stuff was in the guest room, Shy's stuff was at the dump).

I loved our room. I'd gotten inspired. It was totally biker meets biker babe from birth. Black furniture. Deep purple sheets. Chrome accents. A black-and-white picture of me and Shy on his bike, taking off from the Compound, my arms around him, my chin to his shoulder, Shy looking badass cool in mirrored shades.

Sheila had taken that picture and I'd had it blown up to nearly poster size, framed in a black-and-chrome frame and it was hanging over the dresser. It might seem conceited to have a big poster of us looking awesome cool on our bedroom wall but I didn't care. I thought it was the bomb.

Shy did too. I'd kept him away as I was doing up the room and when I unveiled it, he'd shown me he loved the whole thing by starting a marathon session that began on our purple sheets, moved to the floor and ended on that dresser. There was a handprint on the glass of that poster, mine, put there when my hand flew back to steady me as Shy gave me an orgasm. I didn't have it in me to get out the Windex. I wanted to remember giving Shy a room he liked that much for a good long while. That handprint might stay there forever.

The last touch to the room was a wonky ball of pressed-together Christmas candy wrappers that I'd had put in one of those cases where you normally display signed baseballs. They were the wrappers Shy had cleaned up after my Hitchcock marathon right before what was not officially but still was (kind of) our first date. I'd found that ball of wrappers and saved it. I'd buried the reasons why in my pit of denial but I'd kept it and then had it mounted when we moved into our house. It was sitting on my nightstand.

When he saw it, Shy didn't celebrate that in his normal way. He just cupped my jaw, slid his thumb tenderly along my cheekbone, held my eyes, his soft and warm as he muttered, "You were gone for me too."

He was right. I didn't admit it at the time. It was crazy.

But I'd saved a ball of discarded Christmas candy wrappers.

I was gone for him too

Firepower.

Shy took off with zero word from me that I wanted him to do so. He just went off to save Natalie, dragging the brothers with him.

He was off saving Natalie from a drug dealing porn kingpin.

Firepower.

With trembling but quick hands, I dressed, thinking if Shy got hurt, if any of my boys got hurt because my best friend was an idiot, no holds barred, I was going to go apocalyptic on her ass.

* * *

Two hours later, I was in the deserted Compound, drinking coffee I'd made and fighting back the urge to mainline tequila when Rush stalked in.

My brother looked like my father, save for the fact he got Mom's light blue eyes which, fortunately for Rush, were one of the few good things she had to give.

Rush had always looked like Dad but, as time passed, he was looking more like him. He'd always been tall but lean, like Shy. Dad's frame held more bulk. As Rush matured, and especially recently, being a recruit and spending time with the brothers in the storage room at the back of Ride's auto supply store that held a bunch of weight equipment, his body was bulking out like Dad's. It had more power and his muscles were more defined.

He was my brother and I was prejudiced, of course,

but I also knew with the amount of dating he did and the fact that if he didn't want to be alone he simply wasn't, he was hot. He was also lucky that he was one of those hot guys who was hot young and got hotter as he aged.

Just like, from photographic evidence and memories, Dad.

I hadn't seen him much recently, because being a recruit for Chaos wasn't easy. They were on call to the Club 24/7 and still had to do their stints at the store and the garage.

Making matters worse for Rush, he only had one other recruit to help bear the load. The boys had christened the new guy "Joker" mostly because he didn't smile often and never laughed. Club names were random and often ironic. Case in point, Shy was named Shy by the Club because back in the day, with women especially, he was anything but shy.

Although I didn't see Rush much, Shy told me he was "settling in," though he didn't explain this phenomenon. He just said, "Doesn't bitch, gets shit done, is always available, and keeps his mouth shut. He doesn't share but way he's actin', it means somethin' to him to pass that test. Both him and Joker are goin' all out. They'll get through, get their cuts, their ink, and, the way they're showin' their loyalty, it'll be good having them at the table."

This was positive news, so I left it at that, which was good because I knew Shy didn't intend to give me more even if I wanted it.

But right then, I didn't feel positive vibes mostly because my brother looked like he wanted to kill someone.

He, also like Dad, had a short fuse, and looking at his face, I knew the sparks were close to the dynamite.

This meant that Shy and Dad were likely close to the blast.

"Your girl," he pointed at me, stalking behind the bar and heading toward where I sat on a stool, "is a pain in the fuckin' ass."

Not a good opening.

"Is everything okay?" I asked, as he reached up to a shelf and brought down the tequila.

He turned to me. "No."

Crap!

"Are Dad and Shy okay?" I pressed.

"They were when I left," he answered ominously. My heart tripped and before I could ask another question, Joker walked in.

I'd met Joker but I didn't know him mostly because when I was around, he was busy.

That didn't mean I hadn't noticed he was seriously good-looking in a scary way that reminded me more of Lee Nightingale than Chaos. It wasn't learned. It didn't come from dealing with a tough life. It was a part of him.

Joker was tall, built, not bulky but also not lean, just muscled in a powerful way. He held his body and moved like he knew exactly what his frame was capable of and what it was capable of was a lot.

He also had a natural confidence that was kind of bizarre, considering he was younger than Rush, who was twenty-six. He had a thick head of black hair with more than a small amount of wave to it. He wore it long, hanging in his face and down to his shoulders. He also had a full beard that, unlike most of the brothers who sported facial hair, he kept trimmed. The beard made him appear older than his years. The tan he had made him look weathered and again older than he was.

But it was his steel-gray eyes that told the tale. That steel was like a shield, holding everyone back from the mysteries that lay within. This was kind of a weird coincidence, since his name was Carson Steele. And I didn't know him, but I knew from those eyes there was no doubt there were mysteries that lay within.

Watching him stalk in, I thought, although I'd never tell Shy, Carson "Joker" Steele was more than a little intriguing.

At that present moment, however, he was also more than a little frightening.

He prowled around the outside of the bar, eyes glued to Rush, and he stopped four feet from me.

He then growled, "I do not like this shit."

Uh-oh.

"I don't like it either, brother," Rush agreed before he took a slug of tequila.

Joker's eyes raked through me before he strode across the room and disappeared through the door at the back.

The good news was, his eyes raked through me, and it seemed he was just generally angry, not angry at me specifically because my best friend was addicted to drugs, unfortunately chose a dealer who also made porn films and also unfortunately called me in order to extricate herself from a bad situation that involved cameras, sets, costumes, and fluffers.

The bad news was, I didn't know what was going on but I did know it wasn't good.

I turned back to my brother to see he was taking another pull of tequila, and I instantly changed my mind about what I was going to say next. First, I was going to ask for the tequila bottle. Second, after I took a hearty slug (or three), I'd ask what the heck was going on.

I didn't get the chance. The door to the Compound opened, and I felt my eyes get wide when Elvira walked in.

Uh-oh again.

Elvira.

In normal circumstances, this could mean anything.

In the present circumstances, this could only mean bad things.

I'd known Elvira for years. She was a petite, curvaceous black woman who excelled at three things. She really knew how to dress. She put together things called "boards," which were plates filled with fruit, cheese, veggies, and other stuff that didn't sound all that exciting but the way Elvira did it, it was. And if she cared about you, blood, color, religion, politics all melted away, you became her sister in all that entailed and she let you know it. I knew because Tyra had that from her. I hadn't quite been let in but then again, Elvira usually performed her adoptions when you were in the throes of a serious drama.

Something like what was happening right now.

It was also important to know she worked for Hawk Delgado.

I'd known Hawk for years too. He was a friend of Dad's and around, not often, but enough.

I didn't know what he did for a living, but since he routinely wore cargo pants and often sported a loaded gun belt in full view but had no badge, I had a sneaking suspicion he was either a commando or a mercenary. Though I couldn't say what the difference was between those two, I just knew a man was one or the other. I also knew Hawk

Delgado could totally join the cast of *The Expendables* but it was more likely he would act as a consultant on the film because Hawk Delgado didn't playact badass. He just was one.

The presence of Elvira wearing a fabulous wrap-around green dress and spike-heeled chocolate brown boots while strolling into the Compound at five o'clock in the morning meant she wasn't there for the usual reasons she was there: to eat, drink, and raise her brand of hell alongside a bunch of bikers.

Her expression and the phone held to her ear, not to mention the words she was snapping into it said finding fun while dressed to kill was not her current mission.

"I'm tellin' you, Hawk, Tack kicked me out. I was all set, everything was good, then badass biker boy didn't hesitate to blow my cover and send me on my way."

Her cover?

She glanced at me, hauled her ass up on the stool next to mine, moved her gaze to Rush, and slapped her hand on the bar. This meant tequila, STAT.

She also kept talking on the phone.

"Those biker boys strolled in packin'. I knew no good things come to those who suddenly garner Chaos attention at three thirty in the freakin' morning on a porno set and I was right. They made no bones about stating their intentions. They wanted that new girl. Those boys ambled in full force, the whole freakin' Club showed, interrupted everything and launched right in, starting negotiations. Not surprisingly, Benito didn't feel like negotiating. He wouldn't accept a Chaos marker. He wouldn't accept Chaos doin' him a needed favor since you and me know Benito keeps his shit tight and he's got no strings dangling so he don't need no favor. He wouldn't accept anything they were offering. He wouldn't even accept payment with interest for what the girl owed him. The girl was goin' to work. Seein' she owes him thirteen thousand with interest, she's got a lot of work to do. Therefore, negotiations had reached a stalemate and with those boys, well... you know."

I closed my eyes.

Thirteen thousand. With interest.

All for drugs.

God, Natalie.

"Told you she was a pain in the ass," Rush muttered.

My brother was not wrong.

Elvira kept talking and I opened my eyes to watch her.

"That's when things got hot and I tried to hold my cover by not leavin'. Tack was tryin' to be subtle then he got impatient with subtle when I didn't move my ass so he upped and blew my cover in order to get me out of there before negotiations totally broke down. When I left, Benito gave me a look that was *uncomfortable*. Tack sent me on my way tellin' Benito that if anything happened to me, shit that was already makin' plans for the winter would seriously go south and on my heels he sent the Chaos recruits. I'm thinkin' you know what that means."

I didn't know what it meant and I didn't want to know, but I was going to know because she continued.

"Yeah, it's good you're haulin' ass out there, Hawk. Girls in slutty nurse's outfits and boys with big dicks in patient gowns were scurryin'. They felt the vibe deteriorating but then again, that shit was hard to miss." She stopped talking to Hawk and looked to me. "Seriously, can they not get more original with this shit? Nurses and patients? That's been done *to death.* If I was makin' a porno, not that I'd make a porno, but, just sayin', if I was, it'd be all about a UFC ring, sweaty hot guys with tape on their hands and shorts that come off easy, say, with that Velcro stuff at the sides. One yank and *gone.* You get what I'm sayin'?"

I blinked.

I didn't get the chance to confirm or deny I got what she was saying before Elvira's attention went back to the phone.

"I'm here," she stated, then ordered, "You get there." Pause, then, "Take that up with Tack, and get this, I'm gonna take it up with him too. Spent two months hornin' in on that crew for you, such filth, I had to shower about seven times a day. Now all that work is blown with shit to show for it. I don't care if he can kick my ass, Kane 'Tack' Allen is still gonna get a few words from me."

Then she stabbed her phone with a finger that had a long, perfectly shaped, shiny, eggplant-painted fingernail, slammed the phone down on the bar, and trained her eyes on Rush.

"Uh...did you *not* get that I want a shot of tequila?" When Rush moved, offering the bottle to her, she shook her head. "Don't hand me that bottle. I am not a biker babe. I got manners. I drink out of a glass." Then she turned her head to me and declared, "No offense."

"None taken," I muttered.

"And no offense with this," she carried on, "but your bitch is a pain in the ass."

I opened my mouth to agree just as the door crashed open and a long, solid, handsome, chocolate-skinned black man with a bald head, magnificent cheekbones, and a thick black goatee surrounding a pair of full lips that had to be sculpted directly by the hand of God walked in, eyes on Elvira, his long legs taking him right to her.

"Oh lordy," she muttered, her head turned from me, and I knew she was watching the tall drink of chocolate-skinned goodness prowling her way.

"Are you fucking shitting me?" he ground out, still heading toward her.

"Calm down, baby, it's—" Elvira started.

"You are," he cut her off. "You are fucking shitting me." His big frame teetered to a halt a foot away from her and I was a bar stool away with Elvira in between and I still leaned away from his fury. "After I spank *your* ass for this bullshit, I'll be kicking *Hawk's* ass for sending you into it."

Uh-oh.

I failed to mention that Elvira was sassy in a way that she pretty much defined it. When women were sassy, men, no matter how hot they were, didn't threaten to spank their asses. It also didn't matter how angry they were, this would not be met with gentle, calming words. It would be met with rocketing fireworks and even tall, built-hot guys could not control a rocketing firework.

I knew I was right when Elvira slid off the stool which I thought was a tactical mistake seeing as she was taller on it.

She didn't seem to mind, tipped her head back and snapped, "It's my job, Malik."

He moved closer and retorted, "It's your job to answer the phones, do computer work, and herd commandos."

There it was. I was right. Hawk was a commando.

The black guy kept going. "It is *not* your job to go

undercover with a drug-dealing porn producer who targets girls, gets them hooked on junk, and takes payment in pussy."

Uh-oh again.

"It's my job to answer phones?" she asked, her voice soft in a way that made me glance at Rush who was scowling at the pair but, wisely, not wading in.

"Yeah, baby, it's your job to answer fucking *phones*," the hot black guy returned, bending a bit to get in her face.

"You don't get to say what my job is, Malik. Hawk and me decide what my job is," Elvira shot back.

"Woman, you wake up in my bed and after you give me what I need to start the day, I haul my ass out of bed and bring you breakfast so you got what you need to start the day. So do not even *think* of handing me that shit. I get a say when my woman puts her ass in danger," he volleyed.

I had to admit, not out loud of course, that he had a point and also, breakfast in bed sounded sweet. Further, now that it was clear that this guy was Elvira's man, I thought she did a little bit of seriously all right in landing this hot guy.

Elvira clearly didn't think this at the present moment. She snatched up her cell from the bar, shook it at him and asked sarcastically, "You want me to get on *the phone*, big man? Hire a sky writer so all of Denver can know our personal business?"

I thought the appropriate response to this was no.

The gorgeous Malik clearly didn't share my thought process.

He replied, "Yeah, baby. You do that. If you do, maybe

Delgado will read it and get it in his fucking head that he doesn't send my woman out doing crazy shit with drug-dealing porn producers. I cannot believe you kept this shit from me." He blew out a breath and his eyes went to Rush. "Do you feel me? Is this shit jacked?"

"Yeah," Rush answered immediately, male camaraderie and all that, and I knew my brother was hitting serious badass status when Elvira turned her attention to him and he not only didn't move back a step, he also didn't flinch. His badass status would be proved when he went on to suggest, "Though, will say maybe your domestic isn't well-timed. I got brothers out there in an uncertain situation, so maybe you two can suck it up and finish this shit some other time?"

Elvira cut her gaze back to her man, lifted a finger, and wagged it at him. "That works for me but, for you, just sayin', you gettin' what you need to start your day just got cut off for an indefinite period of time."

I chanced a look at Malik and saw him scowling down at Elvira.

Then he pulled in breath through his nose as he held her eyes before he muttered, "We'll see."

"Yeah, we will," she fired back and suddenly he flashed a sexy white smile that shone so bright surrounded by that black goatee, it took him from handsome to such a knockout I had to hold on to the bar.

"Baby, you cutting me off means you getting cut off, and I foresee that indefinite period of time lasting about a day."

I only had the back of Elvira's head but I fancied she rolled her eyes before she mumbled, "Whatever," which, translated by a girl who understood girls, meant he was right and she was saving face. Then she slid back onto her stool, trained her gaze on Rush, and snapped, "Tequila?"

Rush looked at me then grabbed a shot glass. He put it down on the bar in front of Elvira and poured.

He barely took the bottle away before she lifted it and threw it back.

She slammed the glass down on the bar and in an effort not to freak out about whatever was happening out there with my man, my father, and my best friend involved, I leaned toward Elvira and whispered, "Your guy is kinda hot."

She turned to me without hesitation and replied, "Careful what you wish for, girl. One by one my girls went down to badasses, I watched and thought, 'I wouldn't mind gettin' me a little somethin'-somethin' from a badass.'" She tapped her glass on the bar for another refill, Rush gave it to her, she threw it back, then she looked at me again and snapped with emphasis, "*Wrong.*"

"I have a badass," I reminded her.

"Yeah," she returned. "And Tyra told me you two went at it for days over a flippin' fridge. Badasses are capable of and don't hesitate to throw down about a fridge. An IT geek does not care what kind of fridge you buy. An IT geek just thanks his lucky stars he's gettin' it regular. An IT geek would say, 'Whatever you want, honey,' if you told him you were paving the front walk in gold."

I suspected this was true, but still I leaned back and took in Malik, who was now leaning against the bar. What I took in was a tall frame, lean hips, a flat stomach, big hands, broad shoulders, perfect skin, warm, brown eyes, and a brilliant smile even if it was directed at the bar while he shook his head in a way that said clearly he thought his woman was crazy but all kinds of cute.

I leaned forward again and toward Elvira to point out, "True, but IT geeks don't tend to look like Denzel Washington circa *Training Day*. Denzel might have been scary in that movie but his scary was all kinds of hot." Elvira made no reply so I further noted, "And your man isn't Denzel *Training Day* scary. He's more Denzel *Man on Fire* intense with a little sense of humor and a goatee thrown in."

Elvira turned her eyes to me and asked, "You got every Denzel film memorized?"

"Doesn't everybody?" I asked back.

She looked to her glass, tapped it on the bar, and muttered, "Point taken."

Rush poured her another shot, she threw it back, and I reached out and took the bottle from him. I was a biker babe and I didn't mind putting the bottle to my mouth and sucking back, so that was what I did.

I was putting the bottle down on the bar when the door opened again, and all eyes, including mine, went to it. My pulse spiked as Natalie, followed by Hound, Boz, and Speck came in.

She looked freaked. She also was wearing a short, tight nurse's outfit, white stockings, garters, and white, patent-leather, stripper platform, lace-up knee boots. Her boobs were spilling and her hair was a ratted mess of curls contained in ponytails and a nurse's cap.

Elvira was right. That whole gig had been done to death, and as a nurse I took professional umbrage.

But I couldn't think of that as I felt cold start to infuse my system from the outside in because Nat, Hound, Boz, and Speck were the only ones that came in.

No Shy.

No Dad.

I jumped off the stool and locked eyes with Boz, not trusting myself to look at Natalie. Not yet. Not until I knew everyone was okay.

"Where are Shy and Dad?" I asked.

Hound ordered Rush, "Lock her down. My room." He had his hand on Natalie's arm, shoved her forward, and she stumbled on her stripper boots.

Rush moved toward Natalie.

My eyes shifted back to Boz. "Where are they?"

"Tabby," Natalie called, her voice shaky.

I didn't move my eyes from Boz. "Boz? Where are Shy and my dad?"

"Tabby," Natalie called again, her voice breaking halfway through my name and that cold shot through me, freezing me completely.

I looked to her.

"It went bad," I stated and saw tears sliding out of her eyes, mascara going with them. Rush had made it to her and had a hand on her upper arm, but he didn't get the chance to move her before I shot forward and stood in front of her.

"My man or my father?" I asked.

"Move back, Tabby, honey, we need to get her locked down then take care of some business," Boz said from close behind me.

"My man or my father?" I demanded to know, not moving an inch.

"Let's get you to a couch, get you a drink, and we'll talk," Boz went on.

"My man," I leaned in so I was nose to nose with my *ex*-best friend, then I lost it completely, "*or my father?*" I ended on a screech.

"Shy got winged by a bullet," she whispered, and the deep freeze shattered, imploding from the inside and the pain was excruciating. So unbearable, I had to do something. I had to try to let some of it go. I had to lash out.

So I did.

I drew back a hand and slapped her with everything I had. Apparently everything I had was a lot since not only her head but her whole body shot to the side and she again lost her footing on her stripper boots. She only stayed standing because Rush had a hold on her and kept her that way.

I looked up at Boz. "How bad?"

"Clipped, not bad. Tack took him to Baldy to have a look, stitch him up if it's needed," Boz replied.

"What does that mean, clipped?" I snapped.

"Nicked, Tabby, in the neck," Boz answered and I felt my pulse pounding in my wrists, my temples, my neck. "It was a ricochet off a warning shot. Made a bad situation worse. Still, didn't hit anything important. It'll leave a scar but he's fine. Everyone's just pissed 'cause we bought a new problem."

"We bought a new problem," I stated and swung my gaze back to Natalie.

She dropped hers to my shoulder.

"Look at me," I hissed and it took a few beats before her eyes lifted to mine. "You called me tonight knowing. Knowing that for me, they'd swing their asses out there for you. Knowing this was bad shit. Knowing they'd be in danger. And without a thought, for me Shy swung his ass out there for you. He called his brothers and they swung their asses out there for you. My man, my dad, my brother, my family, all getting out of bed to take on your shit. Now, my man bled for you. Now, my family has a problem because . . . *of you*."

"Tabby—"

I shook my head. "No, you don't get to talk. I gave you chance after chance to talk for months, and you didn't take me up on any of them. You left me hanging until you fell so far, you were buried and needed help digging yourself out. I offered you my hand months ago, Nat, you refused to take it. Right now, you are dead to me. *Dead.* The only way you get resurrected is if you kick that shit, for good, Natalie, pay your dealer with your own fucking money and figure out a way to make this good for my family. You pull off that miracle, you breathe for me. Until then, you do not exist."

"Tab, you were right, you—" she started, leaning toward me beseechingly, but I stepped away from her and turned to Boz.

"Take me to Shy," I demanded.

"Honey, shit's hot and Shy wants you at the Compound where you're safe," Boz replied.

"Take me . . . *to my man!*" I shrieked, losing it. I needed Shy, needed to see for myself he was okay.

Boz opened his mouth but Hound moved in.

"Yell, scream, scratch, slap, bite, woman, whatever you do, not gonna happen. We get you, you lost a man, you're tweaked. But we're tellin' you, he's fine and we're yours, Tab, you're ours, we would not shit you about something that important. Now, Shy says you stay here. You stay here. You wanna be away from this bitch, you'll get that. We're lockin' her down so they can't get to her and she can't get into more trouble. What we are not gonna do is take you to our brother when he told us to keep your shit safe. You try to go, woman, you're locked down too. Your choice, sit your ass down and have a drink or find yourself locked in your man's room. Make it. Now. We got shit to do."

I glared at Hound, but even angry I took in the look in his eyes and knew I could throw a fit and not get my way. Anyway, they had shit to do, and I was no old lady if I kept them from that. Since I was Shy's old lady and my behavior reflected on him, I backed down.

But, since I was Tabby and he was Hound, I didn't do it gracefully.

"You're off my Christmas card list," I announced.

To which he replied immediately, "Didn't know I was on it."

My eyes narrowed. "You don't open my Christmas cards?"

"Tab, you want me to stand here talkin' about Christmas cards or do you want me to take care of business?" Hound fired back.

I kept glaring then I declared, "I need a drink."

"Color me a bartender," Elvira stated, hopped off her stool, aimed a look at Malik, who was still leaning casually into the bar, then she strutted her round ass covered in a designer dress around the bar.

"Lock her in Hound's room and get Joker. Speck's here to help out. You boys lock this place down and patrol Ride. You'll get reinforcements soon," Boz said to Rush. Rush jerked up his chin and led a pale-faced, silently weeping Natalie away.

I ignored my best friend's emotion (which was hard) and hitched my behind up on a bar stool.

Malik slid close while Elvira poured coffee.

"Scared straight works, honey," Malik said, and I looked at him. "Seen it time and again."

"Not sure at this moment I care," I replied.

"At this moment, no. I see that." He leaned closer. "Get to that point though, girl. Your man might have shed blood but he's breathing. You need to find forgiveness because you care about her. To get her out of a porn movie nurse's outfit and on a healthy path, she's going to need all the help she can get."

"Not to be a bitch or anything, but what are you, a drug counselor?" I asked.

"No, I'm a vice cop," he answered.

Well, that explained that.

I looked to Elvira. "You're seein' a cop?"

Elvira, done with the coffee, was now pouring shots of tequila. She glanced at Malik then looked at me. "I was."

I turned to Malik to see him grinning at Elvira like he thought she was adorable.

I turned back to Elvira to see her slugging back a shot of tequila. She then chased this with a sip of coffee.

Only after that did she reply, "To get a badass I had a choice. Biker, commando, military, or cop. My clothes do not say back of a bike. Commando screams 'messy' and, trust me, I know this from experience. I do not wanna spend my days learning the different ways of getting blood out of cargo pants. And military men are deployed and I'm sure not takin' out the trash for months and worryin' myself sick while he's off somewhere gettin' shot at, even if it is to keep my people safe. So I got stuck with a cop. He gets shot at and keeps people safe, but at least he's home to take out the trash."

"I'm not sure you did that bad, Elvira. Just saying, breakfast in bed?" I pointed out and her eyebrows flew up.

"Girl, don't tell me. I'll remind you, you held a grudge for three days over crushed ice. You witnessed his transgressions. For that, I get at least a week and you know it."

She was not wrong. He yelled at her in front of an audience. Shy would buy a freeze-out for that, definitely.

To communicate that, I sipped coffee.

"You go a week, baby, we got problems," Malik said low.

Elvira rolled her eyes at me but didn't reply.

"You talk to your girl any longer like I'm not standing right here, we also got problems," Malik carried on.

Elvira transferred her eye roll to him.

"You roll your eyes one more time, you lose my mouth," he warned.

Elvira glared at him.

What she didn't do, I will note, was roll her eyes or talk about Malik like he wasn't there.

I kept sipping coffee.

I watched Rush and Joker walk through the Compound giving Malik looks to which he gave an affirmative, nonverbal, macho man, *I got this* chin lift. I didn't know what he had, but I was guessing what he had was his woman in a biker Compound, so even as a vice cop he was going to do his bit to make sure the Compound was safe.

Then I watched my brother and his brother walk out the front door.

Then I waited patiently for my man to get to me.

As any biker babe from birth would do.

* * *

"Babe, I'm fine."

"Let me look at it."

"Tabby, sugar, *I'm fine.*"

I leaned away from Shy and planted my hands on my hips, staring up at him. "And I'm a nurse, Shy Cage. I'm also your woman. And I'm gonna *look at it.*"

"It's all good," Shy replied. "Baldy knows what he's doing."

Dr. Baldwin, a man I'd known for years, did know what he was doing but he did it for cash and he didn't come cheap. This meant that even though he owned a Harley, needed a haircut, had tattoos, and looked like a bruiser, he also had an extremely well-equipped clinic whose back door saw more action than the front.

Regardless of the knowledge that Baldy knew what he was doing, I took Shy in with a professional eye.

He'd returned about ten minutes before, which was about ten minutes after Malik performed a miracle, got Elvira to lose the attitude, and by the time Shy, Dad, and the rest of the boys strolled in, all seriously pissed off, Elvira was standing between his spread legs as he sat on his stool and they were bar-stool cuddling.

It was cute.

Now, Shy and I were in his room at the Compound. He looked like what he said he was except for a small, white bandage at his neck and discoloration on his black tee under the bandage which I knew as dried blood. His color was good. He didn't appear lethargic, and he'd had stitches with only a local anesthetic.

Still, I wanted to see.

"Honey, sit on the bed and let me see," I requested quietly.

He held my eyes for a few beats before sighing and sitting on the bed.

I got close, gently peeled back the tape and looked.

The boys told no lies. It was just a nick that took only a few stitches. My man was fine.

Thank God.

Carefully, I pressed the tape back and sat on the bed beside Shy.

"Happy?" he asked me.

"That my best friend is an idiot that led my man into a situation that included an exchange of bullets and the Club buying problems?" I asked back. "No."

Shy moved, gathering me in his arms and hauling me onto the bed.

When he had us arranged, him on his back, me mostly on him, he slid his hand into my hair and informed me, "As much as I don't wanna let anything slide with that bitch, Club's been havin' problems with Benito for a while. We got Chaos territory around Ride that's drug and hooker free. This message is clear to everybody, but lately Benito's been encroaching." He held my eyes, took in a deep breath and stated, "You tell him, I won't be happy, but this is why Rush was undecided about the Club."

"I don't get it," I told him.

He rolled me to my back, pressing into me, hovering close. "Right, Tab, the people who keep Chaos territory clean are Chaos."

"Okay," I stated.

Shy studied me then explained, "The brothers, babe. Not the cops."

I blinked then too little sleep, too much tequila mixed with too much coffee cleared away and it hit me.

"Are you saying you're vigilantes?" I breathed.

Shy nodded. "Our territory, our rule, our law, all in our hands. Five-mile radius around the shop and garage. *All* the shops. All Chaos territory."

Oh crap. I didn't know this.

I mean, I wasn't stupid, and I heard my mother and father fighting all the freaking time, so it wasn't like I didn't know the Club had a rocky history. Furthermore, it was a motorcycle club. That right there said a lot. Dad had plans from the start to get the Club clean. I'd been mostly shielded from what it took to get Chaos clean, but stuff was extreme when he went about doing it so it wasn't like it was lost on me.

But Dad did it. He got the Club clean.

"Shy—"

His hand cupped the side of my head and his face got closer. "Baby, leave it be."

"I'm not sure—"

His hand pressed gently into my head. "Not bein' a dick, you know it, but still gotta say it. Sugar, you don't get to be anything. This is Club business. Just know your dad is no fool. He has it goin' on. But Rush is his father's son. He didn't live the nightmare your dad lived with the Club's past history, but that doesn't mean he doesn't have a mission. Tack pulled the Club through some serious shit, but he's still Chaos and is used to doin' it his way, takin' care of Club business, lookin' after what's ours. Rush thinks Tack's job is not done. He wants us to protect what's ours and get our hands clean of all the dirt we gotta rub up against to keep our patch clean. Rush thinks that's the job of the Denver Police Department and our job is to look after our own, not everything within a five-mile radius. My guess is, he talked with your dad about this, Tack knows that shit can encroach if you don't keep a safe perimeter, and they didn't see eye to eye. My other guess is, instead of keepin' his distance and makin' his statement by stayin' out of the Club, he decided to take his chance at making change by joining us."

This did not sound good.

Like, *at all*.

"You mean, overthrow Dad?" I asked, my voice shaky.

"I don't know what it means," Shy answered. "I do know your brother is no fool either. I can tell by the way he's taking his shit as a recruit that the Club means somethin' to him and, gotta say, Tab, that shocked the shit outta me. If I had this as my legacy, I turned eighteen, I'd be workin' toward my cut. He jumped on board when he was twenty-five. But there's no denyin' he's all in. Dog and Brick are in Grand Junction, Hop and me have Tack's ear and he shares. Which is somethin' *you* don't do. As far as you're concerned, you don't know this. You gotta watch it play out just like everybody. You don't intervene. You don't have words with either of them. They're your dad and brother but bottom line, it's Club business, Tabby, and you know what that means."

I did.

I also knew not long after the business went down with Lee Nightingale and the boys had Shy's back, Shy approached Dad to ask if his offer to be lieutenant was still open. Dad shared he was holding the position for Shy until he was ready for it, no one else was even a consideration. This meant Shy was in the inner sanctum, an elevated position within the Club and, at his age, that was huge.

Therefore, as his woman and with his position in the Club, I had to stand by his side.

This meant not getting into his face about Club business.

So I simply stated. "Shy, I don't have a good feeling about this."

"You wouldn't 'cause you're a daughter and a sister. What you aren't is a son or a Chaos brother. They might not see eye to eye but your brother loves his father, he respects him and, when he earns his cut, they'll add a different relationship to that. We all don't get along all the time. There's friction, differences of opinion, politics, even clashes. But there's always the brotherhood and we all know it. That will never die."

Well, at least there was that.

I backtracked, my eyes moving to his bandage then back to his face.

"How big is this problem with the porn guy?" I asked quietly, and I got what I expected.

"That's not somethin' you worry about."

This was something, as his woman and him my man with a bandage on his neck, I had to get in his face about.

"Wrong, Shy," I whispered.

He dipped his face close. "Your bitch is a mess. She hit bottom but, stuff she's into, that won't mean a thing. She might be shaken up and get her shit sorted but she might not. It isn't cool she called you, dragged you and, because of you, Chaos into her mess, but this was going to happen, it just came sooner. You were dragged in, now you know. But that's all you know and you don't worry."

"That's impossible," I informed him.

"If you think this Club hasn't weathered worse storms than this guy, you're wrong."

This was not welcome information.

"Shy, you got shot and you're okay but—"

His head moved, his mouth touched mine and when he lifted his head, his thumb slid to my lips. "Tab, baby, after what you lost, do you think for a second I'd do anything, your father would do anything, to make you lose me?"

This made me feel slightly better, because I didn't think that, not for a second, but that didn't mean I didn't repeat, even with his thumb still on my lips, "Shy, darlin', you got shot."

"A nick," he clarified.

"But—"

"I'm not leaving you."

"But, Shy—"

His thumb pressed against my lips lightly.

"Tabitha, I'm not leaving you."

I held my silence and his eyes.

Then I lifted a hand, curled it around his wrist, pulled his hand away and whispered, "You better not."

He grinned and whispered back, "You're stuck with me."

God, I hoped so.

I took in an unsteady breath.

Then I told him, "Sorry my ex–best friend got you nicked by a bullet."

His grin turned into a smile. "Shit happens."

It was kind of forced but I grinned back.

He pulled against my hold so his hand could come back, his thumb gliding along my lips as his eyes watched. His smile was gone when his gaze again met mine.

"Always and forever, baby, you're stuck with me."

I drew in a deep breath that miraculously was calming and I nodded.

Shy studied me then dipped his head, brushed his lips against mine, and then rolled to his back, taking me with him, tucking me to his side.

"Wiped, sugar," he muttered. "Rest with me."

"Okay," I muttered back, snuggling closer, knowing, after as much caffeine as I consumed, all that had happened and all that I'd learned, I wouldn't sleep a wink.

I was right. I felt Shy relax under me, his breath even out, his arm around my waist going heavy.

I stared at his tee, the pendants resting at his throat, my mind bouncing from thought to thought, not any of them happy.

Then it bounced and landed on, *You're stuck with me.*

My lips curved into a smile.

Then I relaxed into my man, my breath evened out, my weight against him going heavy, pressed deep into his side, wrapped around him, in sleep proving something he was missing in his sleep but that was okay since he already knew.

He was stuck with me too.

CHAPTER TWENTY-ONE

All In

SHY FELT THE vibe, he opened his eyes and felt Tabby's weight pressed against him.

Carefully, he curled up, kissed the top of her hair, then slid out from under her sleeping body. Finding his feet by the side of the bed, he watched his girl adjust, curl into his pillow, never losing sleep.

He wanted to pull her hair away from her face so he could see it, feel the softness run through his fingers, but he didn't want to chance waking her. So he left her in his bed and moved from the room.

When he hit the common room, he saw most of his brothers were congregated around the bar. Hop was sitting on a stool, Tack standing close to him.

Shy approached and when he got close Tack asked, "She doin' okay?"

"Sleepin'," Shy answered.

"She's doin' okay," Tack muttered.

"She'll be out awhile, but I still wanna have this shit done and get back to her before she wakes up," Shy went on.

Tack jerked up his chin, Hop slid off the stool, and they moved out to their bikes, Tack on his phone.

They waited until Tack finished his calls before they started up and roared out, Tack in the lead, Hop and Shy riding side by side behind him.

Tack and his lieutenants arrived at the rendezvous point first. They were off their bikes and waiting when the first vehicle pulled up.

An unmarked cop car carrying Mitch Lawson and Brock Lucas, both detectives with the DPD. Both tight with Tack due to complicated history, this history complicated because it had to do with women and, in Lawson's case, kids.

Shy watched the men exit the car and approach and it wasn't lost on Shy that both men, even behind shades, clocked the bandage at his neck.

Lawson looked to Tack. "Word is, last night, you bought yourself a problem."

"My daughter's best friend got herself a habit. No supplier is a good one with that habit but she still managed to pick the worst," Tack confirmed.

Lucas tipped his head to Shy. "She learn a lesson?"

"We'll see," Tack muttered as a gray Camaro made its approach and all eyes turned to watch Hawk Delgado park and fold out of his vehicle. His right-hand man, Jorge, folded himself out of the passenger side.

Unlike Lawson and Lucas, as he moved to them, Delgado's face was not assessing. He was pissed.

When he stopped at the group, eyes locked to Tack, he stated, "After the meet, we have words."

"Not a big fan of collateral damage," Tack returned, his way of saying there would be no words after the meet. He did what he did and Hawk had to deal.

"You needed that girl, you saw Elvira there, you knew we were working a job, all you had to do was call me," Hawk shot back.

"Do not shit me," Tack bit out. "You're workin' a job, it's about the job, and your job was not about that girl. Fifty-fifty chance you'd let that girl swing and her time was up. She means somethin' to my daughter. I had to move and I didn't have the option of takin' any of the limited time I had to negotiate with you."

Shy watched Hawk's mouth get tight which meant he conceded the point.

"Right," Lucas cut in to change the subject before the mood deteriorated further. "It's not a secret Chaos has been havin' problems with Benito for a while. It's also not a secret DPD has always had problems with him since he's a piece-of-shit scumbag. What was a secret until last night was that Delgado's got somethin' workin' with this and it was blown. Now Benito's gonna be more determined to carve into Chaos territory, and Hawk's out there, seein' as they've probably already traced Elvira to his operation." Lucas trained his shades on Delgado. "Not to mention, Malik is all kinds of pissed because Elvira was made before you did whatever you're gettin' paid to do, you didn't discuss her involvement with him, and she's now seriously vulnerable."

"She's got protection and part of that is sleepin' with a cop," Delgado returned. "The rest of it is me."

This was formidable. They all knew that.

But so was Benito. They all knew that too.

"Now we know the lay of the land," Lawson pointed out. "We also know that the time has come to put an end to Benito's operation."

"That time came about two years ago," Hop threw out.

"Not gonna argue that," Lucas stated. "But that didn't happen and I think it hasn't escaped anybody that this shit was simmering. Now the situation is all kinds of hot."

"Extreme," Tack agreed, then declared, "War."

"Chaos and Delgado," Shy added, looking at Hawk. "I think, man, Benito's more pissed at you, and he's a weasel. Have a mind to your back."

"I always do," Delgado replied.

"Then have a mind to everything," Shy went on. "Weasels are slick motherfuckers who can go underground. He might not come at your back. He might dig up from underneath."

"Not tellin' me somethin' I don't know," Delgado said.

"What he's tellin' you that you don't know is this is now a team effort," Tack announced. "That's why we called this meeting. You're a target. Elvira's a target. Chaos is a target. Benito's an anything-goes man, so right now it is all eyes, all ears, all hands, all firepower . . ." Tack looked to Lucas and Lawson and finished, ". . . all in."

Shy looked through the men and was not surprised when not one said anything.

Tacit agreement.

Lucas and Lawson might be cops, but their bond with Tack was such that it wasn't just about taking down a drug-dealing porn producer. With Chaos in Benito's sights, it was more.

Delgado and Tack were always butting heads, but Tack took Delgado's woman's back during an intense situation, which meant he also took Delgado's. In return, Delgado took Tack's back when things got extreme with Cherry.

Shit like that didn't go down without ties forming. Ties that bind.

Thus, with no further words, the meeting ended. Jorge and Delgado moved to the Camaro, Lucas and Lawson angled into the unmarked cop car.

The three brothers watched them leave, and when they lost sight, they moved to huddle.

"Rush is not gonna be happy about this shit," Hop noted, and Tack sighed.

"Already isn't. We had words," Tack told them. "He thinks we should lay it on Lucas and Lawson and back off. I told him that's not gonna happen. He knows this is gonna get messy. Says it proves his point."

"He's wrong," Shy remarked, and Tack looked at him, nodding once.

"He is," Tack muttered then, "He'll see." He lifted a hand, curled it around the back of his neck, looked into the distance and finished, "We'll all see."

They would. That message was made clear last night.

Take Natalie, declare war.

They took Natalie.

They had war.

Now it was only deciding who would strike first.

"Need to get back to Tab," Shy murmured, Tack dropped his hand and looked at Shy.

"Right," he replied then Shy watched him draw in another breath before he stated, "She's mine, but I get she's yours in a way I don't have anymore. Respect, but I'm askin' you to carry the burden and let her breathe easy."

"She's yours, Tack, which means she's not dumb. That bitch called her direct." Shy lifted a hand to indicate the bandage on his neck. "Last night was not lost on her. She knows we bought trouble."

"I get that, brother. I'm not sayin' that. I'm sayin', *you* carry the burden and let her breathe easy. Are you getting me?"

Shy held his gaze before he nodded.

Tack drew in another breath, this one he didn't hide that, when he let it out, it was relieved.

"Lanie," Hop muttered, bringing the matter back to hand that they needed to get back to their women.

Tack turned and nodded to Hop.

"Right," he repeated. "Later, brothers. Have a mind, it's early, he won't move this quick, but watch your backs."

Shy nodded. Hop did too.

They swung on their bikes and roared off to get to their women.

* * *

Tack

Tack Allen watched his brothers go.

He didn't move as he did. He didn't move for long minutes after they disappeared.

He stood there knowing.

Tyra, Tabby, Lanie, Sheila, the entire family.

Benito Valenzuela was hardcore cracked. Void. Empty. No emotion. No loyalty. No nothing.

Empty of everything but greed.

A man who felt nothing but greed, he gave you only one option for leverage.

But he had many.

"Fuck," Tack whispered, closed his eyes, felt the pit weigh heavy in his gut and opened his eyes.

It wasn't over.

It was never fucking over.

"Fuck," he repeated, moved to his bike, swung his leg over and roared off to get to his woman.

* * *

Shy

Shy opened the door to his room in the Compound, stepped through, and stopped dead at what he saw.

Tabby was sitting cross-legged in his bed wearing his T-shirt. Her head was bowed and she was staring at her phone, her profile a mask of disbelief.

He closed the door behind him, calling, "Tabby?"

Slowly, her head turned his way, the disbelief in her face cleared, her beautiful blue eyes started shining just as her perfect rosy lips started curling up.

Then her body started shaking.

That was when he heard her giggles.

Shy froze at the sight.

There she was, his girl, after a night like last night, sitting in his bed in his room...*laughing.*

Oh yeah.

That was his girl.

On this thought, through her laughter, she forced out, "Shy, darlin', I just got off the phone with Ty-Ty..." She trailed off shaking her head, giggling some more but before he could prompt her, she continued, "She just gave me the latest scoop on Lanie and Hop and, honey, you... would not... *believe*."

She then told him what he wouldn't believe and, in telling, proved she didn't know Hop all that well.

Because Shy believed it.

Every word.

EPILOGUE

Start Now

Two weeks later…

I SWUNG OFF Shy's bike, my eyes to the view.

Denver was lit up, sprawling left to right but beyond, nothing but darkness.

All of it beautiful.

I moved to the edge of the mountain road, my cheeks stinging from the cold that whipped them as I rode up to elevation with Shy, me where I belonged.

On the back of my man's bike.

I felt him move in behind me. He wrapped his arms around my chest, then I felt his lips against the top of my hair.

"What's on my girl's mind?" he asked quietly.

He *so* knew me.

"Natalie," I replied, lifting my hands and curling my fingers around his forearms.

My friend had fallen off the wagon, not that she ever really got on.

It didn't take long.

It also broke my heart.

After that, I broke ties. It killed, but I couldn't save her so I had to save my peace of mind. The problem with that was, it wasn't working.

I felt his lips leave my hair but his jaw replaced them.

We stared at the view silently.

I broke our silence.

"You gave her a chance, she blew it. Went out and scored. You cut her loose and now, I don't know." My hands gripped his arms tight. "Shy, I don't know and as ticked as I am at her, I'm worried."

I felt him heave a breath, his chest expanding, pressing into my back.

"You know what I know?" he asked.

"What do you know?" I asked back.

"I know you can spend your energy and head space worryin', and a bitch who was minutes away from being force fed pussy goes out and scores is not worth it."

I closed my eyes.

He was *so* right.

"You wanna know what else I know?" he asked.

I opened my eyes.

"What do you know?" I asked back.

"No amount of your energy or head space is gonna change her. She's lost, Tabby, in a way it's a miracle if she's ever found. Before you use yourself up, cut her loose. Don't just say it to her, to me, to yourself. *Do it.*"

I swallowed.

Shy was right again.

Therefore I nodded.

His arms tightened and he pressed his lips into the top of my hair.

"You wanna know what else I know?" he asked.

"What do you know, honey?"

"My girl is gonna marry me."

I blinked.

His arms broke free from my grip and he turned me. When I was face-to-face with him, he dug into his pocket. When his hand came out, he grabbed mine and slid the marquise diamond on my left ring finger.

I stared.

It was stunning, beautiful. Not too big that it would catch on stuff and make me worry. Not too small it didn't say what it needed to say.

And what it said was what the sapphire earrings right then in my ears said:

I was loved by a badass biker.

I held my hand in front of my face, fingers extended, Shy's hand wrapped around mine, thumb to the base of the ring, and I stared through the dark at its beauty.

"You didn't get to go with but picking this out was too important, so I took Cherry," he told me and my startled eyes moved to his face.

There it was again.

I was loved.

"She said that would be your thing so that's what you got," he finished.

"It is," I said softly. "It is *exactly* my thing."

He grinned at me. "And that's what you got."

I stared at him then right out of my mouth came, "I've wanted you since I was sixteen, Shy Cage."

Shy's hand moved to slide up my neck and stopped, cupping my jaw.

"Then I'm slow on the uptake, though wantin' that

would be illegal. But I've wanted you since you were nineteen and you stuck your tongue in my mouth," he returned, then muttered, "Thinkin' on it, even before."

"I didn't stick my tongue in your mouth. I touched the tip to yours to show you what you were missing," I corrected, and his grin got bigger.

"Good job, sugar. Taste was so sweet, years passed and I couldn't get it off my tongue."

Suddenly, tears filled my eyes.

"We're getting married," I whispered.

"Yeah," he replied, still grinning.

"We're getting married," I repeated.

"Yeah, babe, and I like it that you like the way those words taste in your mouth, but I'd like it more if you'd shut up and kiss me."

I didn't kiss him. I said, "We're getting married."

Shy went quiet then he let my hand go so he could cup my jaw as he dipped his face close. "Yeah, Tabby, baby. We're getting married."

My head dropped forward, my forehead hitting his. I curved my fingers around his wrists and held tight.

"I'm gonna wear your mom's diamonds at the wedding," I told him.

"Good, I want her and Dad there with you and me," he told me.

A tear slid down my cheek. Shy's thumb shifted and caught it midrun.

I said nothing but I felt everything.

"Tabby, love you, honey but you're kinda freakin' me out," Shy admitted.

"I don't know what to do," I confessed.

"About what?"

"Being this happy."

His fingers flexed on my jaws as he pressed his forehead into mine.

Then he said, his voice rough, "Start now."

"Pardon?" I asked.

"Start now," he repeated.

"Shy—"

"Start now, Tabitha. Start gettin' used to it."

I stared into his eyes as another tear slid out of mine.

"I dreamed a dream," I whispered.

His voice was gruff when he ordered, "Shut up and kiss me."

I didn't shut up. Another tear slid out of my eye and my voice was husky when I repeated, "I dreamed a dream, Shy Cage."

He shifted so his lips were against mine and his voice was now raw when he ordered, "Shut up, baby, and kiss me."

"I dreamed a dream when I was sixteen and here I am, standing with my dream, feeling it come real."

"Fuck me," he muttered.

Then I knew he'd lost patience, because Shy slanted his head and kissed me.

Yes.

I dreamed a dream and there I was, a ring on my finger, my man's mouth on mine, standing with my dream, feeling it come real.

I was right about what I was feeling.

I was feeling everything.

And it was beautiful.

* * *

Six months later…

In front of the altar at our church, I stood next to Shy while holding a bouquet of ivory roses with white hydrangeas at the base, the stems wrapped in ivory satin ribbon, my hair up in a series of elegant curls and twists because, for some reason, Shy requested it be that way.

I was wearing an ivory gown, also sophisticated (to go with my hair), the garter Ty-Ty wore at her wedding to Dad around my thigh, Shy's mother's diamond earrings at my ears.

In this getup, I was getting married to Shy.

Tyra was my matron of honor.

Landon was Shy's best man.

Dad, of course, gave me away.

We didn't bother with a flower girl, since Rider and Cutter both played ring bearers.

Being a now-somewhat-experienced old lady, I managed to hold myself together and not cry when I said, "I do."

I lost it when Shy said it, but I figured that was okay since I could hear Tyra crying right along with me.

The best part of the ceremony was after Shy kissed his bride, and when we were done, he didn't let go. So I stood in his arms, my thumb stroking his jaw, my eyes gazing up at him. The world had melted away, so I didn't hear the hoots and hollers of friends and family.

I only heard what he muttered in a voice that was weirdly raw but unbelievably beautiful:

"Like I'm the only man on the planet."

In that minute, he was, but then again, for me, really, when it came down to it, he always had been.

Though I didn't understand why he said those words and even later, when I asked, he didn't answer. He just smiled at me.

I figured I should let him have his secret. It didn't matter anyway, because the words he spoke were true.

After the ceremony, we had a big blowout. The shindig to end all shindigs.

And the best part of that was after we had our first dance as husband and wife to a lame song I picked, Shy again didn't let me go.

Seconds later, Jose Gonzalez's "Heartbeats" started playing.

A very not-lame song that Shy picked.

It wasn't exactly a song you could dance to, so we didn't. We just looked into each other's eyes, held each other close, and swayed as I let the words of the beautiful poem Shy chose for us wash over me.

It was the best day of my life, and a lot of that had to do with looking into my husband's eyes and seeing, plainly, it was the best day of his.

The only man on the planet.

The only man for me.

* * *

And life was very, very good.

Paradise.

Get lost in the Chaos!
Kristen Ashley's captivating
series continues…

Please turn this page for a preview of

FIRE INSIDE

PROLOGUE

Complicated

HOPPER "HOP" KINCAID watched her winding through the loud, rowdy, drunk bikers and their groupies, heading his way.

Lanie Heron.

He didn't move. He kept leaning against the post that held up the roof over the patio area of the Compound, holding a beer and watching her move.

Jesus, she was one serious class act. Even when she came to a barbecue, to the Compound to shoot pool, or to a hog roast, communing with the brethren of the Chaos Motorcycle Club, she didn't dress down. Designer gear, head to toe. She looked like a fucking model except better, because she was real, right there, walking right to him, her eyes locked to his.

She was also one serious messed-up bitch.

This was not simply because the woman was pure drama. Fuck, he'd seen her create a scene because she wasn't paying attention when she was pouring her Diet Cherry 7Up and it had fizzed over the top of the glass.

No, Lanie Heron was messed up because she stood by her man.

In normal circumstances, Hopper would find that an admirable trait in any woman, mostly because he knew by experience it was a rare one.

Not with Lanie.

This was because before he got shot to death, her man was even more messed up than she was. The proof of this was he was now very dead, and she had scars from the bullets her dead fiancé bought her because he wanted to give her some crazy-ass, out-of-season flowers for their wedding and he got involved with the Russian Mob to do it.

The fucking Russian Mob.

For flowers.

Not messed up, *fucked* up.

Before it all went down, she found out about him working for the Mob. Being a woman, of course, first, she busted his balls. Then she made a tremendously bad decision and stood by him even after his shit got her kidnapped. Then she watched him die and nearly got herself killed in the process.

Fucked up. Your old man gets involved with the Russian Mob, this gets your ass kidnapped, once you get rescued you kick him to the curb. No question. You just do it.

You don't go on the lam with him and get yourself shot.

He watched her move his way, thinking all of this at the same time thinking about the moment he first saw her. It was the night she found out her old man was making whacked decisions in order to buy flowers. Even though, at the time, she was in full-blown drama mode, for once her drama being understandable, the second Hop saw her years ago, he'd thought she was definitely one fine piece of ass.

Watching her come his way, he had not changed his mind.

She was not his thing, normally. Too tall, too skinny, no ass, not enough tits and way too put together with her designer jeans and high-heeled boots that had to cost a fucking mint.

But there was no denying her glossy, long, dark hair was fucking gorgeous. And her green eyes defined what Hop always thought was stupid as shit, but in her case it was true. They were bedroom eyes. They were the eyes any man with a functioning dick would want staring into his as he was moving inside her.

Fuck, her eyes were amazing.

After she nearly lost her life standing by her man, she'd taken off, moved from Denver to be close to her family in Connecticut, and she stayed there for a while licking her wounds. This while lasted too long, according to Tyra, Lanie's best friend and old lady to Kane "Tack" Allen, the president of Hop's motorcycle club, the Chaos MC. Tyra, known to the boys as "Cherry," flew out to Connecticut, reamed her ass, and hauled it back to Denver.

Lanie set herself up again in house and job, and now she was a staple at Chaos gatherings mostly because she was Tyra's best friend. Also because the brothers liked looking at her so they didn't mind her being around, and even Hop had to admit her frequent dramas were pretty damned funny (when they weren't annoying). You had to give it to anyone who was how they were no matter who was around, and that was pure Lanie. She was Lanie, she didn't water that down, and she didn't care what anyone thought of it.

This was the way of the biker, so men like Hop and his brothers could appreciate it.

That said, freaking out because your 7Up overflowed was over the top. Still, a bitch as gorgeous as Lanie Heron...fuck, you'd watch her sitting around and watching TV. Having a fit over spilled soda was definitely worthwhile. Especially if she did it like she did it, jumping around so that hair was swinging, those eyes flashing and what little tits and ass she had moved right along with her.

As she got close, Hop tore his eyes off her and moved them through the crowd.

Tack nor Cherry were anywhere to be seen. This was not a surprise. It was late, things were getting rowdy, but that wasn't why those two had disappeared. Hop knew they were either on Tack's bike going back up the mountain to their house or they were in his room at the Compound. They were married, had been together awhile, neither of them were anywhere near their twenties, they had two young boys, but still, they went at each other like teenagers.

This also wasn't a surprise. Tyra *did* have tits and ass, lots of hair, and a serious amount of sass. A woman like that was built to be bedded and often, and Tack took advantage. Then again, that was why Tack accepted her ball and chain. Actually, not so much accepted it as much as forced her to clamp her shackle on his ankle. Given the choice of waking up to Tyra Allen every morning, not many men wouldn't.

"Hey," he heard Lanie greet him and his eyes moved back to her.

"Hey," he replied.

Her head tilted slightly down, her ear tipping to her shoulder even while her neck gave a small twist but her eyes never left his as she remarked, "Getting rowdy."

"Always does," he murmured, his gaze moving over her shoulder while he thought, Jesus, she was tall. She had to be five-nine not in those heels. In them, she was six foot one. His height. They were eye to eye.

He didn't like this, normally.

Lanie... eye to eye with those fucking eyes?

Shit.

"Wanna fuck?"

At her question, his gaze sliced back to hers as he felt his body jerk in shock.

"Say again?" he asked.

She leaned in slightly, never looking away, and repeated, "Wanna fuck?"

Hop stared at her. He'd just watched her walk to him, winding through loud, shitfaced bikers and their bitches, her gait steady. She didn't move like she was hammered, nowhere near it. Even now, her gaze was clear as it held his.

Still, he asked, "You had one too many, babe?"

"No," she replied instantly and moved closer.

This was not good because, when she did, he could smell her perfume.

Those eyes, bedroom eyes.

That perfume, fuck-me perfume.

Jesus, he'd been catching whiffs of it now for years and it never failed to do a number on him. He didn't know what it was—the fact it smelled expensive, the intense femininity of it that said, point blank, "I am *all* fucking woman"—or the fact that it was elusive. If you got one smell of it, the woman who wore it owned you because you'd do anything to go back for more. Any time Lanie got near him, in the back of his head, Hop hoped to catch her scent. Sometimes he would. Sometimes he wouldn't. But every time, he hoped for it.

Now, though, smelling it now was a very bad thing.

"Not sure that's a good idea, Lanie," he told her, gentling his voice as he gave her the honesty.

"Why?" she asked immediately, and he felt his eyes narrow on her before he answered.

"Maybe 'cause you're best friends with Tack's old lady. I respect him, I respect her, and shit like this, babe, it gets complicated. Any complication sucks but a complication like this"—he shook his head—"no one needs that."

She threw out a hand and declared casually, "It won't get complicated."

Okay, maybe she was messed up, fucked up, a drama queen, high maintenance, *and* a nut.

"Bullshit," he replied. "It always gets complicated."

She moved closer, and Jesus, her scent, that hair, those eyes, all of that close, if she got any closer he'd physically have to set her away or pick her up and carry her to his room.

"Do you want to fuck me?" she asked. Her voice, sweet and feminine normally, was soft now, a little hesitant, a little excited, and that intoxicating combination was doing a number on him too.

"Babe, you looked in the mirror lately?" he asked back by way of answer. "Man would have to be dead not to wanna fuck you."

A little smile twisted her pretty mouth and he knew he

was screwed because that was cute *and* fucking sexy as all fucking hell.

Shit.

She got closer and Hop braced. Any closer and she'd be cozied up to him. She was inches away.

"Do you like me?" she asked.

"Everyone likes you," he answered.

"I'm not asking about everyone, Hop," she told him, and he held her eyes.

"Yeah, babe, you know I do," he finally answered when she didn't move or speak, just waited. "You're funny, you're cute, you're hot, and you got no problem letting it all hang out. That's why everyone likes you. That's also why I do."

To that, she returned, "Okay. Good. Then no complications, Hop. Just you and me and tonight. Tomorrow, I won't expect flowers. I won't expect a belated courtesy date. I won't even expect you to take me out for a cup of coffee. This isn't about that. I don't even *want* that. I just want you and sex. No expectations. Nothing but what we have tonight," she told him. "Tack and Ty-Ty, or anyone, they never even have to know."

He pushed away from the pole, reached out an arm to put his beer on a nearby picnic table and took a huge chance straightening to her because it meant they were closer. But it also gave him the half an inch he still had on her when she was in those heels, and he needed it.

"Don't wanna be a dick, lady," he warned softly, "but bitches say that shit all the time. Then, in the morning, they expect breakfast, coffee, and to come home from work to roses with a note sayin' the guy never had better. You got a man who thinks to buy you roses, he says he's never had better, big chances are he's lyin'. He just wants it regular and he'll take it as it comes."

He knew every word out of his mouth made him the dick he told her he didn't want to be, but she needed to move on. If she was in the mood to get laid, she needed to find herself some *not* on Chaos. Cherry had chosen Chaos, but that didn't mean she wouldn't lose her mind if her best girl hooked up with a brother. She would. Hop knew it. But if that shit happened anyway, Cherry would want to handpick the brother who got in there, and Hop also knew that brother would absolutely not be him.

"Then take it as it comes," she shot back, not appearing offended in the slightest, her words coming out almost like a dare.

"Lanie—" he started but she leaned in and, fuck, if he moved his mouth a quarter of an inch, it'd be on hers. She was all he could see, all he could smell, and all he could think was that she was also all he wanted to *feel*.

"You know my story," she whispered. "You think I want another guy?" She paused then finished with emphasis, "*Ever?*"

He got her. Her dead old man was a moron and she paid for his shit in the worst way she could. Her loyalty bought her nothing but pain, bullet wounds, and heartache. Not to mention, her man might have been good at what he did for a living, the computer geek to end all computer geeks, but he was nothing to look at. So she not only gave love and loyalty but she stepped out of a zone no woman who looked like her had to step out of in order to give it.

So, yeah, Elliott Belova was a moron, and she chose that. He could see her wanting to get back in the saddle but being skittish about buying the horse.

She just wasn't going to do it with him.

Hop started to lift his hands to curl them around her upper arms and set her away but she moved fast, lifting hers to curl them around the sides of his neck, and they felt warm. Her perfume assaulted him straight on and he stilled.

"I do not want that," she carried on. "What I want is... *you*. For one night. Just one night."

Fuck him.

Fuck him.

"Lady," he muttered but before he could say more, she kept talking.

"It was...I know you know where I was back then and who I was with and I know you had a woman then too, Hop, but still, that night I met you, I couldn't help but notice you were good-looking. But you're not with anyone anymore, and I'm *seriously* not with anyone anymore, and I've been thinking about it for a long time, just too scared to do anything about it. Now I've decided I'm doing something about it."

"I gotta say, I like it that you're into me, babe," he returned gently. "Already told you that you're beautiful, and under any other circumstances, I would not hesitate to take you up on an offer this sweet. So you gotta know it's killin' me, even as you gotta trust me when I say this is not a good idea."

"I've had no one since him," she whispered and, acting on their own, Hop's hands came up and settled on her waist, giving it a squeeze and he didn't know why. The move was intimate but comforting. The news that this woman, this crazy-gorgeous woman and all that was her hadn't had a man between her legs in fucking *years* moved him even as it troubled him.

"Lanie, honey," he muttered, not having that first fucking clue what else to say.

"I've thought on it and decided it's you." Her hands at his neck gave him a squeeze and fuck him, *fuck him,* that moved him even more. "I understand why you don't want to, but I promise, Hop, *I swear,* no kidding, seriously, no strings. No expectations. Just us. One night. Tomorrow, it will be like it's always been. Like it didn't even happen. I promise, Hop. *Swear.*"

Her hands slid down to his chest but she didn't move away as she finished laying it out.

"Now, I'm going to your room and I'm going to wait there for fifteen minutes. If you don't show, no harm, no foul. I promise that too. Nothing changes between us. No one knows anything." She sucked in a breath and took a half step back, her hands falling away when she concluded in a quiet voice, "But"—she hesitated—"I really hope you show."

With that, not giving him a chance to say another word, she turned and strutted her narrow ass back through the loud, rowdy, drunk bikers and their bitches, her hair swaying, her arms moving gracefully, her scent still in his nostrils.

"Shit," he whispered when he watched her haul open the door to the Compound.

"Shit," he repeated when the door closed behind her.

He kept his eyes on the door and he did this awhile.

That woman, that crazy-gorgeous woman, was right now in his room.

"Shit," he whispered yet again, right before he made his way to the door.

* * *

Hopper broke contact with Lanie's hooded eyes, eyes that were a fuckuva lot sexier since he'd just come inside her, and he did it hard and he did it long and he shoved his face in her neck.

All he could smell was her. All he could feel was her warm, soft body under his, one of her legs wrapped around the back of his thigh, the other one cocked high, her thigh pressed to his side but her calf was swung in, her heel resting in the small of his back. Her arms were tight around him, one at his shoulders, one angled, resting along his spine. Last, he could feel his cock buried in her unbelievably tight, wet cunt.

He didn't know what it was. Maybe it was that she'd never had kids. Maybe it was because it had been so long since she had a man. Whatever it was, her pussy was close to virgin, it was so tight. Luckily, it was also sleek. Luckier, it tasted like goddamned honey.

He was right when they were talking outside.

This was about to get complicated.

Her head moved, and he felt her lips at his ear even as he heard her soft, tentative words, "Was that all right?"

Hop closed his eyes even as his hips reflexively pressed into hers and he gently fisted the hand he had buried in her hair.

She was worried she was out of practice. She was worried it wasn't good for him. And considering the fact that if she was out of practice, when she got into the swing of things, she'd be off the charts, her worry was both cute and sweet and, like everything else about her, it did a number on him.

Yes, things were going to get complicated.

He opened his eyes, moved his head so his lips were at

her ear, and he murmured, “Lady, I don’t fake it. Not only because I can’t but because even if I could, I wouldn’t.”

All her limbs convulsed around him even as her cunt did the same, and Jesus God, it felt seriously fucking good.

Then it got better when her body started moving under him, her limbs stayed tight around him, and he heard her husky, low chuckle in his ear.

He lifted his head in an effort to watch her face in laughter in the dark. Once she got back to Denver and Tyra got her hands on her, Lanie laughed a lot. He liked watching her laugh. It was always, every time he saw it, a good show.

It was better now because he could *feel* it. Even though he couldn’t see much, the little he saw was still pure beauty.

Totally complicated.

He liked her smell. He liked her feel. He liked the sound of her low laughter. He liked her uncertainty. He liked how hard she made him come. And he liked how hard she came for him, her pussy tightening around his cock, her long limbs wound around his body holding on, her soft pants and moans sweet to his ear, and, best of all, the look on her beautiful face when he gave it to her.

Totally fucking complicated.

He waited until she stopped laughing before he slid his hand out of her hair to her jaw and then rubbed the pad of his thumb across her lips while he asked, “How you feelin’?”

“Uh...good,” she answered, her words meant to be an obvious understatement, her lips moving against his thumb tilting up even as she spoke.

"Good enough for another go?" he asked, his thumb pressing in, pulling at her unbelievably full lower lip and he felt her shift under him.

He knew what that shift meant even before her voice came at him, breathy, "Another go?"

He replaced his thumb with his lips. "Yeah, another go."

"So soon?" She sounded disbelieving.

"You're gonna have to work me up, lady, but . . . yeah. Soon as you're ready, my mouth wants more of that pussy."

She wanted that too. He knew it because her body trembled under his.

"Yeah, I'm, um . . . good for another go," she told him, her sweet voice still breathy.

"Then don't move." He pressed his lips to hers before he lifted his head. "Gotta hit the can and I'll be back."

"I won't move," she whispered.

She better not, he thought. If she did, he'd find her and haul her back. He didn't care if she beamed her ass to Mars.

Fuck.

Complicated.

He knew it and didn't give a fuck as he slid out of her, kissed her throat, feeling her skin, smelling her scent, and rolled off her and the bed so he could make his way to the bathroom to get rid of his condom.

When he got back, she hadn't moved, but seconds later she did, because he moved her.

He parted her legs, swung them over his shoulders, and didn't hesitate a second before he dipped his face into pure honey.

* * *

Hop exited the bathroom and saw Lanie sitting at the side of his bed, her back to him, putting on her bra.

"What the fuck you doin'?" he growled and, shit, that was it. He couldn't deny it. Even he heard it.

He *growled.*

She twisted and he felt her eyes on him in the dark.

"Ty-Ty and Tack are down the hall. They won't come up for air until the morning, and it's almost morning so I should be gone by then."

"You're not goin'," he informed her, putting a knee to the bed and moving her way.

"I'm…*oof,*" she puffed as he hooked her at the belly, yanked her to her back in the bed, and rolled on top of her. She blinked up at him through the dark and finished, "Not?"

"Not done with you," he informed her.

"You're…" again with the breathy something he felt in his gut, chest, and dick "…*not?*" and again with the disbelieving.

Totally disbelieving.

"I'm not," Hop confirmed.

"Is that even…" a pause, then "…*possible?*"

"Is what possible?" he asked.

"Three times in an, erm…night?"

Obviously, Belova wasn't only messed up, fucked up, and stupid, he clearly had no stamina, which was fucking insane. A ninety-year-old man had a shot at that beauty, he'd find a way to get it up and do it repeatedly even if it killed him.

"Yeah it's possible."

Hop watched her head tilt on the pillow. "I…no offense, Hop, but I don't believe you."

Fucking *excellent.*

He slid his hands up her sides as he dropped his mouth to hers. "Right. Good, then, babe. I get to prove it to you."

Close up, he watched her eyes get wide.

"Wow," she whispered against his lips.

"Don't say that now," he ordered. "You can say that later, like you did after I did that thing with my fingers the second time."

Her body shifted under his, her chest pressing up, she remembered something he knew she wouldn't soon forget and she repeated a whispered, "Wow."

He grinned against her mouth and promised, "I'll give you wow."

"You've already given me three wows," she reminded him.

"Four," he corrected.

"Oh yeah," she muttered, her hands moving light down the skin of his back. "I forgot that one because it came so close on the heels of that other one."

Her hands made it to his ass, so he decided their conversation was over and to communicate that to Lanie, he asked, "Are we gonna keep talkin' or do you want wow?"

She moved her head, sliding her lips from his, down his cheek to his jaw and finally his ear.

Once they were there, she murmured, "Give me wow."

With his mouth at her neck, he trailed it down to her collarbone then engaged his tongue and, after, taking his time and a lot of it, he gave her wows five *and* six.

* * *

Hop came out of the bathroom to see Lanie on her feet on the other side of the bed, panties on, hands twisted behind her back putting her bra on.

He didn't say a word. He prowled to her, reached out an arm the second he was close, yanked her to him, twisted and fell to his back in the bed, taking her down with him.

"Hop—" she started, pushing her weight against his arms but he slid her off him then wasted no time rolling over her and pinning her to his bed.

"Sleep," he ordered when he caught her eyes in the weak dawn. "After rest, I'll get coffee, we'll juice up, then round four."

She blinked and breathed, "Four?"

"Got lots more I want to do to you," he informed her and watched her eyes go soft and sexier, her teeth came out to graze her lush lower lip, also fucking sexy, and her arms slid around him.

But she asked, "What about Tack and Ty-Ty?"

"I'll make sure the coast is clear," he told her.

"But they'll see my car," she told him.

"I'll move it," he offered.

Her hand slid up his back, around his shoulder, and then to his neck, where her thumb moved to stroke him. It was light but fuck, it felt good. He'd never had a woman touch him in an unconscious way like that, just a touch, a stroke, giving something that meant nothing and at the same time just doing it and doing it without thinking about it meant everything.

Shit.

Complicated.

"This is just supposed to be one night," she reminded him quietly, but he saw it in her eyes. She didn't even try to hide it. She bit off more than she could chew.

He did too, and he was nowhere near done eating.

"Change of plans. A night and a morning and, maybe,

an afternoon and, possibly, another night," he amended, and her eyes got softer as her hand slid up to cup his jaw.

"I have to work," she told him.

"Call off," he told her.

"I can't. I own the joint," she explained something he knew. "And things are a bit crazy."

Things were always crazy for Lanie. The woman lived crazy, she thrived on it. If there wasn't crazy, she stirred it up because she couldn't breathe without it.

"Babe—" he pressed his body into hers "—told you, got more I want to do to you."

He felt her shiver but her lips whispered, "Hop, I don't—"

He cut her off with a quick kiss then lifted his head and asked, "Where are your keys?"

"We shouldn't sleep together. Sleeping is bad. Sex is good, sleeping together is something else," she stated, and she was right. Sex was sex. Sleeping together was something else.

He just didn't care.

"Where are your keys?" he asked.

"Hop—"

"Lady, we're not sleeping, we're resting then we're fucking some more. Last time I'll say it, not done with you, got things I want to do to you and I'm doin' them. Now, where... are... your... *keys*?"

She stared up at him, her gaze hot, her body bothered, shifting under his, and she whispered, "Jeans pocket."

He pushed into her, pressing down and stretching out to reach a hand to the floor. He grabbed her jeans, got in the pocket, and yanked out her keys. Once he had them in hand, he went back to her and kissed her. He took his time, it was wet, deep, and fucking brilliant.

When she was holding on tight and kissing him back like she never wanted it to end, he ended it. Lifting his lips to her forehead, he touched them there then dipped his chin and looked into her eyes.

"Rest, honey. I'll move your car and be back."

"Okay," she agreed quietly.

He bent in, touched his mouth to hers, rolled off, grabbed his jeans, a tee, pulled on socks and his boots, and he only turned back at the door before he slid through it, still mostly closed.

She was curled in an S in his bed, pillow to her chest, cheek resting on it, arms around it, hair everywhere. Her bare back was exposed, and he could see one leg and her ass in red, lace panties. Eyes on him.

Fucking gorgeous, every inch, and it tasted and felt as good as it looked.

She grinned.

Gorgeous.

He returned it, slid through the door, and went after her car.

When he got back, she was out.

He took off his clothes, dropped them to the floor, and slid into bed with her. Carefully, he turned her into his arms.

She didn't wake. She just cuddled closer, her arm snaking across his stomach then holding tight, her torso pressing into his, her knee cocked and resting on his thigh.

This felt good too.

She was right, they shouldn't sleep together. Sleeping suggested something more. An intimacy neither of them wanted. Sleeping like this with her, it feeling so good, it was, with everything else, enough to make you want a fuckuva lot more.

So it was good, Hop thought, that they weren't sleeping, they were just resting.

On that thought, he fell asleep, Lanie curved close and held tight in his arm, her perfume all over his sheets, and he did it smiling.

* * *

Three hours later, Hop woke and he did not smile.

Lanie's perfume was still all over the sheets.

Lanie just wasn't in them.

* * *

Hop was stretched out on the fluffy cushion on the lounge chair in her courtyard, feet crossed at the ankles, eyes trained to the back door of the garage.

He had no idea how late it was, he just knew it was dark and he'd been there a really fucking long time.

Too long.

Long enough for him to get pissed.

Or *more* pissed.

He heard her garage door go up and didn't move when he heard it or when he heard the purr of her sweet ride moving into it. A pearl-red Lexus LFA. According to word on Chaos, her father bought it for her.

High class ran in the family. So did money.

He only moved off the chair when he heard the garage door going down.

He was on his feet when the outside lights to her courtyard that separated her brownstone from the garage came on, but he didn't move from his spot even as the door opened.

She strode out, sex on heels stilettos, tight skirt, tailored blazer that was unbelievably feminine, hair out to there, slim, shiny, expensive briefcase in her hand, trim, small designer purse over her shoulder.

A cosmo girl tricked out in business gear.

"Yo," he called when she shut the door. He watched her jump and swing around to him, face pale, eyes huge.

"Oh my God, Hop. You scared me half to death."

He didn't reply.

When he didn't, her face lost its pallor, her head tipped to the side, and her brows knitted as she asked, "What are you doing here?"

"Told you, I wasn't done with you," he answered and her head immediately righted with a snap.

"Hop—" she started.

"Told you that," he cut her off, "still, you snuck outta my bed and slunk away."

She took one step toward him, her body moving like she was going to take more, but she suddenly stopped.

"I said just one night," she reminded him.

"And I said I wasn't done with you," he fired back.

"I—" she began, but he interrupted her again.

"You had dinner?"

Her head jerked in surprise then she answered, "Yes, a business dinner. New client."

"Good," he grunted. "Upstairs. Naked. Now."

He felt it coming off her in waves.

She wanted that.

Bad.

Then her head moved again, it was jerky again but she was forcing herself to do it, shaking it side to side. "We agreed. One night."

"I think we also agreed, though the words weren't spoken, one night's not enough."

"This can't get complicated," she reminded him.

"You keep your mouth shut, I keep my mouth shut, we're smart, we contain it, no one finds out, we understand what it is and stick to the boundaries, it won't."

"I don't think—"

"Lanie. Upstairs. Naked. *Now.*"

He saw her breath come fast, her chest moving with it, and Jesus, fuck him, he could taste her excitement and he was five feet away.

"We shouldn't—"

"Fucked you on your back. Like to look in your eyes when I'm inside you. Done that. Now I want you on your knees, gonna fuck your face and your cunt, and I can't do that in the courtyard. It'd shock the shit outta me, class act like you gets into that, but if I got you naked, you're all mine. I don't share with the neighbors."

She stood stock-still, her eyes riveted to him, the only thing moving on her body was her chest rising and falling with quick breaths.

"Lanie," he leaned in, "upstairs. Naked. Right... fucking... *now.*"

She took off toward her sliding glass door.

Hop didn't move but he did smile when she dropped her keys, cursed under her breath, and crouched in that tight skirt to get them.

Second go, she got in and left the door open as she hurried inside.

Hop stared at the door before taking a deep breath and walking to it.

He got inside and saw it was a big kitchen, living,

dining area. He saw the clock on the microwave said it was ten forty-two.

Hc took no morc in.

This wasn't them. To make sure something that could get complicated didn't, he understood that this wasn't what he was going to take or what she could give. He didn't get to look at her shit, check out pictures in frames, see if she was clean or messy, read what he could in how she decorated.

He didn't get that.

He got what was upstairs, naked in her bed.

He turned slowly and slid the door closed. He locked it. Then he moved through the dark space.

He found the blazer on the carpet of the stairs. A camisole on the landing. Her skirt on the next flight. Panties, bra, and shoes leading him to a room from which dim light was coming.

He was hard by the time he made it to her room.

He didn't look around there either. Not because it wasn't what he got from her but because she was on her ass in her bed, knees to her chest, chin to her knees, arms wrapped around her calves, ankles crossed at her ass, hiding everything but still cute as all fuck.

His dick started throbbing.

"Fuck me, I'm gonna come just standing here looking at you," he muttered and watched her eyes close slowly, something moving over her face making beauty so beautiful, it was almost impossible to take it in. Like staring at the sun, if he saw that look on her face for another second, he'd go blind.

She opened her eyes, pushed out of her pose and gracefully moved to the edge of the bed. Feet to the floor, naked, her eyes to his, his going everywhere that was her, she moved to him and stopped so close, he could smell her and feel her body brushing his.

Instantly, her hands went to his tee and she yanked up.

Hop lifted his arms, she pulled it away, and dropped it.

Then her mouth went to his chest, her hands with it, moving, licking, sucking, touching, then down.

On her knees, she unbuckled his belt, pulled it open, unbuttoned his jeans, and gave him nothing through this but the gleaming hair on top of her head.

He knew why when she reached right in, found him, pulled him free, and slid him deep inside her mouth.

She had something she wanted and she was concentrating on getting it.

Fuck.

Fuck.

His head dropped back, his fingers slid into her hair and his voice was hoarse when he ordered, "Baby, up. Woman like you does not get on her knees."

She wrapped a fist around him, slid him out, and he looked down just in time to see her tip her head back, those eyes, those fucking eyes, hooded and turned on, looking up at him.

"I like it, honey."

"Suck me off in bed. Not on your knees. Class doesn't hit her knees."

"Hop—"

"Up, Lanie. Get in bed."

"But—"

He jerked his hips back, she lost purchase on his dick, and he planted his hands under her arms. He pulled her up and then swung her into his arms. He took four strides and tossed her on the bed.

He bent, yanked off his boots, his socks, his jeans and he joined her there.

He pulled her into his arms, rolled to his back, rolling her on top.

"Right, *now* you can suck me off," he told her.

"I get to go back to what I was doing later," she told him and he grinned at the look on her face. She still looked turned on. She also looked miffed.

Cute.

Adorable, actually.

Fuck. It was going to take a serious amount of work for this not to get complicated.

"Maybe," he lied. "Now back to work."

"Ty-Ty told me you guys take bossy to extremes and do whatever it takes to get your way. That was why I snuck out of your bed this morning. I told you we shouldn't sleep together, it seemed you weren't going to take no for an answer so I had to get creative," she shared, and there it was.

Cherry blabbed, so Lanie was prepared.

He'd have to take that into account in the future.

"You're telling me this instead of going down on me because...?" he prompted.

"Because I want your promise I can finish what I started later," she explained.

"Lady, you can do it now. In fact, I'd be obliged if you would," he told her.

She scrunched up her nose. "Like we were before."

Hop shook his head. "I said, no. Not like that."

Her hand came to his cheek and her face got close. "Hop, what you said was sweet and I liked that but I also liked what I was doing and—"

He rolled on top of her and he moved his hand to her cheek, thumb to her lips, pressing in and his face got close.

"I'm guessin' you get what this is. We played with fire, we got burned, now we gotta contain the blaze, but sayin' that, I got no intention of puttin' it out and, babe, I'm gettin', since you left me a trail of bread crumbs to this room, you don't either. We get it, we don't gotta talk about it. We know what we got revolves around bein' naked in a bed so you shouldn't get what I'm gonna give you right now. But I'm gonna give it to you. Never had class. Never had beauty. I'll repeat, never…had…*class.* I'm not gonna fuck over Cherry, who I care about, or Tack, who's my brother, and I know you don't wanna do that either, so this is what we got for as long as it's good. But it's a clean, pure beauty the like I've never had, I'm gonna respect it like I feel like I gotta and you're gonna let me. So, no, Lanie, you are not gettin' down on your knees like every biker skank or groupie or drunk, high piece of ass before you dropped to hers and sucked me off. You go down on me, you do it like who you are. Respect. You don't want that, you're looking to play with rough trade to get you off, find another guy to make you skank. That is not what you're gonna get from me. Now, are you gonna finish givin' me a blowjob or are you gonna fight me on this?"

She laid there and stared up at him, not saying a word, so Hop gave her an alternate option.

"Or are you gonna lie there and stare at me?"

"I think I need to lie here and stare at you for about thirty more seconds," she whispered and Hop felt his lips twitch.

Then he offered quietly, "Have at it, baby."

"Though, while lying here staring at you, I'm just going to say, I really like your mustache," she told him.

"Good to know," he muttered, his lips still twitching.

"It's badass biker cool," she went on.

"Right," he kept muttering, now through a grin.

"And it feels good on my neck and, well...other places," she continued and his grin turned to a smile.

"Also good to know."

"I think I'm done staring at you," she announced.

"So, you gonna get busy?"

She lied.

She wasn't done staring at him. He knew this because she kept doing it for a beat before she lifted her head and touched her mouth to his.

"Yeah," she whispered there.

He grinned against her mouth before he kissed her, doing it while rolling to his back.

When he broke the kiss, she got busy and sucked him off in bed.

Like class.

Like a lady.

* * *

Dressed and sitting on the side of her bed, Hop shifted the soft, heavy hair off Lanie's neck, leaned in and put his lips there.

"Tickles," she murmured. He lifted his head and caught her eyes that had slid to the side to catch his. "In a good way," she finished.

"Good," he murmured back, and dipped his already close face closer. "Sunup, honey."

"Yeah," she whispered.

"Later," he said.

"Yeah." She drew in a breath, then asked, "Tonight?"

"You want that?"

She nodded her head on the pillow.

Excellent. He did too.

He lifted his lips to her temple, kissed her there, moved them to her ear and said softly in it, "You got it."

Then, without another look at her in her bed, sleepy, sexy, and sated, something he knew he couldn't walk away from, he walked away from her, through her house, and out the sliding glass door, putting Lanie Heron out of his mind.

Until tonight.

THE DISH

Where Authors Give You the Inside Scoop

From the desk of Jennifer Haymore

Dear Reader,

When Sarah Osborne, the heroine of THE DUCHESS HUNT, entered my office for the first time, I thought she was a member of the janitorial staff and that she was there to clean.

"I'm sorry," I told her. "I'm going to be working for a few more hours. Can you come back later?"

Her flush was instant, a dark red suffusing her pretty cheeks. "Oh," she said quietly. "I'm not here to clean…I'm here as a potential client."

Now it was my turn to blush. But you couldn't really blame me—she wore a dark dress with an apron and a tidy maid's cap. It was an honest mistake.

I rose from my seat, apologizing profusely, and offered her a seat and refreshments. When she was settled, and neither of us was blushing anymore, I returned to my own chair and asked her to tell me her story.

"I'm the head housemaid at Ironwood Park," she told me. Leaning forward, she added significantly, "I work for the Duke of Trent."

I'd heard of him, and of the great estate of Ironwood Park. "Go on."

"I want him," she murmured.

I blinked, sure I'd missed something. "Who?"

"The Duke of Trent."

"You are the *housemaid*."

She nodded.

"He is a *duke*."

She nodded again.

I shook my head with a sigh. The housemaid and the duke? Nope. This wouldn't work at all. The chasm between their classes was far too deep to cross.

"I'm so sorry, Miss Osborne," I began, "but—"

Her dark eyes blinked up at me and she held up her hand to stop my next words. "Wait! I know what you're going to say. But it's not as impossible as you might think. You see…I am His Grace's best friend."

I gaped at her, for that was almost more difficult to believe than the thought of her being his lover. Dukes simply didn't "make friends" with their maids.

"We have been friends since childhood. You see, the duke's family is quite unconventional. The dowager raised me almost as one of her own."

Now this was getting interesting. I cocked my head. "Do you think he would agree with your assessment?"

"That the House of Trent is unconventional?"

I chuckled. "No. I know the House of Trent has been widely acclaimed as the most scandalous and shocking house in England over the past several decades. I meant, would he agree with your assessment that you are his best friend?"

She folded her hands in her lap, and her dark brows furrowed. "If he was being honest?" she said softly, and I could see the earnest honesty in her gaze. "Yes, he would agree."

I leaned back in my chair, drumming my fingers on my desk, thinking. How intriguing. Friends to lovers, to... *love*. What a delightful Cinderella story this could make.

My lips curved into a smile, and I flicked open the lid of my laptop and opened a new document. "All right, Miss Osborne. Tell me your story. Start with the story of the first time you laid eyes upon the Duke of Trent..."

And that was how my relationship with the wickedly wonderful family of the House of Trent began. I've loved every minute I've spent with them, and I hope you enjoy Sarah and the duke's story as much as I enjoyed writing it.

Please come visit me at my website, www.jenniferhaymore.com, where you can share your thoughts about my books, sign up for some fun freebies and contests, and read more about the characters from THE DUCHESS HUNT and the House of Trent Series.

Sincerely,

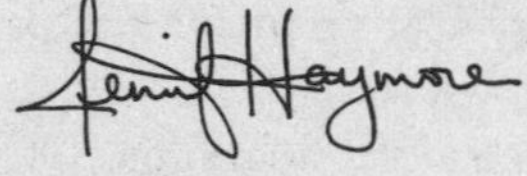

♥ ♥ ♥ ♥ ♥ ♥ ♥ ♥ ♥ ♥ ♥ ♥ ♥ ♥ ♥

From the desk of Marilyn Pappano

Dear Reader,

One of the questions authors get asked most is, "Where do you get your ideas?" I've gotten inspiration from everything—music, news stories, locations, weather, simple thoughts or emotions, from events going on in my own life or someone else's, from dreams, wishes, hopes, fears.

Some ideas take a tremendous amount of work to come together. I don't work on them continuously but rather sporadically while they percolate in the back of my mind. Some never come together.

And then there are the *thank you!* stories: ideas that come fairly complete with characters, location, and plot. A HERO TO COME HOME TO was definitely one of those.

For some time, I'd been thinking about doing a series with a military setting (my husband is retired from the Navy, and our son was in the Army), but it wasn't on my mind at all one summer day when I watched a news segment about military widows. That evening I saw another news segment about a woman who'd thought her dreams had ended when her military husband died in the war, only to find a new love.

By the time I got up the next morning, I knew the seven widows from the Tuesday Night Margarita Club, as well as Dane, the soldier who would restore Carly's dreams, and Dalton, the rancher who'd lost his wife to war as well. I knew the setting, too: my home state of Oklahoma. Of all the places we lived on active duty, Oklahoma is my favorite. I took time off from the book I was writing and wrote the first few chapters, then sent it off to my agent.

The Department of Defense really nailed it a long time ago when they came up with the slogan that "wife" was the toughest job in the service, though since there are plenty of women on active duty, "spouse" is a better choice. Trying to have a career of your own? Good luck when you move at the whim of the service. Need roots? Better learn that home really is where the heart is. Worry too much? Take a deep breath and learn to let go. Never wanted to be a single parent? Start adapting because deployments are inevitable.

But being a Navy wife was great, too. I met some wonderful people and lived in some wonderful places. I learned a degree of independence and adaptability that I never thought possible pre-Navy. Our Navy life gave me ideas and exposure to new experiences for my writing career. Though I already had a lot of respect for those who serve, I also learned to respect their spouses and children and the sacrifices they make.

One of the best parts of writing romance novels is giving all my characters a happily-ever-after ending, and no one deserves it more than the Tallgrass crew. I hope readers agree.

Oh, one final note: that morning A HERO TO COME HOME TO popped into my head? It was the Fourth of July. Fitting, huh?

Happy reading!

Marilyn Pappano

♥ ♥ ♥ ♥ ♥ ♥ ♥ ♥ ♥ ♥ ♥ ♥ ♥ ♥ ♥

From the desk of Molly Cannon

Dear Reader,

The theme of food is woven into almost every chapter of CRAZY LITTLE THING CALLED LOVE. Etta Green is a chef in the big city, but her love of cooking came from her grandmother Hazel. For Etta, the sharing of food represents love, caring, and nurturing—all those things we need and crave our entire lives.

When Etta returns to Everson, Texas, for her grandmother's funeral she discovers her grandmother had been in the middle of turning the old family home into a bed and breakfast. The responsibility of finishing the work on the old family home falls to Etta, and after reading her grandmother's notes on the project she sees that each of the guest rooms has been named and decorated with an old-fashioned dessert as the theme—desserts that evoke comfort and fond memories of days spent with her grandmother.

I love dessert, so deciding on the room names was deliciously fun, and I didn't have to count a single calorie. For the first room I thought back to my school days. Buying lunch in the cafeteria of my elementary school was not high on my list of favorite childhood memories, with one exception. The cherry cobbler was scrumptious with just enough tart fruit to moisten the pie crust on top. I've had other cobblers since then, but that one remains my favorite. So of course *Cherry Cobbler* had to be one of the rooms. I decorated the room in different shades of red and taupe, cozy throw pillows scattered everywhere, and topped it off with pictures of cherries in bright white bowls. A cheerful room that could brighten any day.

Next was the *Banana Pudding* room. Banana pudding was one of my father's favorite desserts, so I always think about him whenever I make it. I still think the recipe on the vanilla wafer box is the best I've tried. And making the pudding part from scratch is simple and tastes so much better than any pudding from a box. With that as my inspiration, I decorated the room in pale yellows and fluffy meringue whites. A light and airy room that wraps the guest in down comforters and soft pillows.

But food can evoke other powerful emotions as well.

When I was a barely a teenager my older brother went to a summer camp, and when we went to visit on family day all the boys greeted us with a meal they'd prepared themselves. The star of the meal was the Ham in the Hole. They dug holes and lined them with slow-burning wood, and then buried the hams, cooking them until they were tender. It was their gift, their offering to the visitors. And it was delicious. The campers were so proud of themselves.

When my brother found out a few years ago that he had cancer, he decided on his own course of treatment and chose the path he wanted to take. As he got weaker we watched him stay strong in his resolve to live the rest of his life on his terms. One of the last things he did was to invite his family and friends over for a special gathering. He'd gone into the backyard and dug a hole. Then he lined it with slow-burning wood and buried a ham. When it was done he fed us more than a meal. It was his last gift to us all. It was a thank-you for loving him and being his family. I let Donny Joe Ledbetter borrow my brother's gift as the gesture he uses to show his home town his appreciation. It makes me happier than I can say to make the Ham in the Hole such an important part of Donny Joe and Etta's story.

I hope you enjoy it, too!

Molly Cannon

Learn more at:
MollyCannon.com
Facebook.com
Twitter @CannonMolly

♥ ♥ ♥ ♥ ♥

From the desk of Kristin Ashley

Dear Reader,

I have an obsession with names, which shouldn't surprise readers as the names I give my characters run the gamut and are often out there.

In my Dream Man series, I introduced readers to Cabe "Hawk" Delgado, Brock "Slim" Lucas, Mitch Lawson, and Kane "Tack" Allen. My Chaos series gives us Shy, Hop, Joker, and Rush, among the other members of the Club.

I've had quite a few folks express curiosity about where I come up with all these names, and I wish I could say I knew a load of good-looking men who had awesome and unusual names and I stole them but, alas, that isn't true.

In most cases, characters, especially heroes and heroines, come to me named. They just pop right into my head, much like Tatum "Tate" Jackson of *Sweet Dreams*. He just walked right in there, all the gloriousness of Tate, and introduced himself to me. And luckily, he had an amazing, strong, masculine, kick-ass name.

In other instances, who they are defines their name. I understood Hawk's tragic back story from *Mystery Man* first. I also understood that the man he was melted away; he became another man with a new name so what he called himself evolved from what he did in the military. His given name, of course, evolved from his multiethnic background.

The same with Mitch, the hero from *Law Man*. The minute he walked into Gwen's kitchen, his last name hit me like a shot. What else could a straight-arrow cop be called but Lawson?

Other names are a mystery to me. Kane "Tack" Allen came to me named but I had no clue why his Club name was Tack. Truthfully, I also found it a bit annoying seeing as how the name Kane is such a cool name, and I didn't want to waste it on a character who wouldn't use it. But Tack was Kane Allen and there was no prying that name away from him.

Why he was called Tack, though, was a mystery to me, but I swear, it must have always been in the recesses of my mind because his nickname is perfect for him. Therefore, as I was following his journey with Tyra and the mystery of Tack was revealed, I burst out laughing. I loved it. It was so perfect for him.

One of the many, *many* reasons I'm enjoying the Chaos series is that I get to be very creative with names. I mean, Shy, Hop, Rush, Bat, Speck, and Snapper? I love it. Anything goes with those boys and I have lists of names scrawled everywhere in my magic notebook where I jot ideas. Some of them are crazy and I hope to get to use them, like Moose. Some of them are crazy cool and I hope I get to use them, like Preacher. Some of them are just crazy and I'll probably never use them, like Destroyer. But all of them are fun.

All my characters names, nicknames, and the endearments they use with each other, friends, and family mean a great deal to me. Mostly because all of them and everything they do exists in a perfectly real unreality in my head. They're with me all the time. They're mine.

I created them. And just like a parent naming a child, these perfectly real unreal beings are precious to me, as are the names they chose for themselves.

I just hope they keep it exciting.

Kristin Ashley